WYLDER TALES, VOLUME TWO

JENNIFER SILVERWOOD

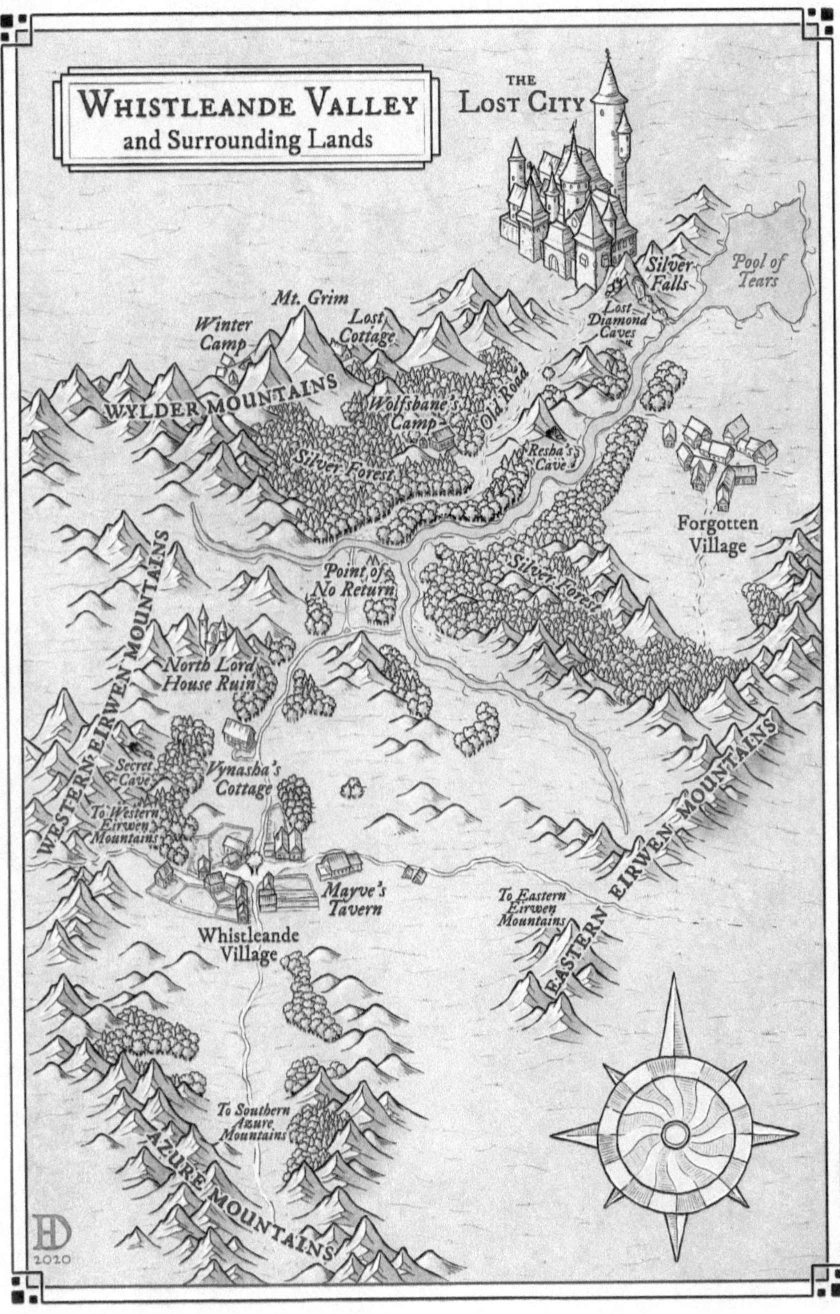

WHISTLEANDE VALLEY
and Surrounding Lands
THE LOST CITY
Silver Falls
Pool of Tears
Mt. Grim
Winter Camp
Lost Cottage
Lost Diamond Caves
WYLDER MOUNTAINS
Wolfsbane's Camp
Old Road
Silver Forest
Resha's Cave
Forgotten Village
Point of No Return
Silver Fore
WESTERN EIRWEN MOUNTAINS
North Lord House Ruin
Secret Cave
Vynasha's Cottage
To Western Eirwen Mountains
Mayve's Tavern
To Eastern Eirwen Mountains
EASTERN EIRWEN MOUNTAINS
Whistleande Village
To Southern Azure Mountains
AZURE MOUNTAINS
2020

Once Upon a Nightmare

HIS LIFE WAS divided into seasons, of before and after.

Before Father brought Wynyth and Vynasha home on one of his many long absences and claimed them his.

After Old Ced drunkenly confessed the truth in a roadside tavern.

"…never was your sister, boy. Wynyth wouldn't tell me who her father was."

Ceddrych watched over Vynasha closely after that, before the war reached Whistleande Valley. It was obvious once he learned the truth. Little signs that she took little after their family became glaring. Her skin was a darker shade than his, her curls tighter and thicker than Tamyra's, and her eyes glowed silver rather than Wynyth's slate gray.

He hated to leave her behind but had little choice when the call for militia went out. And so he went, but he carried Vynasha with him. Letters took time to reach the front, and his were oft writ beneath muddy tarps in the rain or smudged by sweat and blood. Her words pulled him back from the brink of horror every time.

How could he tell her the truth? That the lands beyond the mountains were war-torn and littered with memories he yearned to forget. That the only home he wanted was waiting for him.

After the war, he was uncertain and stripped of the humor she had loved him for. He feared what she would make of his scars and his pained smiles. But Vynasha found him before their family. He was so startled by the changes in her and troubled by the relief he felt as she flung herself into his arms without care. He clung to the scent and feel of her and knew he was finally home.

"Never leave me like this again, you stupid idiot," she said, laughing and crying at once.

"I love you," he said and decided whatever her means of birth, Vynasha was his little sister. Nothing else mattered.

After he learned of the family's failed fortunes and Old Ced's mad schemes to reclaim them, there was little choice left. He would have taken Vynasha and left them to it, regardless. But now there was Tamyra without a husband, and little Wyll to feed. There were his younger sisters who had turned mean and spiteful where they had once been witty and playful. And there was Vynasha, doing her best to look after them all. Could Ceddrych do any less for them, for her?

No, he had little choice. And perhaps… time and distance might set his mind to rights. He had been *off* since the war.

She placed a blue rose in his palm and pressed soft lips to his cheek and begged him to come home with tears in her silver eyes.

Ceddrych clenched the rose too hard, until thorns pricked his palm, but the pain aided him in holding her gently as he was able. Which is to say, not so gently after all. Desperation and some unnamed fear filled him as they led the cart away from the village. The sunset framed Vynasha's curls, a halo of blue-bronze on black, the last glimpse Ceddrych allowed himself before forcing his gaze ahead.

"So long as you promise to come home, that's all that matters."

Vynasha's parting echoed in his mind, a ceaseless refrain over the long weeks spent peddling in villages through the Eirwen Mountains. Ceddrych often woke from night terrors on the road, the same nameless terror that had gripped him ever since leaving her behind.

His need to return home quickly spelled his doom.

Old Ced was a mad, greedy bastard, and never was this more evident than the day they made the turn east and north into Wylderland.

"There's a reason no one ever travels here." Ceddrych had repeated the warning by rote.

"Everyone says so, but our family's ancestral keep was swallowed up by the damned curse, if folk are to be believed," Old Ced had argued back. "Are you going to let countless riches gather dust all on account of rumor and superstition, boy?"

Ceddrych had often wondered, often questioned. But he had also watched Wynyth use magick to make her roses bloom and their crops produce far beyond the normal yield each season. His skin prickled as they passed through eerily quiet forests, and his spine stiffened with every wolf's howl that greeted them.

But Ceddrych pushed aside his misgivings and the unyielding sense something was horribly wrong within these lands because his need to return to Vynasha was far greater.

And he didn't stop his father from pushing on alone to the forgotten city.

"So long as you promise to come home..."

The change came quickly after that, as though it had always been on the cusp, a beast lurking beneath his skin. He was so enraged, so frightened after the pack pushed him to shift that first time, he was unable to return to himself for many moons.

"It's only for a season... We'll start over again, together."

"Together," she had whispered, but her power pressed upon him. Like Wynyth, her words had carried greater weight. Was it any wonder she so easily claimed him before he understood what that meant? Could he be blamed for these unsettling instincts with the beast ever lurking beneath his skin?

Hunting and living as the wolf stripped Ceddrych of lingering guilt and into a basic being. He was hungry and so he ate, thirsty and so he drank from the river. It all might have gone on like this forever, and he could have easily ignored the call of the pack and its bloody alpha.

Until he caught *her* scent in the forest, and the wolf he became merged with the man he had been for one purpose.

He found her beside the mangled body of his dead father, scarred and altered far beyond his imagining. Ceddrych snapped at the others, furious they would dare approach her. She did not belong to them.

He had spent so long hunting her, so many days going slowly

mad as he realized she was a prisoner in that blasted castle like his father had been. It was a miracle they found one another in this limbo between heaven and hell. Yet she had escaped, and they were finally together.

"I thought I would never see you again," she confessed, an echo of his old fears.

"I always knew I would find a way back to you, little sister," he lied.

Better not to tell her of the madness that afflicted him or his weakness as he held her to him possessively. Best if she didn't see the struggle within as he met her golden, beastly gaze.

Vynasha was just as changed as he, a woman grown and something more powerful. The villagers had called her mother a witch, he recalled, once upon a time. Yet Wynyth never brimmed with unchecked power the way Vynasha did. She burned too brightly now, and others would be drawn to her like a moth to flame.

"You're safe now." He sealed his promise with a kiss on her brow.

No matter the truth, or his battle against an ongoing madness, Vynasha was his sister then and so she would remain now.

His to guard and his to protect.

His.

CHAPTER ONE

A Promise Kept

HER FIRST CLEAR memory was of Ceddrych's smiling golden face as he helped her cross the yard to Mother's rose garden. A time when the land was in bloom and the world shone in her child's gaze with an effervescent glow. Vynasha had seen magick in everything when she was still small, before Wynyth's passing the following winter.

"Watch over my little starling," Mother had whispered with her dying breath.

Ceddrych had only drawn Vynasha closer and sworn, *"With my life."*

In the days since she woke in her brother's cottage, Vynasha spoke little of what happened in the castle, too lost in memories and guilt. Had she been so willfully blind she could not see the truth of the matter? She had lived in a luxury she had never known before, but it had been a prison nonetheless. Ferox had trapped her with empty promises, and Grendel bound her against her will.

Why did I not try harder to escape?

Now her faithful horse, Dragos, was trapped in a city of beasts, and her nephew was lost somewhere in the Wylder Mountains. Vynasha nearly spoke of Wyll countless times since waking, yet the walls of Ceddrych's home were far too thin. And they were surrounded by wylderfolk, all too keen and mistrustful of her to loosen her tongue.

Ceddrych didn't seem to mind, content to fill her silences with nonsense and tales of times long ago. Vynasha abandoned all attempts to speak and found herself watching the man her brother had become instead.

"Hold this here for me?"

Vynasha dutifully held down the corner of the hide Ceddrych was stripping of fur and fat beside the crackling fire.

His smile was her reward as he continued. "Do you know the folk within the Eirwen Mountains all believe the Snow Queen was no myth?"

Vynasha smiled back at the small thrill this thought gave her. Tales of the lost princess, driven into hiding by her wicked stepmother only to return home with an army to reclaim her kingdom, had been her favorite. When she wasn't begging her brother to tell the story once more, she'd been forcing Ceddrych to play with her in the forest beyond their home.

Knowing this, Ceddrych waited until she prodded on with the inevitable question. "Truly?"

"Well," he hedged, "to hear them tell, the ruins of her castle can be found between snowy peaks called the Three Sisters. Named after the queen and the sisters she lost on her path to reclaim her rightful throne. It happened like this…"

Vynasha was slow to regain her strength and required Ceddrych's help to cross the limited space within his cottage. "I'm no better than a yearling," she grumbled as they made the slow circle around the central hearth.

Ceddrych's laugh was low and his arm warm beneath her hand. "You're still doing better than the summer I sat on that hornet's nest."

"Oh, Saints, I nearly forgot about that!" Vynasha snorted, and her knee knocked against his as she tugged on his arm. "You refused to come out of the cave until I returned with Mother's poultice to soothe the sting. Cried like a babe the whole time too."

"Have you no heart, Asha? Hornet stings are excruciating, and I was stung no less than *twenty* times." Ceddrych's eyes danced, and his laughter grew as she fell to snorts and giggles.

But Vynasha quietly wondered over the shadow hidden behind his familiar gaze. Best to ignore it for now. Better to steal every sliver of happiness she found.

"I won't be too long," he promised in the hours before dawn. It was the tenth morning since she'd woken in Ceddrych's cottage. A chill permeated the room, and a faint layer of frost coated the walls. The bed was plenty warm from their combined heat, however.

Vynasha shouldn't take advantage of Ceddrych's kindness like this. He had always been softer toward her than the others.

His true sisters, a nasty voice in her head reminded.

She should give him back his bed and take to the furs he had kept spread beside the hearth. But after that first awful night, she had become addicted to the dreamlessness of his embrace.

"I've had good luck the last few mornings, no doubt thanks to your presence," Ceddrych teased as he slung his bow over his shoulder. He did not need these tools to hunt, she suspected, but when asked, her brother had replied, "*I spent too long as a wolf. Now I need to remember how to live as a man.*"

Vynasha dug her claws into her palms as she straightened and declared, "I'm going with you today."

Ceddrych froze in his preparations and twisted his head. His eyes flashed gold and green, and the scent of magick thickened between them. "It's too dangerous." His gaze fell to her legs as she pushed off the covers and stood.

"I'm strong enough to keep up. Wait and see." She lifted her chin and willed him to see her need to breathe. She wasn't sure she could stand another day trapped inside. "Am I not safer with you than alone anyway?"

Vynasha hadn't stopped smiling since they left the cottage behind, dressed in her brother's spare cloak and ill-fitting clothes. She had laughed as he returned to the cottage with borrowed trousers, underclothes, and boots his elderly neighbor's son had outworn.

Ceddrych stole glances at her when he wasn't distracted by the other villagers.

"What?" She kept her voice just above a whisper but couldn't contain her mirth. A restless energy urged her to run, to dance, to chase the joy she felt to be once more with her brother.

Ceddrych's gaze swept over her oddly fitting clothes. "Nothing."

Vynasha tugged at his elbow then slipped her arm through his. "I'm not about to collapse, I promise."

He rolled his eyes and shook his head. "I just… haven't seen you wear trousers before."

Vynasha savored the heat his body offered as the cold seeped into her boiled leather boots. "I wore out your old pairs while you were gone."

"Yes, but you were a child then," he hedged and shifted his arm so their fingers entwined.

"They are more practical than skirts, though not as warm, I suppose," she mused, then she frowned. "You never cared for such conventions before. What's truly bothering you, brother?"

He squeezed her hand and twisted his head so she couldn't see his expression. "I am only reminded you are a woman, and no longer my *little* sister."

I never was.

Vynasha ran her tongue over her slightly too-sharp teeth and turned to study the other side of their path. The village was ringed by the greater forest and the mountains beyond this, and the rush of a nearby river, called the Silver, sang in her ears. Shivers slipped down her spine as she recalled the deadly plunge she and Grolthox had taken down the falls. Wolfsbane had warned her the waters were full of magick. It was a wonder the superstitious wylderfolk should choose to build their home close by.

Ceddrych's home sat snug against the forest's edge, built out of dark logs bent into curves rather than corners, and the thatched roof met at a high point where smoke escaped the air vent. She turned to face the other homes lining the main road a little farther down and wondered why he should choose to live near yet separate from the others.

"Is the well far?" she asked, curious and wary of the figures stepping from their homes with buckets and other tools in hand.

Ceddrych squeezed her hand, and though he smiled, the tension still had not left his frame. "Not much farther. We'll fill our skins and head out from there."

When she turned to take in the snow-laden road, at the rounded cottages several paces across and further down, she noted a similar pattern in their build. Yet where Ceddrych's house was modest, the others were larger to accommodate families. Some had been added onto, other half circles connected to the main home. All the other structures were decorated with paintings in red ochre and sulfur yellows, rich berry blue and smatterings of violet.

Rather than stitched figures cavorting together in luxury and hunts, like the castle tapestries, the villagers painted the patterns of the forest on their walls—veins of leaves had been drawn over shades of dawn, and the trail of invisible vines gave a natural pattern against splashes of color.

Compassion stirred in her chest as she recognized their need for beauty in their harsh world. That same need had driven her to tend her mother's roses, what gave the villagers of Whistleande a reason to want her around. Like these people, she had been considered the monster once.

Shutters slowly turned open, and curious eyes peered at them from within as they passed by.

"This way," her brother murmured, and Vynasha struggled to meet his increased pace.

They rounded a corner and froze to find a huddled group already waiting and watching them warily from beneath hooded cloaks and furs.

Vynasha drew in a sharp breath and tasted dozens of scents in the air, the cloying tug of magick, and something darker she had no name for. Something which made her uneasy and her claws slightly retract and lengthen against her fist.

"*Witch.*" The word echoed among the villagers in a sibilant hiss.

Ceddrych shuddered as he took one step back and then another, keeping her on the far side of the gathered crowd. "I'll bring you to the well another day," he growled. "There's a spring we can use instead."

Vynasha allowed Ceddrych to guide her away from the well and off the main road until they were ensconced deep in the cradle of the forest. She had become so accustomed to the scents within Ceddrych's cottage, to the sense of safety he provided, she had nearly forgotten her unwelcome reception by the village. "I'm such a fool," she whispered.

"You have never been a fool," Ceddrych growled.

Vynasha's laugh was bitter. "You would think I would be used to stares and whispers after Whistleande. I just thought…" She had been an outcast in Whistleande, and now in this land of mythical people. A misfit among misfits.

But the old woman gave Ceddrych clothes for you to wear.

"Do you recall the home we once spoke of?"

Vynasha turned to find his smile returned, and even if it was brittle about the edges, it was still like welcoming the sun. She couldn't help smiling back any more than she could mask the pain his question brought. The future she had dreamed of for so long and given up. "Did you ever find the perfect place in your wanderings?"

Ceddrych ran his thumb along her claws and slowed his gait until they came to a break in the trees. "Would you still like that, a cottage in the woods, covered with roses?"

She blinked away unexpected tears at his words, giving voice to the only dream she had dared keep. A dream she thought would never come true but refused to abandon completely. Hadn't this been the promise she gave to Wyll when they left Whistleande Valley? They would find Ceddrych and finally build the home of which they had dreamed.

"Ceddrych, I need to tell you…" Vynasha startled as Ceddrych released her hand to press his fingertips to her mouth.

A smile was still on his face, but his eyes betrayed darker thoughts as he canted his head to the narrow clearing before them. Shaped like an arrow, the break in the forest became wider as they entered a sea of color.

Snow blanketed the ground, only broken by dozens of winter blossoms in shades of blue, violet, and gold. Fir branches arched over the initial gap, giving way to low brambles shivering in the wind. Between the brambles along the far edge, a white hare lay frozen in one of Ceddrych's traps.

Vynasha's breath caught as Ceddrych allowed her to enter first. The sun warmed her skin and seemed to cast the world in a dreamlike glow. She bent to run her hands over the flower petals, and the dagger hung on her hip seemed to burn, to call for her blood, to make these flowers grow stronger and bolder.

"I thought of you when I found this place," Ceddrych said as he knelt and gently retrieved the hare.

Vynasha licked her lips at the scent of fresh meat and grimaced at the unwelcome hunger. She lifted her gaze to find Ceddrych bathed in the light of dawn, his eyes shifting from gold to green. "It's perfect," she breathed and curled her hands into fists. Now was not the time to bemoan her changed form, not when her brother struggled with the same urges.

She stared at the earth as she sank to her knees and pressed a palm through the snow, to the root of the plants.

"The roses of this garden belong to you and you alone from this moment forward," Ferox once said in a garden covered in glass. *"Nothing is too much for you, Beauty. I promised you your heart's desire, and you shall have it and more."*

It would be so easy to pull Ferox's dagger free, to see what her gift could do. Her other hand was on the ruby pommel when Ceddrych's voice called her back.

"I found it by accident, but I've sketched a dozen different plans for our home over the years. I know exactly which wood we could use…" He hooked the hare to his belt and pressed a hand to the nearest fir. "Not these, of course, but some of the silver birch, maybe?"

All the trees leading to the lost city had gleamed silver in the moonlight the night she and Dragos raced to the castle gates. Vynasha swallowed past the ache in her throat as she shook snow from her hand and stood. "Do you think Balos would let us leave the village?"

As often happened when the leader of the wolf pack was

mentioned, her brother's expression darkened and his form lightly shuddered. A faint growl filled his voice as he replied, "*I* will make it so."

Vynasha rubbed her arms and turned to take in the flowers, and her limbs trembled from pushing too much too far. "Ceddrych, before we head back, I need to tell you something…"

"We still have two more traps we can check," he offered as he came into her line of sight. "Unless you've had enough of the cold for one morning?"

She smiled at his attempt to mask the truth of her weakness. "I may have overestimated my tolerance," she confessed, and the beast within her calmed as Ceddrych covered her fist and wrapped her hand with his.

"Of course, I can check on the others tomorrow. Or *we* can, if you are up for another hike," he offered, his weather-roughened features softening as she tilted her head back to hold his gaze.

Vynasha shook her head and sighed. "I've wanted to tell you since you found me, but it hasn't been safe. The other villagers and the wolves are… I didn't know if they could hear us."

Ceddrych brought her hands against his chest and rubbed warmth back into her palms. "Not everyone has senses like ours," he said, gaze darting between her beastly eyes, "and it's considered rude to listen to our neighbors. But that doesn't stop all of them—"

"Wyll is alive," Vynasha interrupted.

A pained gasp escaped Ceddrych, and his grip on her hands flexed. "Wyllem?"

"I saved him from the fire, but I couldn't heal his scars any more than I could mine. He's only grown weaker each season, and I brought him with me because…" She covered her mouth before her sob could escape, and her vision blurred.

"Vynasha, where is Wyll?" Ceddrych pushed her curls back from her face and pulled her focus back to him.

Tears spilled over her cheeks as she whispered, "I don't know.

I—I had to leave him behind. Wolfsbane warned me it wasn't safe for him, for anyone, but I had to try. I had to find you."

"Wolfsbane," Ceddrych growled. "When did you see him? Is Wyll with them?"

Vynasha nodded and covered Ceddrych's hand with hers. "Please forgive me, but I didn't know what else to do. I thought… Wolfsbane swore they would keep Wyll somewhere safe and protected from…"

"The wolves," he ground out. His hands began to shudder uncontrollably.

"Yes," she rasped.

Ceddrych released her and staggered away as a snarl escaped, and his form blurred before her. Fur sprouted and retreated beneath his skin, and a terrible shout echoed in the clearing as Ceddrych fought back the shift. His chest heaved with uneven breaths as he hung his head and kept his back to her.

"Ceddrych?" Vynasha wrung her hands, hating the distance. She took a step, and two more before her brother held out a trembling hand and growled, "Wait."

Vynasha pushed aside more tears with a rough hand. "I didn't know, Ceddrych. I didn't know you were a wolf. I thought your pack mindless beasts at first."

He nodded, and when he turned, his eyes glowed the same unnatural green as the wolves that had chased her to the lost city. "I know." He huffed and pushed the hair that had fallen loose of its tie back. "Wolfsbane is well-known to us, as you have come to guess. But I'm not angry with you, Asha—I'm furious with myself."

Vynasha shifted in place and wrapped her arms tightly around her chest. Even as a greater part of her heart eased knowing her brother didn't hate her, she still hesitated. "I need to find Wyll," she said. "I promised him I would. But I don't know this forest the way you do. Will you help me?"

Ceddrych blinked, and flecks of gold returned to his eyes as he took her in, as though truly seeing her for the first time. "Ash, of course. I…" His brow creased, and he closed the distance between them, lifting her off her feet and into the safety of his arms. "I'm sorry for making you doubt me."

Vynasha wrapped her arms around his neck and pressed her nose to the crook of his neck. "You are the only thing I'm sure of anymore."

But an amulet dug into her skin beneath her borrowed woolen tunic, a reminder that she was not truly free. For without the amulet's protection, Soraya and her servants would seek and surely find Vynasha. And the wicked prince yet lingered, waiting to devour what remained of her soul.

Chapter Two

A Dream of Monsters

THE CASTLE HAD always been dark and drafty, but now the walls rippled and shivered with moonlight. Tiny blue lights drifted ahead of her path, dancing past tapestries that watched her trek through the forbidden halls. Vynasha met their silent gaze and wondered why she heard no sound from the beasts she had set free.

A dimly glowing figure stepped out of the shadows, and she froze, looking down to see if she could pull out her dagger quickly enough.

"You are not truly here," a rough voice growled, the same that had compelled her to leave and not look back. "Leave me!" He thrust a palm in her direction as though warning her away.

"Grendel." Vynasha moved with every intention of inflicting pain. But she could not lift her feet, could not move at all, she discovered with growing panic.

When she did not move, he turned desperate and shouted at the walls. "She cannot be here! Do you hear me, Mother? I forbid it!" The gatekeeper came to stand arm's-length away from her, close enough she could see regret in his silver eyes and the fresh scrapes along his jaw. He clenched his fists and looked everywhere but at her. "I sent her away, as was my right by your bloody curse." He sucked in a sharp breath and squeezed his lids tightly shut. "Please do not let her in… *do not* let her in."

"How troublesome this must be for you after you sent me away," Vynasha hissed, wishing again for full possession of her limbs. "Why can't I move? Are you doing this, compelling me again?"

He rubbed a hand over his face and let it hang lifelessly at his side. His hair fell into his eyes, and still, he would not look at her. "Not intentionally. This is my dream realm," he confessed, "though it feels more like a nightmare."

"At least we aren't alone in that." Vynasha narrowed her eyes as all he had and hadn't said ran through her mind, all the tiny ways he'd made her believe she needed to escape while binding their blood. No matter how loudly he protested, she knew he'd used her father to bring her there. And once he had what he wanted, he abandoned her as surely as everyone did.

As you abandoned Wyll to strangers?

Vynasha cringed, and some of her anger slipped away. "What have you summoned me?"

Grendel observed her for a moment, face a mask of stone. "Tell me where you are and what exactly what you did before you went to bed."

Vynasha snorted. "I'm not your thrall, remember? Why should I tell you anything?"

"Humor an old monster," he said with a slight lift of his chin.

"Not that you care, but Ceddrych found me after I escaped with Grolthox and…" Her words were quickly drowned by Grendel's exclamation.

"Grolthox! He followed you? Damnable creature. I ordered him to remain behind. He should not have been able to make it past the outer wards…"

"Well, thanks to our little blood bond, you aren't the only magick wielder with power over the curse," she spat as her anger flared back to life. Tiny blue lights spun about them in a fine flurry.

Grendel ignored this as he stepped closer, keeping his fists clenched tightly at his sides. "Where is Grolthox now?"

When she couldn't even move to turn her face aside, her temper boiled to a fever pitch. "My *father* is dead!"

Grendel blanched and averted his gaze, though his posture remained erect.

"What, nothing to say, gatekeeper? You could at least acknowledge you knew he was my father."

His inner light pulsed and then brightened again, illuminating his gray skin as he met her gaze and confessed. "I knew."

Her limbs trembled, and something snapped in the back of her mind, releasing her limbs. She crossed the remaining distance between them, pulled her hand back, and slapped Grendel in the face.

Dream state or not, she felt the full impact in her aching hand and watched as tiny beads of blue blood rose to the surface of his cheek, where her claws had scratched him.

"He *sold* me to you!" She wrapped her arms around her chest and hung her head until her long hair draped over her face. "And he died saving my life…"

"My father was not a good man either."

She peeked at him through her veil of curls and pursed her lips. "You don't have any right to mourn with me. He told me what you did to him, Grendel. Trust me when I say any affection I might have held for you died with him."

He was silent after that, and the burden weighed on her, threatened to crush her again.

"You said your brother found you?" The lights floating nearby seemed to brighten with his careful words, reflecting off his silver irises.

Vynasha took a step back, and the shadows thickened. "Yes."

Grendel turned to pace along the width of the hallway. "Then I am glad. You should both flee these mountains as soon as you are able. Our bond should make it possible."

"Yes, because mortal folk will be so welcoming to a changeling and a woman who favors a demon," she mumbled with a frustrated sigh.

Grendel continued as though he hadn't heard her barb. "You cannot come here again, not if you don't want her to find you. Never think of me before you sleep again."

"That won't be a problem, gatekeeper," she scoffed. "You made yourself clear when you compelled me to leave."

"Good," he grunted. "Because if she finds you, if she brings you back to me…"

Inky shadows encompassed them, blotting out the moonlight and floating blue lights, and a dull roar accompanied it. "What's happening?" she shouted above the growing din.

Grendel seemed unfazed by the howling winds and hissing voices among them. "It would seem you are waking up. Do not think of me again, Vynasha."

The last thing she saw clearly was the emptiness in the gatekeeper's masked features. His loss and loneliness resonated with her long after her dream faded to nothing. A voice was waiting for her in the darkness, however, entreating and pulling her back.

"Ash?" Ceddrych sounded so far away that she did not truly stir until he shook her by the shoulders. She woke in a cold sweat and knew with absolute certainty it had been more than an ordinary dream. She pressed a hand to her chest, where the amulet burned against the skin.

Her brother brushed her hair off her forehead, and she grabbed hold of his hand between her fingers. "Ceddrych." She spoke his name like a prayer. Ceddrych was her tether, the anchor to what remained of who she was before.

"You were shouting in your sleep," he began with a frown.

"I was dreaming," she began, but her mind was still there, in that dark but beautiful place with *him*. Why had she dreamed of Grendel after all he had done to her?

Was it because I was alone?

Ceddrych had brought her back home after showing her the clearing before leaving to speak with the pack. Vynasha must have been wearier than she thought if she fell asleep so quickly after preparing the hares.

"You say things sometimes," Ceddrych said as he pushed more curls from her cheek then added, "in your sleep."

"In my sleep?" Dread coiled in her chest like a snake waiting to strike, but she couldn't help asking. "What have I said?"

Ceddrych's brow furrowed. "It doesn't matter, Ash. I swore you didn't need to tell me until you were ready, and I stand by that." His expression darkened and his grip on her hand tightened. "No matter how much the bloody council threatens."

Vynasha's breath caught, and she pushed it back out as she sat up against the log wall. "What did they say?" she whispered. Ceddrych had said they should uncover what rumors abounded about Wolfsbane, to learn what they could before beginning their hunt.

Ceddrych leaned closer and linked his hands together over her cot, his features almost foreign in the smoky shadows. "Any questions I had were disregarded in favor of *their* questions about you."

Vynasha rubbed her hands over her face and sighed. "Balos."

Ceddrych hummed in affirmation. Since her arrival to the village, the wolf *alpha* seemed to hound their every move. "Back when I was searching for you, he dragged half the pack on some lone crusade hunting Wolfsbane. He refused to aid a *lone wolf*, as he calls me, and now he only cares to make trouble for us."

"Not us, *me*. This village fears me, just like they did in Whistleande, and those people had known me all my life." Her claws pricked her scalp as she dragged her hand over her curls, savoring the pain.

Ceddrych pried her hands from her head with a firm grip and

threaded their fingers together, unafraid. "It isn't *you* they're afraid of, Asha."

Grendel's tortured face haunted her, and the white-furred Ferox lingered on a whisper of a thought. Ferox ruled over the castle Grendel had imprisoned himself within. But had Ferox survived the beasts Vynasha unleashed? And if he had, would the beast come hunting for her now?

Ceddrych ran his thumbs over her claws, and the tension left his shoulders. "The wylderfolk have good reason to fear the lost city."

Vynasha nodded. Odym had alluded to this, to a great war fought between the king against and those who came through the mirror realm. "I know part of the tale, but the king who hunted them is dead, isn't he? Why are they still so afraid? Why fear me?"

You already know the answer.

"And you believe my mother was descended from them?" she had asked the beast.

Ferox's teeth had gleamed with his smile. *"I believe your mother was one who escaped."*

Ceddrych grimaced. "The curse trapped all the souls in Wylderland. Even death is a prison, or so the elders say. Spirits stay and don't move on as they should. As for why they fear you... I suppose it's because you're the first maiden to ever return alive."

A chill prickled at the base of her neck, the silver necklace searing against her flushed skin. She had known others were taken by the prince, and she knew precisely why she was the first to come back.

"You should both flee these mountains as soon as you are able. Our bond should make it possible." Or so Grendel claimed.

Her heart fell before Ceddrych's hardened gaze, for she saw he believed the tale he chose to see. To Ceddrych, Vynasha was another victim of the curse. How would he feel if he knew the unholy bond she had made with their enemy? Or worse, the offer of marriage from the beast who lorded over the lost city?

She opened her mouth to say the words, to tell him the truth.

Bang! Bang!

They jumped as the barred door rattled in its frame.

"Come out, Wanderer," a harsh voice called from the other side. "Come and see the cost of harboring your witch!"

Vynasha wrapped her arms around her curled legs. Her awareness spiked as her new beastly senses took over. "Ceddrych?"

He spoke with the village council. What else has been said?

Ceddrych met her gaze with a flash of guilt burning behind his gaze.

The voices on the other side of the wall grew louder.

"My boy is ill because of your witch, Wanderer!" a woman shouted.

"Yes," growled an older male, "we know you took her outside the village, no doubt to practice her dark magick."

"Who knows what she summoned from that infernal castle!"

"—not one of us!"

"She'll murder our children!"

Vynasha dug her forehead into her knees and placed her hands against her ears as the villagers continued to jeer beyond the walls. Until Ceddrych's hands tugged at her wrists, until she surrendered to his hold. His smile transformed his world-weary face to the boy she remembered.

A sob caught in her throat as he pressed his forehead to hers, at his acceptance, at the reminder that he had claimed her regardless. He would always choose her.

Ceddrych's eyes flashed wolfish green as he pulled away, the only outward sign of his internal fury. He squeezed her wrists briefly in comfort as he released her. Only then, with his back turned, did he seem to grow taller. Magick of the forest, of loam and pine, snow and moss, filled the cabin as her brother crossed the cabin to unbar the door.

CHAPTER THREE

A Den of Wolves

"**W**HY HAVE YOU come?" Ceddrych's voice cut through the din and stunned the villagers into silence. "Why do you threaten us when Vynasha has not left my side beyond the walls of this cabin?"

"If she is so harmless, why did my Asa's cough begin the day she arrived?" the woman from before snarled. "Tell me, how is my boy so weakened he can hardly stand from his bed!"

"What if we are all infected with her curse?" someone called.

"Never suffer a witch to live!" another cried.

"Stay back, damn you!" Ceddrych threw his arms to brace against the doorframe and began to tremor. "Children fall sick every day. My own sister has been recovering from what those monsters did to her."

Vynasha cringed at the unspoken implication. Were the villagers somehow right, after all? Had she carried some dark magick with her?

"Our children never fall ill. Our *blood* has always protected us," an older male growled. "You have been with us a short time, Wanderer, and you do not understand our ways."

"He is not one of us!" the first woman shouted. "The lone wolf has no place among our pack."

"Onya is right," an elderly woman agreed. "You agreed to live among us, but you refuse to protect us."

"Enough, Gira!" Balos interrupted in his deep voice. "You have said your piece. Wanderer, you know the rules of our pack…"

"Vynasha has done no spell! I would have felt it," Ceddrych protested.

"And how do you explain Asa's illness?" Balos asked. "How do you explain the *stench* of evil infecting our village? We warned you what would happen if she called the beast again. Such magick is forbidden in these lands for a reason."

Oh, Saints, the amulet, she thought. It had been burning when she woke. Had Grendel called to her dream, or had she called to his? Bile rose to the back of her throat. Was the boy's illness truly her fault?

"We have survived all these years because we kept noses to the ground and *away* from the lost city," Balos continued. "Anyone who breaks our law draws the city's evil to us. And there is only one punishment for such a crime."

"You can't!" Ceddrych cried.

"We cannot suffer a witch to live among us," Balos snapped back.

"Vynasha is my sister, and she is under *my* protection. And if any of you so much as look at her wrong, I will show you exactly how savage I can be."

"You cannot endanger our lives like this!" the elderly woman from before cried. "Would you sacrifice everyone in this village for that witch? Mayhap you practice dark magick as well?"

"Better her life than yours," Ceddrych growled.

The voices rushed together, overlapping with one another.

Vynasha gasped and stumbled forward until her forehead pressed against the door of the cabin. She couldn't let them harm Ceddrych—she *wouldn't*.

Even if I need to become the monster they fear.

The elder male who had spoken before released a growling shout. "Silence!"

Vynasha's claws bit into the wood and she drew in a breath filled with brewing violence as the male continued.

"We took this lone wolf in as one of our own because he is a protector, by *blood* right. That is enough claim for him to make his home among us. Let him plead his case, but I warn you, boy, do not threaten or lie to us again unless you seek exile."

Vynasha peeked through the crack between the wood and the world beyond. The sun blinded her sight at first, masking shady figures in heavy furs. Yet at the edge of her vision she could also see a woman with scales instead of skin and fire-red hair, three men half the size of the other villagers with beards trailing to their knees, and did she imagine a child with wings? The wylderfolk clung to the outskirts, the shadows, watching with solemn faces. But the closest villagers' eyes were gleaming luminous emerald like the wolves, with the promise of a fight.

Ceddrych's back was to her, his shoulders heaving as he lifted his head and faced the wolves. "All I know is that my sister was a prisoner in that castle, a *victim*... just like your missing daughters."

The crowd shifted, and a soft wind carried whispers of ageless sorrow.

Ceddrych straightened to his full height and turned to face a wrinkled male with feathers instead of hair, and the round eyes of a hawk. "Galtis, you and the other council named me a protector. Now you ask me to turn my back on Vynasha because you're afraid of what you don't understand. If it were your daughter, your sister standing here, could you abandon them so easily? Would you?"

"Our daughters knew the cost of answering the beast's call, far better than you, Wanderer," Galtis replied with a birdlike tilt of his head.

"You speak of what you do not understand," Gira, the elderly woman from before, snarled and her words shredded with her voice into a wolf's bark. "Every day she spends is another we risk bringing the wrath of *her* upon us all!"

The others continued to rave, their protests growing louder, pressing closer. Vynasha closed her eyes and clawed at the amulet burning like ice against her skin.

Balos broke his silence. "Our elders speak true, Wanderer. Whoever your sister was before she entered the lost city is no more. We can all see the marks of her change, the mark of evil. And you know the law. We cannot suffer a witch to live."

Vynasha shifted on her toes and fought the flare of magick heating her blood. She braced her palms against the wooden door so hard her hands bled.

"You want blood, you'll have to go through me first!" Ceddrych snarled as he surged forward.

A moment after, someone shoved Ceddrych back, blocking her vision. The wall rattled from the resulting impact, and Vynasha jerked back with a cry.

"Stay down, boy!" Balos growled.

Ceddrych grunted in pain before rising with a snarl and stumbled back into the fight waiting for him.

Vynasha moved before her mind could catch up. Her palms connected with the cabin door, splintering the wood as it slammed open. She ignored the gasps and outcries of "The witch!" as she stumbled into the ankle-deep snow.

The villagers parted from her, parents lifting children and carrying them away. Vynasha bared her sharp teeth at them and followed the sounds of the scuffle. Their fight had already carried them farther up the street.

Her legs threatened to give out beneath her, but the magick pumping through her blood made her stronger by the second.

Make it quick. Prey on their fear, came the errant thought as Balos threw Ceddrych to the ground before her with a deafening roar. Those forming a circle around the two jeered, yet the villagers nearest to her had staggered back in wary silence, defensive hisses, and growls.

Ceddrych coughed, and blood spattered onto the snow.

Vynasha's vision turned red.

Red like Wynyth's roses, like the blood they'd shed to make new life.

Red like the ruby on the hilt of her dagger, glinting in the sun as she pressed its blade to the alpha's neck.

Her mind rushed to catch up with the consequences of her actions. Utter silence had fallen over the village, broken by a distant babe's cry, the creak of the forest against the winter wind. And Ceddrych's groan as he struggled to stand, to speak. Ceddrych was why she had done this foolish thing, had broken their agreement to keep their heads down.

Noses to the ground…

A gust of breath escaped Balos's lips, clouding the blade of her dagger. His green eyes narrowed briefly at her before widening. She saw her reflection in the black of his pupils—the brilliant golden eyes of a beast, the sharp teeth behind her parted lips. The alpha appraised her with shock, his hand flexed against her throat. When had he grabbed her?

But she had surprised him. A part of her that had been weak for so long in one form or another relished his vulnerability. The thrum of magick pulsed brightly beneath her skin. "You made my brother bleed," she hissed as she dug the blade a shade deeper into his throat. "I should bleed you…"

His lips tugged up at the corners, revealing slightly sharp

white teeth and a beautiful smile. Balos blinked slowly, and his grip on her throat tightened. "You already have, witch."

Vynasha drew in a sharp breath, unable to look away from the bloom of blue trickling down his throat.

The same shade as Grendel's blood.

"This was a warning," she ground out while battling her inner monster. For the beast inside her had struck true and wanted to drown in the scent of blood and pine.

"You should not interfere with pack matters, outsider." Balos leaned into her blade, silver hair falling over his shoulders in wild waves. His beard was closely shorn, albeit uneven as his verdant eyes. The wolf never left his face completely, she mused. A myriad of scars, some like knife wounds, others like claw marks, marred what might have otherwise been considered pleasing features.

Now he has a new scar for his collection, she thought and fought the irrational urge to laugh. *Focus.*

"Ash." Ceddrych laid a firm but careful hand on her shoulder. "Asha, please. You've done enough."

"And if I let him go, what then?" she hissed. "Will he have the others set fire to our home, murder us in our sleep?" Her vision blurred with the memory of the fire that stole her sisters' lives then sharpened to trace the trail of old burns covering her bared arm. "I'm not moving until he realizes I could have done this to him, to *any* of them, at any time." Her gaze flickered up to find Balos had followed her gaze to her arm and appeared… stricken?

Don't you pity me too.

Keeping a firm grip on the dagger, Vynasha looked to the crowd and searched the faces for the one that hated her the most. "Where is the boy?"

Balos's frown deepened as he echoed, "The boy?"

Vynasha pressed closer against him, stretching up on her toes.

"Asa, the one who is ill, the one you're so set on accusing me of poisoning."

The alpha's expressive eyes flattened, and his grip on her throat eased. "Eager to finish the job, little witch?"

"I don't know you or your people, and I trust you about as much as you do me. But I mean your village no harm. And if I can help the boy, I will."

Balos narrowed his green gaze. "Surely you understand if you harm the boy, your life and your brother's would be forfeit."

Vynasha smiled. "Or I could take your life and end us both now."

"Asha, please don't," Ceddrych whispered against her ear while grasping her shoulder. "There's more to this than you understand." Relief filled her at Ceddrych's touch, but the monster inside her wasn't ready to heed his words.

Balos recognized this, her lust for violence, as his smile returned, and he spoke with wonder. "You would do it, wouldn't you, little witch? After all you endured…"

"At least our deaths would hold meaning either way," she managed, desperately avoiding thought of Wyll and broken promises. At least this way, Ferox could never reclaim and bind her to the mirror.

"And what would you ask in return," Balos asked, "for aiding the boy?"

Ceddrych's hold of her shoulder tightened briefly, and the air seemed to thicken around them with something Vynasha could not name.

She swallowed against Balos's grip on her throat. "If I do this, you give us land of our choosing to build a home of our own. Until our home is built, we will stay in the village and protect your people. But if any of you so much as lays a claw or knife on my brother again, I swear by all the saints you will not live long enough to tell others what I am capable of."

For a moment, Vynasha wasn't sure if her bluff had paid off.

And then Balos released her neck with a slow caress. She bit back a gasp at the thrill that laced down her spine.

Balos grimaced as his fingertips lingered over her racing heart, just above the hidden amulet. "Pray you do not regret allowing me to keep my life, little witch."

Vynasha's chest heaved and leaned into his retreat, the monster clawing desperately beneath her skin to take more, to *end this*.

He'll never let you go free. End him now!

Ceddrych slid his arm fully around her shoulders, and his other hand caught her wrist before she could move the dagger.

Balos's expression hardened and he lifted his chin, turning to the elders, the wolves, and other beings, and addressed the crowd. "You have all borne witness to what happened. The witch chose not to take my life and asks that she be allowed to heal Asa."

"Balos, the council should discuss…" Galtis began to speak only for a woman in silver furs to rush past the hawklike elder with slightly sharpened teeth and flashing black eyes. "That witch will not come anywhere near my son!"

"Calm yourself, Onya," Balos snapped.

Vynasha watched in wonder as the woman shuddered and ducked her head meekly, murmuring, "Forgive me, but how can you ask me to trust this witch?"

Balos placed a hand on Onya's shoulder and pressed his forehead briefly to hers. "I understand your fear, but they will not be alone. Should she harm Asa, we will make her suffer tenfold, I swear this." He pulled back, and Onya nodded while pressing her hands together in supplication.

"A storm is coming," Balos told the unsettled mob. "Go back to your homes and trust I and your elders will not allow this witch to harm you."

Many had fallen away, Vynasha realized as Ceddrych pulled

her fully into the shelter of his arms. Only the inner circle, the wolves, and the elders Gira and Galtis lingered.

Galtis collected Onya in his arms and murmured something low against her ear. The mother closed her eyes and nodded.

Gira placed her hands on her wide hips and sneered at Vynasha. "I hope you know what you're doing, Balos. The others will not forgive you for this if you are wrong."

Balos grinned. "I am never wrong."

Ceddrych released a tense breath against the crown of Vynasha's head and muttered, "You don't have to do this, Asha."

"Yes, I do," Vynasha told her brother as she watched the woman, Onya, and the despair she poorly masked with a veneer of hatred as Galtis guided her to a cottage two houses down. Gira followed at a slow pace, flanked by the rest of Balos's pack.

"Come and let us see if you are worthy of life or a slow death, Vynasha." Balos's grin revealed faintly pointed white teeth as he gestured for her to follow.

CHAPTER FOUR

A Taste for Blood

ONYA DID NOT welcome them into her home, a home she shared with her father, Galtis. But she did not scream at them or threaten them in the way Vynasha expected. As before in the street, Onya took Balos at his word with grim acceptance.

"Come and brew an old man some tea, my dear," Galtis urged his daughter. Onya obeyed, nearing the fire while keeping a wary eye on Vynasha.

Galtis favored Balos with a severe look. "Be gentle with the boy. He has suffered much."

Vynasha flinched as the old man's hawklike gaze settled on her and found herself nodding.

"My family is well accustomed with magick, as you will recall," came Balos's unexpected reply. He sneered at Vynasha as he added, "I will know if the witch's intentions turn foul."

"Balos will not lead Asa to harm, Papa," Onya said.

"Pray to the Crafter you are right, my daughter," Galtis replied.

Vynasha clenched her fists, and her claws pricked her palms. Ceddrych had watched her put away the dagger with curiosity and unease. It was not an heirloom of their family, obviously. But a gift from Ferox, a piece of the home she had begun to make for herself, beautiful and terrible as Castle Bitterhelm had been.

Balos grunted and grabbed Vynasha's arm in passing. "This way, witch."

"Unhand my sister," Ceddrych growled low and stepped between them.

Balos glanced down at Vynasha, amusement turning his sneer into a smirk. "Do not start another battle you cannot win, boy. Now, come, I grow tired of this farce."

"And I grow weary of your bark, Balos," the old woman snapped and smacked the back of his head. "Come along, children." Gira opened one of two doors and entered.

Balos pulled her with him after Gira, a furious Ceddrych two paces behind. "Best wait out here, boy," Balos rumbled, an unspoken command behind his sharp smile.

Ceddrych bristled, and Vynasha begged him to not protest with a silent plea.

I know you don't understand, but I needed to see for myself.

Vynasha didn't know if she could help Asa in this altered body Grendel had cursed her with. And even if she reached for the gift the way her mother taught, there was no guarantee she could save Asa the way she'd saved Wyll.

But if it was my fault, if there's even a chance I can help…

Ceddrych's furrowed brow smoothed, and he slowly leaned against the doorframe with a nod. He trusted her.

Vynasha bit back a smile as she passed him, and Balos closed and barred the door behind them.

Here were signs Vynasha recognized. Carved wooden toys in the corner, perched as though waiting for their owner. A basket of children's clothes in need of mending and cleaning, left beside an intricately carved chair and bedside table.

"Aunty?" A small voice croaked, and Gira softly replied, "Hush, now, Balos has come to visit."

The candle burned low, and someone had burned a familiar herb… sage?

Vynasha rubbed her nose at the slight burn as Balos crouched beside the bed. He whispered low, in a tongue Vynasha could barely read yet recognized from the village priest's sermons. When she had dared enter the tiny church at her eldest sister's insistence so long ago.

"Balos?" the boy rasped and coughed, deep and wet.

Vynasha shuddered and rubbed her arms while Balos crouched before the bed. "Asa, you are looking stronger today."

"Truly?" Asa asked.

Balos hummed deeply. "You will be able to train again before the next moon, or I'll be damned."

"Mind your tongue, Balos." Gira slapped the hulking male's shoulder, and Asa's giggle fell to another wet cough.

Asa moaned as the old woman helped settle him back against the pillow. "It hurts, Aunty."

"I know, little love, but it will be over soon." Gira lifted her braided gray head and fixed pale-green eyes on Vynasha. "Balos has brought someone who will help."

Asa turned his head, and Vynasha released a pained gasp. A pair of tiny antlers poked through white-blond hair matted over the boy's sallow face, and sharp wheezing breaths passed his cracked and bloody lips. "Is she a wyldcat?" Asa whispered, curiosity shining from his black eyes.

Balos chuckled as he lifted a beckoning hand. "We shall see, won't we, *Vynasha*?"

He invoked her name like a curse, and Vynasha hated the wild thing inside her that responded to his underlying command. He ruled over these people with magick of his own, she realized. Only Ceddrych and these elders had dared to question or defy him in public. But he didn't know Vynasha or all she had done to come this far. He couldn't cow her or make her bend to his will like Onya.

Deciding this would be the last time she obeyed, Vynasha approached Asa with a closed-lipped smile. "I have heard you are unwell, Asa."

The boy nodded slowly. "Are you a healer?"

Vynasha's smile froze as she carefully placed her hand over Asa's atop his furs. "Something like that." Ignoring the press of Balos and Gira's stares, she ran a thumb over the boy's frozen skin. "Asa, have you heard the tale of the Snow Queen?"

The boy shook his head weakly and squeezed her hand back, unafraid of her claws. Vynasha's smile spread true, yet her eyes burned as Asa attempted to return her smile, and she began, "Once upon a time, in a kingdom long forgotten to the east, there lived three sisters…"

Wynyth said there could be no true power without sacrifice. And so, like she had been taught, Vynasha pricked her hidden palm with her claws and reached within herself. Searching. Seeking. The sharp scent of cinnamon and smoke, of *magick* filled the air as her blood spilled into her palm.

The old woman hissed and lurched forward, but Balos shifted to catch her and whispered, "Wait."

"The eldest sister remembered a time when their mother and father still lived and loved them," Vynasha said. "But the younger twins had forgotten their names, when the Vandal army swept over the Alps and stole their father's kingdom away."

Balos's grasp on Gira tightened as Asa flinched and gasped with pain. But the boy still held her gaze and asked, "How did the sisters escape?"

Vynasha battled the urge to close her eyes as her magick settled over and into the boy and chased after the curse afflicting his flesh. "They did not." Her voice cracked, and she drew in a steadying breath as she continued. "The leader of the Vandals captured the princesses and locked them in a tower only he held the key to. With only their mother's maid to attend to them, the twins accepted their prison as the only world they knew. But the eldest sister did not forget, and with each time the Vandal general paraded her before her people in chains, her promise for vengeance grew…"

The amulet burned cold against her chest, a warning she ignored. She delved deeper and bowed over the bed as a wave of weariness pulled at her limbs. Her claws dug slightly into the back of Asa's hand, and the boy's eyes rolled back as he began to convulse.

"Balos, let me free!" Gira snapped, but Balos growled, "Not yet."

Ceddrych pounded on the door to the room. "Vynasha? Are you all right?"

Vynasha choked back a sob as the amulet burned like frozen fire against her chest. She grasped at the amulet with her free hand and ignored the pull to the presence waiting on the other side of his amulet. The wicked prince pushed so fiercely against her conscience, his panic seeping to the back of her mind, his voice calling her name.

She clenched her jaw and forced her focus to remain on Asa and the magick synchronizing her heartbeat with his.

"How do you make the flowers last through winter, Mama?" The small voice slipped from a distant memory.

Vynasha's eyes fluttered closed.

It was just the two of them in the garden, knee-deep in soft soil and new snow drifting onto the shawls covering their heads. The cold never bothered them the same way it bothered the others.

Wynyth smiled as she ran her hands over the thorny stems. Beads of blood caught along the edge of the thorns, and the snow seemed to thin, the wind to sigh, and the flowers leaned closer to their hidden place in the garden. "*To give life requires sacrifice, you see.*"

Mother's skin was warm as she took Vynasha's hand and showed her how to coax the other roses to bloom. Buds unfurled before them, and though the thorns pricked her palm, Vynasha smiled.

"*I see!*" The air thickened with roses and spices, and her blood burned hotter, her senses seemed sharper. "*Is this magick, Mama?*"

Wynyth nodded and began to sing in the lilting tongue of her homeland.

Vynasha opened her eyes to a cottage in Wylderland, and a dying boy's grip weakened in hers as she found the source of Asa's sickness. A black and twisted thing, a parasite of evil. Asa was barely old enough to hunt, had barely lived at all. She would not allow him to die.

The infection writhed and railed against her magick, no simple curse but a demon. A demon that feared yet struck against her as she learned its shape and purpose. A dead wicked queen had sent this evil to hunt Vynasha after she escaped. But it was greedy, and weary from hunting so far from Bitterhelm's source of power. And so it had latched on to the first innocent it found and made its home. The demon had been sent to find and kill *her*, and she would offer this monster what it had been denied.

Vynasha sang her mother's song in that strange tongue she had mostly forgotten. "*Where will you go, wolf child, when the blood calls you home?*"

Gira gasped and sank to her knees on Vynasha's other side, wrinkled hands scrambling to cover Asa's twitching legs. "Balos," the old woman said through sobs. "How?"

"Hold on to him, Gira," Balos rumbled from Vynasha's other side. He placed a hand on her shoulder, infecting her with his warmth. His other hand covered Asa's chest. "Hold fast, Vynasha."

Asa's limbs continued to move uncontrollably, but Vynasha didn't let go of his hand. The demon did not want to leave it's home, so she would become more desirable. She reached within herself for the well that she had never dared tap into too deeply and sang, *"What will you do, seeker, when all hope is gone?"*

"Vynasha? Balos! Unbar the door so I can… Something is wrong!" Ceddrych pounded against the door.

Vynasha caught the hand at her shoulder and squeezed, an anchor she needed as she reached deeper into the well inside her. Her eyes watered and her nostrils burned as the overpowering scent of magick filled the room like petrichor before a storm.

"Go north, to Castle Bitterhelm, wherein you may taste peace," she rasped, her voice weakening as she caught the demon between invisible claws and pulled it screaming back into herself.

"Before the long sleep," she sang with a whisper as she devoured the monster whole until it was nothing but ashes in her mouth.

"Vynasha!" Ceddrych cried.

"Asa!" Gira sobbed, and then came a boy's weakened and confused voice. "Grandmother?"

A deep rumble against her ear chased her into the fiery darkness. "You did well, Beauty."

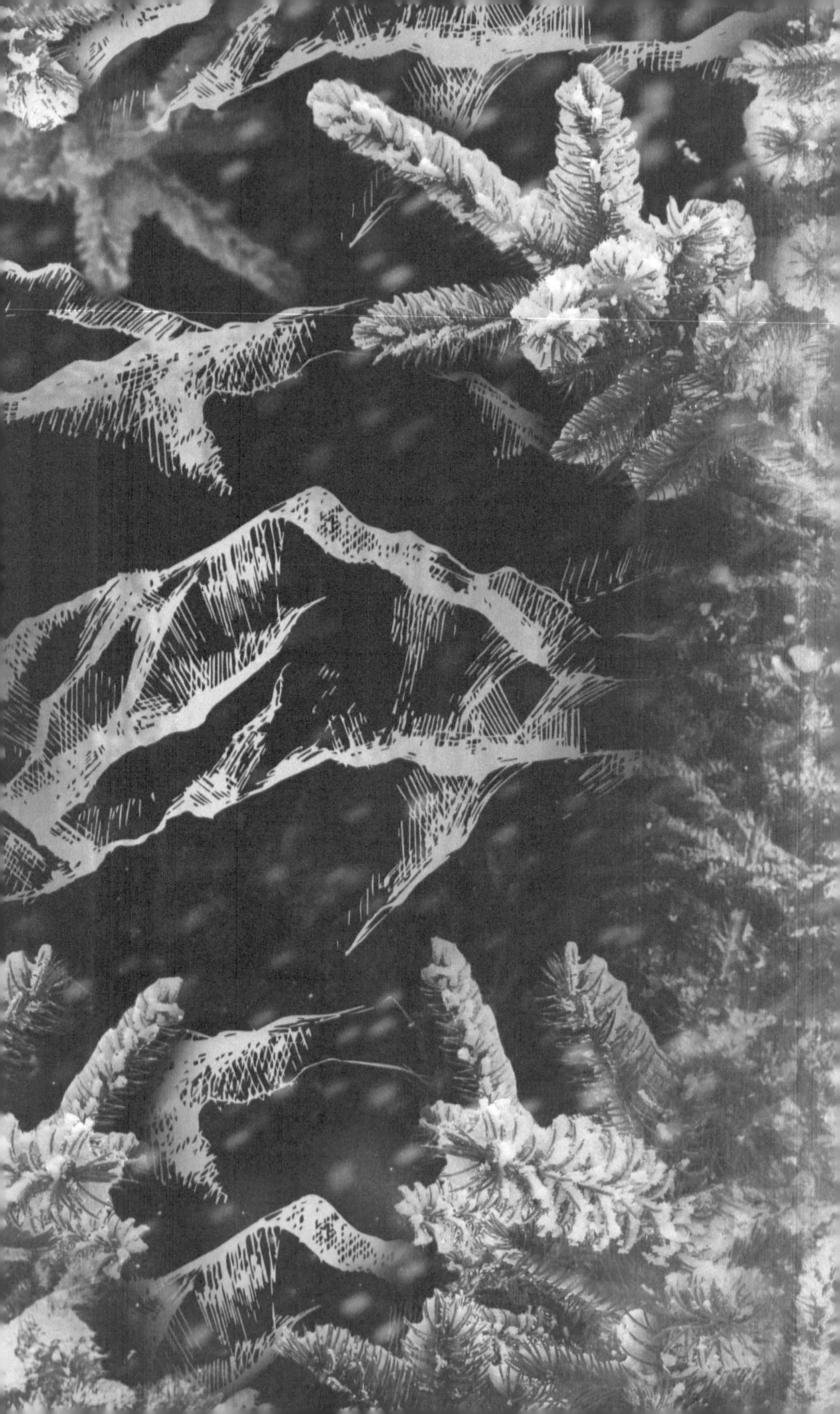

CHAPTER FIVE

A Wicked Bargain

THE DOOR GROANED then cracked against Ceddrych's assault. "Let me in, damn you!"

His blood had been up all morning, from the moment he'd scented the mob surrounding his home. This wasn't the first time the village had deemed Ceddrych unworthy to live among them. He shouldn't have been surprised that Balos went behind his back to stir the people into a frenzy. And after Ceddrych had already persuaded the council Vynasha had nothing to do with the illnesses spreading among the children since her arrival.

"You will bow before me, boy, or you shall die," Balos had warned him after that first horrible moon since the turn. *"Only one can rule Wylderland."*

There was a reason Balos had gone undisputed for so long, after all.

Ceddrych forgot to be afraid the instant the wily bastard threatened Vynasha. She had been his to protect from infancy, and he had loved her all his life. He hadn't the heart to tell her of his own troubles, as he was incapable of causing her undue pain. Best to remain her elder brother, the Ceddrych she once depended on, the one person she trusted.

But he struggled to live as a man after so many months as a beast. And the moment Balos said, *"We cannot suffer a witch to live,"* Ceddrych lost himself to instinct.

Balos avoided his every attack easily, swatting him into the snow as though Ceddrych were truly little more than a pup. Ceddrych had fought and survived a war, learning from warriors far more skilled than him. He still had no answer for why he watched his brothers in arms fall while he survived. With her letters kept pressed against his heart from battle to battle, and the endless journey home, he believed God had saved him for a greater purpose.

To save her.

For days Ceddrych had helped Vynasha rebuild the strength she'd lost from overusing her magick. He had quietly feared she might never recover. And when Ceddrych was thrown aside once again in the village circle, he resolved to end Balos if it kept her safe.

Until she came roaring with a wicked ruby dagger and her claws at Balos's throat.

Hisses and groans expelled from the crowd. Was it fear or anticipation he scented in the bloody air as his sister dug her blade into their lord's neck?

Ceddrych knew the pack well enough, and too little of the other wylderfolk, to trust them. He couldn't even trust himself. He had broken his promise to Wynyth once again. Because Vynasha would surely die for drawing Balos's blood. Surely, the cruel beast would swat her aside as quickly as he had Ceddrych.

Only madness continued to reign, because Vynasha won their

freedom with honey words and a bargain Balos agreed to. *"If I do this, you give us land of our choosing to build a home of our own. Until our home is built, we will stay in the village and protect your people."*

And here she was again, risking her life under the watch of the monster that had made Ceddrych's life a living hell.

"Let me in!" he roared as Gira exclaimed from within, "It is a miracle, Balos!"

"Come away from there, Wanderer," hawkeyed Galtis beckoned with a heavy hand, scarred and wrinkled from a life lived by the claw. "No harm will come to your sister. I am sure of it."

"If she held her end of the bargain," Onya snapped beside the fire where she had begun to cook a venison stew. Two of the pack had managed to take down an elk three days past, and the village ate well because of it.

"Don't think I'll ever forget the way you called for her death." Ceddrych bared his teeth at Onya but refused to leave the doorway in case Vynasha needed him.

Onya lifted her ladle with a white-knuckle grip. "My son is dying because of her!"

"Enough," Galtis barked, returned to his daughter's side with a stern look for them both. "We all heard my sister's praise. If the witch has truly healed my grandson, we will owe you a debt, Wanderer."

Onya scoffed and turned back to her stew, muttering under her breath, "…bleeding sorceress bring whole of Bitterhelm on our heads."

Galtis sighed and ran a hand over the feathers that grew from his head instead of hair. "You are right to fear her, but do not forget the prophecy, Onya."

"I have heard enough of your prophecy, old fool."

"It was not *my* prophecy, as you well know, daughter…"

Ceddrych returned to the door, unwilling to listen to their bickering over a subject he had avoided thinking about for the past fortnight. The priests in the village blithered on about prophecy during his childhood, and the king of Whistleande believed so strongly he started a pointless war.

He ran his hands over the grooves in the door and closed his eyes. Ever since the pack tried to teach him into their ways, he'd heard whispers of a prophecy made long ago. One day, the one born of the old blood would come to break their curse and free them from tyranny. It was the hope whispered at firesides when the white winds howled and wraiths stalked their tracks in the forest. A fool's hope they clung to in the face of endless threat and the siren's lure calling their daughters to a fate worse than death.

Ceddrych should have been afraid of the claws on his sister's hands, the points in her teeth, and beastly wyldcat eyes. But all he saw was Beauty.

Something shifted against the wood he leaned against, and Ceddrych lurched back as the door unlatched. The beast beneath his skin clawed at Ceddrych, urging him to follow his sister's scent, to make sure she was safe. "Where is my—"

"The witch sleeps," Gira announced from the open doorway, a thin but smiling Asa at her side.

Ceddrych gaped at Asa and thought once more of what he could no longer ignore. Of Vynasha's burn scars and her confession in the clearing. Of how she had saved Wyll.

"Asa!" A clash of metal hit the wooden table behind him, and then Onya barreled forward, knocking Ceddrych aside.

The wolf sank to her knees with a sob as Asa stumbled into her arms with a cry. "Mother, she swallowed the demon! She took it out!"

Galtis placed a firm hand on Ceddrych's shoulder once again. "Easy, Wanderer." Tears fell down the elder's wrinkled cheeks, pulled taught with his own smile. "Remember our debt," he added with what felt like a promise and a warning.

Gira pulled Galtis away, whispering, "We must speak, brother. Her blood… and she sang. Did you hear her song?"

Galtis murmured low, "In the mirror tongue."

Ceddrych shuddered and slipped around Onya and Asa, away from the elders whispering of things he pretended not to understand.

Whatever they believe, they're wrong. She's not their bleeding savior. She's no one to them, and everything to me.

Regret followed him the instant he entered Asa and Onya's bedroom. Ceddrych's hair stood on end at the thick scent of magick cloying in the room, overwhelming the stench of sickness.

Balos sat on the edge of the bed, Vynasha lying unconscious in his arms.

"What have you done?" Ceddrych breathed, something inside him breaking at the horrifying sight. The beast in his blood fell silent.

Balos flashed a sharp smile that didn't match the fervor in his green eyes. "Great magick requires sacrifice, pup. Your *sister* needs her rest." And the bastard had the gall to brush her curls from her face, to cradle her as though she were something precious and not a hellion intent on killing him as she had been.

This more than anything compelled him into action. "I'll decide what she needs," Ceddrych growled as he reached for her.

Balos ignored him, standing with his sister's added weight as though she were no more than a child.

Ceddrych followed him, seething.

If he drops her…

If he so much as looks at her in an unseemly manner…

But a darker voice taunted him, snarling like his inner beast. *And what will you do, fool? What can you do that you have not already done?*

Ceddrych hated feeling helpless and vowed he would find a way after this. Whatever it took, he would make Balos pay for making fools of them today, for demanding too much of his sister when she'd already given too much. He'd make them all pay.

Onya's sobs had ceased, and she sat at the dining table with

Asa in her arms, Galtis and Gira sat on either side. The elders stood as Balos carried Vynasha past them.

"Is she well?" Galtis began, a hand coming to rest on his grandson's head as the boy watched with wide eyes.

"The twins have already been by with word of the other children," Gira said, an oddly soft expression on her normally sharp features.

Balos halted just shy of the door, drawing Vynasha even closer so her head settled beneath his chin. "Tell me."

Ceddrych's jaw ached from clenching too hard, his muscles strained from restraint.

Gira approached him with a beatific smile and hands hovering over Vynasha as though fearful to touch and yearning all the same. "She healed them all."

"All?" Balos choked. Vynasha didn't stir, and Ceddrych battled the need to steal her away once more. To hide her from the way these monsters looked upon his sister like she was the answer to their prayers.

Gira nodded. "Yes, Balos."

A pause, as Balos held her gaze, something unreadable passing between them. The energy in the room shifted along with their scents. Ever since his turn, Ceddrych had discovered his new senses picked up far more than the broader world around him. Emotions held a scent too. Not all, of course. Some were easier to track, like fury and fear. Whatever unnamed emotion filled the cabin was not joy as he expected but something else, something greater.

Ceddrych bent his knees and forced himself to loosen his fists so they didn't notice his anger. He needn't have worried.

"Open the door, please, Gira," Balos finally said before turning to smile at Asa. "And you must eat well so you will be ready for training, boy."

Asa smiled, but his eyes remained fixed on Vynasha. "Is the lady okay? I want to hear the end of her story."

"You will, Asa. She just needs a bit of rest, that is all," Balos replied with warmth before nodding to the others.

Ceddrych followed their progress out the door and sneered at the rest of the pack gathered to hold vigil in the new-fallen snow. Several prowled in wolf form closer to the trees. The watch had doubled since Vynasha's arrival. More than shadows had been appearing in the deeper parts of the forest, creatures stirring to life that had slept an age.

"Is she ill, Balos?" one of the twins called. The boys appeared no more than fifteen summers, but appearances were deceiving in Wylderland.

"We heard Asa say she swallowed the demon harrowing the little ones," the other twin added. Both Dadas and Tarbus were lean with heads of bright-red hair and almost impossible to tell apart.

Balos grunted low before replying. "You boys, stay near Asa and Onya. The rest of you, keep watch on our borders. Those thieves will come sniffing out the source of her power soon."

"Yes, Balos," the pack echoed with whispers, growls, and bright exclamations from the twins.

Ceddrych's limbs shook with the effort it took to ignore Balos's command. The old bastard found great amusement in forcing Ceddrych to obey. The more he fought against the command, the more Balos's smile grew.

He kept his focus on the steady beat of Vynasha's heart as he rushed ahead and opened his cabin door. "I'm staying with her," he snapped as he tended to the dying fire. At least the coals hadn't gone out while they were distracted. Most of the village kept their coals warm even after putting out the flames. Hardy as the wylderfolk were, winter would come for them all if they weren't cautious.

Balos chuffed as he placed Vynasha on the single bed and covered her body with furs. "Of course you are staying with her." From the gleam in his green eyes, the bastard was well aware of the instant relief his approval gave Ceddrych.

Ceddrych fed the fire to avoid giving in to his more violent urges. There was little he wanted or should say, not after Vynasha sacrificed so much to grant them their freedom. To give Ceddrych *his* freedom, though she was unaware.

"So much trouble, over so fragile a creature," Balos murmured under his breath.

Ceddrych turned to find Balos brushing aside his sister's unruly curls while eyeing her with what could only be fascination. The log in his hand cracked from his grip. "You said yourself she needs rest."

And you need to leave.

Balos smiled as though he heard what Ceddrych hadn't spoken aloud. "Rest she needs but also constant watch. That was no lesser demon your sister took upon herself. It still haunts her dreams, you see."

Ceddrych shoved the log into the fire pit with greater force than necessary. Sparks spun and danced before him. "I have been watching after Vynasha all her life."

"*All* her life?" Balos quietly intoned with a mocking tilt of his silver head.

Ceddrych rolled his shoulders back and refused to meet the male's eye. "I knew her before your cursed kingdom made us into monsters."

Balos turned his smile to Vynasha and traced the dried violet blood that still coated her open palm. The wounds had already sealed. "If you knew the things I knew, boy… if you had seen the true depths of wickedness I have known, you would not be so eager for me to leave your sister's side."

Ceddrych slowly approached the bed, as near as he dared. "I will never leave her side again unless she wishes it. And yours is the last face she'd want to see after what you forced her to endure."

A curious thing. The way the male's smile instantly fell and the mask of careful arrogance failed. Just a moment, yet long enough to show what looked like pain crumpling the alpha's face. The beast beneath Ceddrych's skin stirred at this rare show of weakness.

Balos turned back to Vynasha, his thumb brushing her healed palm once more. "Her blood is tainted, did you know?"

Ceddrych stiffened, as recent memories of words called in her sleep, of the violet blood she'd been covered in when he found her, the same violet that stained her hand today…

Balos nodded as though Ceddrych had shared everything in his mind, all the things he could never speak aloud. Not in this village. "Oh yes, she has been marked. It is why the demon came to our village, the reason we should have killed her rather than let her live. It would be a kindness in the end." And he leveled a hard, ageless glare at Ceddrych as he said, "Never trust her again, and you might save both your lives."

"But she risked her life to save Asa's," Ceddrych growled back. "Vynasha would never harm another person unless in defense. I know she would never harm me."

Balos absently lifted his stained fingers, the violet blood faintly luminous in the firelight. "And the song. Did you know she sang in the elder tongue? Did you *know* your sister practices blood magick? Or that in the old kingdom, she would have been slain for such an offense against nature? Make no mistake, what Vynasha has done today is forbidden with good reason. It is for our bargain alone she still lives…"

"To hell with your old kingdom," Ceddrych replied. "You have no king, only a ruin full of ghosts and monsters."

Balos shook his head as he rose with heavy sigh. "When she wakes, you will *both* honor the agreement she made, Wanderer."

Ceddrych managed a simulacrum of a smile. "And you will give us our due reward when we've met your pithy bargain and are finally free of you."

Balos laughed and shook his head as he turned to leave, an arch to his brow and a flash of malice meeting his green eyes. "None of us is free, boy. Least of all her."

CHAPTER SIX

A Cruel Temptation

GRENDEL WAS WAITING for her within a watery-gray reflection of the bedroom Vynasha once occupied in the castle. His back was to her, facing a hearth filled with blue flames. Floating lights danced about the edge of her vision as she rose from the side of her bed. She'd been crouched in the same position in Asa's bedroom, she recalled.

"Asa," Vynasha gasped and rushed to her feet, then pressed a hand to her stomach as a wave of nausea crashed over her.

"Vynasha?" Grendel was before her in a flash, firm hands catching her by the waist as he helped to settle her atop the bed. "Thank Crafter you finally came. I called for you—did you not hear my warning?"

"I heard… Let me go," Vynasha groaned as she pushed away from him until her back rested against the headboard.

Grendel flinched and pain crumpled his features as he sat back on the edge of the bed and his features seemed to glow brighter than anything else in the room. "What has happened? You were drawing too much attention to yourself. It was only a matter of time before you drew *her* creatures to retrieve you."

"One of her *creatures* has already come to destroy everything in their path to reach me," she spat back.

Grendel straightened, fury in his violet gaze. "What do you mean? Was it one of the beasts?"

"It was a demon, a being of shadow," she spat. "It tried to kill every child in the village and then me before I ended the bastard."

Grendel ran a hand over his tired face and turned back to the blue flames. "I had hoped…"

Vynasha fisted the bedsheets. "Hoped for what? That your bitch of a mother would care for the innocents that suffer because of her curse?"

A bitter laugh escaped her as she savored his discomfort. "You bloody royals care so much for your own grievances but so little for the plight of common folk. Did you never consider the consequences of sending me away before *she* could trap me under her thrall?"

Grendel leaned forward and placed his hand near her thigh, too close for comfort. "You are *mine*, Vynasha. She cannot bind you without destroying me, and I will never be weak again."

Vynasha refused to be intimidated by him, this price she was bound to. His eyes widened as she leaned forward. "If you're so strong, why are you hiding in this dream realm and not reclaiming your birthright from Ferox?"

Grendel's gaze swept over her features and dipped past her neck. "It is not so simple as that."

Vynasha scoffed and gritted her teeth against the lurch in her stomach. "It's obvious you are a *coward*."

Grendel snatched her leg and sharply tugged. A gasp ripped

from her throat as Vynasha fell against the sheets, and the prince loomed over her with a hand inching around her waist, his thumb grazing her breast.

It's not real!

But she felt every part of his body pressing against hers, and her blood sang to be reunited with its other half.

"Get off of me," she hissed and dug her claws into his chest through the fabric of his shirt.

"I *warned* you before, did you not listen?" Grendel pressed his forehead to hers, his skin cooler than hers, like an impression of new-fallen snow. "I have endeavored to keep you safe from her, from him, and every beast that would try to use you." His lips brushed hers with every word. "And still you do not understand…"

Vynasha's breath hitched, and a part of her burned to close the distance, to press her lips to his, to pull him harder against her until they were one flesh. Did she truly want *him*, or was this their bond, drawing them together against her will? Could Grendel's magick work even here in this shadow realm? How much worse would it be were they truly together?

She bared her teeth at the prince but clenched her thighs together beneath him to relieve the growing ache. "Stop talking in riddles and tell me, then," she snapped, desperately clinging to her mask of fury.

"You already know," he murmured and grazed his nose along hers. "You *know*, love…"

Vynasha hesitated at the devastation in his eyes, the unspoken apology. "The bond," she breathed.

Grendel smiled as he lifted a hand to trace the path her scars took over her neck, along her jaw and the side of her face. "And you know what will happen if I waken?"

Vynasha felt so little where the fire had deadened and warped her skin. Magick hadn't saved her beauty, and it had been worth the chance to save Wyll. Grendel's touch broke past that numbness now, the same way he had broken through her walls before. She hated him, oh, how she hated the reminder she no longer belonged to herself.

"You wouldn't be able to stop." Despair bled into her voice with the truth. "You would send everything and everyone in your possession to reclaim me."

"No, love, I would come for you myself." Grendel's smile twisted with avarice as his touch firmed at her neck and he drew her against his mouth. "And I would raze everything in my path because I would not care. Do you not see? My *cowardice*, as you called it, may be the only kindness I can offer you, Vynasha. Please do not squander my sacrifice again."

"I hate what you've done to me," she said through sobs and dug her claws deeper into his chest, just to watch the way he bled violet instead of blue now, the same as she did. His fault.

My fault, Mother…

"I love your claws. Will you show me your teeth?"

"My…" she sputtered, fury and confusion warring within her.

Grendel smiled as he surged forward and covered her mouth with his.

I hate him, she thought as euphoria claimed her senses. Every inhale became his exhale until she could not tell where she ended and began. There was only this moment.

Bliss relieved the burning she'd been plagued with as she moved her lips against his, unsure but accepting. Her bloody hands slipped over his shoulders and around his back, holding him in place.

Grendel groaned as he pulled her knee aside and slotted their hips together.

Vynasha gasped at the shock of feeling too much, of everything he would give. But it wasn't enough in this shadow realm of dreams. The sensation was muted yet still dulling her senses with ecstasy.

Grendel deepened their kiss, his tongue stroking hers and

tracing her slightly sharp teeth. He devoured her moans and pulled away to press her name against her raw lips.

Here was the danger, the warning made flesh. Would she wake with his taste on her tongue, with his blood on her claws?

"Vynasha, stay here with me," he begged and traced her with his tongue before biting lightly down.

Her hips rolled instinctively as she tugged his head back and met his fevered gaze. "This isn't real," she said, panting.

Grendel ran his fingers over her breast and smiled at her moan. "Does that not feel real, love?"

Vynasha shook her head and reached within herself for the rage she still held for him. "We're dreaming, and even if we weren't, I wwould *never* be your lover."

Grendel stiffened and then his hand slipped to encircle her neck. "You forget we are bonded, Vynasha. I know what you fear to feel."

There it was again, the fury and fire he had compelled away with his kisses. Vynasha wouldn't make this mistake again. "You see only what you want to see, you cold bastard."

She swiped his cheek with her claws, and Grendel reared back with fury burning his eyes the same shade of violet as their shared blood.

"Stay out of my dreams and stay away from me!" she roared and kicked Grendel off of her as she should have done from the beginning.

Her vision began to fade as he pulled his bloody hand from his marred cheek and reached for her, her name a distant echo on his lips.

CHAPTER SEVEN

A Blood Witch

YNASHA WOKE WITH a gasp, her hand at her throat and her body aflame. "I didn't... it's not..." She pulled her shaking hands away and stared at the fresh violet blood coating her fingers. "...real."

"Easy. Don't try to get up, Ash." Ceddrych's worried voice cut through her panic. "Here, let me see."

"Ceddrych?" She lifted her head, and her brother was suddenly there beside her, a bowl of herbal water and cloth in his lap.

Vynasha stared into his golden-green eyes with wonder as he began to gently clean her hands and claws. "What happened?"

Ceddrych stilled, and his jaw clenched as he held her gaze. "I nearly lost you again," he said before moving the cloth to her neck.

Vynasha blinked back tears and tilted her head back. "Asa?"

Ceddrych sighed, and his shoulders slumped as he replied,

"He woke the moment you passed out and has been telling the whole village about his *new friend*, the witch."

Vynasha laughed so she wouldn't cry. "I'm still alive, so I take it Balos will honor our bargain?"

"For now." Ceddrych returned the cloth to the bowl and set it on the floor beside the bed. "Talk in the village is in your favor…"

"And yesterday they were a mob at our door," she scoffed then frowned at Ceddrych's grimace. "How long have I been asleep?"

Ceddrych leaned forward and ran a hand over her unbound curls, brow creasing once more. "Three days."

She gasped. The dream hadn't lasted so long, surely.

But he wanted you to stay.

Had giving into Grendel, even for a brief moment, prolonged her time in his shadow realm?

"That's not all," Ceddrych added as he took her hand in his. "There were others who were ill like Asa. And I don't understand how you did it, but they were all healed as well."

"Others?" she whispered.

Ceddrych offered what should have been a reassuring smile and said, "Yes, four that I know of. They have come by asking to meet you."

Vynasha struggled to breathe. She knew she should be relieved to hear this, that losing three days and a little blood was nothing compared to the lives of children. But they could never know she had almost called ruin upon them by saving Asa.

Grendel had warned her, hadn't he? She'd drawn too deeply when she attacked the demon poisoning Asa. Had the same being attacked the others as well, or were they connected like branches from a single vine?

No matter. What's done is done.

Her offer to heal Asa had been genuine, and in the end, she'd had no choice but to use her magick. Balos had ensured that.

And you drew too much magick to save the boy. Drew from him.

Vynasha turned from her brother's steady gaze. Ceddrych had become her anchor since dragging her from the river. They had been so close, once. To have that closeness with him again meant everything to her, and she feared what he would see in her expression now.

"I've always known you had magick, Asha. I know Wynyth taught you all she could, but what you did for Asa and the other children is beyond…"

He hesitated, and Vynasha bit down on the inside of her cheek. The sting kept the tears threatening to spill behind her eyes. "I was stupid to put us at risk like that," she whispered.

"No, no, Ash." Ceddrych squeezed her hand, and tapped her chin, coaxing her to look at him. She marveled at the wonder in his brilliant smile. "Saving that boy's life wasn't stupid. Healing a half dozen others wasn't stupid. You saved our lives by saving theirs, little sister."

"But I drew too much attention to us. The… *they* will sense it, and what happens when they come looking for me?"

He shook his head as her tears spilled over her cheeks and caught the beads with his fingertips. "If they come, we will fight the way you fought your way out. You won't be alone, and now we have a real chance. Thanks to you, the council has agreed to let us build on the land I brought you to. All we need do is find…"

Wyll.

Vynasha smiled at the lovely picture Ceddrych painted, a tale she longed to come true. She closed her eyes and pictured the cottage they would build together. She pictured Wyll's laughter and roses encircling a stone-walled garden in full bloom.

A knock on the door spoiled the vision and jolted Vynasha from the cusp of sleep. She opened her eyes and sat up with a groan. The nausea from her dream persisted, and the weariness she'd been battling since waking in the village pulled at her aching bones.

Ceddrych eyed her slow progress with concern as he stood

and crossed the room. Tension kept his broad shoulders taut as he lifted his chin and scented the air.

Vynasha ran her thumb over her claws and tensed as her brother opened the door.

"What are you doing here, Onya?" Ceddrych's greeting sounded more like a threat.

Onya leaned past Ceddrych to eye Vynasha. "We heard the witch was awake and wanted to pay our respects."

"I see," Ceddrych replied, tension bleeding from his broad shoulders. The door creaked as he pulled it wide, snow slipping past Onya and Asa into their home. "As you can *see*, she's doing well."

Vynasha's breath caught as Asa lurched forward and exclaimed, "She is awake!"

"Wait," Onya hissed as she reached to catch the boy. "Asa!" Onya groaned as she chased her son inside.

"I see your son is as well-mannered as you are," Ceddrych muttered as he quickly shut the door.

Asa plopped onto her bedside. "I waited and waited for so long! I told Auntie Gira I thought you would sleep forever!" Firelight glinted off the small prongs poking through his silver hair and his black eyes were bright as he bounced in place.

"Watch your tongue, Wanderer," Onya snapped. "My son has not stopped asking after her since the witch saved his life."

"Do you feel well?" Vynasha asked with no small amount of wonder. It was one thing to create magick, to exchange life for life as Wynyth once taught her. But the boy before her brimmed with life in such contrast to the sallow creature she'd first met.

Asa nodded and took her hand in his, much as she had done before. "The demon wanted to keep us forever. I asked the others who were sick, and they all said it told them terrible things. But you burned it out of us, and now we are all better than before!"

Vynasha's breath hitched as she realized Wyll hadn't moved so freely or without pain since the fire. But she found herself squeezing the boy's hand and slowly returned his smile. "Better?"

Asa drew his legs onto the bed, and Onya's fluttering hands fell to her sides as the woman kneeled beside them. "Oh, yes! I told Grandfather and Auntie that I should be ready to join the hunters soon. I just know Balos is going to let me once he sees how much stronger I am." Asa lifted his pointed chin and squeezed Vynasha's hand for emphasis.

Onya sighed. "You will do no such thing until I finish training you myself, little love."

"But mama, I *am* ready! I carried the water jug from the well to our house all by myself yesterday!"

Ceddrych shuffled on his feet at the foot of the bed, his grimace twisting into a reluctant smile as he met Vynasha's amused gaze.

Asa squeezed her hand again. "Do you not think I am ready, Vynasha?"

Vynasha leaned forward and held his hand between both of hers, careful of her claws. "I am certain your mother will let you join the others one day. But you were so very ill, you see, much as I have been these past days. And we can't begrudge our families for wishing to keep us close until they're certain we're safe."

Asa slumped forward and idly played with her thumb. "I suppose so," he muttered then straightened with a grin. "Could you tell me more of the story about the Snow Queen? What happened to the three princesses? Did they ever escape the tower?"

Vynasha's sudden burst of laughter, coarse and raspy from lack of use, surprised her. Ceddrych stood very still as both Onya and Asa chuckled along with her. "Shall I tell you how the eldest princess found revenge against the general? Or how the twins first discovered their magick?"

"Another day," Ceddrych interrupted. "We've had more than enough excitement for the evening."

Asa groaned, but Onya dragged her son away with a firm hand. "You will see her again soon, mayhap tomorrow? If you are feeling well enough, Witch?"

"If Asa promises to be good," Vynasha offered with a softer smile for the boy.

"Oh, yes! I swear it by tooth and claw," Asa quickly piped up.

"Shush, boy," Onya growled, "before you swear your life service to the witch by accident."

Vynasha snorted at Onya's use of the title she had so long feared and dreaded. Somehow, the meaning had changed, creeping upon her unawares. She no longer feared being a witch if it meant seeing Asa's smile again, and if it could save others.

"Perhaps after you learn proper manners, we'll invite you for supper," Ceddrych drawled as he led them to the door.

"I can finally learn manners, right, Mama? Just like Auntie Gira says I should?"

Onya's put-upon sigh was belied by the crooked smile that favored Vynasha as they crossed the threshold once more. "Thank you for allowing our visit."

Vynasha opened her mouth to reply, but Ceddrych had already shut the door with a firm "Good morrow."

Vynasha hid her growing smile behind her hand as Ceddrych leaned heavily against the doorframe. They waited as a brightly chattering Asa could be heard beyond the walls of their cottage, greeting anyone who would listen about his visit with "our witch!"

Ceddrych turned the moment her laughter bubbled past her lips, and she gave up trying to hide her smile. Something softened in his gaze at the sound, and he ran a hand over his face as he returned to her side. "I don't know whether to thank the boy for making you smile or wring his scrawny neck for bothering you. Though I'm not surprised, it being Onya's whelp."

Vynasha caught his hand and tugged. "Don't be mad at Asa. He's just a boy, and it's a miracle he's so well."

Ceddrych chuffed. "No miracle, Asha. Just you…"

"And where does this power come from, if not God, the mother, or the saints?" She whispered the question she had long feared.

"I stopped listening to that damned village priest long before your first word, little sister," Ceddrych replied. "And I am unsure any god we know lives here. This is a land for all the creatures and beings the rest of the world has forgotten. If we can make Wylderland our home and I can keep you… if you can be safe, then what does it matter where your power comes from?"

Vynasha swallowed past the lump in her throat and tugged at his arm. "Will you hold me?"

Ceddrych's brow creased, and then his expression shuttered, as it often did since their reunion. It meant there were things he would or could not say to her, things he was keeping from her.

Much as Vynasha wanted to force him to speak and break the wall between them, she understood. For there was much she hadn't told Ceddrych and much she couldn't bear for him to learn. And this was fine—it was *safe*. They were together, and nothing else mattered besides finding Wyll and building their home.

Yet when she closed her eyes, she saw the way Balos had flung Ceddrych aside with little effort. And the fear she felt then returned with her vengeance.

"Asha, what is it?" Ceddrych's free hand pushed her curls behind her ear.

She breathed more easily once Ceddrych had settled beneath the covers and furs with her. Only after he had tucked her against his chest did she dare meet his hazel gaze and whisper, "Promise me."

"You only need ask." Ceddrych squeezed the fist she placed over his heart.

"Promise you'll never do something so stupid as challenge someone over me again."

Ceddrych flinched, and she pressed her fingers to his mouth before his protest could crawl out.

"Because you may have almost lost me, but I almost lost you before that. And I *can't*… I won't survive losing you, don't you understand?" She didn't know she was crying until he carefully wiped away her tears, and his chest shuddered beneath her hold.

"You think I could survive losing you? I only challenged *him* because I would rather both of us die than watch them *burn* you." His chest heaved as he struggled for another breath.

Vynasha shook her head and pushed his hand away with a wet laugh. "Saints, listen to us. Are we truly arguing about who would grieve the other more?"

Ceddrych's answered laugh came out as more of a sob, and he squeezed his eyes shut before pressing a kiss to her forehead. "I promise," he whispered, and it felt like a benediction, something sacred and heavy with the press of magick in her veins.

"Thank you," Vynasha said with a sigh as he tucked her beneath his chin. His scent surrounded her, and the beast beneath her skin settled once more.

CHAPTER EIGHT

A Glass Prison

NO SOONER HAD she closed her eyes than she opened them to the glasshouse gardens of Castle Bitterhelm. Snow swirled over the glass with an invisible wind and hovered unnaturally before dancing slowly through tiny cracks. The air was thick in the true glass gardens, filled with the perfume of roses and magick. In this shadow realm, the place between waking and dreams, Vynasha could only smell the decay of a thousand petals shed, the stench of a dying curse.

Vynasha cursed under her breath, "Bloody gatekeeper."

The garden had been Ferox's gift to her, and she would always associate it with the beast she tried so hard to forget. Her gaze darted over the hedgerows as she slowly walked the familiar path. But no pair of golden gilded horns appeared. Her beast didn't belong to this plane.

"Is it just us?" she wondered aloud. "Did you make this place to torture me, Grendel?"

In the liminal space between dreams, there was no sun or moon, only drifting stars. The lights cast pale, lavender shadows over everything and made the roses blooming upon every hedge gleam bright as blood.

Vynasha's breath hitched as she ran her hands over the outstretched blooms. Buds blossomed as she passed, shedding fresh petals, which fell and rose to hover like the snow above.

When Ferox first brought her to the gardens, the roses were dead. Vynasha had used her gift to bring them back to life.

"My blood," she said as the hedgerow shivered and rippled as she passed.

A soft voice began to sweetly hum a familiar song that set Vynasha's teeth on edge.

Petals clung to her hair and clothes as she reached the inner garden and gasped in surprise. "Hvalla?"

The girl seemed even smaller than she had before. Gray skin and dark, blue-black locks a tangle, with blossoms braided into the strands. Hvalla had tended the garden as best the girl could, and slowly gone mad since Soraya cast her curse.

Vynasha blinked and found herself standing beside the maid. "Hvalla?"

Hvalla's humming stopped and the girl's head tilted in a birdlike manner as she cupped a heavy blossom between her hands. "Have I done well, mistress? It was very difficult to tend your garden when Master broke the hedges after you left…"

Vynasha's full velvet skirts spread like a wine stain around them as she sank to her knees. A weight filled her as she took in the shadow garden, the blossoms, and the maid anew. "I'm sorry I left you all to face his wrath alone."

Hvalla had been barely more than a spirit, transparent in the way many servants had been in Castle Bitterhelm. But the weight of the girl's hand was solid and surprisingly warm.

Her dark eyes seemed to look past Vynasha yet filled with sorrow. "They hunted him, our kind Master, the one who tried but could not hate us. The beasts hunted him, his own kin. And he wanted to destroy it all," she hissed, hand clamping down with sudden pressure. "He could not destroy the mirror, so he came here and hurt himself trying to destroy your roses, his gift…"

Vynasha shuddered and pulled her hand free as Hvalla's expression smoothed and her voice faded. She rubbed her eyes and frowned at her tears. "I shouldn't have let Grendel send me away. I should have fought harder to stay and tried to stop them."

She hadn't allowed herself to dwell on that day, least of all on the beast that saved her life by taking the brunt of their fall and dragging her to the river's edge.

"*Wynyth's girl…*" Old Ced had begged before the end. "*Forgive me for failing you.*"

Hvalla startled her from the bitter memory. "My queen would have assuredly become consumed by the curse had she stayed. The curse breaker must be strong of will to face their reflection in the mirror. And claim the mirror you must before the end…"

"Ferox's attempts to make me didn't go so well before." Vynasha grimaced at the memory of the beast's desperation and his great hand forcing her hold until the runed arch seemed to set her bones afire in fury.

Hvalla moved slow fingers to trace the petals dropping from the fresh buds and hovering in the air between them. "He wanted to go home."

Vynasha looked to the skies, to the swirling stars trailing silver dust in their wake. "So do I," she whispered.

"My queen is home," Hvalla argued with a giggle.

Home was Tamyra's songs while she baked in Grandmother Mayve's kitchen, little Wyll's hands around her neck as he begged her to carry him on her back. Home was Wynyth's rose garden and

Ceddrych… And for a time she would rather forget, home had been a haunted castle with a glass garden, a lavish prison.

Vynasha buried her face in her hands, amazed to find more tears spilling down her cheeks. "I should have listened to you before, Hvalla." She sniffed and lifted her head to find the girl already watching her solemnly. "You tried to warn me what was to come, didn't you?"

Hvalla leaned toward the roses. "None could speak the truth, but you are my queen."

Vynasha smiled and placed a hand over Hvalla's trembling arm. "I'm sorry I didn't try harder to listen. But I'm here now. Can you tell me why I must claim the mirror? Grendel believed it was safer for me to let the curse die on its own. He said I'd be safer if I stayed away."

Hvalla swayed slightly and her voice dipped low as she shook her head. "Safer for Vynasha of Whistleande Valley… yes, and there is happiness to be found in a cottage in the woods. Until the beasts come knocking and the shadows a-haunting. Once the curse fades, nothing will hold them back. And none can tame them but the curse breaker." The girl thrust her hands in the tangled briars with a groan. "All will perish and be devoured in their wake!"

"Stop! What are you doing?" Vynasha struggled to pull Hvalla free from the vines. But the briars lashed up Hvalla's arms, and the thorns dug in deeply.

Blossoms sprouted where the girl's silver-blue blood pooled. Her pale eyes filled with unshed tears. "I am unafraid to die, my queen. I will tend the roses as promised, will keep the garden safe until you return."

"Stop that—no one is dying today." Vynasha clawed at the vines, yet the thorns only tightened their grasp. She froze at Hvalla's pained cry. "Oh, Saints! I'm so sorry, Hvalla, I don't know what to do or how to stop this!"

"You will know, my queen." Hvalla smiled, and the glass garden dimmed as snow fell heavier, blotting out the dancing stars above. "You will know once you feel love and hatred in equal measure."

Vynasha tried to use her claws to snap the briars nearer to the soil, but they passed through instead. "What the hell?" She lifted her hand and watched in growing horror as her form began to quickly fade. "Hvalla, what's happening?"

"Stay away from this realm, my queen. The master sleeps, and we are drawn deeper into the shadows with him. He gathers them close to his side so they will not hunt you. Avoid the shadows, lest you be forced to join him."

"Wait!" Vynasha lost her grasp of the girl's arm. Her hand passed through her as though it were no longer there. "Hvalla, hold on to me! I can't leave you alone in this cursed place!"

Yet Hvalla drifted deeper into the rosebushes and did not fight the thorned branches wrapping tenderly around her neck. "Find the lost stars, my queen. Bring us home as was promised."

In the distance, a lone wolf began to howl a mournful song.

Vynasha's scream was lost to the sound of breaking glass and the roaring of beasts.

She woke to hushed voices whispering by the door, and her hand wrapped painfully over the amulet hidden beneath her tunic. Vynasha's heart raced with lingering panic as she took in the coals in the fireside, the empty bed, and Ceddrych speaking to someone through the crack in the cabin door.

She closed her eyes and focused on the familiar scents of recently cooked stew, animal pelts, and the underlying wolf sleeping beneath her brother's skin. The wolf was nearer to the surface now, as it often was whenever Ceddrych was upset.

"My sister has only just recovered from saving *your* village, yet he commands I leave her alone to clean up his mess?"

"Apologies, Wanderer," a young male began, "but it was Wolfsbane's scent he caught too near the border, sure enough. He's already taken Onya and half the pack ahead before the trail gets cold. He ordered Vilhelm to bring you with the rest to join the hunt."

"Aye!" an identical voice butted in. "Because you spent so long roaming the forbidden lands as a wolf before…"

"Before the day we found the witch," the first voice added. His brother?

Vynasha frowned and watched Ceddrych's reaction carefully.

"*I spent too long as a wolf,*" he once said, "*Now I need to remember how to live as a man.*"

Her own beastly instincts rose to the fore the heavier the scent of rage and magick thickened the air.

"I see," Ceddrych finally replied, his voice unsteady. "Anything else you pups care to tell me?"

Vynasha peered between his legs at a pair of dirty, identical faces. Brothers, indeed. The boys looked so alike there was no telling them apart. She ducked lower to claim more than a glimpse. Youth marked them by their scrawny limbs, faces caught in the crux between boy and manhood.

"Anytime today, pups." The doorframe groaned under Ceddrych's hold.

The twins eyed one another.

"We should not tell you here," one said.

"Yes, anyone could be listening," added his brother.

Ceddrych grumbled under his breath, "Dropped on their heads at birth…" Then, to the twins, he spoke slowly. "Dadas, Tarbus, while I appreciate your loyalty, your prattling has already awoken my sister…"

Dadas and Tarbus startled then ducked to peek at her through Ceddrych's legs. Vynasha froze, and the twins favored her with wide, identical smirks.

"And I keep no secrets from her. Any warnings you have for

me, she should hear." Ceddrych pushed off the doorframe with a deceptively easy motion and turned around to follow their gaze. His attempted smile was tight about the edges. "Asha, I'd hoped to spare you from these miserable mutts, but I suppose there's no stopping them." He inclined his head and waved his hand. "Come inside, then."

Dadas and Tarbus stared, mouths slightly gaping, as Ceddrych stepped aside, and then bowed at one another. "After you, brother."

"Oh, no, after *you*." They pushed and cajoled one another until Ceddrych grasped them by the backs of their fur collars and dragged them inside.

A chuckle escaped Vynasha's lips as the twins scrambled to regain their footing while Ceddrych shut the door firmly behind him.

"Tarbus! Straighten up, you mangy hare." Dadas elbowed his brother.

Tarbus nudged him back harder with a scowl but kept his mouth shut when Ceddrych came to stand before them. Side by side, the twins weren't much shorter than her brother, yet Ceddrych still seemed to fill the room and command attention.

"Done ogling my sister yet?" Ceddrych crossed his arms over his chest. "Tell me the rest."

Tarbus kept his head tilted and his gaze down in a submissive manner. "Balos asked the council for permission to continue his hunt for Wolfsbane. Now that the children are healed, he wants to use your bargain to flush out our last enemy."

Dadas piped up, "Aye, and the elders approved."

Ceddrych's posture stiffened, and Vynasha recognized the effort it took for him to contain his anger. "Our agreement was to patrol our borders and guard the village. And we have finally been given leave to build our home. So for the last time, you can tell your *alpha*, I will not join his damned crusade against Wolfsbane."

"Wait!" Vynasha flinched at the sudden force of their attention. Curiosity from the boys, and the promise of violence in

Ceddrych's green-gold gaze. "You should join them in case they find… something important."

Like our lost nephew.

Ceddrych's rage dampened to a simmering coal as he grimaced and sank on the bedside to take her hand. "These bloody hunts can last from a week to a full moon, Asha. I can't leave you unprotected for that long."

Vynasha forced a bright smile and squeezed his hand. "So don't leave me unprotected," she said with a glance at the squirming twins.

Ceddrych arched a brow, and his mouth tilted up at the corner. "What an excellent idea, dear sister."

Vynasha pushed aside the furs and willed strength into her limbs. The rushes beneath her feet crackled, and Ceddrych steadied her rise with a hand clasping firmly around her waist.

"I've got you," he murmured low as she looked up and caught his warm gaze. Suddenly, playing the part became far more agonizing.

But I promised Wyll, and until I'm well enough to join the hunt, Ceddrych needs to believe I'll be safe.

Vynasha's smile turned brittle as she said, "What say you, boys?"

Tarbus shuffled in place and rubbed a hand over his arm. "Will we… be safe from your magick?"

Ceddrych growled deep in his chest. "I believe we've already settled the matter with the entire bloody village, wouldn't you agree?"

Vynasha stiffened. It shouldn't hurt, their doubt and fear. Fear had kept trouble from her doorstep when she was left alone to protect Wyll. She was a fool to hope for more after Asa and Onya's visit.

Dadas shoved his twin and grumbled. "Nice going, soft belly."

"No, he's right to be afraid," Vynasha found herself saying, to Ceddrych or the twins she wasn't certain. "I've been afraid for most of my life. Fear keeps you alive…" Her gaze met Tarbus's, and the boy slowly straightened. "I know I'm an outsider—I'm not even from Wylderland—but this place is our home now. And I swear I will do everything I can to honor my promise to Balos and protect the village. That includes you."

"And if these two lummoxes do as they're told, you won't have to." Ceddrych pressed a kiss to the top of her head and squeezed her shoulder then turned to the twins. "Give us a moment. Wait outside for me."

"Yes, Wanderer," the boys murmured in unison and slipped back into the snow.

"Come, I want to show you something." Ceddrych beckoned her across the room to the mess of vellum parchment and books stacked on his neglected worktable. He spread a fresh roll of stretched animal skin over the table, revealing carefully inked mountains, the Silver River, and a vague impression of the lost city.

"You made this?" Vynasha leaned against the table to support her weight and ran a careful clawed finger over the trails leading from Wylderland to his family's ancestral ruins above the valley of Whistleande. Her finger stilled just over the last stronghold of the northern lords, a reminder of Old Ced's desperation to reclaim his family's honor.

"Always wanted to explore new lands, didn't we?" Ceddrych said. "This may not be entirely accurate, of course. I only know what I've seen in books and with the southern army during the war."

She looked up at him, instantly aware of his careful wording, of the fact this needed to be kept secret. "Why are you showing me this?"

"I want you to have this, just in case something happens."

"In case *what* happens?"

Ceddrych ducked his head and tugged at one of her long curls. "Don't let anyone else see this while I'm away?"

Vynasha nodded and shifted uneasily as her brother rolled the map back up. "Of course. You know I won't." She frowned as Ceddrych slipped the map to a shadowed nook within his small bookshelf.

He glanced at her over his shoulder with a shadow of his usual mirth softening the gravity in his face. "Please stay close to home while I'm away?"

Vynasha nodded and pressed her palm over the impression of the amulet beneath her tunic.

Appeased, Ceddrych tilted her chin to meet his pensive gaze. "I swore I wouldn't leave you again."

She smiled the way she would have before the fire ruined all promise of beauty. "Wylderland isn't so vast a country as the flatlands were from Whistleande. If you aren't home in a fortnight, I'll just have to come find you."

This was the reason for his map, she suddenly realized. In case he didn't return, in case he didn't find Wyll, or worse. Her smile faltered, and Ceddrych breathed in sharply, as though he read the truth behind her false smiles, but then cast a glance at the door.

The twins were waiting, and all the wolves had excellent hearing.

Vynasha swallowed and caught his wrist, felt the rapid pulse beating beneath her fingertips. "You will come home," she whispered.

Ceddrych's jaw worked as he nodded. He drew in a deep breath then slowly straightened and released her. "Come back inside, pups," he called to the door.

The twins entered, heads down and cheeks flushed from the cold, shaking their heads to release a dusting of snow onto the floor.

Ceddrych squared his shoulders, authority settling into his voice as his breath clouded the air. "The two of you will stay here until I return. Obey her as you would me."

Dadas paled at this. "You mean us to… stay inside?"

"With her?" Tarbus blurted. "Alone?"

"Naturally, though you are welcome to sleep in your other forms if that helps you feel safer." Ceddrych arched an eyebrow, and a disarmingly easy grin transformed his face into the handsome warrior he'd once been. "You won't bite, will you, sister?"

The sight warmed her heart with happier memories, and she couldn't help but return his confidence. "Only if they ask," Vynasha replied with a click of her sharp teeth.

The younger wolves flinched, and the fleeting thought of how the twins would have managed Ferox in all his monstrous beauty made her smile grow.

Dadas and Tarbus kept a wary eye on her and their backs to the wall as Ceddrych approached the door.

Her brother pulled his fur cloak over his shoulders and attached a bone-handled blade to his belt. "Stand guard outside if you prefer the cold." Ceddrych stepped out into the snow. "Only remember this. No one else goes in or out without her permission. First sign of trouble in the village, and I don't care what promises we made to Balos, you get her out and come find me, understood?"

"Of course!" The twins spoke over each other. "You can depend on us, Wanderer!"

The clouds were trapped in a veil of gray masking the dawn, raining a steady veil of thick snow. Something about it set Vynasha's teeth on edge, and her hand pressed harder to the amulet.

Don't leave, please.

Ceddrych shared one last look with Vynasha over his shoulder, eyes flashing green as he shuddered, then stalked away from the village and into the woods.

Chapter Nine

A Time to Hunt

OME BACK!

The words sat at the tip of her tongue, desperate clunky things she refused to let escape.

"No," he hissed instead.

Tarbus tripped, and his shoulder knocked against the doorframe with a *thump*. "What?"

"Idiot," his brother grumbled and set him to rights on his feet.

Vynasha blinked and was painfully aware she was scowling at the forest, as though the trees and not Balos were responsible for calling her brother away. At least this time he left her with bodyguards.

"Could you…" She paused as they pulled away and immediately ducked their heads, watchful and ready for instruction.

Vynasha shook her head and wrapped an arm around her waist

as she stepped back into the cabin. "Why do you do that? Obey so quickly? Truly, you're unlike any boys I've ever met."

One twin nudged the other, and it was the more composed Dadas who cleared his throat and answered. "We are pack, and our nature bids us to obey."

"Pardon my rudeness, Witch," Tarbus blurted suddenly to his twin's groan. "But has not Wanderer told you about the wylderfolk?"

Painted shutters from the cottage next door slid open, curious eyes reflecting the firelight behind them. Vynasha dug her claws in and muttered, "I need to dress… wait here."

Only after she shut the door and leaned back against the wood could she let her mask fall. She pressed the heels of her hands against her eyes until the tears ceased, and her ragged gasps seemed to echo as loudly as her heart.

"We're fine," she hissed as she removed her hands and drew in the scents of home. Her hand twitched as it reached for the amulet hidden beneath her tunic. "He's going to be fine." Words fell on a too-silent room, devoid of Ceddrych's warmth and smiles. Times like this she missed the familiarity of the whispering castle walls with their shifting tapestries and watchful shadows.

Vynasha took unsteady steps to the table and chair where her brother spent many an hour accompanied by sticks of charcoal and precious paper. She glanced at the shadows where his map lay hidden then ran her fingers over the edge of pages covered in the old tongue he had once begun to teach her. The rest were in the trade tongue of her village. Every available corner was covered in little sketches of familiar things. Pieces of home, the turn of little Wyll's smile before the fire, Tamyra's warm eyes, and Vynasha…

She pushed another paper aside, her chest constricting as she found more drawings of the girl she had been and even more as she was now. A portrait all too lifelike, of a scarred young woman with curls escaping her braid. And a pair of wide eyes with irises shaped like those of a wyldcat.

Vynasha lifted a trembling hand to hover over the portrait's eyes. She had seen her reflection briefly in Ceddrych's eyes. She knew she was monstrous. So why had Ceddrych made her beautiful?

Another paper caught her eye. Vynasha smiled as she shoved the drawing aside and unveiled a beautifully sketched cottage, drawn the way a craftsman might, with smaller sketches to show his final vision.

"Home," she murmured, the home Ceddrych wanted to build for them. If Balos kept his word, the home they could build, on land they had already chosen.

Vynasha clenched her jaw as she pulled the plans free from the pile and quickly folded the paper in quarters and slipped it in the pocket of her breeches. If Balos had his way, nothing would change, and they would remain trapped with the same folk so eager to condemn her days before. Perhaps some of them secretly still did.

Vynasha moved with purpose now, ignoring the countless aches and twinges in her body. Reaching the bedside in two strides, she pulled the ruby-studded dagger she'd kept hidden beneath the pillow. Ferox's gift was warm to the touch, the tang of Balos's blood still caught on the blade.

She tightened her fist over the dagger's hilt and searched quickly through Ceddrych's chest of clothes until she found a belt and enough leather she could adjust to fit the dagger to her hip. She would never be without protection again, thanks to her claws, but the dagger was made with something more, an ancient magick she didn't fully understand but had served her true. The blade felt right once secured to her thigh.

Strange how a gift from Ferox, who wanted a loveless marriage, could bring her comfort.

He was nothing more than my jailor, she told herself, but there had been so many small moments of... kindness between them. A slow-burning ache formed in her chest, beneath where Grendel's amulet rested, as she recalled Ferox's last words to her.

"A pity you could not love a beast."

Blinking against the burn in her eyes, Vynasha tugged on a dry pair of leggings then wrapped waterproof leather boots over her calves. She slipped her arms through Ceddrych's spare coat and bound it tightly over her tunic. The door loomed ahead, daylight peeking through the cracks, beckoning her, yet for a long moment, she hesitated.

Life was harsh and bitter here, so near the top of the world, and yet the sounds of children playing in the street and wylderfolk speaking outside proved otherwise. Some people were born with ice in their veins. A part of her feared the ones who came for them with ill intent and the blind hatred she had tasted as she'd pressed her dagger against Balos's neck.

These are not mortal folk as you knew them, she reminded herself. *These are skin-changers, beings of air and earth like Odym told you about.*

These were the descendants of Soraya's kind, the ones who had come through the mirror. And now Ceddrych was out there, somewhere, trying to reason with a madman bent on hunting their kind down. Vynasha lifted her chin as she lifted the latch and opened the cottage door.

Twin shadows stepped in front of her, blocking the weak sunlight. Dadas and Tarbus spoke at once and over one another.

"We can't—"

"Can't just let you wander about!"

"Not without—"

"Wanderer will skin our hides for sure!"

Vynasha took a step onto the snow and closed the door behind her. "And here I thought I was the scariest thing in this village."

Snow crunched beneath their boots as the twins stumbled back several steps. Standing this close, she could see the faint differences between the otherwise identical brothers. The one standing to her left avoided eye contact and wore slightly darker furs, while his pale skin was dusted with freckles over his almost childlike nose. The other twin's gaze was more direct, his complexion slightly clearer, and his single blue eye stood out beside the other brown.

"Dadas, yes?" She made sure to smile with her lips closed. Tarbus, with the mismatched eyes, grimaced in turn. "I believe my brother said none could enter or leave without my permission, correct?"

Tarbus narrowed his eyes and rubbed his forearm across his nose with a sniff. "But… I thought he asked you to stay near the village?"

Dadas rolled his eyes. "Do you *want* her to pluck out your eyeballs?"

Pressing her advantage, Vynasha took another step, and the boys caved, heads slightly bowed to her as she parted them. "My brother also told you to obey me as you would him. And I've decided to check our trap line before another storm blows in. Are you coming or not?"

Vynasha did not wait for their answer as she charged down the short path Ceddrych had taken and entered the woods.

The valley had been trapped in an endless winter, yet the curse kept Wylderland from a permanent death. There were reprieves when the snows fell less often and flowers miraculously blossomed, when beasts and fowl populated as though spring had come. Yet even then, the land remained blanketed in a sea of white. Ceddrych told her the people within the village claimed this is the way it had always been. If there had been a difference before the curse, few of them remembered it.

Much like the last time Vynasha had followed Ceddrych into the forest west of the village, her spirits lifted with every step which carried them away from civilization. Yet she missed the weight of her bow in her hand, the quiver of arrows she had made herself. All lost in the journey or left behind.

"No more looking back," she said as she ducked around a snow-laden branch. Two pairs of footsteps echoed hers, though their tread was remarkably soft for such tall and lanky boys.

Not boys, wolves, she thought with a darting glance over her shoulder. True to their word, Dadas and Tarbus kept close but not too close. They had taken to scouting either side of the surrounding forest, and a part of Vynasha was grateful they had followed her. Much as she hated to rely on anyone from that village, Ceddrych seemed to trust them. That was enough for her.

"Before," she called, smiling at the sound of the twins tripping on their feet, "you seemed surprised I didn't know more about your people. You do realize Ceddrych and I aren't from Wylderland?"

The twins didn't quite close the gap, yet their shadows leapt ahead to match her uneven stride.

"But that cannot be true," Tarbus blurted. "Do not look at me like that, Dadas. Everyone has been saying it, even if Uncle told us to keep silent."

"What do they say?" Vynasha focused on the trail, on breathing steadily in and out. She had turned a blind eye to the village before, trusting Ceddrych at his word. Next time she would be prepared.

Dadas sighed then began in his more subdued tone, "The curse blocked all outsiders from entering our land. Only those of the blood could break through and survive."

Vynasha frowned at the echo of what Grendel and the Beast told her before. Rumors had persisted for generations in Whistleande Valley about the lands to the north. It was known that none who entered that road ever returned. But why would anyone come back to Whistleande after the war? Or so she had believed when she was still a girl.

"Has Wanderer told you the prophecy?" Dadas pressed when she gave no answer.

Vynasha slowed her gait as they approached the first trap. "I've heard more than enough about bloody prophecies."

A white-furred hare jumped against its constraints. Vynasha pulled her dagger free as she darted forward and caught the hare. "Thank you," she whispered before claiming the creature's life. Her nostrils flared as the rich scent of blood cloyed in the air, and she closed her eyes.

The beastly thing Soraya's curse had made of her shivered with sickening pleasure. A mad urge pressed against her mortal instincts, the need to rip and bite and drink.

The crunch of snow brought her back to find her lips already pressed to stained pink fur and the twins watching her warily. Hunger brightened their eyes, too, blood calling to the wolves beneath their skin. Neither dared meet her eye, nor stand higher than she.

Vynasha clenched her teeth together as she lowered her hand slowly. She tied the hare to her belt and kept close watch on the wolves. "Why do you serve my brother?" Her voice creaked, the words odd and clunky on her tongue.

Tarbus spoke first, his curiosity winning over fear. "Wanderer is the first wolf to challenge our uncle's rule."

"Your uncle?" Vynasha reset the trap and swept the snow until all traces of blood were wiped clean.

"Balos," Dadas replied.

"I see." Vynasha rose and slipped her dagger back in its makeshift sheath then picked up her feet. She needed to keep moving, to check the next trap. And she refused to let these wolves smell her fear at the mention of the alpha she'd dared bleed. "So they've fought before?"

Tarbus laughed. "Of course not! Uncle is far more powerful in a fight."

Dadas jabbed at his twin. "What the hare-brain is trying to say is that Wanderer was strong enough to hold to his will. He did not heed Uncle's call when he tried commanding his wolf to obey."

Vynasha's breath escaped in a heavy cloud. "And it's harder to ignore the call when you're in your wolf forms?"

"It is impossible to ignore the alpha's call." Tarbus leaped over a fallen log, and Dadas held a steady pace on her right side. "All obey."

"But not Ceddrych," she said, the missing pieces sliding together. Ceddrych must have the old blood through his father's family. Old Ced hadn't really been Vynasha's father and had shown little interest in raising her after Wynyth's death. But how had Ceddrych fought the call to obey, when Old Ced became a thrall to Bitterhelm?

If Ceddrych wasn't her brother, who was he? She wasn't sure if she could bear the look in his eyes when she told him all their *father* had confessed at the river. Would she ever be ready?

"Stop looking back," she growled, nearly missing the troubled glances the boys gave her.

Tarbus loped ahead and backpedaled to face her as they reached another bend in the trail, leading to slightly higher ground. "Wanderer is of the blood, so the elders had to allow him to stay. And Uncle would rather have a close watch on the lone wolf who can challenge him."

Dadas cleared his throat. "No one said anything about challenging Balos for the pack. That is why he lives among us."

Tarbus chuffed. "When he bothers to live as a man, that is… Ow!" The stick hit Tarbus squarely in the back of his thick red head, and he turned an affronted glare to his brother. "Fine! I was only trying to help."

Vynasha coughed and then laughed, startling both boys. "Please don't stop on my account. I'm just a mad witch to your village, so I won't be repeating any of this."

Tarbus returned her smile and managed to hold her gaze for all of three seconds before a resounding *crack* echoed in the wood.

Dadas growled and put his back to Vynasha while Tarbus did the same at her left.

Vynasha glanced at the snow raining thickly through the treetops. No birds sang, though creatures seemed to pass quietly through these woods before. A different kind of stillness had fallen upon them, an unnatural quiet.

Crack, the sound came again from slightly farther away.

Vynasha placed a hand on the jutting hilt of her dagger and turned her head in either direction. "We should move," she whispered.

"Not if we are being hunted," Dadas grumbled low.

Vynasha's lips curled over her sharp teeth, suddenly furious with the thought. "Anything hunting us is getting more than they bargained for. Come, there are more traps to check."

The twins ducked their heads slightly to the sides as she added, "Keep a close eye on the trees."

Whatever stalked them wasn't using magick—that much she was certain of. Anything with tooth and claw, she refused to fear after all Bitterhelm had thrown in her path. Her legs trembled slightly from the effort as she resumed their slow climb. Tarbus stayed near as Dadas stepped off the trail silently.

A series of smaller shuffles and cracks followed them, discernable now they weren't speaking or focused on their path. Vynasha bit back growing suspicion and kept a hand on her dagger just in case. "So my brother won't challenge Balos for the pack, but he risked everything to claim me."

Tarbus huffed. "The elders wanted to kill you, but not Uncle. He…"

"He what?" Vynasha startled the boy as she caught his arm and forced him to meet her eye.

Tarbus worked his jaw and then reluctantly whispered, "He wanted to watch you and see if you turned like the *others*."

Vynasha jerked her clawed hand from the boy's arm, flinching at his obvious relief. "I'm sorry… I shouldn't have grabbed you like that."

Tarbus shrugged, and a genuine smile split his face in two.

"Oh that was nothing. You should see the rounds Dadas and I go during training with Uncle."

"Gotcha!" the missing twin's voice echoed behind them, followed by a piercing shriek and beastly snarl.

Vynasha and Tarbus stumbled back the way they'd come and slipped through two great tree trunks.

"Look what I've found, brother." Dadas kept a familiar little boy aloft and pressed against the other side of the tree.

"Set me down, you mangy hair!" Asa hollered. "I only wanted to see where you were stealing Vynasha away to."

Vynasha shook her head as she stepped between the boys. "Set him down, Dadas."

Asa scowled at the taller boy and brushed snow off his furs. His head was bare, wild silver hair sticking up around his horns. He turned a beatific smile upon her as she knelt to face him.

"Asa, what are you doing here? Your mother is going to be worried sick," Vynasha scolded.

Tarbus nudged his twin and muttered, "Or try to murder her again."

"Shut it, soft belly," Dadas growled.

Asa's smile faded as his brow creased, but then he picked up a child's practice bow and quiver and stood as tall as he could. "Mother's off with the pack. I slipped out while Aunty was busy checking on you and found *those* two herding you in the middle of the woods. I had to make sure you were okay! Please let me stay! I can protect you, see?"

Vynasha gently helped Asa reattach his quiver and couldn't help her growing smile. "The twins are a menace, I agree." Her smile grew at Tarbus's scoff, and she met Asa's hopeful gaze. "We were just going to check on my brother's trap line. We have a few more to check if you'd like to join us?"

Better the boy stayed with them this far from the village than be sent back, she reasoned. She didn't expect the air to leave her lungs as Asa threw his arms around her neck.

"Oh, thank you! I have not been outside in *ages*, except the two times mother brought me to see you."

"Okay, that is enough, you runt," Tarbus grumbled as he pulled the boy back by the shoulder. "If you come with, you need to listen to your elders and not smother our witch."

Vynasha climbed to her feet and stared at the twins and Asa.

"Just 'cause you are part of the pack does not mean I need to listen to *you*, Tarbus," Asa argued while Dadas ran a hand over his face.

"It does if you plan on joining, pup," Tarbus sputtered.

Our witch.

Vynasha turned back toward the trail and breathed the calming scent of winter into her lungs. "Asa, if you're coming with us, I'd like you to walk with me. These lummoxes can check our flank in case anyone else tries to surprise us."

Asa skipped to her side and placed his hand in hers, and Vynasha blinked against the sting of tears. "You already caught one hare." The small boy pointed with awe. "Are we going to make a stew? Coney is my favorite."

"Oh for the love of… *ow*! Dadas, you know a warning would serve just as well," Tarbus muttered as the twins followed them back to the trail.

Vynasha squeezed Asa's hand and offered as warm a smile as she could manage. "If we find two more of these, we'll make a feast of it."

CHAPTER TEN

A Time to Build

VYNASHA HADN'T INTENDED on telling the twins or Asa about the clearing or what Ceddrych planned for it. But no sooner had they entered did Asa whoop with delight on finding their third hare. And as the twins created a fire and Vynasha guided Asa on how to clean his first kill, the truth poured past her lips so easily it frightened her.

"This is where Ceddrych and I plan to build our home."

Three pairs of bright and innocent eyes found hers. Asa's questions were only compounded by Tarbus's snark and Dadas's watchful interest.

She pulled the drawing from her pocket and showed it to the others. "Here. And there," she turned to point to the place where the house would stand one day. Soon, if she had anything to do with it.

Asa jumped to his feet. "When do we start?"

It began like this. Two wolves and a faun aided a witch in drawing lines in the snow, using the drawing as their guide. None of them had experience with building something on this scale. But Vynasha had spent a season turning a barn into a home she and Wyll could safely live in. And the twins were old enough to have aided others in repairing cottages. In a land of always-winter, there was a never-ending need for replacing thatch and boards. Asa darted around the surrounding brush and winter flowers to gather as many sticks and markers as he could. The sun was high in the sky, peeking brightly through the gray clouds, by the time they had a rough approximation of what it would take.

They stood together before what would one day be the entrance, weary but happy.

"Well, it's a good start," Vynasha declared as Asa slipped an arm around her waist and bounced on his feet. She found she did not mind the casual touch.

"We should bring tools next time," Dadas mused aloud.

"And just where are we going to steal tools no one will notice?" Tarbus said.

The twins paused to share a trepidatious glance, swallowed, and nodded. "Uncle."

"This is a stupid idea," Vynasha grumbled as she glanced back to find Asa keeping watch farther back, where they had chosen to trek into the woods past an outlying village trail.

Only the boy's horns peeked through the dense underbrush before he lifted his hand in the "all clear" sign.

"Do not worry," Dadas said. "Uncle is not home, only the old woman. And no one ever comes here when he is away."

"And that's supposed to make me feel better?" Vynasha hissed.

"The old hag is harmless... mostly." Tarbus grinned and winked as he crouched low and pulled back the tangle of low-hanging fir branches.

A lone house rested in the clearing not ten paces ahead, a small stable leaning against the side they faced. Smoke rose in steady puffs from a large chimney which spanned both stories of the grand log home. The walls were painted with patterns reflecting ferns and creatures in sun-bleached layers of paint. The peaked roof appeared in good repair but in a fashion no one built beyond Wylderland. Like so many things she had seen since venturing to this strange place, Balos's house seemed out of time. A relic of an age long passed.

Vynasha glanced at the fading sunlight casting deeper shadows to their right, to the side facing the trail that would lead toward the village. It was strange yet somehow unsurprising the wolf alpha would choose to make his home apart from the pack.

"Say a prayer for me, brother," Tarbus whispered, then turned to Vynasha with a cheeky grin. "A kiss for luck?"

Vynasha snorted and blushed. "Aren't you a little young for kisses?"

Tarbus sighed and placed a hand over his heart. "You are truly a cruel mistress to deny your knight this boon."

Dadas shouldered his twin. "Get a move on, you hare-brain, and pray Wanderer never learns you asked."

Vynasha grinned as a harried Tarbus shoved his brother back before crouching low and padding silently to the shed. "If he does ask, say I bit Tarbus instead."

Dadas coughed and ducked his head to hide a smile. "Mayhap you should have." He frowned then and studied the shuttered windows of the house. "Why do you call him brother?"

Her breath froze in her lungs as she watched Tarbus open the shed door with a cringing creak. "What do you mean?"

Dadas twisted his head and eyed her carefully, his tongue darting out to soothe a crack in his lip. "Your blood does not smell like his."

Vynasha released a puff of warm air and drew the cowl of Ceddrych's cloak further over her head. "The curse... altered me before I could escape the castle," she lied. How else could Dadas know? Unless Ceddrych told him.

But that would mean...

CRACK!

The shed door flew open with a bang.

Tarbus practically fell upon them then with a heavy grunt and trembling limbs. "Run! The old hag is onto us!"

A beam of candlelight spread through the open curtains by the window directly across from them.

Dadas cursed and grabbed Vynasha's hand. Tarbus scrambled back to his feet, and together they raced as quickly as they could back to Asa's hiding place.

"Bloody hag left a nasty trap for me," Tarbus huffed as they raced through the woods then lifted his stolen bounty. "But I got the tools!"

Vynasha didn't realize she had been laughing until the four of them fell heavily against the wall of Ceddrych's cottage.

The twins turned to favor her with wicked smiles, and Asa bounced around them like a fawn until Vynasha firmly nudged him in the direction of his home. "Go before your elders miss you. We'll have plenty more adventures tomorrow," she promised.

By the time she fell into bed not long after, breathless and aching yet victorious, the twins had shifted into their wolf skins, sleek, gray creatures with faintly glowing green gazes. Their forms were vaguely familiar, as though she'd seen them before in a dream. Vynasha made sure to bank up the fire before placing a hand on either beast's head, and whispered, "Thank you."

Neither wolf reacted to her touch but for the slight swishing of their tails over the rushes.

Vynasha slept heavily that night. Her dreams were filled with memories of her mother's songs and the garden of roses.

When they returned to the clearing the following morning, Vynasha was surprised to find Asa had brought two of his friends, a boy and girl with raven feathers in place of hair and pitch-black eyes.

"This is Hugyn and Munyn. You saved them the night you banished the demon," Asa explained. "They are my cousins." The siblings whispered among themselves but spoke to no one else but Asa.

"So long as they are here to help and not play," Tarbus grumbled and winced as Vynasha dug her claws into his side.

She made sure to keep her sharp teeth hidden as she smiled and said, "We are here to build, but you can also help me keep an eye on the forest and set traps."

Hugyn and Munyn nodded and, sweeping feathered arms to their sides, bowed their heads in reply.

The twins opened the sack they had risked so much for to unveil gleaming silver tools.

"Told you we would come through!" Tarbus said with a grin.

"Only because Uncle is not home. They must be returned before the pack," Dadas warned.

"Oh, shove it, you ninny. No one is going to find out. Besides, the elders are too busy to notice we are even away from the boundary."

Vynasha ran a finger over the runes etched into the haft of an awl. "This land is past the village boundary?" She smiled as the twins nodded. Of course Ceddrych would have wanted them to live apart.

"With our enemy so close, we should have never wandered this far," Dadas said. "Wanderer said—"

"Wanderer told us to watch over his witch, and that is what we are doing," Tarbus argued.

"We found more wood to grow!" Asa ran past them, more gathered limbs in his arms, the raven siblings fluttering behind him like winged shadows.

Vynasha cocked her head at the slight hum the tools emanated and gasped at the shock sliding up her arm as she lifted the awl. "What magick is this?"

Asa laughed. "How do you grow a house where you come from?"

Dadas lifted a larger axe and lowered his voice to explain. "The villagers outlawed the practice of magick years ago, to keep us hidden from… you know. But we still use runes everywhere we can."

Vynasha turned the awl in her scarred hand. "It's light as a feather."

Dadas hummed in agreement. "And the blade never dulls or breaks."

Vynasha tightened her grasp on the awl and looked at the outline of the home she wanted to build. "Good. Let's begin."

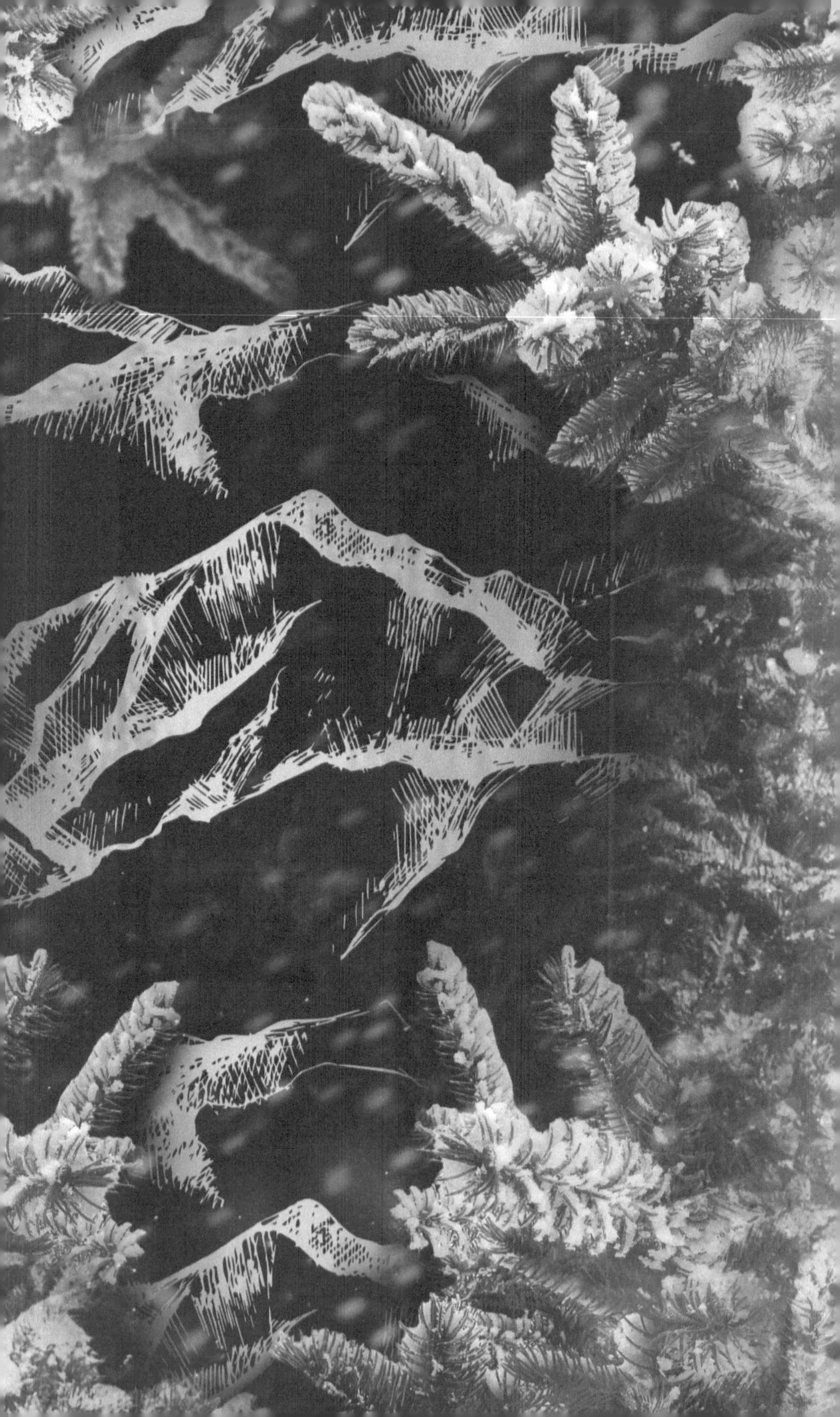

CHAPTER ELEVEN

A Pact of Blood

POWER HAD RETURNED to Ceddrych's limbs the instant his body broke and reformed into that of the wolf. A rush of repressed instincts nearly overwhelmed him. The urge to rip into Balos for using what little sway he held over him, for tearing him from Vynasha's side.

She wanted you to go.

Yes, he had a purpose in searching the wilds of Wylderland. The scent he had been tracking for days now, barely present and only known to him. Because he alone knew to seek the scent of his lost nephew rather than that of the hunters. Bloodthirsty barbarians, those mortals. He may not agree with Balos about much, but he had seen the leftovers of their cruelty firsthand.

A skinned wolf carcass with horror-filled eyes staring vacantly in the night.

Wolfsbane and his daughter wore the skins, it was said. And Vynasha had left Wyll in their hands.

Mortal fears seized his heart in his chest, emotions that didn't belong to the wolf. Fear that Wyll had inherited whatever had turned Ceddrych into a beast. Fear that the hunters would destroy an innocent boy because of their prejudice. How could he face Vynasha if that happened? And if their family watched over them truly, if the priest had spoken true, how could Ceddrych face Tamyra for allowing her son's brutal murder?

A deep threatening growl built in his throat. He bared his teeth as the wolf beside him yipped in question. Ceddrych turned his head to meet the watchful gaze of his bloody minder.

Rather than let him split from the pack as they often did, Balos had insisted Ceddrych remain with them from the start. Had he been alone, Ceddrych was convinced he could have already found his nephew. But any attempts to push beyond the edge of the pack's run, and Balos's piercing howl called him back.

Bloody bastard.

Ceddrych pushed harder against the snow and created greater distance between himself and the *beloved* alpha. Balos was the largest of the wolves, taller and broader than even Ceddrych's dark form. But not by much. His tongue lolled out in a semblance of a smile.

Not much longer.

He would honor the pact Vynasha made for their freedom, and once he found Wyll, they could make a true home together. He had to believe that or he would do something foolish.

A sleek silver-furred female darted through the trees just ahead of him, turning her head briefly to bark at him. Onya kept just as close an eye on him as her master.

Ceddrych didn't hold back his snarl and dipped his nose lower to the ground to push the presence of the wolves from his senses. It was not easy. The pack was twelve strong, though more had stayed behind to guard the village in their absence. Not counting the youths and elders.

Focus.

They had crossed the partially frozen river the day before, and the overwhelming taste of magick clung to his fur still. It had been a full day since he last caught traces of Wyll's scent.

Balos split them into groups of four and sent the other two north and south. Their group pushed farther west.

The valley rose before them in a series of cliffs and caverns filled with creatures best left to their slumber. His last encounter with the forgotten ones had ended with gashes so deep in his sides and his mind so addled he had barely made it back to the village.

A warning howl at his right flank told him Balos wanted them in close file and to remain wary.

Ceddrych turned his head and nearly came to a standstill as an all-too-familiar scent hit his nose. A faint whimper escaped him. The scent was of Whistleande Valley, the same traces Vynasha carried.

Onya appeared with a firm brush against his side and warning growl urging him to move.

Ceddrych snapped aggressively back as he lifted his nose to the air and released a long howl from the back of his throat. The scent was leading to the hilltop above them.

An answering howl sounded to their right.

Another soon followed to their left.

Please be alive, Wyll.

Ceddrych wasn't sure what he would do if they managed to find Wyll. He hadn't told the pack or the village elders about Wyll. Truth be told, he had been far less involved in the boy's life than he'd like to have been.

Will he fear me the way Ash feared us?

The wolf's instincts grew stronger as they climbed to the top of the hill. Tracks littered the snow. Small prints, likely Wolfsbane's daughter, and something like sled marks. The taste of Whistleande, of his shared blood, grew stronger and fresher.

Balos growled with anticipation, and Onya yipped happily.

An odd *thwack* and *thump* echoed off the thinned trees ahead. A faint cry of surprise, and then the *shh* followed, kicking up clouds of snowdrift in their wake.

Ceddrych barked a laugh as they reached the hill crest only to find freshly disturbed snow and the distant pass of a sled dropping into the pass below.

Clever, he thought as Balos practically roared.

Of course they gave chase.

No rest for the wicked.

The sled had gained the hunter a small advantage. But the winding forest thickened the deeper they descended. Sure enough, they heard a resounding *crack* maybe fifty paces ahead.

The sled had broken to shattered slivers against a copse of fir trees. Branches shuddered, and the undergrowth was disturbed.

There were no clear tracks.

The scents had disappeared. Well… almost.

Ceddrych's ears twitched as he fought the instinct to turn back the way they'd come.

Balos howled with frustration, and the other wolves echoed his cry as the rest of the pack closed in.

Ceddrych breathed deeply as the wind blew west and carried the faintest trace of Whistleande Valley again. The others didn't sense it.

Would it be better to tell them or lead them away and circle back when we make camp?

The trees swayed against the wind, always watching them, as if waiting for something to happen.

"We make camp!" Balos wasted no time returning to his

mortal form, and Onya followed as she always did. "Three will circle our perimeter in case we catch scent of the hunters again."

Ceddrych stepped forward but didn't bother changing skins. He had no desire to feel the full weight of longing that other form suffered. All for the mate he could never truly have.

Balos narrowed his green eyes at Ceddrych. "You are to remain with the camp, Wanderer."

Ceddrych snarled and tossed his head. He ignored the faintest of pulls, the *command* layered in the alpha's voice.

Balos growled at his disobedience and through gritted teeth said, "Very well. Onya, remain here. Vilhelm, you will join Wanderer in patrolling the eastern perimeter."

A mixed gray-and-white-furred wolf silently padded to Ceddrych's flank. The warning in Vilhelm's glowing green eyes said there would be no wandering off as he was wont to do.

"What about you, Balos?" Onya approached and placed a too-familiar hand on her alpha's arm. "You have pushed harder than all of us. Should you not rest?"

Balos grunted as he shook off her touch. "Wanderer is the only thing keeping our witch in line. I will not let him out of my sight."

"As you say." Onya ducked her head but couldn't hide the way her face fell. It was known she had wanted Balos since before his wife died.

Ceddrych tossed his head and snapped at Vilhelm until the smaller gray wolf let him pass.

The pack split though the majority lingered behind. Balos overtook Ceddrych before he reached the thicker tree line hugging the mountain face.

Ceddrych had not lingered in this territory for long in his wanderings, not after his run-in with the forgotten one. Here, the air grew so thick that it was suffocating and maddening. Even for a wolf.

Balos howled with frustration as they slammed into a patch of thorny briars.

More howls answered from various positions around them in the valley below the mountain.

Ceddrych clenched his jaw and tried not to whimper as briars clung to his coat. The forest was so dark ahead not even shadows of creatures moved in the underbrush. And the trees watched over them, mockingly.

Balos paced back and forth, and Vilhelm growled deeply as he circled back seeking a way through.

Yet through the cloying scents of sap and evergreen, Ceddrych caught the faintest trace of Whistleande. And he knew it was not the trees watching them this time.

Onya appeared suddenly, her coal-black coat only broken by the white streak across her nose. It was in the same position as the scar on her mortal face. She bowed her head to Balos, ignored his furious bark, and pushed farther into the painful underbrush.

Damn.

He couldn't allow Onya to find them first. His fur bristled as Onya suddenly tilted her head back and released a deep howl.

Balos growled as he followed, until they reached a tiny clearing barely large enough for the three of them to squeeze through.

More howls answered Onya's cry, those who had split to check their perimeter. Vilhelm was nearest, half a league away.

Onya snarled as she circled the clearing but could find no way to press forward.

Balos snapped at her hind legs until Onya froze, fur bristling. And then the alpha broke through his wolf skin. Clawed paws became almost-human hands with long-tipped, black nails. His snout shrank, and his eyes drew closer together to meet the new nose. Fur fell in clumps with shredded skin. It peeled from his inner flesh painfully and yet easily, shedding to the forest floor and partially cloaking his mortal form.

"Enough!" Balos bellowed, and the snarls immediately ceased. "Your blundering about has given us away, Onya."

Onya's tail slipped low between her legs and Ceddrych kept his head down and averted.

"If the hunter was nearby, she is long gone now," Balos seethed.

Onya shed her wolf skin with a pained groan and kept her head ducked low as she gathered her skin over her shoulders. "But she cannot have gone far. Allow me to chase her scent alone. I will find a path. I swear it by the Crafter."

Balos broke the distance between them in a single stride. Onya yelped as he caught the back of her tangled hair and forcibly exposed her neck. "Do you know how long I have hunted Wolfsbane and his offspring?"

Onya visibly swallowed. "Lifetimes."

Balos favored her with a cruel smile. "Remember this before your next attempt to break your oaths. When I give an order, I expect it to be obeyed. Do not mistake my respect for you as my second as an invitation for your pithy affections."

Onya ducked her head and her arms stiffened at her sides. "Forgive me, Balos."

Ceddrych had never cared for Onya, though he pitied her boy, so clearly not of the wolf's blood. Which made his choice to slip back into his mortal skin irrational in hindsight. He cursed as his broken fur draped over him as a cloak and strode forward, breaking Onya from Balos's line of sight.

Balos's smile grew amused at this unforeseen challenge. "Have you something to say, Wanderer? Nothing will ease Onya's punishment once we return to camp."

Ceddrych grit his teeth against the sharp bite of snow on his bare feet. "We all know the pains you have suffered at the hunter's hands. You tell us every time, as though they are our greatest enemy." He paused and glanced briefly at Onya. "But what of the enemy my sister fled? What about the demons that prey on your village, *her son?*"

Balos chuckled and shook his head. "You have not lived among us long enough, Wanderer. You do not know what our lives were like before we destroyed Wolfsbane's village. The decades we lived in fear, in fear of them adding our children's furs to their twisted trophies. No, I will not allow them to take advantage of our weakness, as you so *eloquently* pointed out."

Ceddrych swept his arms wide, inviting the bitter cold and keen of the invisible press of eyes watching them from the forest. "Even you've admitted the oracle has confirmed it. Magick has returned to Wylderland, the beasts and forgotten ones are stirring, and your people are in greater danger than ever before. Tell me why you choose to fixate on this damned blood feud when we should be protecting the valley."

Onya shifted in place behind him as Vilhelm slinked silently to the alpha's side.

Balos sneered at Ceddrych, some great emotion flashing and then settling behind his green eyes. "Vengeance is the only thing that matters anymore. Mayhap one day you will understand this, pup. For now, you *will* obey my command and return with us to camp on all fours where you belong."

Ceddrych flinched as the weight of the alpha's order passed over him, and the change came to him as unwillingly as the first time.

Damn him, he thought as fur sprouted over his skin and his jaw extended. Within moments, the wolf had taken over, snarling and snapping with all the fury Ceddrych was unable to release.

"Onya, you will watch over Wanderer until I return," Balos growled. "Vilhelm, sweep the border of the wood once more before taking rest with the others."

"Where will you go?" Onya's voice trembled, and she didn't dare lift her gaze to meet their alpha's.

Balos gritted his teeth and turned his head to the east. "I have unfinished business to tend to. In my absence, you will continue the hunt as faithfully as you swore to me, Onya. Hunt well!" With this final command, the alpha slipped into his wolf skin with a low rumble and tore through the underbrush.

Vilhelm eyed him with a warning growl before lowering his nose to the earth.

Onya shook her head then shivered as Balos's powerful howl seared through them. She returned her attention to Ceddrych as fur slowly grew over her skin, her golden eyes glowing like twin coals in the moonlight. "This is all your fault, Wanderer. You and your witch. We might have been free of the hunt, and now we shall never know peace."

Vilhelm barked briefly, a warning Onya did not take kindly. "I am still his second!" she snarled as she fell to her hands and knees with a shout. The change took her fully then, and Vilhelm left them before she could turn her wrath upon him. All the deference she'd given Balos was replaced by fury that had her snapping after Ceddrych's heels until he moved.

Ceddrych couldn't fight an outright command, especially when the alpha put all his power behind it. So he didn't bother snapping back at Onya, but he continued seeking the scent of home as they skirted the tree line. And he didn't tell the pack that the scent had been strongest in the clearing they just abandoned.

Balos leaving offered a rare and perfect opportunity for Ceddrych, if he was clever and brave enough. He would steal away the instant Onya's guard was down and before Vilhelm, the pack's best tracker, returned.

I will find you, Wyll. No matter how long it takes. I will find you again. And this time I will bring you home.

CHAPTER TWELVE

A Song of Home

TIME PASSED QUICKLY as Vynasha and the children worked to mark and fell trees, and the youngest gathered saplings and shrub to weave rushes. Every day they toiled together to lay the foundations. Every day more of the village youth she had healed appeared to help.

Vynasha struggled to put names to all the faces, too lost in wonder at children of every form and shade, all with smiles ready for her. After the fourth day and finding their small group numbering thirteen, Vynasha forgot to hide her sharp teeth behind her answering smiles.

The trap lines shouldn't produce so much so quickly, yet they found enough each day to help feed those who wanted to help. As if the land was looking out for them, too. Many used the excuse of checking their own lines and hunting near the village. But the ones who worked longest and hardest were the wolf twins and Asa and his cousins.

Dadas and Tarbus took it upon themselves to guide the others, though often argued with a thick-boned girl named Katya, a year or two below the twins.

"That is *not* the way you form a notch," she claimed with a tilt of her hips after the rest returned home before twilight.

"Oh, and I suppose you could do better, could you?" Tarbus grunted as he set his axe against the nearby log.

The axe looked far too large for Katya, until the stout girl proceeded to swing the blade true. The instant the axe head hit the log, the air hummed like the strike of a church bell. When the fine silver dust cleared, a perfectly cut notch remained. Katya flashed a sharp-toothed grin, fangs poking down into her lower lip.

Vynasha laughed at the dumbfounded look on Tarbus's face. "Perhaps Katya should handle the axe from now on?"

Tarbus kicked at the morning snowdrift with a groan. "Fine, you may notch the logs, but Dadas and I are setting them."

Katya proceeded to make another notch, another strike and clang of the bell, and then said, "Are you certain you are stronger?"

Tarbus sputtered and waved his hand in the younger girl's direction. "You are *younger*."

Dadas exchanged a knowing look with Vynasha and shook his head. Though often silent, he was by far the more perceptive twin.

Katya lifted an end of the log she had just notched with only a little strain. "I am a child of the earth, remember, wolf boy?"

Asa cackled as Tarbus was quick to follow her lead in picking up the other end of the log. It must be said he struggled far more to carry and slip the log in place than the younger and shorter girl.

"What did she mean?" Vynasha asked Dadas as she followed him to their small fire pit. The area had fast become their preferred cooking station. One of the children had even crafted a makeshift table using small limbs and a thick layer of bark.

"Hmm?" Dadas checked the mixture they had been fixing that would be used to seal the logs once they finished the foundations.

"Katya said she was a child of the earth," Vynasha spoke low, though Hugyn and Munyn worked steadily nearby with ever-watchful black eyes. "I've heard something like that before…"

"Oh, yes." Dadas cleared his throat and turned to make sure Katya was far away before leaning in closer to explain. "You heard the tale of how the wylderfolk came to this land?"

Vynasha nodded and pressed a hand to the amulet weighing against her heart. "The mirror," she whispered with a glance for the trees. She could never shake the feeling of something watching them in the forest. The reach of a long-dead enchantress had proved indeed far.

Dadas hummed in affirmation as he stirred the mixture in the bowl they had crafted the day before. "In this other land, there were many kinds of folk. Folk of the air could have feathers or wings of any kind. Folk of the water had gills or scales and could breathe just as easily below or above the seas and rivers. Folk of the earth have the strength of mountains and can shape any metal as if it were clay."

Vynasha wrapped her arms around her chest and took in the rag-taggle band that scattered about the clearing she and Ceddrych would call home. "What about the wolves?"

Dadas froze then set the stick aside to meet her eye. "The wolves are something other. My uncle could tell you more."

Vynasha barked a sudden laugh. "Can you honestly picture Balos sitting down for a fireside chat with *me*?"

Dadas grimaced and cocked his head. "You may have a point… but Uncle really is not so terrible as he would like everyone to believe."

Vynasha bit her lower lip and hid her expression behind her loose curls. "I suppose you must respect your elders."

Dadas chuffed but didn't press her argument, or so she believed. He followed her to inspect Katya and Tarbus's newest handiwork while the pair had left to choose another tree to fell. And there he chose the relative privacy behind a wall three logs tall to speak in his uncle's favor once more.

"Uncle helped raise us after our father was killed." Dadas pushed against the newest log, testing its grip on the notch beneath, and steadily avoided Vynasha's surprised gaze. "He is harsh because we need him to be strong to keep the village safe. The curse has been upon us for a long time, Vynasha… longer than you may know."

"You all look younger than me." She studied his youthful face and asked the question which had pressed upon her for days now. "How long have you lived in the body of a youth?"

Dadas slowly lifted his gaze, and the weight of far more years than he should have lived was suddenly present and all too tragic. "No one is born in Wylderland, and nobody dies of natural causes. It has been so long we do not keep track of the years anymore. Only the elders know the true count of days, and no one speaks of it. Most of the children are not even aware of this. We live our lives as best we can, but nothing has changed. Not for an age. Not until *you* came."

Vynasha couldn't hold his gaze anymore, couldn't quite look at any of them. "I ran away before I could be made to break your curse," she confessed. "I'm afraid I haven't done enough, but you don't know… not even Ceddrych knows what it was like."

What they were like.

Gilded golden horns like a trophy on a white wolf's head.

Kind eyes and fluttering lace cuffs on quivering ghostly hands.

Soft hands and careful whispers while they believed she slept.

Silver eyes flashing and bones breaking as a prince gave in to his cursed nature.

Black fur surrounding her while great claws kept her pressed close as they fell what felt forever down the pounding falls.

Vynasha blinked, and tears spilled over her cheeks. She had sworn not to think of Old Ced. The old man hadn't truly been her father, yet he was the only father she'd ever known.

She turned her back to Dadas and faced the woods, faced whatever watched over them from the shadows. A faint gleam of silver and violet darted behind a tree in the thicket, and Vynasha stiffened.

But Dadas pressed a warm hand to her shoulder carefully, as though he thought she might break or bite, and said, "I am sorry."

Vynasha turned to face him and frowned. "I should be asking your forgiveness."

Dadas smiled, and the contrast of ancient eyes in a youthful face struck her once more. "Time passes differently for us than the lowlanders, or so Wanderer has told us. Even if you had not come, we may have gone on living shadow lives. Now you have given us a chance."

"A chance for what?" she asked.

Dadas's smile turned his ever-solemn, careworn features into an impish reflection of his twin. "Do you feel that?"

Vynasha frowned. "Feel what?"

"The roots are taking!" Asa crowed with delight as the ground began to tremble beneath their feet.

Vynasha caught Dadas by the shoulder as the earth jolted again, knocking the boy against her side. The mixture in the pot sloshed over the sides as a terrible groaning and cracking rent the air. Panic struck her and she turned wildly about. "What is this? What's happening?"

Is it Grendel? Has he wakened? Has he come for me?

"The roots have taken." Dadas laughed, bright and boyish. "The land has accepted us. Now we can mold the house into any shape you wish!"

Vynasha's breath caught in her throat as she watched the younger children approach the foundations and lay their hands upon the shifting wood. Wood struck and fashioned with rune-enchanted tools.

Tarbus and Katya laughed as they raced one another from the forest to join them.

"Come! You should have the final say," Dadas said.

Vynasha allowed him to guide her to the unfinished home.

Each step seemed to echo in her ears to the thud of her heartbeat, or was it the forest?

Already, the first floor seemed to rise above their heads, logs stretching and limbs wrapping around the cracks, reaching up to the roof they had yet to build.

She hesitated then pressed her scarred hands against the wood. The thud of her heartbeat was echoed by the earth and magnified by the power hidden within each child around her. She turned to meet Asa's smile. Hadn't Asa claimed they *grew* houses?

Vynasha had not believed him.

Was the enchantment imbued by the runes?

"Stop thinking about how it is and imagine what it can be!" Asa called to her above the rumbling din.

Vynasha gaped at the boy, at his laughter and the face he made at her incredulity. Had he read her mind?

Asa rolled his eyes at her as if in answer and leaned heavily into the logs with both hands. She shook her head amd followed his instruction.

Stop thinking of what is.

Closing her eyes, Vynasha bit down gently on her tongue, just enough for a few drops of blood to pool in her mouth.

Imagine what it can be.

And she recalled Ceddrych's drawing to her mind's eye, traced over every detail he had lovingly sketched.

Vynasha gasped as the others pushed their will into the foundations, sharing their strength, enough that she could avoid drawing more of her gift.

Let it be enough, she prayed. And she imagined the look on Ceddrych's face, the way he would smile and twirl her about as he had done when their lives had been simpler. She imagined Wyll safe beside a fire and using her magick to make him whole again. She could almost hear their laughter and Wynyth's songs.

Mother's song echoed on the wind and snow stinging her cheeks as trees bent and groaned beneath their hands. The steady rhythm of their hearts reached into the walls, the rooms and first-floor ceiling taking shape with every crack and snap.

And then a sudden flux of power came from beyond them that felt like snow and the mirror Ferox made her touch...

"Our fate would always have led us to this." His horned helm had brushed the top of her head, and then his nose pressed desperately to her neck.

The house stretched with a great heave, dragging her back to the present, and settled with a rumbling louder than any beast, the ripples knocking them to their knees.

The wind hissed, and then the earth heaved a great sigh as they fell back into the snow with a collective groan. Peals of laughter escaped Asa, Hugyn, and Munyn. Katya and Tarbus cursed colorfully in the old tongue.

Vynasha blinked numbly at the peaked roof leaning into her vision and the twinkling stars taunting her above. Her attempt to sit up caused the stars to swirl, and she released a groan as she pressed the heels of her hands to her eyes. "Saints..."

"Vynasha?" one of the twins called, and her hands were pulled away.

One of the children gasped. "How is she glowing?"

"Violet," another hissed, "like the old queen."

"Vynasha!" Asa threw his arms around her neck, and the motion sent a wave of fresh nausea through her. "I knew you were magick! You made it happen just like the songs."

Tarbus called Asa's name, and the boy's fierce hold eased. "Give our witch more room, you soft belly."

A calloused hand brushed her curls off her forehead. "She looks ill," a worried Dadas added.

That's because I am, she tried to answer. But the stars only swirled faster in patterns behind the crowd of young faces hovering over her. "Don't let me sleep," she murmured as her eyes fluttered closed.

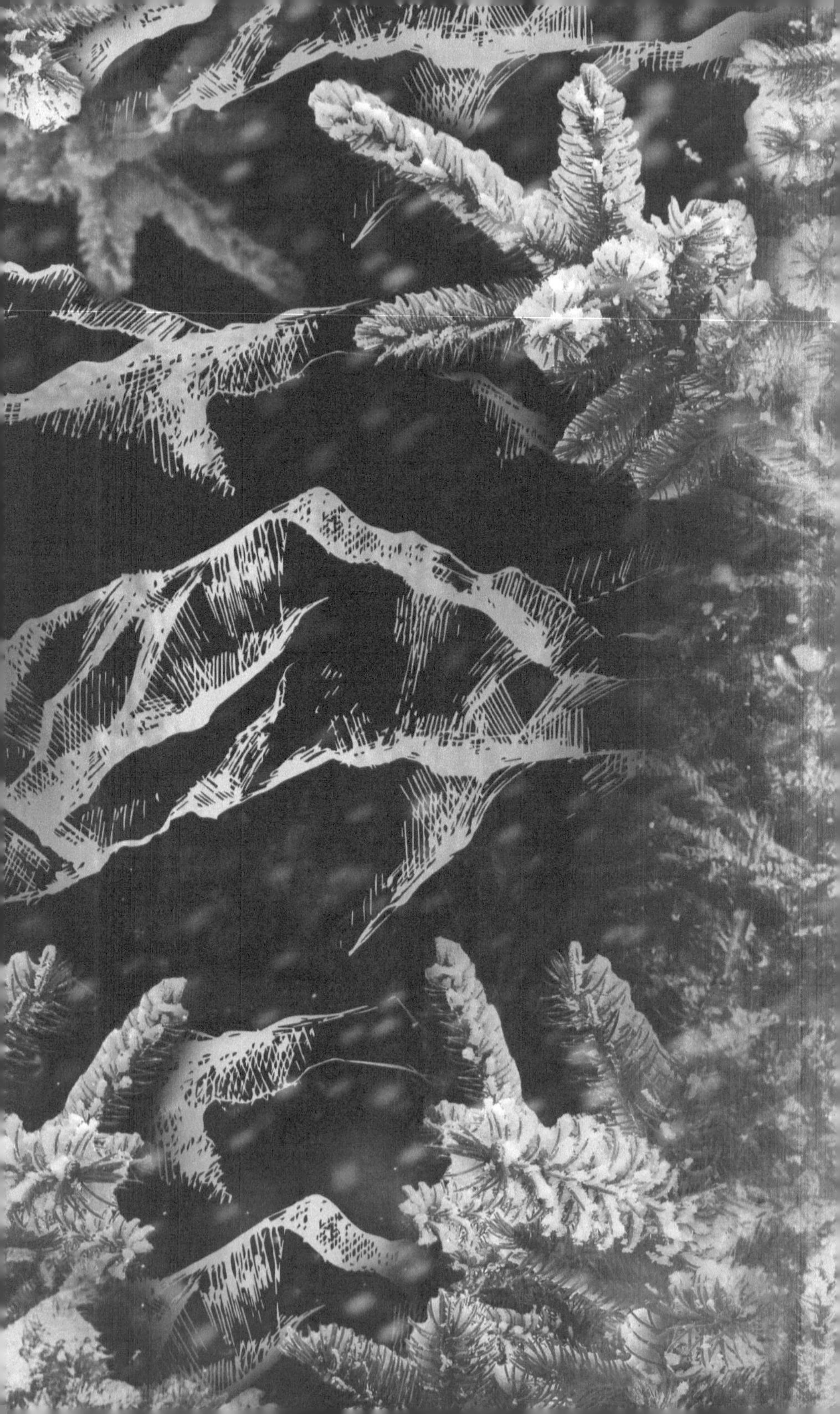

CHAPTER THIRTEEN

A Dream of Vengeance

BALOS'S ABSENCE SHOULD have made it easy for Ceddrych to slip away. Without the alpha's punishing drive and power of command, the pack was listless, many eager to return to their families. But Onya and Vilhelm pushed them even harder, rabid in their personal need to continue the hunt.

Ceddrych had asked Vilhelm once why they should be so afraid of an old hunter and his crippled daughter. And the other wolf had coldly replied, *"When your family has been hunted to the last child and your mate's pelt worn over your enemy's shoulders, then you will understand."*

Vilhelm spoke rarely, more wolf seeping into his mortal skin than any other besides Balos. This was something Ceddrych could relate with. Before Vynasha's return, he had found comfort in his wolf form. Now he had to keep trying to find a way to be both beast and man, if not for her then for Wyll.

The first night, after they lost the trail and Onya was forced to escort Ceddrych to camp, was the worst trial. With Wyll's scent so fresh and near and this rabid she-wolf snipping at his heels. And once they shifted forms in camp to eat a fire-cooked meal, she took her humiliation out on him.

"You will sleep in my tent, Wanderer, or you will not sleep at all," Onya demanded once she had finished her meal.

Ceddrych lost his appetite and set his bowl on the ground. "I will remain on watch."

Her dark eyes flashed as they found his across the fire. "You will not be taking watch until Balos returns. Until then, you will remain where I can watch over you."

Two wolves sleeping nearby twitched their ears but didn't bother lifting their heads. If they heard, none gave any indication, though Ceddrych was aware little privacy was afforded among the pack.

The other pack who remained in camp had settled into makeshift tents, carried by those chosen to hold their weaker form. Balos kept them in shifts, wolf and mortal flesh in turn. It was best to use all senses and means available to the pack, as they believed. No male or female was forced to a specific duty in the way Ceddrych had seen in the world beyond Wylderland. All tasks were split equally.

Onya commanded respect, though not the same fearful awe as Balos or wariness Vilhelm inspired. But she had earned her place as second, for reasons Ceddrych struggled to understand. She was quick to anger and the first to dole out punishments. Yet she raised her son alone, save for her father and aunt, and cared for the younger pups like a protective mother bear.

Ceddrych studied her as she stood and urged him to follow her to the tent she usually shared with Balos. The air was blessedly free of any evidence of coupling. But to his shock, he found two separate pallets instead of one like other couples in the pack shared. Onya's pack lay between the furs. They were forced to crawl in closely together, and Ceddrych's skin itched to turn into the wolf. He would feel far better in fur than vulnerable skin.

"Stop looking at me like that," she snapped.

Ceddrych's head jerked up, and he grimaced. "I wasn't looking at you."

"Perhaps not with your eyes, but you look all the same." She chuckled as she gathered her wolfskin fur around her shoulders to cover her form and settled onto her pallet. "You may rest easy tonight. If I wanted to bite you, I would have the instant Balos left."

Ceddrych snorted and settled uneasily on the pillow, wrinkling his nose at the alpha's pungent scent. "You did bite me once, the first time I refused to bow to *him*."

Onya smiled, transforming her features into an echo of the beauty she must have been. "Ah, I had nearly forgotten with the arrival of your witch. I suppose Balos returns to her now."

So focused had he been on finding Wyll, Ceddrych never considered the reason behind Balos's sudden departure. "He returns to the village. But why?"

Onya met his eyes in the darkness, only cleared by the gift of wolf sight. "That is no business of yours, Wanderer. You are not fully *pack*, remember?"

Ceddrych gritted his teeth, as his skin suddenly felt too tight, too mortal. He needed to change, to stop Balos and...

For what?

The voice in his head sounded far too much like Vynasha's, and once more he was returned to his true purpose in joining the hunt. Not to appease Balos as they had agreed.

Bide your time and find Wyllem.

Onya rolled over, giving her back to Ceddrych in a show of arrogance. She did not see him as a threat. He glared at her back and forced his body to recline. Vynasha was strong. She had survived the journey to Wylderland, and she had survived the cruelties the curse wrought upon her. She wasn't alone in the village—he'd made certain of that. It would have to be enough.

A woman's wail broke him from a series of nightmares.

"Vynasha?" He turned, reaching for a body that was no longer there, and frowned as his head hit a rough hide. His vision sharpened as the beat of snow hit the outer layer of the tent, until the twitching form of the woman opposite him proved the nightmare continued into the waking, and not only for Ceddrych.

"N-noo," Onya whimpered. "Aslov, please waken!" She thrashed against the pallet, sobs bursting from her throat, tears tracking over her gaunt cheeks.

Her despair drove him to cross the distance, to place a hand on her arm and speak her name. "Onya? Onya, wake up. It's only a dream."

She shook her head, her eyes moving quickly beneath closed lids. "No, no, no, you cannot!"

Ceddrych caught her hand as she suddenly lurched to slap him. "It's a dream," he repeated more firmly. "Open your eyes, Onya."

"Aslov!" she twisted in his grip, forcing him to release her hand or break it. "Do not leave me, my love, please…"

Compassion was not a feeling he was accustomed to, not after the war and especially since becoming a wolf. What else could this be, he decided, as he drew her into his arms and spoke as gently as he could. "You aren't alone, Onya. You're safe."

"Safe…" she repeated, nuzzling against his chest with a shuddering sigh.

"I swear it," he said. He had heard the story from Galtis, her father, the night the elder asked him to forgive his only living child for attacking him. They all carried similar tales, like Vilhelm, even Balos. Onya lost her husband when Asa was just a babe to Wolfsbane's people. Her hatred ran deeper than most.

If she found peace in sleep for this night, she didn't need to know he had given it to her. It didn't mean anything. So why did her relieved sigh rattle him so?

Her breath hitched, her back suddenly rigid beneath his hand. Another nightmare?

"Unhand me," she growled.

Ceddrych released her and scrambled back onto his side of the tent. Onya was just as quick to create distance between them, her dark hair half hanging over her face, only disturbed by quick pants in the growing painful silence.

With a huff, Ceddrych ran a hand through his loose hair and turned his head. "You were... upset. I only wanted to help."

"Never touch me again," she snapped back then lowered her voice to a hiss. The camp was small, and the pack had excellent hearing even with the snowfall. "You do not have the right, Wanderer."

Ceddrych nodded, clenched then unclenched his jaw as more words pressed against his throat. Foolish words that she did not deserve. He clearly lacked control in his mortal form, for they came regardless. "For what it's worth, I am truly sorry... for the loss of your mate."

"Do not mock me," she hissed.

"No, that's not... I only meant to say I can't imagine what it's like for you, having to continue without him while raising Asa. I think..." He swallowed against the pressure building at the back of his throat, the need to reach for someone who wasn't there and hadn't been since he left the village. Damn Onya for forcing him to sleep in this weak skin, for the feelings he had been able to keep at bay until now. "You're far braver than I could be," he confessed.

"You would know," Onya whispered, so softly he struggled to catch her words near to her as he was. "Your defense of your mate was most *touching*."

Ceddrych froze, fear and lingering guilt and self-hatred twisting his innards. "You know nothing."

Onya leaned closer to him, a smile and a taunt behind her words. "I know what the witch you call *sister* is to you. Everyone in the village knows but for her. I wonder what she would say, your precious Vynasha, if she understood what it means to be a wolf's mate."

Ceddrych flinched and twisted away, digging his fingers into the hard ground. "And I wonder how Balos has withstood your company for so long."

He grunted as the she-wolf was suddenly upon him, shoving him back onto the ground. Sharp fingernails dug into his shoulders as she shared his breath. "Watch your tongue, Wanderer," she growled, her chest rumbling with the truth beneath her flesh. "You will *never* understand what Balos has sacrificed for all of us. He deserves your respect, not disobedience."

Ceddrych's blood thrummed against the threat she gave him, all because he made the stupid mistake of comforting her. "You're right, I don't understand it, and I don't bloody care. I'm here because of my mate as you rightfully called her. And Vynasha will never hear of this or know what I am to her. Because it doesn't matter what I want, so long as she has everything she needs."

Onya scoffed and slowly slid back onto her palette. "And what if she never learns you share no blood?" she hissed. "Will you remain incomplete forever?"

Ceddrych worked his jaw and resisted the urge to claw at the hole in his chest, the hole that was only ever sated when Vynasha was near. "If that's what she needs."

"You are a fool, Wanderer," she muttered bitterly before curling into her furs.

Maybe he was, Ceddrych reflected days after that first cruel night.

A fool would not leave the safety of the pack behind to wander alone once more. This fool understood he would be far more likely to find his nephew alone than with the others chasing the boy away.

The forest seemed to close in around him so far from the river, but this was nearest the place he last caught Wyll's scent. And so he began his hunt from there.

It had been so long since he was last alone like this, with only the trees and shadows for company. Not since he chanced upon Vynasha's scent by accident and it was enough to bring Ceddrych back into his mortal flesh. Wyll's scent was similar yet subtly different, not sweet but tasting faintly of ashes in his mouth. Wyll did not have magick.

No sign of Wolfsbane, nor his daughter, at least. Whatever magick protected the cruel mortals, Ceddrych didn't understand nor care. They had done nothing to him. Yet. Should he find Wyll harmed in any way, Vilhelm's and Onya's vengeance would become his.

CHAPTER FOURTEEN

A Cursed Nightmare

VYNASHA SHOULD HAVE known better than to tempt fate. For no sooner did she close her eyes than she appeared in her bedroom in Castle Bitterhelm.

She rose from the bedsheets with a curse and froze. The room was altered. Where the shadow realm had been dimmed, the fire burning in the hearth was now a hearty rosy violet. Candles of a similar hue illuminated the wall sconces, and the candelabrum scattered about the room.

Grendel was nowhere to be seen, but this gave Vynasha little comfort.

The dress she wore was softer than anything she'd become accustomed to in the village, deep emerald velvet-trimmed silk. She ran scarred and calloused fingers over the emeralds and pearls sewn into the bodice. Her upper chest was on full display, mottled skin more prominent here than anywhere on her body.

Vynasha cursed as she rose from the bed and searched for a robe or anything that would keep her from exposing herself, only to find a distinct absence of clothes in her once brimming wardrobe. "How did he manage this?"

A dry laugh and weakened voice sounded from the armchair before the hearth. "This is *my* shadow realm, Asha. I can do as I please, and it pleases me greatly to see you dressed as your station demands."

Vynasha dug her claws into her palm as she stalked around the chair to stand before the fire. "What do you mean my *station*? And why did I wake up here and not in the garden?"

"Why indeed…" Grendel smiled beatifically at her from his slumped and far too casual pose in the high-backed chair. His silvery-violet eyes drank her in with an indecently slow perusal, and his smile grew.

Impatient with his games, Vynasha planted her hands on her hips. "Answer me, or I'll rip your gifts to shreds."

Grendel swallowed and his tongue darted out to trace his lower lip, as though tasting the air. "I find it comforting to rest here most days. None come looking for my spirit so near to where you linger."

Vynasha pulled her shoulders back and resisted the urge to cover her upper chest, if only to mask the shallow rise and fall of her chest. She willed steel into her voice instead. "Where I linger?"

"Indeed." Grendel sat up so suddenly Vynasha took a small step back into the false heat of the hearth. "So long as we are bound together, a part of you will always remain, even if it is the part you prefer to keep furthest from me."

Vynasha's hands fell to her sides. "That's why I keep dreaming of the gardens. Even if I don't touch my magick, even if I left Wylderland, I'd still dream of this place, wouldn't I?"

Grendel's gaze slid from her heaving chest to her mouth, but he gave no answer, only waited.

Vynasha blinked against the sudden burn in her eyes and turned her back to him. "When I die, will my spirit come here?"

Trapped forever.

"Tell me, does that sound so terrible?"

A bitter laugh escaped her. "How can you ask me that? You know why I left, what I wanted." She stiffened as his hand slipped around her waist. He had moved so quickly, silent as the specter he'd become.

His breath heated her cheek as he replied, "An eternity with me need not be torture."

Vynasha flinched. "Don't," she hissed, turning her head aside, before he could sense the way her body was already beginning to betray her.

This is a dream. It's not real.

Yet the want she had felt before returned with a mere brush of his thumb over her bodice, at the way his tall frame settled against hers.

Rather than be dissuaded, Grendel buried his face in her curls and breathed deeply. "Vynasha, how I have longed for you," he groaned and slipped his other arm to draw her hips back against his.

Vynasha shuddered at the firm press of his desire against her backside. "I don't want this," she snapped but still could not bring herself to break away. Not from the slow trace of his hand along her arm or the heady rush of magick pulsing between them.

"You do not *want* to want this," Grendel insisted.

Vynasha twisted in his embrace and caught the ruined prince by his jaw, digging her claws in just shy of drawing blood. "I think I've made it clear the last thing I could ever want is an eternity with *you* in your cursed castle."

His eyebrows pinched, yet the want somehow remained in his almost feverish gaze. His throat contracted, and his voice was thick as he managed to reply. "Hate me as you will, but nothing you say will stop my needing you, Vynasha."

"You hardly know me," she snapped.

His hand caught hers before she could pull away. "I have searched for you most of my life."

"*Ferox* found me and saved my life long before we ever met, Prince."

"You would defend the beast that tossed you into a dungeon like a petulant child when he did not get his way?"

Vynasha ripped her hand from his grasp. "Ferox was honest about my choices from the beginning, but you? You took my freedom and damned my soul and have called it kindness."

A slow smile tilted his face into something frighteningly beautiful. "I have hated the idea of you, that my salvation should come from any other creature than myself."

"At least we can agree on something," she muttered, but her lips parted as he ran a hand over the back of her wrist, and her hand fell limp in his.

"I was more powerful than you can begin to fathom before my mother enacted her bloody curse." Grendel took another step closer, forcing her to tilt her head as his free hand rose and a single finger traced the skin along the low collar of her dress. "I sensed you long before you crossed our borders. I chased you in my cursed form to the castle, desperate for any taste of your scent. And every hour after your arrival was perfect agony for me. Hating and wanting you in equal measure."

Vynasha's breath stuttered as he brought her limp hand to the back of his neck. "I can never love you."

"Oh, darling." Grendel chuckled low, a sound that tightened the coil in her lower belly. "Who said anything about love?"

Vynasha's protest was stolen by the sudden brush of his mouth against hers. Her hand flexed around his neck, drawing him more firmly against her.

Oh, Saints.

She wanted to rip him to shreds. She wanted to cleave herself to him until they were one. She wanted…

Vynasha moaned as Grendel tugged the collar of her dress just enough for her breasts to spill out. A broken sound escaped him as he rubbed his thumb against a taut peak.

"Perfect," he huffed, and her lips parted in a silent cry as he dipped his head and covered her breast with his mouth.

Vynasha caught his head and she pulled at his hair, scraping a claw against his slightly pointed ear.

His rumbling groan drew an answering shudder down her spine as his tongue laved over first one peak and then the other.

She squeezed her eyes shut as the room seemed to spin around them, and her weaker leg was the first to give out.

Grendel caught her fall, laying her upon the rug before the hearth, the same rug they had once sat on and spoken late into the night. His mouth left her breasts to press reverently over the scars littering her skin, and he amurmured, "Beautiful."

Tears spilled from the corners of her eyes. "I'm not," she weakly moaned.

Grendel shifted so he lay against her side and slowly, purposefully kissed from her upper chest along her neck, where the flames had scored her skin deepest.

Vynasha squeezed her eyes shut and her chest shook from the effort to contain her sobs. A weak hand fisted the hair at the back of his head, and her mouth parted as he rose to press kisses against the corner. Her scars kept her smile from blooming into the bright thing it had once been.

"Every part of you is beautiful," he said then claimed her mouth again.

Vynasha opened her tearful eyes to find him watching her between kisses. The thrill of his skin against hers, even in this shadow of a dream, drew her blood to racing, her heart pounding in time with his. And she found herself caressing his pointed ears, savoring the way his eyes rolled to the back of his head and the arch of his hips against her leg.

She devoured every kiss he gave her and hummed happily as his tongue traced her lips, opening to let him in.

Her skirts had spread a maddening poof between them, and Grendel chuffed as he pulled away in a vain struggle to peel the layers back.

Vynasha couldn't help but answer his frustration with a satisfied grin. "Serves you right for dressing me in this ridiculous contraption without my knowledge."

Grendel's eyebrows arched, and his grin gleamed in the firelight as a hand dragged firmly over her stocking-clad thigh. "Well, I could not have you dressed in nothing while you slept, could I?"

Vynasha shoved her skirts back down, halting his progress. "What do you mean while I slept? This is the dream."

Grendel hung his head and sighed heavily as his gaze flicked longingly for her exposed breasts. "And a part of you remains," he simply said.

Vynasha's heart fell through her throat, and she brought her hands up to scrub away her lingering tears. "But this is a dream. I— Grendel, why does it *feel* so real?"

Grendel's eyebrows pinched together as he slowly ran a soothing hand over her covered thigh. "Our bond makes it real. You are not simply dreaming, love. Your spirit is drawn here, as I said before."

"Am I even in my body still?" Vynasha sat up, forgetting her indecency as panic filled her chest. Was she an empty shell, then? Still breathing but not fully alive? "Oh, Saints, what would happen if I didn't wake up? That isn't possible. None of this should be possible," she growled and gripped his arm, but didn't remove his hand from her thigh. Even now she could no longer deny the wretched part of her that *wanted* his touch.

Grendel brushed her curls behind her rounded ear, tracing the curve with something akin to awe. "We are both sleeping in a way, I suppose. But this is safer for those you love. You asked me why I brought you here, when you continue to toy yet again with magick you do not comprehend."

Vynasha batted his hand away from her ear. "You forced me to sleep, didn't you?"

Grendel's smile stiffened. "I did you a favor you have yet to return. Are you not aware how the terms of our bargain work, love?"

Vynasha scoffed. "You speak of bargains when we both know you tricked me into sharing your blood. You *made* me into this." She gestured to her too-sharp teeth and beastly eyes. And no matter that she knew it could have been far worse if Grendel hadn't intervened, the truth was difficult to face.

"I have been more than gracious, more generous than most. If you only knew the terms, I could have made… the things I could have made you *do*," he said with a press of his lips to hers. "Accept my love as the gift it is and remember what happens if you break the terms."

The last bargain Vynasha made with Ferox had ended with her in a dungeon. Was Grendel's offer any better?

Not for the first time, Vynasha wished she had not crossed paths with Wolfsbane and his daughter and left Wyll behind. She wished Ceddrych had found them first.

Vynasha jerked her chin aside before Grendel could kiss her again and squeezed her eyes shut. "This was a mistake. It won't happen again."

Grendel carded gently through her thick curls and cradled the back of her neck. "Whatever you wish, so long as you keep me in your dreams."

The blue firelight shivered and flickered, and Grendel turned his head with a frown. "What…"

He covered her body with his as the walls groaned against a sudden *thrum* which shook the walls.

"Grendel!" Her claws dug into his tattered overcoat as a foreign power seemed to wrap around her navel and *tug*.

His luminous gaze found hers, and his mouth took the shape of her name as the world shattered around them.

CHAPTER FIFTEEN

A Taste of Violet Ice

YNASHA WOKE WITH a shuddering lurch. A cool hand held back her curls as she retched over the side of her pallet.

"Easy, all will be well. Your spirit has returned." A tentative voice accompanied the gentle press of fingers against Vynasha's brow. "You are safe again."

Vynasha caught the child's hand in a tight grasp and choked as she tried to swallow air. Had she stopped breathing? "Wh-who are you?" she managed as the small girl helped her lay back on her furs.

"Erythea," the girl whispered then held a cup of water before Vynasha's lips. "Drink. You have had nothing for a whole night and day. Only your magick sustained you."

Vynasha drank, grateful to rinse away the lingering bile at the back of her throat. The water tasted like pine and newly fallen snow, a taste oddly familiar to her tongue. She quickly took in her surroundings, momentarily lost by the high wooden ceiling, the roaring stone hearth, and carvings of creatures etched in the ceiling and walls. And then her gaze skittered from the cup in her hand to the girl's faintly glowing blue skin, the same way Vynasha's skin glowed violet when using her magick.

With a sickening rush, she recalled Grendel's warning, the way the dream had suddenly shattered. And then she met a pair of ancient lilac eyes framed by a braided crown of silver hair. Erythea. The girl who had used magick to break Grendel's hold over their bond.

Vynasha flinched and accidentally knocked the water aside, ignoring the way Erythea's face fell and her shoulders hunched to make herself appear smaller.

"I-I am… s-s-sorry," the girl stuttered as the glow emanating from her skin faded.

Vynasha pressed a hand to her gut and felt the echo of the tug her spirit had sensed in Castle Bitterhelm. "*You* brought me back."

"You went so far away for too long." The girl wrapped her arms around her legs. Finely woven leggings and beaded boots, clothing of a quality Vynasha had not seen on most of the other children.

Vynasha frowned at the knowing in the girl's lilac eyes. "Who *are* you? Why haven't I seen you before?"

Erythea's full mouth quirked up at the corner in a tentative smile as she whispered, "I am very good at hiding." Her smile fell as she added, "But Grandmother's grimoire says it is not safe to stay away from your body that long. The others were afraid of what Wanderer would say if he returned before you woke. So I tried the spell, and it worked!" The blue glow returned to her skin with her growing excitement.

Vynasha clenched her fists to avoid the urge to recoil from the girl. A girl who used magick freely and willingly in a village where all others were too afraid to touch it. A grandmother who kept a grimoire when Vynasha had nearly been burned for being *rumored* to be a witch.

"You!" Tarbus suddenly stalked through the nearby doorway with a snarl. "I thought we told you to go home, you little rat!"

Erythea leaped back until she was pressed against the opposite wall, lilac eyes blown wide with panic.

"Please tell me that is not who I think it is." Dadas groaned as he followed his twin inside.

"Oh, it is." Tarbus bristled and stalked carefully into the room until he stood at Vynasha's bedside. "And she was just leaving, before she could bring more of her bad luck into our witch's home."

Erythea blinked and tears streamed down her face. "P-please," she rasped. "I was only trying to help."

"You are the reason she drew too much in the first place." Dadas snatched Erythea's wrist and dragged her from the room. "You want to help the witch? Go home, Thea."

The girl yelped as the other children crowded around them, calling insults after her.

"Witch!"

"Witch's brood!"

"Take your curse with you, rat!"

Erythea sobbed as she tripped and fell to her knees with a cry.

Like Wyll cried when the villagers threw mud and saints know what else the one time I brought him to the village.

Vynasha had been powerless then, too afraid to unleash the prickling of magick rising beneath her skin, the fury that had seemed to choke her as she screamed back at the boys and half dragged, half carried her nephew into Mayve's Tavern. Their cousin Stye had taken one look at them and proceeded to rain fury upon them. Stye and a handful of his strongest brutes that lingered at the tavern. Wyll's tears hadn't stopped until they were escorted far enough from the village to be safe.

"Am I so ugly, Auntie Asha?" Wyll had asked.

She had wanted to run as fast as her broken body would allow her, to let go of the tether her mother had insisted she maintain. To keep herself safe from a pillory or a pyre. And then the voice in the wind had begged her, "*I know you crave vengeance, but please do not put yourself in harm's way.*"

Ferox was not here to stop her this time, and Grendel could do nothing from his self-imposed prison.

"Enough!" Vynasha growled low and deep, an inhuman sound that would have frightened her once, as she leapt up from her covers. In two strides, she reached Erythea and stood between the frightened child and her tormentors. The children Vynasha had come to view as friends, children she had risked her life to heal and protect.

"Vynasha?" Tarbus shared a look with his brother.

Dadas crouched, poised to rush to her side. "Are you in any pain?"

The twins flinched as she snarled and shoved them back. "What should any of you care? Why give me any concern when you're all perfectly fine casting stones at an innocent little girl?" Vynasha scoffed. "And all because she used magick. You're all bloody hypocrites!"

Asa and his feathered cousins slipped back into the room with rounded eyes. "But she could have killed you," the boy whispered.

Erythea whimpered, and cool hands clasped around her legs. The winter kiss of the girl's magick greeted the violent storm waging within Vynasha enough to calm her. Enough for her to see through the red haze her rage had brought her.

"She's a little girl," Vynasha said. Only moments ago she had seen the vicious curl on Asa's lip as he kicked Erythea out. She wouldn't be fooled by his innocent façade, by *any* of them, anymore. Vynasha took time to look each of them in the eye and only found something akin to remorse in the slump of Dadas's shoulders. "From what I have seen, each of you can touch magick. What makes Erythea any different?"

Tarbus grimaced and kicked his foot against the hardwood floor. "We are forbidden from using in the village because it keeps everyone safe. But the rat has no control over her power. *She* is a danger to herself and everyone in the village."

Erythea gasped behind her, and Vynasha found her hand combing through windswept curls. When had she lowered her hand? The girl breathed harshly, and through their timid connection, the girl's magick did feel… wild.

"What did you mean she brings bad luck?" Vynasha glanced at the spilled cup of water between freshly cut floorboards beside her fur pallet, knocked aside in her haste. It was cool within her new home, but it shouldn't have been cold enough for the water to have already frozen solid.

"Bad things happen around her constantly. Sometimes it is little accidents, other times a bad harvest," Tarbus grumbled. "Ask anyone in the village. She may as well be cursed."

"*Are we cursed, Auntie?*" Wyll once asked. "*Is that why the forest swallowed up Grandfather and Uncle Ceddrych, and the fire…*"

"I see," Vynasha ground out, the memory of her nephew too near. "And why did you say she caused me to draw too much?"

"But I did not, I swear it!" Erythea suddenly cried, her grasp too tight on Vynasha's leg. "I was only trying to help."

"Liar! We all felt you watching us," Tarbus snarled.

"It is true, Vynasha." Dadas took a knee before her, favoring the girl at her feet a dark look. "She was watching at a distance from the forest when the house caught root. But instead of keeping away, she came closer and tried adding her magick to yours. It caused the house to grow too quickly. And we lost control."

Gooseflesh broke out over the back of her neck at his ominous words. She couldn't deny her fear as she realized the child had somehow broken Grendel's hold over her. Was the children's fear any different? She forced her trembling hand to steady as she threaded her fingers through tangled curls. "And none of you thought to bring up that you knew she was watching? You could have told me, had you truly trusted me as you claim."

Tarbus took a reluctant knee beside his twin and sighed. "Forgive us. We wanted to snatch up the rat the moment we realized what had happened, but we were too late. Rat has always been too good at hiding."

Vynasha frowned as Erythea stiffened and seemed to curl into herself even more. "She said something like that too." She lifted her gaze again to the completed room, the beautiful and strange carvings etched into the walls, and the steady *thrum* of a pulse beneath her feet. Now that she knew to look for it, the same taste of winter lingered in the boards, the eldritch power of the mirror. Erythea's magick.

"All this time, I've felt someone was watching us," she murmured as she looked down into a fearful pair of lilac eyes. "But I thought it was… something else."

The wolf twins looked at one another briefly. "Something else?" Dadas asked.

"Come, on your feet." Vynasha aided Erythea to stand and led her to the hearth. The little witch wouldn't release her hand but kept pressed tightly against her side, keeping her front to the room. "The same reason you fear the shadows, the reason so many fell ill the same time I arrived."

She leaned against the stones built around the fireplace to take pressure off her bad leg and turned a hard eye to the twins. "Ask my forgiveness all you want. But remember this. You've spent so much time fearing a scared little girl, you haven't stopped to think about the real threat at your backs. And if *they* send any more demons or beasts to the village, it will be witches like Erythea, like *me*, who save your sorry hides."

"Trouble!" Katya burst suddenly into the room, a fresh dusting of snow on the hood covering her cornsilk hair. "Something chased me all the way from the village boundary. Shit, what is the rat doing here?"

Tarbus caught Katya by the shoulders, guiding her over the threshold. "What did it look like? Was it one of the pack or…"

A grating howl rent the air suddenly, stealing their collective breaths. Erythea bit back a cry and buried her face in Vynasha's chest. Asa and his cousins, Hugyn and Munyn, rushed across the floor to press against Vynasha's sides.

"That *thing* is no kin to us," Katya snapped back, her grip tightening on the runed hammer in her hand as they turned to face the door.

The open door.

"Bar the door!" Dadas shouted, but it was too late.

CHAPTER SIXTEEN

A Foul Hunger

THE FOUNDATIONS AROUND them rattled as a massive force suddenly pounded against the wall. Erythea screamed as Asa covered his ears with his hands.

Another howl followed the first, this time fully upon them, a cry unlike anything Vynasha had heard before.

Except for when she lived in Castle Bitterhelm. When she had woken to strange beastly cries in the night. A dark curse slipped past her tongue as Dadas joined Katya and Tarbus in attempting to seal the door.

"What in seven hells is that?" Tarbus shouted.

Vynasha squeezed Erythea and Asa briefly and then looked down at them with wide eyes. She had Ferox's dagger hidden in the pocket of her coat, had pricked Balos with the blade. But could she take down one of the castle's beasts? Thanks to her bad leg, she had relied heavily on traps to provide fresh meat for herself and Wyll. Now her leg was renewed, and her claws were sharp, but her magick wasn't made for brutality like this.

The beasts were people once, like Old Ced.

Hugyn and Munyn wrapped tentative hands around her arm, lifting their solid ebony eyes to meet her gaze. And a strange surety fell over her, wiping out her bitterness over the children's actions. They had been taught to hate, just like those boys in Whistleande. None of them deserved to die.

"Get it closed so the house can seal itself," Katya said over the beast's latest assault on the walls.

The beast was assessing them for weaknesses, but it hadn't managed to break down the door yet. A crack remained, open to the deep grating bellows of a monster, caught between the howl of a wyldcat and a bear.

"Even you cannot close this bloody door!" Tarbus grunted as the twins and Katya pushed back against the door yet again, and the beast's massive, furred head. A flash of a scarlet eye peeked through and seemed to find Vynasha immediately.

Another bellow sounded as the beast renewed its efforts, and Vynasha bit her tongue until blood filled her mouth. Tears blurred her vision as her heart thundered in her chest.

Each thump sent dust and rose petals falling from the rafters, another reminder of the castle.

Mother, give me strength.

"Stay here," Vynasha ordered as she pushed Asa and the raven siblings back.

"Wrong… all wrong," Erythea whimpered as Asa howled, "Wait!"

"Stay," Vynasha repeated through gritted teeth. She pulled her dagger free and stalked forward on unsteady limbs.

Dadas and Tarbus grunted as they struggled against the weight of the beast's head. Tears spilled over Katya's cheeks as she bared all her strength to keep her back against the door and her boots on the ground.

"We must turn, brother, before the beast breaks through!" Dadas growled.

"We cannot take it down with just the two of us." Tarbus laughed, a bitter and helpless sound.

"Shut up, you hare-brains, and get the door shut!" Katya argued. "It cannot break through if the house is sealed."

Vynasha tightened her grip on the dagger to keep her hand from shaking. Dadas noticed her first, despair flashing through his wolf's eyes. "Let me through," she said with greater calm than she felt.

"Are you mad?" Tarbus barked. "It will gut you alive!"

"No, it won't." Vynasha squeezed her eyes shut then opened them as the beast barged against the door once more, a bloody snout breaking through. She looked down at the dagger and muttered a prayer as she sliced a shallow cut into her palm.

"Please, stop." Dadas's nostrils flared and his lips curled to reveal sharp teeth. They were near to turning, but she was a monster too.

Vynasha leapt forward and pressed her palm against the beast's nose, and the creature's snarl fell to a whimper. "That's it… you know this scent, don't you? You followed it all the way here—well, here I am." She shifted on her feet and tested her grip on the dagger then looked down at Tarbus. "Let me pass."

The twins shook their heads in tandem. "We cannot," Dadas sputtered as his brother hissed, "We swore oaths to protect you!"

"And you have. Now let me protect you," Vynasha said, her gaze dropping to Katya. "Trust me."

The girl's mouth worked for a moment before she swallowed and nodded. "Let her through."

"I bloody will *not*," Tarbus began.

"Now, you lummox," Katya snapped.

Dadas gasped as the smaller girl dragged them both from the door, just enough for Vynasha to push through the crack.

The beast was massive, at least as tall at its razorback spine as Grolthox had been. Its head was a cross between a bull and a bear, with bright ruby eyes shaped like a wyldcat's.

"Seal the door shut behind me," she said, softly, to not spook the creature.

A whispered argument erupted behind her before Katya shut the door with a resounding *snap*.

The beast snarled and lifted its head, sniffing at the house, at the prey waiting inside. But Katya had been right. The instant the door shut, a wave of magick passed over the structure at Vynasha's back.

"Easy, eyes on me," she said as she brought her bleeding hand before its face.

The beast cocked its head aside, and its shoulders hunched, brown fur bristling as it pressed its wet nose into her palm.

She bit back a cry as the beast ran a rough tongue over her wound with a rumbling purr. The rubies in the dagger bit into the hand she kept ready behind her back, just in case. "That's fine, take what you need. But not too much."

As though the creature heard her, it suddenly lowered its head, licking its chops.

Vynasha lowered her trembling arm as quickly as she dared. "You are very far from home," she said, drawing the beast's gaze. With careful steps, she began to step into the snow on her stocking-clad feet and ignored the stabbing chill. "How did you make it past the gate and the wards, I wonder?"

The beast took a lumbering step after her. She turned her head but maintained eye contact and reached a palm behind her to avoid the trees. She just needed to get the beast away from the house, then she could…

What? What will you do?

Her eyes welled, and she tamped down on the fear rushing through her blood.

"*Keep talking,*" a voice that sounded too like Ferox whispered to her head.

Vynasha squeezed her fist, and droplets of her violet blood spilled on the snow. The beast followed the trail, taking careful licks after her. "Do you remember who you were before?"

The beast growled low and lifted a narrow, hungry gaze upon her before following the next drop of tainted blood.

"My father became a beast like you. Only death released him in the end…I'm so sorry, what's happened to you. I'm sorry…" Tears blurred her vision, and Vynasha stumbled, catching her fall on a tree trunk.

The beast's hackles raised, lips curling over teeth as long as her fingers.

"I'm sorry I didn't save you," she confessed as the beast drew back on its hind legs. Spittle and the scents of death mixed with her blood billowed from the creature, and Vynasha crouched, readying the dagger and her claws. She looked past the beast and could barely make out the light from the cottage. It would be enough.

The beast stumbled forward and brought its massive paw down over her much smaller form.

Vynasha swung her arm in an arc, and a scream passed her throat, more wyldcat than woman.

Blood black as soot spilled over the snow, and the beast roared. But it wasn't enough to keep its paw from catching her shoulder and tossing her aside.

All the air was knocked from her lungs as her body was flung against a tree. She lost her grip on Ferox's dagger, but it didn't matter, not anymore. Not as she struggled to breathe, to see the blurred form of the beast run for her.

"Get up and fight!" Ferox's voice seemed to cry out against the wind.

I'm sorry I couldn't keep my promise, Wyll.

She had cheated death too many times, had gone on living for her nephew's sake. But he had Ceddrych now... oh, Saints, Ceddrych.

A sob passed her bloody lips, but she refused the call of magick in her blood. She couldn't risk it, not again, not after her last mistake had nearly cost the lives of innocent children.

The beast's hot breath was upon her, and she waited for the inevitable.

Only, she didn't die the gruesome death she justly deserved.

A beautiful white creature burst from the forest at her back so suddenly, the beast had no time to react.

All bodily pains seemed to dim to a separate place in Vynasha's mind as the moonlit creature attacked the beast with such speed her dulled senses struggled to keep up.

The beast turned about with a furious roar as the white creature bit its leg, its back, and its arm, ripping and tearing with frightening ease.

The beast unleashed a pained, pitiful groan as it fell. The end, when it came, was shielded by her savior.

Vynasha blinked, and the creature turned, its beautiful silver fur turned bloody. Bright green eyes seemed to brighten as the wolf approached her.

She blinked again, and the wolf was a white-cloaked man, his bare chest and arms covered in black blood.

"Vynasha?" The deep, rasping voice was familiar to her.

She smiled. "Balos."

An unreadable look passed the alpha's chiseled features. Yet those burning green eyes traced over her form with greater intensity. "You are injured and have exhausted your power, little fool."

Vynasha chuckled and winced at the pain in her shoulder. "Would you believe me if I told you I've felt worse?"

The corner of his mouth tugged in a ghost of a smirk. "Pain can be a great teacher, I have found."

"You would, you old masochist." She groaned as she braced her good arm against the tree at her back. The tree the beast had tossed her against. Oh, Saints, did everything ache.

"Would you accept my aide?" A pale, dirty hand entered her vision, and Vynasha found that unreadable look again in his eyes.

Vynasha hesitated, thrill and dread in equal measure tugging at her heart. "How are you here? Is… the pack with you?"

Balos grimaced but kept his hand outstretched. "They continue the hunt."

Vynasha frowned at his half answer. "Aren't you angry with me?"

"Did you not lead the beast away from the children with your own blood?"

"Yes…" Her vision blurred as her hand rose, dripping luminous violet, and the cloyingly sweet scent of her blood thickened in the air. When her vision cleared, Balos had wrapped an arm around her upper torso, and he drew her to stand against him.

"Easy," he murmured as they began the slow progress back to her home.

Deep clawed tracks and broken bracken disturbed the once pristine forest, a clear path the way she had come. Vynasha shuddered and rasped, "The children?"

"The house locked them inside the moment you left." His voice deepened with an edge of something she was too weary to understand.

"The house?" She blinked, and they suddenly stood before the two-storied frame.

"I see you have been busy in my absence," Balos said.

Wood the same shade as the dark fir bark of the surrounding forest, with veins of violet and silver threaded throughout the house in runic patterns. Roses bloomed in defiance of winter, bursting from every crack and crevice. With every breath, she could feel the power coming from within, magick which seemed to resonate within her weak heartbeat.

"The children…" Vynasha listed to the right, but Balos caught her fall.

"They are well as can be. Vynasha? Open your eyes!" Balos commanded as her world tilted. Large hands caught her and tucked her into a comforting heat. "Help me! Vynasha, you must open the house, or none can enter nor leave."

They shifted, and the cut in her hand burned as her palm was brought firmly against rough wood.

"Please, Beauty, just a little more. Then you may rest, I swear it."

Vynasha tried to speak the word, but her lips didn't obey any more than her eyes.

Open.

"Beauty!"

Chapter Seventeen

A Trail of Blood and Snow

THE PACK'S FURIOUS howls followed Ceddrych for the first three nights after his escape. There were moments he half expected Vilhelm to suddenly appear as the older wolf was wont to do.

Only a fool would stop moving to test the pack or ignore this boon. Without Balos to use his limited power of influence and command on Ceddrych, nothing could hold him back anymore. The others would be bound most to Balos's parting command: hunt Wolfsbane.

Any game he might have hunted was scarce, but Ceddrych wasn't hungry after the last hare he consumed whole. The taste of flesh and blood was as delicious as it was abhorrent to the man within his skin. But the longer he hunted, the more his instincts took over. He would eat a proper meal later.

After…

His time as a wolf was different than that of a man. He slept little, as shelter was sparse, often in a thicket or the hollow of a great tree. He woke just before first light, not that the nights lasted long in this part of the world, and returned to hunt the scent of home.

Avoiding all caves and places in the wood where the shadows were too deep to be natural, Wanderer clung to the memory of Vynasha.

Soft curls, like silk ribbons.

The wolf was closer to that scent, closer to his true pack. He lost the scent for a time. It faded, and he searched instead for signs of man: fire, cleaned bones, clumsy tracks. Tempting to forget this futile hunt, to give in to the urge to run, run, keep running away until he was finally free. But the thought of her…

Eyes once silver moonlight, now bright gold like a wyldcat's.

Wanderer slowed as he reached a rare break in the trees. The sun shone unusually bright over a patch of undisturbed snow glistening like diamonds. And as he opened his mouth to breathe deeply this new place, he caught something beneath the clean snow and prey of the forest. Something acrid like ashes after a fire had been stamped out and like *her.*

Shining claws upon delicate hands covered in scars and callouses. Rough and smooth at once.

He found himself within the sunlight before he realized he had moved.

Only a fool would forget himself in Wylderland. Forgetting made one susceptible to enchantment.

No, came the errant thought of the man inside his skin. *Not enchantment.*

His paw slipped through the gap in the snow, through the hidden snare.

A trap.

He came back to himself suddenly, fully, painfully. How long had he wandered, searching? The wolf's howling snarl escaped his throat as ropes snatched him up and into the trees, dangling easy prey from above.

He snapped and clawed at his binds in a blind rage, but Ceddrych's mind raced. It would be simple to break through with a knife. But though they brought their wolf skins with them through the turn, a cloak to protect them, they could not carry weapons.

Blood rushed to his head as he swung, trees blurring and slowly falling still as he came to a stop broken only by the wind. Twin figures appeared through the trees, then. One covered in black furs, not much taller than the thin one beside her. A child.

His heart seized in his chest.

"We got one, Resha!" the boy said.

Wyll.

Ceddrych laughed, but the sound came as a bark that startled the girl with his nephew.

The girl's face was largely obscured by a black wolf's fur, but he sensed the weight of her wary glare. He froze as she pulled a white-bone knife free from her belt and lifted her other hand to warn Wyll to stay back.

Ceddrych was more vulnerable in his mortal form, but he had no choice. He drew in a deep breath and focused on the man within himself to trigger the change.

But Resha was nearly upon him, knife raised and a snarl on her lips.

Wait, he tried to scream. The ropes groaned against his weight, never intended for game as large as he.

The wolf howled, long and mournful.

Resha flinched and her arm slowly dropped to her side.

She was not ready for the attack that came from the woods until it was too late. The wolf was smaller than him, dark and far too familiar.

Had Onya been following him all this time? Had the pack?

But no others came as he'd expected. Onya fought alone, with a speed and viciousness Ceddrych had never seen. She was a blur of fur, sending snow flying in every direction as she whirled and snapped at the girl.

"Resha!" Wyll screamed but still scrambled back behind the nearest tree.

Onya's head darted briefly to the boy then back to the girl.

Ceddrych wouldn't have believed it unless he saw the way Wolfsbane's daughter—for who else could this be?—dodged every attack, pulling a second dagger free and wielding both like extensions of her arms. Like longer, sharper claws.

Onya yelped as the bone dagger drew her blood to line the forest floor.

Ceddrych struggled against his binds once more. He had to do something, had to stop this! He bit and clawed at the rope and ignored his bleeding jaw as the first snap gave way.

"Resha, the other wolf!" Wyll shouted, a mistake.

Wolfsbane's daughter hesitated, and Onya took full advantage, slamming the girl into a tree trunk so hard snow rained from the branches onto the ground.

A pained hissing sound escaped Resha as the girl slumped to the earth.

Onya snarled with triumph, ready to make the kill.

"Don't hurt her!" Wyll came rushing from behind his tree with only a shaved and polished tree branch in his hand. "Please! She's my friend!"

Onya tossed her head, looking between Resha and Wyll before growling low and slowly prowling toward the boy.

Snap!

Another piece of rope broke free, enough for him to slip through in a sodden heap onto the snow. He barely felt the fall. He was already up and running.

Onya leaped forward, knocking Wyll to the ground. His nephew screamed.

Ceddrych released a roar filled with all the fury and fear

driving him to attack Onya. His jaws clamped around her throat as he forced her off his nephew, and they fell back into the snow.

Her startled yelp was belied by her renewed fury as their eyes met briefly. Her claws raked into his chest, threatening to spill his guts, but he didn't let go, only clamped down harder. She tried to kill Wyll. She was going to murder him, the last of his blood, his *pack*.

They rolled in the struggle for dominance, and Ceddrych struggled against her desperate frenzy to force her beneath him into the muck. He glanced up, and his gaze caught and held his terrified nephew's.

Oh, Saints, Wyll.

If he was going to die from his wounds, Ceddrych wanted his nephew to know him. He wanted him to see the truth. Had Wolfsbane and his spawn ever told the boy? Or did they honestly believe they were hunting cursed beasts as Vynasha once thought?

Ceddrych closed his eyes and pushed down the wolf's need to finish his kill. The shift came easier than it ever had before as pain threatened to overcome his growing remorse. Instead of teeth, his arm was wrapped tightly against Onya's bloody neck.

Wyll yelped in shock, but Ceddrych renewed his hold on the struggling she-wolf. The pain and blood pooling around them made his breath hitch and his vision whiten before he pushed it aside to growled, "Onya, stop this now! He's just a child, like your Asa. He… he's my nephew," he said with a sob. "Do what you want to me, but please don't hurt him!"

Onya froze, her eye finding his once more, and something of the woman inside her flickered within her wolf. Her paws slowly retreated, and he sensed her agreement to cease their fight, even as she whimpered from the pain of the wound he'd inflicted on her.

"Thank you." Ceddrych sighed with relief and relaxed his hold on her neck as gently as he could. "I couldn't let you hurt him but went too far. Forgive me," he said, knowing this was more than Onya would be willing to give.

Onya rose on trembling legs over him with a keen whine then suddenly yelped and fell upon him with a violent jerk. Her eyes rolled back as an almost human cry passed through her open jaws.

"No!" Ceddrych caught her head as Onya's blood began to spill in a hot gush over his torso.

A sickening squelch and rasping breath followed as a girl with amber eyes and horrible scars appeared over Onya's fading form with flat teeth bared and her bloody bone dagger raised overhead.

"Don't!" A small body fell over Ceddrych, obscuring his view, surrounding him with the scent Vynasha had carried across the mountains. Home. Tears stung his eyes as he clutched his nephew as best he could. "Please don't hurt him, Resha!" Wyll begged. "He's my uncle."

Ceddrych waited for Wolfsbane's daughter to pull his nephew away, to finish the kill she clearly longed for.

Silence followed instead.

Silence Ceddrych did not understand, as Wyll continued to speak, and only the rasping breaths of the girl answered.

"I… I don't understand, either. But. But your father said you met my brother and grandfather when they came, didn't you? He said my name, and Wolfsbane said the wolves took Aunty Asha. Maybe they don't really want to hurt her if Uncle Ceddrych has been with them."

Another pause, and then Wyll replied, "Fine. Believe what you want, but he stopped that other wolf from hurting me. And he's hurt. Can't we bring him to camp at least? The others won't find us there."

Ceddrych closed his eyes and released a pained groan. "Blindfold me if you wish, but if you don't plan on carrying me, we should go now, Wyll."

"Oh! Sorry, Uncle." Wyll pulled back, and Ceddrych was met with the same horror he felt the first time he beheld Vynasha's burn scars. Only, Wyll's were far worse. Half of the boy's face appeared almost waxy in texture, and hair struggled to grow on his scalp. His eye on this side of his face was milky, but the opposite shone brilliant blue, the same shade Tamyra's had been.

Ceddrych tightened his grip on his nephew and bit back the sob at the back of his throat. "My boy, we've found you at last... Do you know how long I have searched for you?"

Wyll's mouth didn't open fully on the scarred side, but the opposite tugged at his ruddy cheek. "I could say the same to you, Uncle. Aunty Asha never gave up on you, thank the saints."

A shadow fell over them, and Wyll's smile fell, but the boy's grip on his cloak tightened as he twisted to face Wolfsbane's daughter.

She stood over them a grim, wild specter of the forest, a black wolf pelt over her head. Blood dripped from her knife, and she pressed a gloved hand against her wounded side. The wind tugged at the onyx strands that escaped her pelts. But her amber gaze burned through him right to his core.

Ceddrych trembled beneath that gaze, the hatred she held for him equal that of Vilhelm or Balos... or Onya. Onya, who would never return from the hunt again. Onya, who had accused his sister of witchcraft and then brought her healed son to them in supplication. As though Vynasha was truly the one their bloody prophecies had promised. A queen.

"Please?" Wyll begged once more, drawing that searing gaze away. To Ceddrych's surprise, the girl softened almost immediately, her thick eyebrows pinching together as her full mouth pressed into a thin line. Finally, she nodded, sneering at Onya's cooling body as she pointed her knife at her fresh kill.

Ceddrych swallowed back bile and forced his attention to Wyll as Resha pulled Onya's corpse from him. She died as a wolf. She died fighting like her husband and all the fallen who came before her. She died because he chose his family over the pack. His chest burned as he struggled to sit with Onya's claw marks littering his chest afresh. Balos would never forgive this. And what of Asa?

"Can you stand, Uncle?" Wyll asked as Resha dragged Onya's body over to the trap he had been caught within.

Ceddrych couldn't bear to watch what the monstrous girl did next. He couldn't stop her when he was weakened like this and reliant on them for shelter. He needed to protect Wyll.

"Uncle?"

Ceddrych clenched his eyes shut and pictured Vynasha's face and wasn't sure when he would make it home to her. He'd made a promise to her. But Wyll…

"Resha? Come quick! Uncle doesn't look so well."

"I'm *fine*," he growled and opened his eyes at the boy's flinch. "Forgive me, Wyll. I may need to wrap my chest before we leave."

"Resha? Do we have anything to spare?" Wyll's features pinched, and he stood on too-thin legs for a boy his age. In fact, he should be far taller for a boy of nine. And there was something else, something about his scent Ceddrych had missed before beneath the blood and ash and promise of home. Something was wrong.

Wolfsbane's daughter appeared suddenly on his other side like a shadow, and she thrust wrappings that might have been part of the trap's netting before. "Help me, would you, nephew?" He grunted as he grabbed fistfuls of snow to rub over his torso. Hopefully, the cold would help slow the bleeding and prevent illness.

"She really hurt you," Wyll said as he pulled the binding around Ceddrych's back, his hands trembling. "Why did you let her hurt you, Uncle?"

Every shift of his torso sent a fresh wave of agony through him, saving Ceddrych the need to reply. He shook his head and struggled to stand. Wyll was stronger than he appeared, helping to steady him. "Here, lean on me, Uncle. I can finish."

Ceddrych nodded. "Thank you," he wheezed as his nephew tied the bottom tight near his hip and tucked his dark fur cloak over his chest. It would be covered in blood. Would Onya's blood be on his fur the next time he shifted? Would they all smell her death on him if he dared show his face in the village?

He turned to find Resha had reassembled the trap and hung Onya's wolf form by the neck, despite the girl's injury. Bitterly, Ceddrych wished Onya had done more to harm the wretched girl. But he needed time. He needed to put aside the wolf and remember he had been an uncle once.

Resha grunted as she set the trap's mechanism in place, her chest heaving with effort. Her hatred burned thick with her scent in the air, as rotten as anything Ceddrych had smelled near the lost city.

"You asked why I let her hurt me, Wyll?" He waited for his nephew to lift his head, his single bright blue eye curious and aged far beyond his nine years. "She has a son, a little younger than you. And now that boy has no parents."

Just like you.

Wyll's face fell, and Ceddrych should have felt guilt over this. He should have been smarter instead of walking right into the girl's trap. And he should have never left home a year ago.

"I'm sorry for her boy," Wyll whispered.

Ceddrych blinked back tears and decided he was more affected by his wounds than he thought. But he drew Wyll against him and ignored the ache to press his lips in the boy's messy curls. "I'm sorry too."

Resha grunted again and motioned with her hands to Wyll, sending a dark, cursory look to Ceddrych he read loud and clear. As if he would do anything to risk his nephew, he wanted to scoff.

Wyll nodded and slowly urged them to the west, farther away from the village. "Is Aunty Asha well? Is she safe?"

Ceddrych glanced back over his shoulder to the forest beyond them. "She is well enough for now. We'll be safe once we're all together again."

Wyll turned his face into his chest and sighed. "Do you think we can go home soon?"

"Soon," Ceddrych promised and prayed to anyone listening he would not fail them again.

CHAPTER EIGHTEEN

A Sea of Shadows

DYNASHA DIDN'T DREAM. She floated in a sea of flame and shadow, but she wasn't alone. Something was carrying her in that shifting kaleidoscope of light and dark. In this place, she could see the tether stretching from her to Grendel, two entwined strands of ruby and sapphire light braided tightly and pulled taut. A sphere of soft indigo surrounded her, trapping the connection, keeping her here in this present in-between.

In the dream, she was aware of the weakness in her mortal flesh, a searing pain in her shoulder. And someone outside her body kept her from escaping to Bitterhelm as she had before. The part of her tethered to Grendel ached and yearned. Whether it was his or her longing, she could no longer say. She should be grateful they were keeping her from connecting with him. She *should* be grateful.

Whispers seeped through the sphere of light, voices familiar and strange, speaking in a tongue she felt as though she should understand. She listened harder, and the words took shape.

"—*cannot* remain here," Balos growled. "You have already worn my patience enough, nephews."

"We swore an oath to guard her," one of the twins said, and his brother quickly added, "To Wanderer and to you, Uncle."

"You broke into my shed and stole what was never meant to be wielded with a child's hands."

The rumble of Balos's reply was nearer, surrounding her as surely as the light. Her tether to Grendel shuddered and pulled tighter. What if it snapped?

"But we knew it would be fine," Tarbus argued, and his twin said, "The Oracle would not have let us take them, or we would have asked. And Vynasha needed—"

"Those tools were never yours to command," Balos argued. "Have I not told you time and again why we no longer use them? I had not thought you needed lessons in how to avoid the attentions of the lost city, but it appears I was wrong. Know that only her power alongside your cousins saved your lives, pups. You nearly called ruin upon yourselves and might have done far worse if I had not come."

Silence fell, and the words which followed were muddled, fading back into unintelligible babble waxing lyrical to her ears.

For a time after the voices quieted, Vynasha floated, listening to the steady *thud, thud, thud* which lulled her to peaceful rest. Not sleep. Not truly. Better to float in this sea apart from nightmares and the castle that was her soul's eternal prison.

Voices returned much later, how long she could not say. She listened then *listened* harder until the words became clear.

"I am sorry, Father." A girl's voice, soft and tremulous. "I only wanted to help, to keep her safe as you would have."

Balos's voice loomed over Vynasha, deep as the sea and just as lovely. "You were told to remain with Grandmother. You were *told*, Thea. I cannot keep you safe if you do not remain in the boundaries."

"I know, Father," Erythea whispered. "But I heard what you said to my cousins. If I had not been here, it could have been far worse. And Vynasha cannot leave her skin if I hold her here. Are you not happy?"

An oppressive silence followed, and the beating *thud* surrounding her picked up its pace.

"I am happy you are all safe and alive," Balos finally said. "But you cannot hold Vynasha any longer. You are too untrained, and she will wrench back control the instant she awakens, little rose."

"Yes, Father…" the girl said. "Now that she is safe, will you return to the hunt?"

"No, little rose," Balos replied. "I shall not leave you again unless I have no other choice. I believe I am done hunting shadows and vengeance."

The shadows deepened around Vynasha. Sensations she had been unaware of steadily seeped back to her awareness.

Vynasha was no longer floating but held against something warm and powerful. The world tilted and shifted. A soft *crunch, crunch* met her ears, followed by the cool kiss of snow.

She blinked and saw the underside of a strong jaw, the faint ticking of a pulse at the base of the man's throat. A throat marked by a long pink scar, newly healed from the cut her blade had inflicted. Silver hair gleamed in the dappled sunlight filtering through the trees. His nostrils flared, and the chin tucked until a pair of fierce green eyes met her gaze. His lips parted, briefly, a flash of uncertainty passing over his face as he adjusted his hold on her body. The *thud, thud* of his heart beat loudly against her ear. Her ear pressed to his chest.

Balos frowned at her sharp inhale then grimaced as he lifted his chin and resumed his pace and said, "You exhausted yourself, defeating the demon which threatened our children. Did you know that?"

Her fingers flexed against his shirt, and her shoulder ached, but her throat was too dry to form sound. How could she have known? Wynyth's lessons in magick had concerned flowers, and her mother died before she could teach her more. Vynasha stumbled upon healing animals. It was instinctual, and after the first time she fixed a bird's broken wing, Vynasha hadn't dared test the gift further.

Balos continued as though she had spoken her thoughts aloud. "You were commanded to *rest* and recover, but instead you took it upon yourself to lead children to make a new home using tools far beyond your knowledge. And like a *child*," he snarled, his arms tightening, drawing her closer to his chest, "you grew the house within a single day instead of the *weeks* as intended. Bleeding yourself out to lure a starving beast…"

"I had no choice," she rasped, claws tightening over his chest as he barked a bitter laugh.

"Yes, as if you had not exhausted your magick, draining your very *life force* before. Well, you certainly did an admirable job in spilling your precious blood and finishing the job."

Vynasha shook her head. Weak. She was so weak. Why was she always weak when this new cursed body was physically strong? "I had no choice," she repeated between gritted teeth and closed her eyes lest he see the sudden well of tears.

Stupid.

Balos released a heavy sigh, and his steps slowed. "You saved my daughter's life, and my nephews and kin. For that, I owe you a boon, Vynasha."

She blinked up at him, startled. "A boon?"

Balos's lips tugged up at the corners into a devastating grin. "I have sent the others home and my daughter just ahead to warn her grandmother of our arrival."

"Where are you taking me?" She tore her gaze from him to the forest ahead. Snow drifted from the sky with a gentle kiss to her skin as Balos carried Vynasha between curtains of tree branches and snow.

"As I have heard tell, you visited before." Balos adjusted his grip on her thigh, a sharp reminder she was at his mercy.

As they emerged on the other side, the wind swept over them, and Vynasha cringed at the familiar sight. The shed where Tarbus had sneaked inside to steal tools from their uncle… the great house rising before them as though part of the forest.

"Oh," she said, inwardly cursing herself for sheer stupidity. "This is your home."

Lovely, now you truly sound like an idiot.

"Indeed." Balos chuckled and flashed a sharp, white grin that stole the breath from her lungs.

Vynasha opened her mouth then bit her tongue to keep from saying anything else. A strong scent washed over her, and she blinked, surprised by the height of the house before them. Had it been so grand before? She had barely thought of more besides fear of discovery the last time she was here with the twins. Her eye caught the details she had missed as Balos drew closer.

The style of the wooden structure reminded her of Ceddrych's drawings of their ruined family manor, at the foot of Whistleande Pass. It was built in a rounded shape like many of the other village houses, but no fresh paintings adorned its sides to gift it with color. Instead, vines bearing an indigo flower bobbed in the same breeze that carried their scent to Vynasha's sharpened senses. The flowers reeked of magick, and all she could think of were the roses that now grew within her new home.

"Father! You are late." Erythea came bounding from the glowing golden doorway of the house, a brilliant smile that turned her amethyst eyes into crescents. "Grandmother was forced to keep supper over the hearth."

Balos chuckled, a warm sound Vynasha found far too inviting. "I had to see to the others, and our guest needed greater care than simply being tossed over my shoulder."

Erythea's smile turned shy as she bowed her head to Vynasha. "Welcome to our home. I hope you like your stay. I helped Grandmother prepare our guest room and everything. Oh! And I promise I will share my tarts with you. Do you like berry tart?"

"I… don't know," Vynasha blurted, digging her claws into Balos's shirt as his chest shook with fresh laughter. For the girl who had tried to save her, misguided as she'd been, Vynasha offered a smile. "But that's a very generous offer, thank you."

"Yes, a *very* generous offer," Balos taunted. "Especially when she will undoubtedly use this as a ploy to convince my mother to bake more than necessary."

Erythea gasped. "Of course not! Father, I can help bake them too!"

"Off with you, then, little rose."

Erythea danced back to the doorway. "I shall tell Grandmother you have come." The glow of fire and lamplight swallowed her up, her fair hair gleaming gold as she darted inside.

Vynasha turned to Balos the instant his daughter was out of sight and hissed, "What are you playing at, you old bastard?"

A wry turn of his lips stole the genuine smile he shared with his daughter. A strange man, Balos of Wylderland. Vynasha truly struggled in that moment to recall the way he had taunted Ceddrych into blind rage.

She yelped and caught his broad shoulders as the much larger man set her gingerly to her feet at the wooden stoop just beyond the door. The motion made her shoulder twinge and reminded her of her pitiful state once more. The beast had torn through her flesh like butter, and it was a miracle she had use of her arm. To make matters worse, she was only wearing stockings. "Where are my boots?"

"You will earn your boots as soon as I am confident you will take no more trips to that bloody house you made without my consent."

"I hardly needed *your* consent," she growled and caught his wrist as he gripped her waist.

Balos ducked his head until his silver hair spilled over her cheek. "Our original bargain, as you will recall, means you *will* remain within the boundaries of the village. And yet in less than a fortnight you have forsaken your oaths." His lip curled into a sneer. "A common fault of yours, I have learned. Tell me, do you ever keep your promises, witch? Or are you merely craven?"

The chirp of Erythea's voice accompanied a deeper, huskier tone farther within, but their words fell on deaf ears. Vynasha didn't care who heard her, didn't care how her legs shook with the effort to stand. "I'm *alive* because I'm not afraid to say or do whatever it takes. And if that makes me craven, so be it. Better a craven than dead and of no use to my family."

Balos clenched his teeth, and his nostrils flared as he took another step into her space. Vynasha found her back against the doorframe, and it might have been all that held her up. "Until I can trust you will not go running off attracting strays," he snapped, "you will remain in my home, where I know you will be protected."

"Why?" She found her strange golden eyes reflected in his green irises, the telltale trek of scars in the nearby lamplight. "Why do you care?"

Balos flinched, as though her simple question had struck a physical blow, and his grip softened at her waist. His throat worked, and his lips parted. "I—"

"Balos, what could possibly possess you to stand there with the door open? Trying to invite every beast and fowl to our doorstep?" A slightly hunched-over woman appeared at the door, flour-dusted hands propped on her wide hips. "Well, are you going stay there all night or bring our guest inside before she freezes, pup?"

Balos sighed. "Mayhap I merely wanted to prepare her before meeting *you*, Mother."

CHAPTER NINETEEN

A Wylderfolk Welcome

ANY AMUSEMENT VYNASHA found at hearing the big bad alpha called "pup" faded against the startling gaze of Balos's mother. The old woman's eyes were a startling black that filled her entire iris. A braid of snow-white hair framed her careworn face, yet something of her former strength rose with her chin as she studied them. A slow smile vanished beneath her apple cheeks as she flashed Vynasha a sharp grin. "Welcome to our home, little witch." The old woman backed into their home and pulled the door open further.

Vynasha took a slow step then another and dug her claws into her fists as her knee buckled. A strong arm slipped around her waist and lifted her against a body made of iron. "I have you," Balos murmured.

Vynasha tried not to notice the way the old woman watched

their every move as they walked inside. She gritted her teeth and accepted the alpha's aid and silently vowed she would avoid using magick until she was at her full strength again.

There must be a better way.

"Supper is on the table!" Erythea announced as she bounded into the room, tugging at her thin fingers. The terrified child from the cottage was absent behind the safe walls of her home, something Vynasha understood too well.

"The food does smell delicious," Vynasha offered.

Erythea grinned, her woolen skirts swishing about her ankles as she swayed. "Our rooms are upstairs. Our house is not the tallest in the village, but it is the oldest, right, Grandmother?"

"Yes, Thea, it is," the old woman replied as she returned to a rounded fireplace at the center of the main room, the chimney rising through the ceiling above her head. Dried herbs hung overhead, and a round rug lay beneath cushions surrounding a low table for eating.

"That is Grandmother's loom," Erythea pointed out as she darted from one side of the vast room to the other. "Our village keeps a few dozen mountain sheep for wool, and Grandmother's the best. She is going to teach me one day. I still must use the spindle."

Vynasha stared at the floor loom with fascination. Neither Wynyth or Grandmother Mayve had used a floor loom, and few matrons in Whistleande continued the practice.

"Oh, and look, those antlers are from when the greater elk still roamed our forest. Do you like our table?" Thea continued as Balos guided Vynasha to a seat at the head. "Grandmother's father built it."

"Actually, I've had elk before. It's good, if a little gamey..." Vynasha sank into the seat Balos pulled free for her. She glanced at the simple but beautiful shine of the wood beneath her hands and thought back to the lavish meals Ferox had served.

She blinked, and she was sat in a vast hall at a long, gilded table with crystal goblets and exotic dishes. And a beastly prince smiling at her across the table.

"*I know I'm not the first guest to your halls.*" She had once taunted Ferox.

"*And yet you are the first I am asking to become my wife,*" he had calmly replied.

"Vynasha?" Balos called to her from a distance, and she blinked, startled to find his much larger hand covering hers. Her claws had dug into the precious tabletop, and her shoulder twinged. She flinched and allowed Balos to pull her hand free.

"S-sorry," she muttered, blinking rapidly as she slipped her hand from his hold and into her lap. At the sudden stillness in the room, she ducked her head so her loose curls spilled into her face to safely observe her hosts. Unwelcome or not, she would do well to not insult them. For Ceddrych's sake at the very least.

"The stench of Bitterhelm lingers upon you, child," Erythea's grandmother said.

Vynasha shifted and avoided the old woman's penetrating stare.

"Mother," Balos growled in warning.

"Do not *mother* me, pup. Her scent is polluted. No wonder stray beasts hunt her now."

"Mother, you will not speak of this any longer." Balos's voice did not rise, but his presence seemed to expand, stretching past his skin.

Grandmother cackled as she set a bowl of stew before Vynasha and pressed her hands on the table to lean forward. "You dare to command *me?* I speak only the truth of what I see. If you are unprepared to listen, then you may leave. Return to your futile hunt. Go and command your pithy beasts and return when you are ready."

Erythea dropped her bowl two seats down too soon and gasped, hurrying to mop it up.

Balos aided his daughter with a rumbling growl. "Vynasha escaped the curse unlike every other marriageable daughter in the village. You will treat her as an honored guest and keep your *truths* to yourself."

Vynasha pressed her palm over her wounded shoulder, attempting to wipe the excess surge of power buzzing in the air. The scent of the stew was suddenly too strong, too much. She turned her head and studied the details she hadn't noticed before, the bolts of colored fabric braided together near the fire with rag dolls and the loom. Carvings had been etched into the rafters of animals and plants that scrolled all the way down to the walls. Flowered vines from outside had crept within as well and hugged the old tapestries hanging on the walls. For a moment, the people sewn on the old fabric seemed to point and giggle at her, whispering behind their hands. She blinked, and the walls returned to solid wood again. She grasped the amulet hidden behind her tunic.

"I shouldn't be here," she hissed, startling herself and her hosts. Balos's dark eyebrows drew together, another flicker of feeling in his green gaze. Vynasha shook her head. "You saw what happened before. I'll only draw trouble to your doors. Maybe it would have been better if I hadn't escaped after all…"

"No, please do not say that!" Erythea covered her mouth as they all turned to stare at the girl. She hesitated, lilac eyes shining as she slowly lowered her hands again and said, "You are safer here than anywhere in Wylderland. The runes used to build this home are the strongest anywhere in the valley."

The old woman surprised Vynasha when she sat in the seat opposite her son and took Vynasha's clawed hand. "My granddaughter is right, and my son has good reason to keep you here—blight him for making me say it. As for *you*, little queen… You are naught but skin and bones, and healing, to boot!"

Vynasha flinched at the title Ferox had often tossed carelessly around when she lived in the lost city. "I'm not very hungry."

"Oh, and you are the authority on how to heal a magickly drained body, girl?"

"I…" Vynasha shook her head, the old woman's words striking a bitter chord. "My mother didn't have time to teach me much."

Grandmother hummed low, and the hand covering Vynasha's suddenly grew unnaturally warm. A warmth that slipped into Vynasha's hand and up her arm, to the crux of her wounded flesh. The warmth of hearth fires on the coldest nights, stinging and welcoming all at once for its heat. Grandmother's onyx eyes glowed faintly like blackened coals as she said, "You will rest safely, and rest deeply under my roof, little queen. I swear no beast nor demon will reach you under my roof."

Vynasha swallowed past the lump in her throat and turned her hand to grasp the old woman's in return. She nodded. "Thank you."

"Good!" Grandmother squeezed harder with a strength that belied her age then released her and turned to her own bowl. "Now, no more excuses," she said, pointing her spoon at Vynasha. "Eat!"

Vynasha rolled her shoulder, surprised to find it already moved more easily. She glanced curiously from the old woman to the child and lifted her spoon to her lips. Her eyes fluttered shut as a burst of spice and flavor hit her tongue.

Erythea giggled, and Grandmother shushed her.

Nearly choking on her bite, Vynasha swallowed painfully and covered her mouth. "Sorry," she rasped.

Balos's smile held no hidden malice. "Not hungry, are you?"

Vynasha rolled her eyes and tucked into the meal with gusto. It was a revelation. When was the last time she had enjoyed a meal? Grandmother's black eyes glittered in the lamplight, burning with eldritch intensity.

A niggling feeling pressed at the back of her mind, something she was missing. Vynasha pushed the instinct away in the face of her hunger as she savored the stew. Her spoon scraped rudely against the bottom of the bowl, but she didn't care. She was ready to lick the bowl clean.

"Allow me, little witch." Balos snatched her bowl free from her tight grasp, and Vynasha came back to herself.

Grandmother and Erythea also stood, retreating to the hearth. "Come, child, we must find something that fits our guest better than those filthy rags."

Balos chuckled as he refilled her bowl and carried it back to her. A single eyebrow arched over his amused gaze when she refused the urge to devour the second bowl. "You need not feel ashamed. I doubt you have seen better fare than my mother's cooking since…"

Bitterhelm.

Vynasha gritted her sharp teeth against the delicious smell wafting from the bowl. "None of you are eating seconds."

A casual lift of his shoulder, and he eased back in his seat. "You have spent a great deal of magick in so little time. Greater magick than you should be capable of, I might add. Is it any wonder your body has turned on itself when you refuse to replace the energy you have used up?"

"That's why I've been so weak," she muttered under her breath.

Balos heard her, of course. Likely everyone in the house could. "You have no control. You were cursed with too much too quickly, and it has been slowly killing you." He ground out the last.

Vynasha took a tentative sip of the stew, determined to take it in slowly this time, and glanced up at him through her lashes. "Why are you helping me?"

The alpha shifted then leaned forward, the table groaning under the weight of his muscular forearms. "Who says I am not helping *me?*"

Vynasha snorted. "You're impossible."

Balos's hands curled into fists on the table. "And here I was, thinking you were the impossible one, Beauty."

Vynasha dropped her spoon as she stood, her chair nearly toppling over in her haste. "Never, *ever* call me that!" she growled.

"Do you hear me? I'm so bloody sick of being called something I'm not!"

Balos looked up at her, an impenetrable mask hardening his features and dimming the light in his gaze. He made no move to stand, though he was easily a head taller than her. The silence following her demand charged the air between them. His lips slowly tugged at the corners, a ghost of a smile. "Look at you, dead on your feet from magick and ready to take my head off just like the day you bled me with this…"

Vynasha gasped as he pulled her dagger free from his shirt, flipping the blade by the hilt and pointing the gleaming silver end toward her. "Where did you find that?" She had attempted to harm the beast with her blade and lost it in the chaos after.

Balos's lips thinned as he flipped the dagger again so the hilt was bared to her. "Careful you never lose this again, Beauty."

Vynasha narrowed her gaze at him as she carefully took the hilt in hand, forced to close the distance between them. Balos didn't immediately release the blade.

"You never know when this steel might save your life." He breathed his words like a benediction, the black of his irises expanding as she pushed the dagger toward him instead of ripping it free as she wanted.

"Pray you don't regret giving it back to me, then," she said, troubled when the alpha allowed the razor-sharp end to prick the bared skin of his chest where his shirt parted.

"We both know you do not need steel to end my life," Balos rumbled. "But it is such a pretty thing, is it not?" And she knew not if he meant the dagger or not, the way he stared at her, the way his chest rose and fell with a sudden heave.

Her nostrils flared as the sharp tang of his blood scented the air. It was only a drop, but the hunger she felt before returned tenfold.

Monster, the voice in her head whispered. Vynasha shuddered and licked her lips as she pulled the hilt back with a jerk. This time, he let her free with a wicked smile on his face.

"Father! Are you hurt?" Erythea reappeared with Grandmother hobbling closely behind her.

Vynasha hid the dagger beneath her brother's blood-stained cloak. Saints, she was filthy, wasn't she? How could Balos look at her and call her beautiful when she was like this?

Unless he likes the sight of blood…

"I am well, little rose," Balos assured the girl, his gaze holding Vynasha's a moment too long to be considered polite. But he allowed Erythea to bring a cloth to his chest and carefully dab the bead of blood away.

Vynasha forced her gaze away to find Grandmother appraising her with knowing black eyes. "Well, if you are done ogling my son," the old woman said.

"I wasn't!" Vynasha blurted.

"We have a bath prepared for you," Grandmother continued. "Come quickly, girl, as the heat will fade quickly in this cold."

"And I should make my way to the village," Balos announced as he finally stood.

"At this ungodly hour?" Grandmother barked with a hand on her hip.

"The elders demand an explanation for my return and the beast at our door. Do not worry, Mother. I shall return and find time to sleep. Keep the hearth warm for me."

Vynasha stiffened as his gaze swept over her, and her fist tightened on the hilt of her dagger. She felt stronger for it, enough to ignore the way her blood quickened under the weight of his focus. She had only felt this before in dreams, in nightmares she should be grateful to have escaped for now.

"Bah, take yourself to Galtis and his council of fools, then,"

Grandmother said as she waved her son away then took Vynasha by the elbow. "We shall do our best to find the girl beneath the muck."

"Beauty is more than skin deep," Balos replied.

The dagger's hilt dug painfully into her palm as Vynasha watched the alpha turn his back to them and disappear into a swirl of white.

CHAPTER TWENTY

A Drop of Magick

THE AMULET AROUND her neck pulsed painfully, and she quickly realized bathing would be a problem for two reasons. Her countless scars, and Grendel's talisman. But the old woman ushered her to the large tub set before the hearth and took turns with the girl to fill it with buckets of steaming water. When they attempted to aid her in stripping, Vynasha snarled and lifted her dagger.

"I can undress and bathe myself." She did not like baring herself before anyone, not even before the fire. Her sisters had teased her mercilessly for her modesty.

Grandmother arched an unimpressed silver eyebrow. "Your bedraggled appearance does not inspire my confidence, child. Allow us to help you. Have you not suffered enough?"

"Please?" Erythea echoed, tugging gently on Vynasha's wrist.

"Do *not* throw away or burn my brother's cloak," Vynasha warned. "I will clean it myself."

Grandmother pursed her lips but nodded, and Vynasha put aside her shame long enough to pull the bloody cloak free and set the dagger beside it. To their credit, neither Grandmother nor Erythea said anything as she shed her borrowed layers.

"What a pretty necklace!" Erythea was quick to say as she paused with the heap in her arms.

Grandmother's black gaze sharpened and then flared wide as she snapped, "Where did you get that bauble?"

Vynasha covered the amulet with a palm and glared back at the old woman. "A friend. It stays on."

Grandmother bristled, and the room seemed to grow too hot, then so frigid Vynasha was eager to step into the offered bath. Yet no sooner had Vynasha turned her back on the old woman, one foot into the scalding hot water, when Grandmother declared, "Great Crafter! Not even the curse could do away with those scars."

Vynasha forced herself to slip into the water and pushed the pain the woman's words inflicted to the deep place inside her. The place she stored all the things that hurt her, the place that simmered hot as an inferno, asleep all her life. Until the curse turned her into half a beast and the dark place became increasingly difficult to suppress.

Despite her harsh words, Grandmother and Erythea tended to her kindly, but not nearly so gently as the ethereal maids from Bitterhelm. Grandmother was too brusque in her manner and prone to speaking her mind in the candid way of most elders.

Erythea was a curious blend of bouts of enthusiasm and suddenly quiet timidity. The girl watched her grandmother most carefully, taking her cues from the old woman. This much was considered proper, even in the village near Vynasha's home, the way of most families in Whistleande Valley. But there was something about the girl's darting glances from Grandmother to Vynasha's amulet, the nervous twitch of small and slender fingers which betrayed something else.

"*Watch carefully and listen,*" the voice in her head seemed to say. But Vynasha was numb from a full belly and the glorious heat of the scented bath to ask questions.

Can't I have this one night? Just one night to rest and feel normal again.

Yet the voice in her head only laughed. "*You have never been normal from the moment you were born.*"

"Tilt your head back, please," Erythea whispered.

Vynasha's eyes fluttered shut as the girl poured warm water through her curls, rinsing the potion they had used to cleanse them. "I can't recall the last time I washed my hair. It takes too long to dry. Too dangerous in the winter."

Erythea hummed. "What did you do instead? Your curls are very lovely."

Vynasha glanced back over her shoulder with a huff. "You are as prone to false flattery as your father."

Erythea's pale cheeks blushed a delicate rose and she ducked her head as she carefully wrung out Vynasha's sodden strands. "Forgive me. I am too curious, Grandmother says."

Vynasha glanced over to the stairs where the old woman had disappeared after a battle over why she was quite capable of cleaning her own body, thank you. "I combed it with an oil made from the roses I grew," she finally said, resting her cheek on her forearms as she drew her knees closer to her chest. She didn't want to know what the girl thought of her mutilated form.

Erythea stilled and then continued to wring out her hair, draping the drying curls over the end of the tub. "How do you make oil from roses?"

Vynasha chewed on her lip, careful of her sharp teeth. "My

sister Tamyra showed me. She worked in the village and was curious about many things as well."

Her vision blurred as she closed her eyes and struggled to bring her sister's face to mind. Eyes blue as little Wyll's and hair nearly as black as Vynasha's, only falling straight as a pin down her back. Kept braided around her head like a crown beneath her cap most days. Little Wyll had loved to comb his fingers through it after a long day, when Tamyra was done cooking or serving at Mayve's tavern and it was just the two of them. Vynasha had tried teaching him to braid it, but he had been so young, too young. And then…

"What happened to her?" Erythea's voice wobbled, and her cool hands tightened over Vynasha's hair. The kiss of violet magick spilled into the water, dancing like tiny rivulets.

Vynasha twisted around and caught fresh, luminous, violet tears slipping past the girl's cheeks. Her throat ached as she forced herself to say, "She died… and it was my fault."

Erythea gasped and dropped part of Vynasha's curls into the water. "Oh, no, please forgive me!" The girl moved quickly to lift her hair free from the tepid bath and wrung it out again. "Grandmother tells me I am always getting lost too often. It was only—your pain is so strong. You have been so sad for so long…" More violet tears spilled over her cheeks, blending with the water.

Vynasha shivered and gently tugged her hair free. "It's all right, Erythea. You didn't do anything wrong." Or at least, she didn't think the girl had. Unexplained things happened around Erythea too often, the other children had warned her. Her emotions were tied strongly to her magick, a dangerous thing indeed. Pushing aside her uneasiness, Vynasha snatched up a nearby cloth and stood.

Erythea's face fell as she took in the shimmering bath water. "I have ruined your bath."

"It's fine." Vynasha stepped onto the nearby woven rug, her

back to the hearth and smiled. "You did nothing wrong. And you were right about me—I have been sad."

But not just about Tamyra.

The creaking of stairs was their only warning.

Erythea leapt to her feet and dumped more of the hair potion into the water. Vynasha took another step, as near the flames as she could stand, and pulled her curls over her shoulder to finish wringing them free of water.

Grandmother clucked her tongue as she appeared on the landing, a parcel held in her thin, knotted hands. "Thea, put a kettle of tea on, girl."

"Yes, Grandmother," Thea whispered as she ducked her head and shuffled to the opposite end of the room.

Vynasha grimaced as she released another drop of shimmering violet liquid from her curls.

"Shame on your brother for letting you walk around in those hideous things," Grandmother said as she slowly approached. "About time we remedy this sad state of affairs, yes, little witch?"

Vynasha covered the amulet against her breastbone and turned to meet the old woman's depthless gaze. "I don't need your charity. The clothes I came in were fine."

Grandmother huffed and arched a knowing brow. "Covered in blood so thick the stains would never come out, you mean?"

Vynasha lifted her chin in unspoken defiance. "I already owe your son a debt for my life," she ground out. "I won't be beholden to you as well."

Grandmother bowed her head and squeezed the cloth-covered parcel. "I understand, far better than you know." Fierce black eyes rose to pin Vynasha in place. "I am an old woman. I have seen over seven hundred winters now, I suppose. I lost count years ago, but I like to think I am not so old and bitter that I can't show kindness to those who deserve it."

She pressed the parcel in Vynasha's hands. "My son owed you a debt already for saving his daughter's life, and so you need not fear."

Vynasha nodded, unable to thank her or accept the old woman's reassurances. She didn't know these people, and what she understood of Balos alone made her leery enough.

Erythea's thin arms strained as she set a full kettle on a hook beside the wide hearth, then set it near the flames to boil. She pushed back her silver hair and eyed them curiously.

The old woman nodded with a ghost of a smile tugging the corners of her mouth, as though she heard the girl's unspoken question. To Vynasha, she said, "Do let me know if they need taking in. You are much naught but skin and bones, and my girl was more endowed, but they should suffice."

Grandmother turned to the tub and placed a fingertip at the end. The rune glowed suddenly, a brilliant red. "I shall see to this. Thea, show our guest her room so that she may change without an audience."

"Yes, Grandmother." To Vynasha, the little girl offered a tentative smile. "Come, it is just up the stairs. Your room is next to mine."

CHAPTER TWENTY-ONE

A Silver Tongue

VYNASHA PICKED UP her brother's cloak and the dagger, ignoring the pungent stench of the unwashed fur, and followed Erythea. As they ascended the stairs, the girl continued at a whisper, "I keep Mother's old spell books upstairs. Father insists we keep them in our rooms because of the villagers."

"The villagers?"

"All but the smallest magick is forbidden."

Vynasha glowered at the tapestry hanging on the wall against the stair, at the rich scent of the flowers which snaked across the rafters above. The alpha had been ready to condemn her to burn along with his bloody village. And all the while, his daughter was far more volatile and his mother used runes for seemingly simple yet complex spells. Seemed the rules applied to all save his kin. Vynasha would remember this the next time Balos looked at her with hungry eyes.

Erythea's bedroom was the first door to their right down the narrow hall. There were five bedrooms total, Grandmother's being the largest, she learned. The ashen-haired girl told her that before she was born, all the rooms had been filled with her family. Now it was just her grandmother, her father, and herself left. Vynasha didn't ask her why, and the girl forgot to be sad the moment they entered the door after Erythea's.

An odd concoction of scents met her nose upon entering, recently cleaned dust, a slightly tangy scent of magick, and an underlying scent beneath it all. For the person who had once lived here?

The bed was much larger than anticipated, and a tall chest sat at the foot, carved in patterns of flowers like the ones growing outside.

"This was my aunt's room," Erythea said as she set the parcel upon the chest. "Our village has a tradition of keeping a chest for all the things you want to take into your new home. For when you find your mate."

"Mate?" Vynasha pressed the cloak and dagger more securely to her chest and was grateful a portion of the chimney wall bordered her new room.

Erythea shrugged and wrapped her arms around her chest. "Some of the wylderfolk never find their mate. We do not know why. And some folk find more than one."

"What about the wolves?" Vynasha ran a hand over the soft fur blanket covering the bed.

Large violet eyes darted up to meet hers. "Wolves only mate once. Once and for always, forever."

Gooseflesh rose over the back of Vynasha's neck, and the cold seemed to fill her wholly with the thought. She didn't know why, and she didn't want to. She only wanted to sleep on this soft featherbed and return to the safe place she had floated in before Balos woke her up.

"I… am not supposed to speak of mates, Grandmother says. It is considered rude to ask, but… have you found yours, Vynasha?" Erythea tugged at her fingers and reached for the parcel to fiddle with the faded blue ribbon.

Vynasha turned her head to hide her grimace and the biting words ready at the tip of her tongue. Erythea was a child. She didn't and couldn't know what happened to her at Bitterhelm. Not even Ceddrych knew, and Vynasha suddenly sank onto the bed with a huff as everything that had happened slammed into her with brutal clarity.

"I have no mate," she growled, digging her claws into the fur coverlet.

Only a master, and he will be waiting for me in my dreams.

"Forgive me?" Thea shifted nervously and slowly backed out of the room. "Please, I put my foot in my mouth at every turn, I know. I just—have never had a friend before or met anyone like me! And I… I do not blame you if you hate me too." The girl's voice faded to a whisper.

Vynasha closed her eyes and drew in three slow, deep breaths. Until she remembered the little girl in the room, the magickal child that might have saved her life. She had owed the girl a debt, indeed, and hoped at least on that account they might be considered even.

"I am very tired," Vynasha finally replied.

"Oh." Erythea stifled a pitiful sob as she reached the bedroom door. "Of course, I should see if Grandmother needs help and let you dress."

"Wait." Vynasha glanced up to find the pale silver girl staring back at her with luminous violet eyes, and her heart thawed. "I would like to be your friend, too, Thea."

The girl blinked, and a single tear escaped, following the sudden curve of her cheeks as she smiled. "Truly?"

Vynasha nodded and practiced a smile she did not feel. "Yes. But you're right. I need to dress and then sleep. Maybe you can show me the spell books you mentioned in the morning?"

Erythea bounced on the balls of her feet, suddenly bristling with joy. "I cannot wait! Good morrow, Vynasha!"

"Good morrow."

The door clicked shut, Grandmother's voice barking muffled orders from the floor below.

Vynasha ran a hand over her face with a groan as she reached for the parcel at the end of the bed, set it in her lap, and pulled the ribbon holding it together loose. Too pretty for her but in a different way than the castle's fine silks and linens. This clothing was clearly handwoven but more brightly colored and lovely than anything she'd seen the wylderfolk wear. Even Grandmother and Erythea wore darker shades than the leggings and tunic they gave her, theirs stitched with simpler patterns. She much favored the simple boy's clothing Ceddrych had borrowed for her, but she hesitated to refuse a gift from Balos's family. Had these belonged to his sister as well?

Don't forget Ceddrych is still out there at the pack's mercy.

Resigned, Vynasha pulled on woolen undergarments that hugged warmth to her skin. She ignored the gleam of Grendel's amulet hanging from her neck as she pulled on a cream tunic embroidered with scrolling vines and flowers that hung below her waist. She secured a layered skirt the same shade as the fir trees outside with a blue and yellow beaded belt. Her woolen legging-covered feet poked below the hem, and she ran her hands over the soft fabric. It would keep her warm beneath her brother's fur cloak. This much she could cling to.

She laid the cloth before the fire, along with her brother's cloak. She would find a way to clean it tomorrow. When she woke, she would take advantage of every spell Erythea was willing to show her and be as pleasing as she needed to be until she was ready to stand alone.

The mattress sank beneath her, like sleeping upon a cloud. A true featherbed, she marveled, like those in the castle. And the stuffing had been replaced recently. How long had they been planning for her to stay here?

Vynasha didn't remember falling asleep, and she did not recognize the shape of her dreams. No safe bubble or familiar replica of the castle as she had come to expect. This was a storm of thunder and hail, a torrent of violence and rage, beasts and claws, painted in shades of blood.

She woke to near darkness, choking on terror. The amulet flashed, and she struggled to make out the strange room she found herself in. The bed was too soft, and the clothes itched on her skin, wool rather than supple leather and fur.

Vynasha pushed aside the covers and flung her legs over the side as she took in the ornate chest, the scent of someone long dead, and the fine beadwork on her skirt. "It was just a dream," she whispered and wiped the tears from her cheeks. "You're safe."

But the bed no longer seemed inviting, and she shivered, suddenly eager for warmth and something to wet her throat. No light broke through the tiny, shuttered window on the far wall beside the chimney. The others would be asleep, hopefully unaware of her nightmare. How thin were the walls?

She shivered again as she stood on feet bare but for her new woolen stockings and took slow, measured steps across the room. Her legs were stronger, at least. Perhaps that bath and whatever Grandmother had poured into it aided her more than she thought. Or Erythea's tears.

The latch on the door was soundless, and yet the instant the wood gave way to the home beyond, voices traveled to her ears from below. Was the room spelled somehow? She glanced at the frame and found several runes etched into the wood.

"Tell me you did not plan for this, Mother." Balos's words caught her attention, and Vynasha gripped the doorframe.

"Plan for what, pup?" Grandmother replied, her voice deeper and as gravelly as her son's.

"You *know* what," Balos snarled, paused, then continued at a rasping whisper. "You allowed my brother's boys to take the runed tools, when I left everything locked and warded for this very reason."

Grandmother cackled, uncaring whether she disturbed their guest. If the rooms were spelled, she needn't worry. "Are you accusing me of allowing the children to play with your pithy tools, Balos?"

Something shifted, clattered, and Balos, too, did not bother to contain the fury in his reply. "I am accusing you of meddling in affairs you had no business to, *Oracle*. Now tell me, did you plan for the witch to use those tools and lure one of those bloodletting *beasts* to our doorstep? Did you hope the beast would finish her off? Did you *see* it in one of your damned dreams?"

"Bah! That is absurd. I have no more wish than you to bring any of *them* near my grandchild."

"Yet you allowed Erythea to wander away from the safety of our home yet again, placing her in danger. There are times, woman, that I do not wonder if you hate us, for the cruel manner you profess to love us."

Vynasha's breath caught, and she willed herself to shut the door, to return to the blessed silence. But she had to know. She needed to be prepared if the safety she had been promised was nothing more than an illusion. And oh, how badly she wanted to believe it was not an illusion. The part of her that had crossed the wilderness alone with her nephew was disgusted with the coward she had become.

Grandmother's reply, when it finally came, was dripping with sincerity and a weight Vynasha didn't understand. "What use is love when you can craft the perfect tool?"

"Tool, or weapon?" Balos pressed. "I have told you many times before, my daughter will not step within a league of that thrice-damned castle. What my *sister*..."

"When will you open your eyes and acknowledge the truth of what your sister was? What your daughter is?"

"I know who Erythea is." Balos's voice cracked, and something lurched within Vynasha's chest at the sheer vulnerability behind that sound.

She should not still be listening.

She still pressed her ear to the crack in her door.

"I will not sacrifice my daughter like a pawn for *any* reason. You will honor our bargain as you agreed, before I went hunting and overcome your prejudices. Vynasha is the key to everything, and she is the only one strong enough to survive what is coming for us. If you need a weapon, look better toward the one I have brought under your roof."

Grandmother scoffed. "What use have we for a reckless witch who could not even be rid of the monster sleeping in that blighted castle when she had the perfect opportunity?"

"That *monster* has awakened because of your carelessness," Balos growled. "And now the only thing keeping it from razing our home to the ground is sleeping above our heads. Have a care how you treat her."

The old woman laughed again, bitter and rasping as her words. "You are a fool, Balos. A covetous fool for wanting what can never belong to you."

Vynasha pushed the door shut as quietly and quickly as she could manage. She barely made it to her bed before she gave in to the needle-sharp pricking in her gut. She covered her mouth and retched, but nothing passed her gullet. Tears streamed down her cheeks.

Awakened. Grendel is awake.

The amulet pulsed against her chest, a throbbing, incessant reminder of the fool's bargain she had unwittingly made with its owner. Was it protecting her from him, or was it a beacon for him to find her? If she weren't more terrified of losing the damned thing, Vynasha would rip it off her neck in a heartbeat.

But she was not brave enough. Not when she knew *he* was coming for her. Hadn't he warned her?

"*I would come for you myself,*" he had said. "*And I would raze everything in my path because I would not care.*"

Even if the amulet didn't draw Grendel and his beasts, the blood bond they shared might be enough to spell her doom.

Vynasha slammed her palms against the soft fur coverlet with curse. "Ceddrych, why didn't you come home instead of *him*?"

If there was ever a time she needed her brother, blood or not, it was now. She pressed her clawed hands over her eyes and pushed until stars erupted in the pitch black.

"What am I supposed to do now?" she wondered aloud, taking in the room of a dead girl.

What happened to Erythea's aunt? Had she, too, been drawn to the castle like the other young women in Wylderland?

Vynasha hugged her stomach until the last traces of nausea slipped away and laid atop the coverlet, staring at the cast of lamplight seeping beneath the crack in her door. No sound betrayed who might be outside her door, but shadows soon replaced the light.

First, she needed a way to keep anyone from walking in without her permission. She pushed off the bed and gritted her teeth against the lurch in her belly.

A chair sat against a nearby desk. Vynasha propped the chair beneath the door jamb. This may not keep an alpha like Balos out, but surely his bitch of a mother couldn't break through. And in any case, the sound would alert her. Enough to slip a hand under her pillow for the dagger she placed beneath her head.

This done, Vynasha retreated to the bed and wrapped her arms around her legs, rubbing against the slight twinge she felt in her bad leg. It was better since the curse, ironically enough, almost like new.

But there were moments, especially since using her magick as she had, that the aches returned, echoes of the girl she had been.

Vynasha dug her chin into her knee. "Come home, Ceddrych," she whispered into the night. If the magick in her blood could bring a child back to life, surely it could bring her brother home. "Don't leave me alone," she whispered into the suffocating silence.

CHAPTER TWENTY-TWO

A Tale of Lies

"*COME HOME.*" THE voice haunted him into the waking. "*Don't leave me alone.*"

Ceddrych woke from troubled dreams the same way he had since allowing Onya to die. Cold, weak, and with his hands tied in front and a swift kick of a boot to his back.

The slow but steady *drip, drip* of the caves made the thirst in his throat burn, but he had grown used to ignoring it. He groaned as he turned, blinked, and found a familiar shadowed figure standing before him. No sound escaped her, but Resha's cool disdain practically oozed from the flick of her amber gaze over his broken form.

"Good morning to you, too, you wicked harpy," he growled.

She smiled, pale, flat teeth in a face that might have been

lovely beneath layers of grime. Wolfsbane's daughter cared not for appearances, and only cursory cleanliness, if the state of Wyll and their camp were anything to judge by.

Her hands formed several quick, simple, and clearly rude gestures before she turned back to tend the low fire already burning in the deep pit on the other side of the small cavern, close to the thick fur palettes Resha and Wyll used. Nothing like the single fur they had given Ceddrych to use over the stone slab which made his bed. Wyll had tried to argue in his favor, but there was no arguing with Wolfsbane's cruel daughter.

"Where's my nephew?" Ceddrych rasped.

Resha ignored him as she prepared a pack and other sharp tools. So she was to go hunting this morning. The young woman barely lost a day to escape the cave and her prisoner.

Wolfsbane's daughter kept Ceddrych bound every night, without fail. Even as broken and injured as he had been after the fight. Wolfsbane had taught his daughter no kindness. Or perhaps kindness along with all other feelings had been torn from her by the wolf that marred her throat. She had reason to hate the wolves, but this is why Ceddrych had tried to keep out of Balos's endless war with the hunters.

"How long has Wyll been gone?" Ceddrych tried again, anxious that he couldn't hear the familiar rustlings and often low humming that accompanied his nephew.

Resha stood and hefted her pack over her shoulder. With her free hand she used her white bone dagger to point to the exit.

Ceddrych rolled his eyes. "Obviously he's gone outside. Maybe you would consider letting me out for longer than relieving my bowels?"

Resha bared her teeth again and drew her dagger tip along her throat in clear threat as she walked past him.

"Yes, yes, over my dead body," Ceddrych grumbled.

Resha raised an eyebrow and pointed her dagger at him again, motioning with it in two quick flicks.

Ceddrych gritted his teeth as he climbed to his feet. His vision spotted as cramped muscles and newly healed flesh reminded him of how weak he had become.

Resha huffed and returned to his side, one hand on her dagger, pressed to the perfect place to take out his heart. Her other bony hand snatched at his shirt. It was all he could do to stumble along with her.

The cavern was tall enough for him to stand and wide enough to move easily around within yet not so large as to invite more of the cold in. Heavy stones blocked off the back passage leading to other caverns, and the entrance was so narrow that Ceddrych was forced to press his back along the passage wall.

"Easy, you mad harpy," he hissed as she dragged him at a steady pace so the rock scraped his back and threatened his stomach. He should be used to this after the past several days of routine torture. But he was too weak without the ability to shift into his more powerful form.

No more than thirty winding paces from the cavern did the narrow rocks break to open skies halfway up the mountain. Thick undergrowth and gently swaying fir trees obscured the entrance. Had Resha and Wyll not led him directly to it, Ceddrych might have never found their camp.

Ceddrych's arms and wrists ached, but Resha made no move to untie his hands, merely watched and waited for him to relieve himself ten more paces away from the entrance. She smirked slightly and pointed again with her dagger.

The humiliation made him furious, of course. Each time, he leaned awkwardly to avoid pissing himself and struggled to contain his temper. And every time, she watched with grim satisfaction. He couldn't quite ignore the burn of her heavy gaze now as he finished and tucked himself back in.

The burning need to shift was strongest here, near the forest. His nostrils flared as he caught traces of Wyll's scent, an echo of home.

Resha pressed the sharp edge of her knife to his side, and he gritted his teeth, grunting as she forced him back into the belly of the beast. Hateful woman.

She forced him to sit beside the fire, making the motion Wyll had told him meant *stay*.

Ceddrych hunched his shoulders and hung his arms over his bent knees to hide the way his legs trembled. Even a short walk drained him. He glared at his jailer as she hefted her pack more securely over her shoulder, made the motion again, and turned her back to return to the world beyond.

He tended the fire because what else was he supposed to do?

Kill the bitch keeping us prisoner, for one.

But Ceddrych had never been bloodthirsty, not during the war or as a wolf. And damn him, but he cared too much what his nephew thought to scar the boy any further than he was. Like it or not, the hunter had kept his nephew alive in this wilderness for months. His debt to her was far greater than he was comfortable with.

What you want doesn't matter. Keeping Wyll safe is more important.

"Uncle Ceddrych!" Wyll called, appearing with a fine dusting of snow over his dark curls and a smile on the unmarred half of his face. "How long have you been awake?"

"Not long," Ceddrych lied and affected an easy smile to hide his weakness and his fury with his nephew's savior. "I see your traps were empty this morning," he added, hating that Resha allowed his nephew to wander alone.

"No luck." The boy sighed as he reached the fireside. Wyll moved more at an uneven gait but with surprising strength for one so ill. Over the past days, Ceddrych learned to look past the horror of his nephew's scars. It was easiest like this, with Tamyra's compassion shining from the boy's good blue eye.

"Maybe something's got the game spooked," Ceddrych said, taking in the camp once again, the rugs and rushes beneath fur palettes, the drawings etched over the walls in paints and charcoal.

"Resha found me soon after I checked the last trap. She's going to see if she can hunt bigger game."

Ceddrych arched an eyebrow as he accepted Wyll's water skin and drank deeply. "Amazing how well you understand our lovely host."

Wyll snorted and shrugged. "She says a lot with her eyes, and Aunty Asha always said I was a fast learner." The boy couldn't hide the spark Vynasha always brought to his eye. They had spoken much of her, and Ceddrych had to hold on to the hope they would find their way back to her soon.

"You're smart to cleave to Wolfsbane's daughter as you have. She's protective of you." Hopefully, that wouldn't be a problem when the time came to leave her behind. Ceddrych owed her a debt, and he would repay that debt by letting her live when Balos demanded every hunter's death.

"Resha's taught me so much. Want some porridge? I made it myself earlier this morning," Wyll offered as he checked the pot set to the side of the hearth, lifting it to sit against the coals. His bad side was weaker, but the boy compensated for this with little trouble.

"Thank the saints." Ceddrych pushed up to sit on a short wooden stool beside the hearth and pressed a hand to his tender stomach. The wounds Onya had inflicted no longer needed bandages, but the scarred flesh felt raw. Had they allowed him to change skins even once, there might not have been any scars… evidence of his betrayal. "I don't know if I can stomach another meal cooked by that woman," he added, pushing his more troubling thoughts to the back of his mind.

Resha was an inspired hunter, but she burned most meals she oversaw. And she bared her daggers at him each time he commented on this fact. Wyll was far better, having lived part of his life above Grandmother Mayve's tavern with his mother.

Wyll grinned but glanced nervously toward the tunnel that led to the mouth of the cave. "She should be back before nightfall."

Ceddrych hummed around his spoonful of porridge. Still hot and filling as he had come to expect. "That I don't doubt. She wouldn't risk leaving you alone with the big bad wolf too long."

Wyll laughed at this, a short and faintly rasping sound so like Vynasha that Ceddrych's heart squeezed in his chest. "You're my uncle. And besides, you fought that other wolf to save us. Resha knows you're on our side."

"Our side?" Ceddrych gripped the bowl and was careful to keep his temper in check. His nephew shrugged a shoulder and stirred the pot, and so Ceddrych pressed on more firmly, "Whose side do you believe we're on, Wyllem?"

The boy glanced up at Ceddrych through the fringe of curls spilling over his forehead. "Didn't you run away from the pack? Wolfsbane told me all about what they've done to the other mortal folk in the valley. People like…" Wyll's remaining eyebrow furrowed as he studied Ceddrych.

"Like us?" Ceddrych set his bowl aside, his guts tying into knots. "If you believe for even a moment those hunters consider you part of their little *tribe*, you're wrong."

"But Resha promised she'd help us get Aunty back when the time came," Wyll pleaded. "If you're fighting the pack, too, then we can work together for Aunty Asha's sake."

Ceddrych bit back a growl. "We are *outsiders* in this land, Wyll. It does not matter what any of them say or what magick lies in our blood. We don't belong here. The sooner you understand there is only *one* side, the better."

Wyll cleared his throat and ducked his head, suddenly interested in the pot. "You mean our side."

"Our side," Ceddrych echoed as he grabbed the boy by the shoulder. "We are family, Wyll, the only family any of us has left.

That is the only side we need, and your aunt and I are the only ones you can trust. Because I swear to you, Wyll, if those hunters come within a league of the village, the pack will know. And once they learn what happened to Onya, they won't allow Vynasha to step one foot outside the boundary wards."

Wyll cocked his head slightly. "How will we get to her, then? Resha says a storm is brewing in the north. What if the snows are so bad we can't leave the caves and Asha's trapped?"

Ceddrych eased his grasp and settled back on his stool with a nod. He had thought he smelled snow in the air, more than usual. This could cause problems, but when did anything worth having in his life come easily?

"We will return as soon as we can, but we return alone. Do you understand me, Wyll?"

Wyll turned toward the cave exit and then to Resha's drawings covering the cavern walls. A crude tapestry of her life, from what Ceddrych gathered.

"She won't like this," the boy sighed. "She'll probably try to follow us."

"Will she tell Wolfsbane?" Ceddrych pressed. He was almost certain part of the girl's *hunting trips* she frequently took were to meet and report to her father.

Wyll shook his head. "Not if I ask, she won't. They don't always get along."

Ceddrych's brows rose at this information. Wolfsbane had given shelter to his nephew and Vynasha, and Resha risked her life to help Wyll survive. What reason could they have to quarrel when they seemed so united in their wicked purpose in exterminating his kind?

Wyll rubbed his hands together over the flames, not too near, though. Neither he nor Vynasha were fully at ease around fire. "If we go to the village, won't the pack be mad about the other wolf, Uncle Ceddrych? Won't they smell the hunters on us?"

Ceddrych pushed his hair out of his face and tucked the strands behind his ears. "Oh, they most certainly will. But if I return with you beside me, they will know you are my kin by scent. They will see you are a child and I had no choice but to protect you. And… it might be best if we let them believe Resha killed Onya alone as I remained in the trap."

Wyll frowned, and his shoulders hunched beneath his furs. "You want me to lie."

"I want you and Vynasha to be *safe*," Ceddrych replied. "I know you are afraid of the wolves and that they seem monstrous to you. But never forget I'm a wolf now as much as I'm your uncle. And I will lie and kill whenever and however many times I need to keep our family together."

Wyll rubbed his eyes and nodded. His voice was thick as he reached for the bow and quiver of arrows resting on his pallet. "I understand, Uncle. I just want to go home."

Ceddrych covered his nephew's hand and thought of the changes in Vynasha's appearance, the ever-present itch beneath Ceddrych's skin. "We can never go back to Whistleande. But if you put your trust in me, I swear to you that I will make a new home for us, where we never need to worry about anyone hurting us ever again."

Wyll threw his arms around Ceddrych's neck so suddenly, he wasn't prepared and nearly toppled into the fire. Laughing, Ceddrych righted them and held the boy back. "What's this for?"

Wyll shook his head and only buried his face in Ceddrych's chest a moment longer. "Thank you for finding me, Uncle."

Ceddrych's heart stuttered, and he held his nephew tighter. "You found me, remember? You're strong, Wyll, so much stronger than you know. Soon as I'm healed enough, we'll go home, I promise." He would make it so, whatever way he had to.

They had been lost to each other, three candles adrift in this cursed winter landscape. Wylderland held no churches, no priests.

Its people prayed to their Crafter and God only knew what else. But there was magick in the land, magick in their blood, whether Wyll knew it or not. They would light their own way now.

It hadn't been easy for them to shake the wolf pack in the wake of Onya's slaughter. They had nearly been caught twice before reaching the cliffs and the cave system. The caves littered this mountain, Wyll had told him. Caverns haunted by deadly, forgotten beings of shadow best left alone. Did Wolfsbane or his daughter tell the boy the reason the pack never came this far west? Had he noticed the watchers in the shadows?

Ceddrych had scented the creatures from the moment they first reached the camp after days of running from the pack. He sensed them even now behind the barrier Wolfsbane's daughter had erected, listening to the aimless stories Ceddrych told to Wyll to pass the time. Suffocating silence seemed to thicken when they drew near, and their scent was that of ancient places and the bitter iron tang of blood.

"How did the sisters escape the warlord?" Wyll asked after Ceddrych added a fresh log to the fire. It was ironic that his nephew had asked to hear the same old tale Vynasha favored. Had she told Wyll the pieces she remembered on cold nights when they'd been alone in Whistleande Valley?

"You recall how the eldest sister was cleverest," Ceddrych said, clearing his throat and blinking against the sting of smoke in his eyes. "Well, she was also the most unselfish of the three sisters. And she knew the warlord found her beautiful. Every day, he would summon her before the court, dressing her in clothes meant to show off his new trophy to his generals and to humiliate the former heir to the throne. Every evening, she returned to her sisters and told them pretty lies so they wouldn't know how bad the kingdom had become."

Wyll tilted his head to the side, such a clear reflection of Vynasha that it made Ceddrych smile. "Why would she lie? Wouldn't it be better to tell them the truth? M-mother always said I should tell the truth."

Ceddrych's smile faded. "Your mother was a very wise woman, and you should do all the things she told you if you can. The princess knew that to tell her sisters the truth would only hurt them. Better she carry the burden for them all until she could find a way to reclaim the kingdom for them all."

Sparks drifted from the flames as Wyll poked a long stick into the smoldering fire. "I think… Aunty Asha did that for me, after the fire." One murky and one sky-blue eye rose as Wyll's brow drew together. "Every day, she told me you would come home soon. After a while, I asked her why you and Grandfather hadn't come back yet. She had different reasons every day. And I think a part of me knew she was lying, but I wanted to believe it so bad."

"And maybe Vynasha wanted to believe it too." Ceddrych clapped his nephew gently on the shoulder.

Wyll nodded and wiped his face with his sleeve, sniffing as he stood. "I should go check on Resha. Sun's going down soon."

Ceddrych grimaced as he glanced at the cave entrance. He had been not exactly *concerned* but certainly mindful of the passing hours. It wasn't unusual for Wolfsbane's daughter to disappear for large portions of their days, but there was storm brewing on the horizon, and something about it had Ceddrych on edge.

Wyll slipped his bow and quiver on, along with a water skin filled with recently melted snow. "I won't go past the first trap, I promise." The boy paused. "Uncle Ceddrych?"

Ceddrych reached within himself, just enough to bring the wolf close to the surface, enough to stand on his feet and bring his senses alive. He shook off the urge to shed his human skin and breathed in the familiar blend of fear and kin. "I'm coming with you," he growled and stalked forward until he could see the eerie green glow overtaking his brown eyes.

Wyll swallowed and shifted on the balls of his feet, but he didn't turn away. He had grown used to the changes in Ceddrych as well, it would seem. "She showed me the boundary once. We'll go there first?"

"We'll find her." Ceddrych nodded his head and shuddered as he allowed Wyll to take the lead.

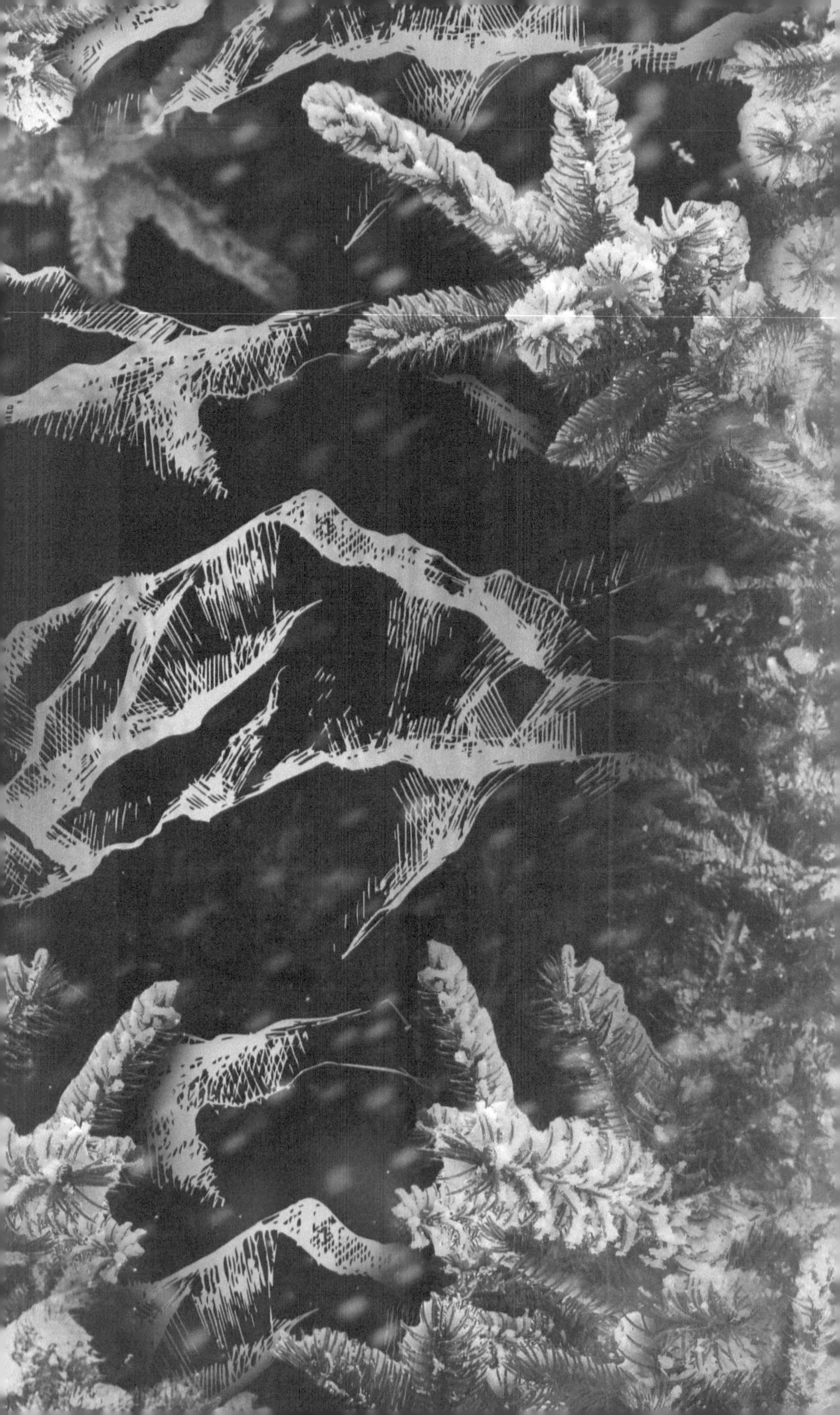

CHAPTER TWENTY-THREE

A Midnight Hunt

THICK CLOUDS COATED the sky in a dim shroud, and the shadows within the trees had deepened to a shadow of nightfall. Ceddrych followed Wyll's careful climb down the narrow path that hugged the mountain, bringing them deeper into the valley between peaks. They had lost the pack in that valley after a full day of walking with little rest.

No howls ushered their return, only the thickening fall of snowflakes and suffocating silence of the forgotten ones. Ceddrych once asked why some wylderfolk came to live such solitary lives apart from their kin. Galtis had explained the truth whispered but rarely spoken of in the village.

"Some that came through the mirror from our people's first home

did not come by choice. They were banished or outcast, and some were too horrible to be allowed to remain on the other side. Soraya gave them all sanctuary against the king's wishes, and they have been dormant since the curse… for the most part."

Stories persisted of wolves venturing too deep in certain parts of the forests or mountains, usually to the west, and never returning. Ceddrych wondered if Resha's people told similar tales. He sniffed the air, catching traces of her scent, but only lingering traces. Whatever power the hunters held kept them nigh invisible to even a wolf's nose. In this skin it was much harder to track her by scent alone.

He kept his nephew in sight, no more than ten paces ahead, and took to meandering around the brush, following tracks in the snow.

No footprints, save one nearer the cave and another farther down into the valley.

Wyll paused, his breath catching as he bent over and picked up a familiar pack. "Uncle…"

Ceddrych reached him in two strides and took the pack from his nephew. He breathed in deep, mouth open to catch all of her scent. "She was afraid," he muttered.

"Look over here," Wyll whispered, pointing with the tip of the arrow he kept loose in one hand, his bow held tight to his other side.

In the growing dark and deepening chill, the tracks were harder to make out, but Wyll would know the shape of that paw anywhere. Cursing inwardly, Ceddrych ducked and sniffed the earth, shuddering as the instinct to shift gripped him again. He squeezed his eyes shut, biting down elongating teeth until blood touched his tongue, then lifted his head to meet Wyll's shining gaze. "She was being hunted."

"Pack?" Wyll barely breathed the word, but in the unnatural silence around them, the sound seemed to echo. The trees creaked and swayed toward them.

Ceddrych stood with a heavy sigh. "We should go back. It's too dangerous to track her in the night. You know she wouldn't want you to risk yourself." Much as he hated to admit it, this much Ceddrych understood about the young hunter.

Wyll stared at the deeply set tracks left in circles around Resha's single footprint and shook his head. "She would come for me no matter what. She saved my life, Uncle Ceddrych. I have to keep going, please?"

He fisted the leather strap of the hunter's pack and followed the trail of heavy prints leading deeper into the valley. "I don't know what we're walking into, Wyll. Please at least let me take you back to the cave, and then I can search for her on my own."

"I know I'm only nine, but I'm not a *child* anymore, Uncle. I know how to survive this land because Resha taught me how. I was sick and dying and she kept me alive until I grew better. I know what's out there, and I know she can't come with us to the village. But I won't leave her behind, not like this!"

The urge to take away the boy's choice was very much on the tip of his tongue. He wasn't so weak that he wouldn't sling Wyll over his shoulder and carry him back to camp. But Wyll looked up at him with Tamyra's features bleeding through his scarred face. And Ceddrych hadn't the heart to break his trust.

He turned his head away and worked his jaw as he took in the swift snowfall and rapidly declining visibility of the forest.

Vynasha's going to kill me.

Ceddrych sighed again as he hefted Resha's pack with a grunt and set it on a nearby low-hanging branch. "Best to leave this behind, then."

"Does that mean…" Wyll took a step toward him.

Ceddrych turned and flexed his hands, until he felt the familiar burn itching beneath his skin. "Wyll, remember what I said about trusting me?"

The boy nodded quickly, and Ceddrych knelt, placing a hand on his shoulder while keeping an eye on the surrounding forest. No creature betrayed itself to his senses and he was through with being blind. "Without sunlight, I can't track her in this form any longer, not with what's hunting her. I can't protect you when I'm like this, but I can as a wolf. Do you understand?"

Wyll trembled beneath his hold, but then lifted a stubborn chin in imitation of his aunt. "I understand. Our side, right?"

Ceddrych smiled. "Our side." He clapped the boy's shoulder. "You should step back and give me a moment. But I should be large enough to carry you on my back in my wolf form, and we can cover more ground more quickly this way."

"On your back?" Wyll reeled and widened his eyes. "Like Dragos?"

Vynasha had mentioned the horse that helped bring them into Wylderland, now at the mercy of Bitterhelm. Ceddrych hadn't had the heart to tell Wyll yet. He smiled. "Yes, just like Dragos, only hang on to the fur around my neck and keep your legs tight."

Wyll released a puff of warm air then nodded quickly. "Okay." He took several steps back, clutching his bow and arrow against his chest and waited.

The change came swiftly, as Ceddrych had known it would. A low, desperate barking growl escaped him as his bones broke and reformed so quickly it was nearly painless. His vision sharpened, the world coming alive with hundreds of new scents. His chest heaved as the ruined flesh Onya had left behind reformed into fully healed scars.

No game lingered nearby, not after the greater predators moved through their territory. Only those already ensconced in the safety of tree trunks or underground burrows. Ceddrych was still man enough that he withheld the urge to howl with the exhilaration this body offered him. He lifted his head and huffed as he found his nephew watching him, slight frame taught with tension and wariness. No fear, not this time.

Ceddrych bobbed his head in what he hoped looked enough like a nod then loped to the boy and sank to the earth. He turned to watch as Wyll blew a heaving breath then slipped his arrow back in its quiver, tightened a strap binding the arrows tightly together, and slung his child's bow over his shoulder.

Wyll hesitated only a moment before reaching for Ceddrych's back, and with a grunt, heaved his leg over the side. True to his word, the boy gripped the fur at Ceddrych's neck, his legs gripping his sides the same as they might a horse. Then his nephew whispered, "Ready."

Ceddrych stood as slowly as he could, moving at a careful stride through the trees. Wyll held onto him with surprising strength for a boy so near to death months before. Had he felt that ever-present itch under his skin too?

The wolf instincts guided him to press his nose to the earth and listen. Notice the scents layered beneath the snow. The stray branch bent at an unnatural angle.

As night fell, Ceddrych's eyes adjusted, and the heat of his predator's body kept Wyll warm on his back.

This way they followed the nigh invisible trail Resha had left behind.

As a wolf, Ceddrych was never blind. The world only shifted to endless shades of gray. Moonlight sifted through the trees, casting light he avoided. The beast stalking Resha could be anywhere, but the unseen watchers had his fur standing on end.

The old ones roamed beyond their caves at night, it would seem, and their silent vigil was filled with whispers warning him to *Listen. Look. See what is hidden.*

Releasing a heated puff of air, Ceddrych paused and lifted his snout to the air. Wyll's grip tightened at his neck in silent question.

A faint crack echoed through the forest.

There.

Wyll tensed against his back as Ceddrych prowled toward the sound. Until a pinprick of golden light blazed through the shadows, and all they could do was follow it.

This is stupid, the voice that sounded too like Vynasha's seethed at the back of his mind.

Did they have a choice? Ceddrych recognized the tracks they followed, the scent growing stronger as they reached a break in the trees, a tiny clearing waiting at the inevitable end.

A choked whimper escaped Wyll, and Ceddrych crouched low to the earth just shy of the tree line.

Resha was tied to a stake pitted beside a small fire. Her bloodied leg was a mess and her wolf cloak missing, revealing ragged black hair and tears cutting streaks over her cheeks from terrified amber eyes. Terror reserved for the large man hunched over the flames.

If he were an honest man, Ceddrych would admit that he had been expecting Vilhelm. Of all Balos's great wolves, Vilhelm was the best tracker, the most patient, and when needed, even more ruthless than Onya. But Ceddrych was a liar when he needed to be and suspected that need, that *skill* he had been forced to learn the hard way, might be the only thing to save them now.

The crackle of the fire seemed even louder in the watchful silence. And the shadows seemed to press more firmly against him, whispering, *See what is hidden.*

Ceddrych frowned, lifted his head, and breathed in deeply, and a lead weight dropped in his chest. The scent he had known… the scent of her blood…

"I know you are there, Wanderer," the deep, gravelly voice called. "Unless you wish for more blood to be spilled this night, you *will* shift skins so that we may speak like men."

Wyll shook his head against Ceddrych's back and barely breathed the word "Don't."

"Oh, and bring the boy," Vilhelm added, as though it were an afterthought and not a fact he'd been immediately aware of.

Ceddrych hung his head but did not look away from Vilhelm's deceptive repose for a second.

Resha's gaze quickly darted around the clearing, seeking them out, before returning to Vilhelm. As if she couldn't bear to keep her gaze from him long.

There was only one choice he could see that didn't end in their deaths. Carefully as he could, Ceddrych crouched and turned until Wyll slid off his back. The boy scrambled toward him, but Ceddrych bared his teeth and slunk back far enough to embrace the change. Pain barely touched him, too lost in the cold at his feet as he rose and wrapped his dark fur coat around his shoulders. His chest was littered with the scars Onya gave him, but if he was careful and clever, Vilhelm never needed to see them.

He glanced over his shoulder to meet his nephew's eye and hoped the boy saw his unspoken warning as he said, "Come."

Careful.

They entered the clearing together, Wyll lurching forward, only for Ceddrych to catch the back of his cowl and keep him in place. The whites of Resha's eyes gleamed brightly as she shook her head at them. Vilhelm had yet to turn around.

"Sit," the other wolf commanded, none of the weight of an alpha's command, just frigid ice.

A fallen log sat on the other side of the fire. Ceddrych urged Wyll to sit and kept his arm a constant weight on the boy's shoulder. With his other hand, he held the cloak over his chest, grateful he'd thought to change skins on the hunt. At least the flesh was no longer as tender, but the echo of old wounds lingered as a constant reminder of what he could never betray.

Vilhelm's long, braided-back hair was pale where Resha's lay a streak of black. But as the other wolf straightened and lifted his sharp chin, the signs were painfully obvious. The arch of his darker eyebrows, the tilt of his mouth both grim and amused. Even the feral light in Vilhelm's eyes was eerily familiar as he began to speak. "You have no doubt heard the rumors of how I lost my wife and son, Wanderer."

Ceddrych tightened his grip as Wyll gasped, and Resha looked on with gaping horror. He shook his head. "Only rumors."

Vilhelm hummed low and turned his too-bright gaze to Resha. "I was not born in the village. I was an *outsider* much like you, Wanderer. But the pack took me in when the witch's curse changed me, as it comes for all of us with the blood." A terrible smile deepened the scar nearly bisecting his cheek. "I did not expect to find my mate among the villagers, but we were happy."

Resha flinched at his sudden, bitter laugh, and she glanced at Ceddrych, all earlier animosity driven away by shock. If his nose was right, if what he scented between them was correct…

"Happiness is not something monsters are allowed, would you not agree, Wanderer?"

Ceddrych grimaced and thought of the blissful time spent with the sister he thought to never see again. Would they be the last peaceful days he knew?

Vilhelm continued as though Ceddrych had answered aloud. "Of course, you understand better than most." Again, that vicious smile turned to Resha. "She was heavy with child when my father learned of our union. I was away on a hunt when the hunters attacked our camp… I was simply hunting game to feed my wife and unborn child, and *he* found her in labor. And he slaughtered them like rabid *dogs*."

A pained wheeze passed through Resha's throat as she dug her fingers into the mush and sludge before the fire. More tears spilled down her cheeks, and Vilhelm leaned eagerly forward, as though scenting them.

His smile widened but didn't reach his lifeless eyes. "Killing one's own kin is considered the highest treason among our kind. Tell me, *sister*, did you know Wolfsbane's choices were what spelled the hunters' doom?"

Ceddrych released the breath he hadn't known he held, and his grip on Wyll shifted as the boy buried his face against Ceddrych's side. So it was true. Vilhelm was born a hunter, and if his instincts were correct, Wolfsbane's daughter hadn't known her brother was still alive. What had Wolfsbane told her?

Resha covered her face with her filthy hands, and Vilhelm surged to his feet with a snarl. "NO! You will look at me and answer me when I speak to you!"

Near silent, wheezing sobs shook Resha's chest as she lowered her hands to her lap and stared at her brother. She shook her head again and held up her hands as though to say, *What would you have me do?*

Vilhelm crouched before her and tilted her chin up to meet him. "Do you even remember, little sister? The night the village burned to the ground and I ripped apart *Father's* world as he ripped mine apart? Did you know the only reason you still live is because Balos allowed me to spare you and Mother?"

Resha's features tightened, and her hands clawed together as the sheer utter despair ripped her apart on the inside before their eyes.

And Vilhelm relished his sister's pain as he lifted the wolf skin that had been on the girl's head. "This trophy you bear belonged to Onya's mate." He cut his gaze to Ceddrych and bared his teeth. "All this time, hunters have been killing and maiming their own kind. And they did not even know it."

Ceddrych had heard of the village the hunters once dwelled in, when their numbers were large enough to make a much greater threat. When hunting parties went out and slaughtered whole families of wylderfolk. Until the night the wolves found their village and only Wolfsbane and his daughter survived.

What happened to the mother?

"You should have fled with what remained of the hunters when you had the chance, sister," Vilhelm growled as he slowly stood, fists clenched and flexing his bare forearms. "Though nothing will save those cowards from my teeth before the end."

"What will you do with her?" Ceddrych spoke the words

before he could stop himself, but he needed to know, for Wyll's sake at least.

"Worry less what I will do to my own blood, Wanderer. What will I do with *you* and the lovely *present* my sister left for me to find?" Vilhelm didn't leave Resha's side but seemed to grow larger as he lifted his chin and favored Ceddrych with that horrible smile promising retribution for their loss. "Have you any idea what Balos will do once this is known?"

Ceddrych braced himself but didn't dare rise to meet Vilhelm's stance. He needed to believe Ceddrych was still weakened if they were to have a chance. "I fell into your *sister's* trap, Vilhelm. There was nothing I could have done to save Onya."

The lies tasted foul upon his tongue, a taste he would suffer again and again. And pretend he didn't still see the betrayal in Onya's eye as Resha plunged a knife in her back.

Vilhelm trembled, his nostrils flared, and spittle escaped as he roared, "She was *pack*!"

Resha cringed and sank nearer to the snow, wide eyes riveted on the wolf that had once been her brother.

"Onya is dead! What's done is *done*," Ceddrych ground back. "Nothing we can do to change that, only bring her home for burial." The urge to shift skins prickled the back of his neck, drew a layer of sweat to freeze against the bitter midnight wind.

Vilhelm narrowed his gaze to the boy at Ceddrych's side. "The pack preserves her body back as we speak. But I was… curious." He tilted his head. "After Wolfsbane's daughter slaughtered our pack sister and cut you from her trap, how did you not overwhelm these two pitiful *mortals* the first chance you had, Wanderer?"

Snow crunched beneath his heavy tread as the wolf approached them, nostrils flaring again. "At first, I thought you allowed yourself to be captured, to finally uncover the hunters' secrets and *end* them from within. Anything to return to your precious *witch*."

Wyll turned his head from Ceddrych's chest and curled into as small and unthreatening a posture as the boy could manage.

Ceddrych sighed, the tension unbearable, and he was so very weary. "I know that you can scent the blood I share with this boy."

Vilhelm bared his slightly sharp teeth. Those who spent too much time as wolves became less and less like their mortal selves, more like the beasts beneath their skins. "The blood does not lie. And if this boy is your kin, you have right to mercy, but this will not completely save you from punishment, Wanderer."

Wyll's hand reached up to cover Ceddrych's at his shoulder. With a quavering voice, he dared speak. "My uncle hasn't done anything wrong! He's just trying to protect me!"

Vilhelm's gaze flickered between their hands to their features, and the madness in his eyes faded. "If you seek any hope of keeping your heads, you will both come with me now. And you will not interfere as I bring my sister to her long overdue *justice* for the many lives she has claimed."

CHAPTER TWENTY-FOUR

A Wolf and a Witch

AFTER HOURS OF attempting to find rest, Vynasha finally gave in to the ache in her parched throat. Surely everyone had retreated to their rooms and it was safe.

Her hands curled as she glanced from the door to the dagger hidden beneath her pillow. She didn't need it.

Her hand moved before she could stop herself, and Vynasha sighed. Her fingers closed over the ruby studded hilt in a comforting grip. She lifted her skirt and used a leather thong to strap the blade to her thigh. She'd think of something better later.

Hours of forcing her body to lie still had at least seemed to restore strength to her limbs.

Or maybe it was the runed bath? Maybe even Thea's tears.

She was grateful sound was muffled within each room, for

the chair beneath the door jamb clattered as she pushed it aside. Yet when she opened the door without a creak, nothing stirred in the hall beyond.

Vynasha held her breath as she stared down the yawning maw of stairs leading below. Her cursed eyes allowed her perfect vision as she carefully descended to the first floor landing. Enough to see figures in the tapestry lining the staircase shifting and turning to follow her progress.

The last step creaked as she rushed to escape the too familiar magick. Eyes had followed her wherever she went in the castle, and she didn't care to know who watched her now. Were there trapped spirits here as well? Or were they simply echoes, enchanted to confuse and intimidate?

Why would he have these tapestries in his home but condemn me?

Vynasha glanced toward the shadowed entrance and boarded windows. No sunlight peeked through the slats. Was it so early yet?

The glowing hearth adjacent to the kitchen was much more inviting. She had barely crossed the threshold when the pale furs before the fire shifted, and a white wolf turned to bore piercing green eyes right through her.

Balos.

The beast stared at Vynasha, and she stared right back. Not so long ago, she would have been afraid. But there was something so familiar about the shape of his maw and the intelligence burning through eyes that shouldn't belong to a wolf. Gooseflesh rose to the surface of her scarred skin, but she pushed her thoughts violently back under the surface.

She crossed the room, and Balos watched her steady progress with a keen eye. He watched as she reached the cupboards and tables lining the wall, filled with herbs and dried meats. Her hands shook as she checked different wooden containers until she found what smelled like tea leaves. "And they called me a bloody witch," she muttered under her breath.

There was a washbasin equipped with a pump nearby, and she was pleasantly surprised when clear water poured through the spout into the basin below. She ran her finger over the contraption until she discovered the etched rune that most likely kept the water from freezing. Or perhaps it kept the water flowing?

Balos's eyes burned into her back as she carried the bucket and tea leaves over to the hearth. He took up the entire span of the fireplace, and much to her surprise, curled his long torso and front paws to make room.

"Thanks," she whispered before filling the iron kettle with water and tea leaves. She was stronger than she had been before what little rest her body found. The kettle was not so heavy as it should have felt, so she set it on the hook and pushed the hook over the low fire with ease.

The logs looked mostly burned out, so she reached for another log and added it atop the flames then picked up the nearby rod to poke at the coals. How long had Balos been sleeping here? Why was he sleeping here and not upstairs in the room she understood to be his across from Erythea?

The wolf's chest rumbled as he slowly set his head over his front paws. As if he could make himself less intimidating by lowering his posture.

Vynasha snorted and glanced at him from the corner of her eye. She shouldn't feel so at ease around someone she had threatened and who had threatened her. But he had come back, not a moment too soon, and had saved her life. There were times she had wondered if he had saved her life that day in the village with her blade at his throat. Her throat ached, and the kettle wasn't steaming yet.

"I never thanked you." The words tumbled past her lips of their own accord. She ducked her head until her curls spilled over her shoulders in a comforting curtain. "For saving my life," she added. She lifted her shoulder. "Or what's left of it."

The wolf said nothing, but she felt his attention focused solely on her, and the even heave of his breathing was soothing in its own way. She jumped as the kettle whistled and was quick to pull it out of the fire, careful to pour a cup into a mug sitting nearby.

For a moment, she stood half-facing the fire and the wolf, a steaming mug in her hands, uncertain. "I should go upstairs," she murmured.

The wolf's ears twitched, and he curled his body again, leaving just enough space for her to sit before the flames.

Vynasha swallowed, tasting the strange floral and pine blend on her tongue. She should go upstairs. But Balos stood up for her against his mother's wishes—he even seemed to care for her. Vynasha needed to know why, what he wanted from her. She would never learn the answers by fighting him at every turn, though Saints knew she yearned to.

She sank to her knees and settled onto the rug, taking a sip of Grandmother's blend, and watched the wolf watching her. "You know, I think I like you better in this skin."

Balos chuffed, faintly, what might have been a wry chuckle had he been a man.

Vynasha bit back a grin. "I don't understand you at all. You live in this house, with an *oracle* as your people say, with a daughter who can't control her magick. And runes covering every surface, tapestries just like…" She shook her head and faced the flames. "You are surrounded by magick. It's in your blood. But you were so ready to throw me on a pyre. No different to the people of my village. Somehow, I expected more from my mother's people, if Wynyth really was from here."

She drank more of her cooling tea and drew her knees to her chest. The wolf rumbled and then, to her surprise, shifted nearer.

Startled, Vynasha nearly dropped her cup as she felt the beast curl his body around hers, almost… sheltering. He couldn't speak, but there was so much emotion burning brightly in his green eyes, that Vynasha's lips parted, and she found herself leaning back against the soft silver fur.

"Is this an apology?" she whispered, smiling faintly as the wolf's chest rumbled again, and the sound echoed beyond them, faint thunder like an oncoming storm. Vynasha glanced up and toward the nearest boarded window and shivered, leaning into the wolf's side. "Tell me when you're a man, and I might believe you," she muttered as she set her empty cup to the floor.

Balos arched his head into her side until she lay fully against him. Her body rose and fell in a soothing lull, like she imagined rocking upon the waves of the sea might feel.

Thunder rumbled again in the distance, drowned by the wolf's breathing and the crackle of flames, and Vynasha's eyelashes fluttered closed.

No dreams of Bitterhelm or otherwise haunted her, and the peace she felt saturated her limbs, so she woke to the steady rise and fall of the ocean at her ear. Comfort like she hadn't felt in at least a moon made waking difficult.

If not for the steady *tap, tapping* dragging her from honey-sweet sleep to sudden wakefulness, she could have slept this way forever.

Only, when she woke, she realized she was cuddling with the same monster that nearly had her burned at the stake, and the tapping was coming from outside Balos's house.

Vynasha rose as carefully and quietly as she could, half expecting Balos to open his eyes at any moment. The wolf slept soundly on. She grimaced as the chill of morning air bit through her layers and rubbed her arms. Gingerly, she stepped over his tail and on the balls of her feet across the cabin to the source of the tapping.

Not the front door and not the window along that same wall but somewhere above them. Vynasha reached the door and glanced back over her shoulder. The wolf's chest heaved at a steady pace.

The door creaked faintly as she cracked it open and scanned the dimly lit yard. Fresh snowfall masked any tracks she may have followed, but the telltale hissing and subsequent *tap, tap* betrayed them.

Vynasha slipped through the door but didn't dare close it completely, letting it rest on its hinges as she darted down the steps and around the side of the house.

The twins stood huddled together, their shocks of red hair bright against the white landscape. They took turns tossing pebbles they'd found Saints knew where at what looked to be Erythea's window. Vynasha shook her head but was surprised to find the smile spreading across her face. She crept behind them until she could hear them whispering.

"You are certain this is the right window?" Dadas asked.

"Of course I am sure! Do you think if it were anyone else we wouldn't know by now?" Tarbus blustered as he reeled his arm back and prepared to toss another pebble.

"Morning, boys." Vynasha bit back a smile as first Dadas then Tarbus whipped around.

"Witch!"

"Vynasha!"

Each ducked their heads in the odd manner the wolves had, tilting so they could meet her gaze.

"You do realize you were throwing rocks at Erythea's window, don't you?" Vynasha rubbed her arms and looked to the heavy clouds gathering above. The rumbling she'd heard before sleep sounded closer but still distant, the sky crackling and heavy with the scent of rain.

"Told you," Dadas hissed while elbowing his brother.

Tarbus jabbed him back and huffed as he straightened and leaned forward. "We had to come see you."

Dadas nodded, hand twitching as though to reach for her. "To make certain you are well and safe."

Vynasha arched an eyebrow. "Why wouldn't I be safe?"

The twins gaped at her, struck before rushing on together. "Because you are staying with *Uncle.*"

"And our cousin who brought that beast upon us."

"That is not even the worst of it," Tarbus hissed.

Dadas shivered. "Oracle…"

Tarbus made a quick motion across his chest like the villagers used to cross themselves when they saw Vynasha in the streets.

She held up a hand. "Would you please slow down and explain to me why Grandmother is called an oracle? And if your village knew she was a witch, why were you so hostile toward me?"

Dadas and Tarbus cast furtive looks at the forest and the shadow of the house they lingered beneath.

"We do not fear magick," Tarbus blurted too loudly, then softly, he added, "We fear the castle and the great hunt beginning again."

Dadas attempted to explain. "And the oracle's not a witch, she's something different. One of the old ones who traveled through the mirror."

Vynasha's gaze turned inevitably north and east, where the darkest clouds gathered over the tallest peaks. The mirror had been covered in runes, like those etched all over Balos's home, in fact.

Ferox had begged her to unlock the mirror, to claim it with him and break the curse. And she had refused like a coward. What might have happened if she had given in that day?

Would Father be alive?

"So she's very old," she whispered. "But she's been good to me so far. What aren't you telling me? Why are you all so afraid of her? If Balos is your uncle, isn't she your grandmother as well?"

The twins shared a weighted look. Tarbus tilted his head toward Vynasha, but Dadas vehemently shook his head. "No, she has not claimed us."

"Shut up, hare-brains," Tarbus groaned then said to Vynasha, "Look, just be careful, okay? Do not insult her and do not trust her."

"But *why?*" Vynasha battled the childish urge to stamp her foot. She was weary of riddles and secrets.

Dadas offered a weak smile and tugged on the cap in his hands. "The oracle knows things that were, are, and will be. Every prophecy she has made came true. So *be careful.*"

Vynasha frowned at the genuine fear in their eyes. She had once shied away from touch and hated it after the fire. But these boys continued to surprise her, or maybe she surprised herself? Whatever the reason, she didn't hesitate to place careful hands over their shoulders. "I'll promise to be careful if you two will look after yourselves and the others until I return."

"Of course!" They said together.

Vynasha smiled. "Very good."

Dadas blushed, and Tarbus straightened to his full height.

"Why are you lurking before my home this early, nephews?" Balos's deep voice cut across the yard.

The twins hunched as their eyes widened and their heads arched to the side, exposing their necks instinctively.

Vynasha dropped her hands to her sides, fisting her skirts as she turned. She kept her chin as high as she could raise it without looking ridiculous. Balos would get no submission from her. He was not *her* alpha. "No doubt you heard every word they just said," she countered.

Balos stood in the shadow of the overhang porch shielding the door and covered with inches of snow. Violet flowers swayed in the wind, and the silver of his hair and the paleness of his skin made him nearly blend into the snow as he stepped barefooted in place of her tracks. "Indeed, I heard my nephews harassing my guest and luring her dangerously outside the boundary line keeping you untraceable to our many *enemies*." Balos glanced pointedly to her feet, only a faint twitch of his mouth and arch of his brow betraying his amusement.

She was in her stockings, she realized with growing dread, wet to her knees now. Vynasha kept her head high and released her skirts to dig her claws into her calloused palms. "They were worried about me."

Balos canted his head and crossed his thick arms over his chest, only a white fur cloak covering his bare skin. "And now that I have returned, my nephews can cease worrying over matters that do not concern them." His green eyes flicked up and pinned the boys at her back.

"S-sorry, Uncle," Tarbus muttered, and Dadas echoed, "We have not forgotten our place."

Vynasha narrowed her eyes at this. What did he mean? She placed her hands on her hips, drawing the alpha's focus back to her. "They are clearly hungry and in need of breakfast, wouldn't you agree?"

Balos leaned back and his lips thinned as he appraised her for a moment, nostrils flaring. The faintest smirk dimpled his cheek, surprising on such a harsh face.

The twins held their breath, and Vynasha held her ground, arching her own brow as she silently challenged him. And for a moment they were before the fire again, the wolf and the witch. And the wolf moved his paws, inviting the witch to lay with him.

Balos chuffed and shook his head. "Very well, nephews. Come in, out of the cold. Tarbus, tell the other children waiting at the tree line to come in as well."

Vynasha stiffened and whirled on the twins. "Others? Don't tell me…" She turned her head and peered at the empty forest.

Tarbus rubbed the back of his neck and cleared his throat. "Yes, Uncle."

"Come along, Beauty, and let us warn my mother about our uninvited guests."

Vynasha ignored his offered hand, snatching Dadas's elbow instead as she returned to the porch. "I thought your mother was an oracle. She'll have foreseen this, won't she?"

Balos's rumbling chuckle chased her inside, where Grandmother was already putting Erythea to task. "Stir the batter, girl! These hungry mouths won't feed themselves, but they *will* clean their own dishes, will you not, Dadas?"

Vynasha bit her lip and released the younger wolf, who favored her with a wry grimace. Only then did she realize she might have asked before dragging the twins inside to face the being they feared.

CHAPTER TWENTY-FIVE

A Bane and a Boon

VYNASHA'S GUILT WAS quickly swept aside by Grandmother's ability to put the children to work. Everyone had a job to do, including the witch responsible for dragging them under the roof of their feared oracle.

Balos began cutting fresh firewood outside, thankfully after donning a fresh shirt and boots. Even wolves wore clothes, or Vynasha wasn't sure how she would concentrate on the task Grandmother gave her.

She had only ever been a passable cook, not inspired the way Tamyra or even little Wyll had been. Her heart ached for her nephew as she set to work cutting meat with the cleaver Grandmother had passed to her. She was to mince the fresh hare as best she could for the pottage already brewing over the hearth.

Katya had seemed relieved when the younger girl caught sight of Vynasha, a fleeting smile flashing across her face before she turned a wary glare at Erythea and Grandmother. She tended the fire and handled the heaviest pots now. Her deep brown eyes found Vynasha's across the room, and her brow rose in clear amusement.

Vynasha couldn't help her grin as she turned to where Asa was warily helping Erythea roll out fresh dough. The younger boy had thrown his arms around Vynasha's waist the moment he darted across the threshold, shouting, *"I missed you so much! Grandfather said I needed to leave you alone, and Tarbus kept telling me to go away, but I made them bring us along."* And into her ear he had whispered, *"Hugyn and Munyn came, too, but were too scared to come inside. They're still watching the house just in case…"*

Some of the pain from missing Wyll eased to have the children around her again. There were others who had helped them build, who had come to thank her in small ways for saving them. But besides the raven twins, it was Dadas and Tarbus, Katya and Asa, and Erythea who had bonded together to bring magick back to the land. Together they had done the impossible, and she would have happily died for them. Part of her felt stronger to have them nearby again, and she wondered if they hadn't made a kind of bond of their own that day in the woods, bringing Ceddrych's dream to life.

"Watch your fingers, girl! Or do you want to slice those pretty claws off?" Grandmother snatched the cleaver from Vynasha. The meat was minced, perhaps too well. "What are you waiting for? Go take that to the pot, or we will be waiting until sundown to eat."

Dadas and Tarbus had been perhaps the most uncomfortable of all, one delegated to plucking feathers off a fowl intended for supper later, the other meant to bring wood from outside to the hearth to keep the flames high. Each time Dadas returned from his uncle's domain outside, his features seemed more drawn and pinched, and his brow furrowed. What was that brute telling his nephew?

Vynasha dumped the meat too quickly, and Katya leaped back with a shout as the boiling pottage sizzled and popped back at them. "Shit! Katya, I'm so sorry." Vynasha laughed and braced a hand on the faintly trembling girl.

Katya had a hand up to steady her as well, she realized, and with a raised eyebrow, she leaned into whisper, "We had thought she might cook *you* in that pot."

Vynasha snorted then covered her mouth as the door opened and Dadas returned with another load of tinder, Balos trailing silently after his nephew. The alpha's gaze searched and fixed on the harried state of her, and his mouth tilted up at the corner in amusement. Naturally.

Katya ducked her head as Dadas passed Vynasha without meeting her eye.

"Do you have that dough ready yet?" Grandmother asked Asa and Erythea.

"Look at what we made!" An overly enthusiastic Asa held up powdered hands, while Erythea seemed to flag and sit on her stool with a feeble smile.

"Hmph, it will do," Grandmother declared. "Boy, you are not busy doing anything, come and help me set this over the pot. Careful, Katya! You will burn it to pieces if you are not paying attention."

Balos's cold hands startled Vynasha as he guided her away from the hearth. "Mayhap you would like to clean up, put on shoes?"

Vynasha bit back a growl as she stepped aside. "Whatever do you mean? I feel quite refreshed." Her feet ached, and the stockings were still wet in odd patches on her skin. She wasn't about to give in and leave the others alone when she had brought them into the oracle's den.

Balos twisted his head quickly, but not before she caught a glimpse of his growing smile, damn the man.

As the meal was set at the long table and the children were forced to take their seats, an unexpected transformation took place. The long table was filled with Balos, his mother, daughter, and Tarbus seated on one side of Vynasha. At the other sat Asa, Katya, and Dadas. The children exchanged tense looks with one another, especially the twins. Yet as spoons scraped bowls, and Asa asked for seconds. "Can I have more, Oracle?"

Grandmother's laugh made Katya jerk in her seat and Tarbus jump. "Well, of course you can, child. Thea, you aid the boy, would you?"

Erythea bowed her head. "Yes, Grandmother," she said and lifted her lilac gaze to Vynasha, a hidden smile tucked at the corner of her mouth.

"Thank you!" Asa jumped to his feet and practically ran around Vynasha's chair to meet the girl they had all been so afraid of the other day. "I never knew a witch's brew could be so de-li-cious!"

Katya snorted, covered her mouth, and then Vynasha burst into a series of giggles. *Giggles.* She smiled, for once not bothering to hide her sharp teeth as Katya shook her head and Grandmother cackled. Dadas and Tarbus stared with wide eyes but had growing smiles on their faces.

Yet it was Balos who caught her gaze and held it longest. Warm affection turned his severe features into something she could only describe as soft. No mocking in the turn of his smirk, no smile to rival hers, but his green eyes seemed to peer through her and hook at something deep within her. Vynasha's laughter faded.

Asa flopped back onto the bench to her left. "I wish mother knew how to cook like this," the small boy said, offering a sheepish grin as Katya lightly chided him. "Well, it is true! Even Aunt Gira says the whole village knows it."

"You come and eat at my table whenever you wish it," Grandmother leaned in and offered with a wink.

"Mother," Balos warned. "You know why this must be the last meal they share at our table."

Grandmother tutted. "Nonsense. The wards are holding perfectly well, the girl is stable enough, and are these little ones not best kept close than left to haunt our wood?"

Erythea shifted in her seat nervously, and Vynasha frowned as a different tension seemed to build and thicken in the room. A familiar scent filled the air until it began to overpower the delicious meal. Erythea used her apron to wipe sweat from her forehead.

Katya turned to whisper something to Dadas that Vynasha couldn't quite make out, something about "…out soon… know we cannot."

Balos sighed and ran his hand over his face. "Your noble efforts are commendable, but now is not the time, as you well know."

Grandmother grumbled under her breath then slapped a palm over the table. "Enough of your blithering, Balos." To the children, she offered a sharp yet kind smile. "You are welcome, whether your alpha likes it or not. This is still my roof, and I declare who is and who is not welcome."

Glittering black eyes fell on Vynasha, and it was the unnerving stare of a collector pinning butterflies to a board.

Thea's voice was small and faint. "Grandmother?" The icy spike of the child's magick rose to a fever pitch.

"Up!" Grandmother rose surprisingly quickly for a woman of her apparent age. "All of you, up and get to cleaning your mess while I take Thea to her room."

"But we just…" Tarbus started.

"I was not finished!" Asa whined.

Balos stood to his feet, his fists clenched as he grunted, "Thea?"

"No, no, you will just be in the way, boy. Escort the children to their homes." Grandmother again surprised them as she lifted Erythea into her arms as though the girl weighed no more than a doll. "I have you, little rose."

Vynasha sat poised on the edge of her seat, heart racing and the amulet beneath her dress burning cold against her scarred skin. She had the oddest sense that she should be following them as the old woman carried the girl past the kitchen area and to another room hidden in the shadows. The door closed with an ominous thud, and the crushing press of the girl's magick faded instantly.

Vynasha drew in a deep breath and noticed the way Dadas and Katya also eased back in their seats. Asa hurried to finish the last of his seconds.

"Knew something like this would happen," Tarbus grumbled, eyeing his uncle nervously.

Balos ran a hand over his unbound silver hair, and his chest heaved. He ducked his head, and though he did not raise his voice, the clear command filled the room. "Do as she said and clean up."

"Yes, Uncle," Dadas was the first to murmur, dragging a reluctant Katya and Asa to carry their bowls back to the kitchen after him.

Vynasha dug her claws into the tabletop and slowly stood. "I should help."

"No," he snapped then turned to face her, his grim features softening as he repeated, "No, you should rest. You are not yet fully healed and already helped enough in preparations."

Vynasha shifted to lean against the table. "Is Erythea okay?"

Balos turned away, his jaw tightening as he looked past the kitchen. "In truth? My daughter has been suffering much of her life."

The whispers faded, and only the faint swish of brush and water over bowls and spoons followed. Vynasha released a breath, hating the faint rasp she could not contain. The smoke from the fire had damaged her voice and it was never as strong after. Wyll was the same…

"I'm sorry," she blurted, wincing inwardly as he took a step toward her, verdant gaze frighteningly dull.

"Yes. I suppose you, too, know what it means to suffer," he said and trailed a gentle finger over the mottled skin marring her neck.

Her pulse leapt in her throat as though to meet his touch. She frowned and swallowed as she batted his hand aside. "No, that wasn't what I meant. I… used to take care of my nephew. His mother is dead, and it was just us, alone, after the… fire. He never recovered the way I did."

Her voice wavered as tears spilled over her cheeks. His hands braced her head, and the rough pads of his thumbs were gentle as he brushed the tears away. Her hands tightened over his fists. "You—don't need to do that," she hissed and pulled, but she might as well have been pulling roots from the earth.

Balos leaned into her, and a slow smile caught at the corners of his eyes and dimpled his cheek. "You must not weep, Vynasha, not anymore."

She choked on a laugh. "I feel stupid, crying when I was trying to…"

Vynasha paused and grimaced. What was she trying to do, comfort her enemy? Wasn't he the enemy still, no matter if he had saved her and had shared a fire with her as a wolf? She should never forget the callous way he offered her up as a sacrifice the first time they met.

The clinking of bowls had ceased, and the room was too silent. She turned as far as his hold allowed and caught a glimpse of the children huddled beside the fire and pretending not to stare at them.

Oh, Saints…

"When your brother brought you to our village, I fully believed you to bring ruin upon us all," he began with another stroke of his thumb over her cheekbone. His smile grew. "But then you banished a demon and saved those children again when no one else could. So I wonder…"

Her breath hitched as he leaned down until his forehead nearly touched hers.

His smile faded as he moved a hand to tuck an errant curl behind her ear and whispered, "I wonder if you will be the making of us, Beauty."

"Don't call me that," she said, but the lack of conviction in her voice betrayed her.

Balos nodded. "Thank you for your tears and your kindness, Beauty. I have not had a peaceful rest for longer than I can remember, until last night."

The absence of his warm touch had the opposite effect on Vynasha, then. She ran her fingertips over the place his left hand had lingered and watched him order the children to follow, then held the door for them to pass through.

None of them would leave without telling her goodbye, of course.

"Remember what we said," Tarbus began.

"Stay vigilant," Dadas added with a quick squeeze of her hand and furtive glance at his uncle.

Katya's embrace lifted her off her feet though the girl was a head shorter. "Do not let the old hag push you around. Same for the wolf and his brat. You are *our* witch."

Vynasha smiled, blinking as she seemed to come to from very far away. "I promise if you promise to watch over Asa for me."

Katya beamed, and then Asa's thin arms wrapped like fierce vines around her waist. His horns dug into her breasts, pressing against her heart.

"Do you really need to stay here, Vynasha? We miss you so much! We want you to come home soon, please?"

Vynasha crouched down to brush back the silver hair from his forehead and pressed a kiss to his brow. "Just a little longer, until we're sure it's safe, okay?"

Asa chewed on his cheek and tilted his head slightly in a fawn-like manner before nodding. He threw his arms around her neck, kissed her cheek, then whispered against her ear, "Light a candle in your window if you need us to help you escape. Someone will be watching."

She blinked, and the boy was already darting through the gap Balos's arm left over the door. Green eyes found hers as he said, "Behave, little witch."

CHAPTER TWENTY-SIX

A Spellbound Child

THE DOOR CLOSED with a soft thud, leaving Vynasha in heavy silence. She turned, wincing at the ache in her bad leg. The table and kitchen area were spotless.

The fire was dwindling. Vynasha crossed the room, eager for any task. In the absence of voices and people, every creak and groan of the wooden house amplified. If she let herself listen long enough, each deep groan sounded like a breath.

"I wonder if you will be the making of us, Beauty," Balos had said. What right did he have? How dare he place such high expectations upon her shoulders?

She stabbed the log with the poker too hard, shedding hot coals and sparks over the massive hearth. Nothing was so grand as the main hall within Castle Bitterhelm, with its hearth standing higher than a grown man. Compared to her former home, this house was almost cozy.

"I'm not *anyone's* savior," she growled.

A faint sound buzzed in her ear, and Vynasha turned her head toward it.

She stared at the shadowed corridor the Oracle had disappeared into. The darkness hissed and seemed to whisper, and gooseflesh rose on her arms.

The buzzing grew louder, rising in pitch until the unmistakable echo of a child's scream pierced her ears.

She fisted the poker and carried it with her into the darkness. Later, she would bemoan her new willingness to rush headlong down a short dark hall into unknown peril.

The scream cut off abruptly as she reached a slim door, raised the glowing poker to illuminate the runes lining the door, and snarled.

"Erythea?" she called as she dared press a hand to the wood. A surge of energy stung her hand, but Vynasha gritted her teeth and pushed back against the pain. She had endured far worse.

"Thea!" she cried. "Hold on, I'm coming!"

The energy binding the door would not relent. Vynasha snapped, "Let me in, you old bitch, before I break this door down!" She raised the poker, prepared to hit the locked handle when the door clicked then creaked slowly open.

Shifting on her feet, Vynasha held the poker before her like a sword and entered the room.

She expected a larder or another bedroom, certainly not clusters of candles dripping wax on the floor or candlesticks set beside stacks of books and scrolls. Runes coated every conceivable surface of the four walls. Power pulsed and swirled in thick ebbs and waves from the chalk circle at the center of the floor, from the child floating lifelessly midair.

"Come back to us, child." Grandmother's voice cracked, and she paused in her chanting to speak the slightly archaic common Vynasha could understand. "Do not forsake us now when we most need you!"

Vynasha lost her grip on the poker. The old iron dropped with a resounding clang. This was far beyond any magick Wynyth had shown her, far nearer to the dark power that held the castle in its cursed grasp. So why wasn't she afraid? Why was her blood racing with excitement instead?

The Oracle's gnarled hand shook as she reached for Vynasha. "Do not just stand there, girl, help me!"

It was instinct for Vynasha to close the gap and take Grandmother's hand. But this was nothing like the moment she linked with the children to raise Ceddrych's new home.

The Oracle's hand gripped hers so tightly her bones ached. And then the heavy scent of cloves and moss burned her nose as she inhaled. As she exhaled, the pulse of power in the room doubled, flowing between Vynasha to the Oracle and pouring into the circle binding her cursed grandchild.

For Vynasha could see it clearly now, the mark upon Erythea to bind her magick, the way those bindings were frayed at the edges and threatening to unravel.

Erythea's back bowed too far, and her limbs splayed in midair as she screamed.

"I need more, girl!" Grandmother crowed.

Vynasha bit her tongue with sharpened teeth. Her blood was bittersweet and tasted of *him*. The amulet burned suddenly hot against her skin, and the magick was too much too soon. Vynasha had barely recovered and would see the stupidity of her actions later. But she did not hesitate, not when the girl was clearly in pain. Not when Vynasha was able to do *something* rather than let her magick consume her.

Grandmother cackled as she pulled Vynasha's power through their physical connection. "Oh, my dear, is this what you have been hiding?" Golden candlelight reflected off her black eyes.

Vynasha winced as the aches she had overcome returned and her body began to weaken. "I can't!" She tried to tug free and for a moment wondered if the old witch would let her go.

The Oracle smiled and released Vynasha's hand. Erythea fell to the floor with a heavy *thud,* and several candles snuffed out.

Vynasha sank to her knees and caught her breath. "What in the name of all the saints was that?"

Grandmother did not seem at all affected, though the old woman stood straighter than she had before. "I shall give you a lesson as soon as you help me make my grandchild comfortable."

Vynasha climbed onto unsteady legs and hobbled to a nearby pile of furs and woven blankets. Together, they broke the circle to carefully ease the unconscious girl onto a makeshift pallet. Grandmother brought a small bowl of fragrant water and cleaned sweat and tears from Erythea's face.

"Very good, my little love. You have done well." Grandmother met Vynasha's gaze as she finished tucking a fur over her chest. "I suspect you already know what has happened here this day."

"No!" Vynasha grimaced and lowered her voice as she ran a soothing hand over Erythea's chest. "I have never seen magick like this, so how could I know?"

"How could a daughter of Wynyth not know?"

Vynasha's hand stilled. "Did you know my mother?"

Grandmother sighed and settled back on her haunches, wringing out her cloth and returning to the girl's neck. "Yes."

Vynasha closed her eyes and fought the urge to unleash the questions ready to burst from her tongue. An old ache, never forgotten and numbed with time, returned. She was a small child again, Ceddrych's arm around her shoulders, and her mother withering away before their eyes.

Tears spilled over her cheeks as she opened her eyes and found the Oracle watching her with an unreadable gaze. She could ask her questions, but could she trust the old woman to speak truthfully? So many secrets, such knowledge in those black eyes.

Vynasha scrubbed her cheek and ignored the stabbing pain in her heart as she put her mother back in the box those memories belonged. "What was the lesson you promised to give me?"

Grandmother flashed a brilliant smile, and somehow Vynasha knew she had just passed an unspoken test. "All magick comes at a cost. Erythea was born with too much, and due to the curse, her body was never allowed to mature into a being capable of wielding it. Yet still she persists. Still, my grandchild studies her mother's grimoires and practices magick that harms her and inevitably others."

Vynasha watched the gentle way gnarled fingers carded through silver locks. "You bound her magick to protect her," she said.

Grandmother hummed happily. "And can you guess why the bindings frayed yet again?"

Vynasha ducked her head and slowly lifted a hand to her chest, where Grendel's medallion continued to burn with lingering icy heat. "She pulled my spirit back into my body," she whispered with growing dread. "Has she been keeping me *here* every time I have slept since then?"

The Oracle beamed and inclined her head. "Very good, dearie. She should not have interfered and paid the price. I cannot allow her to continue. Do you understand?"

Grendel.

Vynasha nodded. "I never asked for her aid. If I had known the cost, I never would have." She should have known Thea never stopped shielding her dreams. She shook her head and watched the rapid flicker of the girl's eyes shifting behind closed lids. "Why would she do this for me?"

"Why indeed? Mayhap you will ask and she will answer. Only promise me now you will say whatever you must to make her stop." The Oracle rose slowly yet gracefully to her feet.

"And if I do?" Vynasha lifted her gaze to the dangerous woman standing over her.

Grandmother flashed another one of her sharp predator's smiles, all teeth and pleasure for being drawn out. "Then I will teach you how to shield your own dreams, and much more."

CHAPTER TWENTY-SEVEN

A Price Paid

THE CANDLES SHOULD have withered down to stubs by the time Erythea woke from restless sleep. Grandmother had left hours before to tend to supper, leaving Vynasha to keep vigil by the girl's side. But not without warning, "*I shall know if she wakens, or if any foreign magicks interfere with her bonds. Do not rouse my grandchild until she is ready, little witch.*"

A short stack of books made from bound vellum and animal hides kept Vynasha company. She could barely make out the words from one grimoire written in faded brown ink. Pictures of herbs and other ingredients for potions were interspersed with runic diagrams. Every page she touched was filled with the faintest traces of emotions, like ghosts of a memory of the ones who wrote and wielded the old magicks. Boundless pain, desperation, and sorrow poured from the tome until Vynasha pushed it aside in favor of one written in the common tongue.

Would you have understood these words and how to read them, Mother? Would you have taught me if I had been a little older?

She could only pray she hadn't made a deal with the devil when she ignored the Oracle's bribe. For that was what it must have been. The old woman might have told her everything she ever wanted to know about her mother. Perhaps she never would know, or perhaps she might if Vynasha earned her knowledge.

Nothing is freely given without a price.

Erythea gasped then curled closer to Vynasha seated at her side. "W-where is Grandmother?"

Vynasha took the girl's cold hand in hers. "She left to cook supper. Would you like me to fetch her?"

Violet eyes blinked rapidly as the girl took in her surroundings, then slumped against her furs with a sigh. She glanced at Vynasha and the corner of her mouth quirked so similarly to her father. "Now I am the one in need of aid. Did Grandmother tell you?"

"Yes." Vynasha squeezed her hand briefly and fought back the surge of anger at all the girl had done. By keeping her from Grendel, had Erythea inadvertently summoned the beast? Would Vynasha be a prisoner behind the Oracle's wards if the girl had never interfered?

Erythea sighed and her face fell. "Grandmother warned me to leave you be. I did not expect the spell to be so difficult to hold on to."

"Why did you?" Vynasha studied the silvery features of Balos's girl, the scent of frost permeating her skin, and wondered how long she'd been trapped in the body of a child. What happened to a person bound to live an immortal childhood, with a child's whims and feelings?

Erythea's other hands twitched and tugged at the weave of her blanket. "My aunt left for the forgotten city and never returned... She was my most favorite person in all the world, the only one who ever listened to me, or had time for me. And when you came to us it was like… like she had come home again."

Vynasha's claw ran over the girl's palm, and the child was unafraid. Would Wyll fear her now? "You've all lost someone to the curse, I know. I'm sorry they took your aunt. I'm sorry you lost your mother. But your grandmother was right. You should have released the spell after I woke. Big magick attracts them, and you couldn't understand…" She laughed and gritted her teeth. "None of you know what I went through to escape the castle. I—had help getting away. One of the ones who helped is still trapped and sacrificed much so I can live freely with my brother."

Erythea swallowed as Vynasha tightened her grip and leaned toward the girl. "Now they know something powerful ripped me away. Now they know you're here, and you'll never be safe. That's why I need to find the spell you used myself."

Erythea pulled her hand free slowly, and Vynasha flinched as she realized she'd been holding the girl too tightly. "This one," Thea whispered as she pulled free the more recent tome written in archaic common. "This was my mother's grimoire."

"Show me the spell," Vynasha said as she set the book on the girl's lap.

Pale fingers turned quickly to a page marked by a faded ribbon. "Here," Erythea said as she pointed to a simple diagram written in runes in the shape of an arrow. "Spells can be written with anything and on any surface so long as you mean it. But the best are written in blood, or with ink on the skin." She turned her hand and revealed markings Vynasha hadn't noticed before now. The same pattern smudged and drawn over and over.

Vynasha took Thea's hand and studied the markings then the diagram. "You know what the runes mean?"

Erythea's smile was weary. "I am still learning. Grandmother has been teaching me, but it is difficult. Their meaning is taken from a language no one speaks this side of the mirror."

Vynasha froze, and she turned from the book to the door the Oracle had disappeared through. "That's where she's from, isn't it? She's one of the ones who came through long ago."

"Yes," Erythea whispered, so low she could barely hear her reply over the flickering candles.

Vynasha took the book from the girl and sank back into her seat. Odym had told her the tale when she lived in the castle, of Soraya's people, the ancient kind that were survived today by the wylderfolk in this village. And Erythea was one of their descendants. But had the wolves come from the mirror world as well? Or were they already here? And if so, did that mean Old Ced and their family carried the blood as well?

"I don't have time to learn another language," she murmured. "If I copy these runes onto my skin like you did, will it work?"

Erythea chewed on her lip. "I used a different rune on myself since I meant to sever your bond and not my own. But if you use what my mother wrote, yes, it will work. Mayhap we should wait for Grandmother before you try it?"

Vynasha closed the book and slipped it to the bottom of the stack the Oracle had left her. "No. I will do this alone. For now, let's get those runes off your skin before the ink sets in permanently."

"Father would be displeased if I marked myself like the old ones." Erythea giggled as Vynasha pulled over the scented bowl of water and cloth and began to clean her inked skin.

"The old ones?" Vynasha asked, but already her mind wandered to the possibilities. She had seen tattoos on men in her cousin Stye's tavern before. She knew they needed to bleed and add ink to make the design stay upon the skin. Could she do the same and keep her spirit grounded to her body?

"Some of the elders are covered with runes, same as they use to protect the village or to make small magicks. But I overheard Grandmother say once that the forgotten ones even placed them on their faces, and some became mad from binding themselves or trying to steal dangerous power. It is forbidden to do this in our village now."

The ink stained Thea's hand still, and the water turned blacker, but Vynasha persisted. "Promise me you won't try any more spells unless you tell me first, yes?"

The girl blinked rapidly, violet eyes shining in the candlelight with surprise and a depth of feeling she wouldn't expect from a child so young. "I promise."

Grandmother warmed the stew they ate the night before, adding fresh herbs to the pot and ordering Vynasha to settle Erythea in a seat before the hearth. "We shall sup here this night," she announced, not bothering to look up when Vynasha aided the weakened child into the main hall. "Put my grandchild there, then come over here, girl. I have work for you."

"Wait, before you help Grandmother, could you bring me my fur, please?" Erythea's weak smile and fierce gaze found Vynasha while Grandmother nattered away about village matters.

Vynasha frowned but nodded. "One moment." She turned her back on the cursed child and the Oracle, and wondered if the girl had the gift of foresight as well.

The room was far more forbidding with only the dancing candlelight casting curious shadows on the rune-coated walls. The shadows trembled, shimmering together and then apart, taking shapes of hooded figures and beings with great wings.

Vynasha shuddered as she knelt beside the palette, then hesitated. The pressure of unseen eyes raised the hair at the back of her neck, but she would not have an opportunity like this again. "Forgive me," she whispered as she found the page in Erythea's mother's grimoire and used her dagger to rip the diagram free from its binding. She sheathed the dagger quickly then carefully folded the spell and tucked it into the pocket of her skirts. She snatched the fur Erythea requested as an afterthought.

Did she plan this? Did she know? But she's only a child, no more than eight at the most.

And she had been trapped in the body of a child for longer than Vynasha had been alive.

There was no room for guilt or fear, not now.

Never again, Vynasha silently vowed as she was quick to obey Grandmother's instructions. She would keep her head down and obey the witch, hoarding every scrap of knowledge she gleaned like the dragons of old.

Perhaps she shouldn't have been surprised when Grandmother's tales shifted from the village to the curse. After they had settled before the hearth, the world beyond the windows dimmed with the oncoming twilight. Vynasha sat on the rug between Erythea and Grandmother's chairs, keeping them between herself and the smoking hearth.

"I have seen what magick can do to ordinary folk," Grandmother murmured between sips of honey ale. "I have seen beasts that walk on two legs and speak like men…"

Ferox, Vynasha thought with a shudder and prickle of guilt.

"I have seen spirits that live and breathe but are fading to dust. Such a shame that the land nearest Bitterhelm thrives but the castle itself is dead." The old woman shook her head and gathered her shawl over her shoulders.

Thea sighed and leaned her head against the cushioned headrest in her chair. "I do not know why, but I always feel sad when I think of the lost city. Everyone else in the village is afraid of it." Her violet eyes flickered to Vynasha.

Grandmother hummed. "The fools fear justly, child. There is naught but death awaiting our kind in that cursed place… not anymore, at least. And yet they will never confess how they all long for it just as strongly."

The wood of Vynasha's cup groaned beneath her harsh grasp. "Because the curse makes us long for it."

"No," the Oracle snapped, black eyes illuminated by the inferno beside her. "Because each of us longs for *home*."

Vynasha arched a brow, the question at the tip of her tongue.

"The mirror," Erythea murmured.

Vynasha hid behind her loose curls, and the guilt she had felt for abandoning Odym and Grendel, for denying Ferox, turned to horror.

"*Our fate would always have led us to this. Forgive me, Beauty.*" And waves of unending violet light had broken over her as Ferox had forced her hand to the arch, consuming her until her heart cleaved in two.

Her inability to bond with the mirror had forged a path leading to her father's death, and so long as she left the mirror untouched, the curse would keep drawing the wylderfolk to their deaths. But surely, she wasn't the only one capable of this. Hadn't Grandmother insisted Erythea was the key, after all?

"Vynasha?" Erythea's soft voice pulled her back to smoke and ale, and the potent scent of too much magick in too small a space. "Are you well?"

Vynasha glanced between Grandmother's keen gaze and Erythea's furrowed brow. "I... am a little tired from earlier."

Grandmother smiled. "You are growing stronger, though you may not feel so. Power comes with a price, but it is also like skin calloused from hard labor. The more you grow accustomed to wielding, the greater you will become capable in time."

Erythea's worry didn't ease. "I do not think she slept well the night before, and I am also weary, Grandmother."

Vynasha pressed her lips together and forced her gaze away from Balos's strange child. Again she couldn't deny the feeling Erythea was trying to help. What puzzled her even more was her own worry over the girl's well-being. She had cared only for her surviving family since escaping the castle.

But that is not entirely true, is it? The voice that sounded like Ceddrych prodded at the corner of her thoughts.

Vynasha nodded her head and rose to her feet with a groan. "I will clean up if you need to take Erythea upstairs."

Grandmother hummed. "How very thoughtful of you, dearie."

"May the gods watch over your dreams," Erythea urged as Grandmother helped her rise.

The Oracle cackled. "The gods no longer live here, not in this cursed land."

Vynasha might have believed it. She had never found much faith in the god Whistleande, but she had admired and even adored tales of the saints. She liked to think they had saved her the night she rescued Wyll from the pyre that killed her sisters.

Only she had come to Wylderland and learned the voice in her head was no saint, but a beast. No saint had protected her as she tried to escape, just the cursed father that gave his life so she might live. And for what?

I'll protect Ceddrych and Wyll, no matter what it takes.

Vynasha pressed a hand over her skirt pocket and set to work, making the kitchen as spotless as she had once done for her vain and spoiled sisters.

Chapter Twenty-Eight

A Fever Dream

BALOS STILL HAD not returned home in the time it took Vynasha to finish scrubbing the pot and table. She pretended she didn't drag out the work, waiting for him. The exercise felt good even though her back ached as she lit a candle with a weary sigh. She glanced at the door one last time as she climbed the steps, to avoid looking too closely at the whispering tapestry. And she was most certainly *not* listening for the alpha wolf as she hesitated just outside her bedroom door.

Clenching her jaw, Vynasha turned her mind to the runes and what she needed to do.

The silence that greeted her was welcome after the endless nights and days spent in constant company with people she could not trust. Her heart ached for Ceddrych's attempts to make her smile and, most of all, for little Wyll and their long silences. They had gone hours without speaking, the quiet broken only by softly spoken words or her attempts to sing the old songs. Only after supper in the evenings would she allow Wyll to coax stories Ceddrych and Wynyth had once shared with her or read by dwindling candlelight.

Vynasha sat on the edge of her unmade bed and carefully lit the short lamp on her bedside, then blew the candle out and set it aside. She pulled the stolen parchment free and unfolded it on her bedside then slipped the ruby dagger from its sheath.

Her breath came in uneven gasps as she studied the pattern. Blood would be best. Blood was the way Wynyth had taught her. Vynasha's blood had been tainted by the Gatekeeper of Bitterhelm, and tonight she would seal her own freedom. She would not fear the beasts or his veiled threats any longer, or her spirit fleeing her body each night in her sleep.

I'm nobody's savior. That's Erythea's fate, not mine. It was never meant to be mine.

Still she hesitated, the blade pressed against her forearm. She tightened her grip on the hilt until the rubies pinched her skin, then bared her teeth. "Just do it, you coward."

Vynasha pressed the blade deeper, until the first drop of blood welled at the tip of her blade, gleaming the same violet shade as Grendel's eyes.

She growled as she pulled her dagger back and pushed her curls from her damp forehead. Vynasha squeezed her eyes shut. She wasn't afraid of the blood or the spell. But she didn't want Grendel to send any more beasts. One was enough to nearly kill *her*. Would one of the children be next?

Vynasha cursed as she set the blade and parchment on the table.

The Oracle's home was riddled with spells of protection, but Erythea no longer guarded her spirit or her dreams.

Only one way to know for certain.

Vynasha settled her head onto the pillow, closed her eyes, and thought of *him*.

It was far too easy in the end. A sharp tug at her navel, and she fell.

Could she breathe, Vynasha would have screamed, as she seemed to fall forever: through snow and ice and a howling storm of rose petals.

She fell until she floated, petals of black and crimson caressing her skin until her bare feet met solid ground.

Her bedroom in castle Bitterhelm was destroyed. Broken furniture littered the room, as though a beast had rent every object to shattered pieces. In this static dream world, the walls were blotted out by great slithering shadows, tapestries rising like tattered flags upon an invisible wind in the air.

Vynasha covered her mouth as she took first one step and then another to the bed where she had been ripped from Grendel's arms. Nothing but tattered fabric remained, clear claw marks rent so deep as to reach the stone beneath.

She turned rapidly as her vision blurred and gritted her teeth as she turned her back on the room and fled. "Please let it still be there," she prayed as she stepped out of her room and instantly into the glass gardens.

Vynasha stumbled into a sea of rose petals, thick scented layers like snow, and like snow, the petals rained down over broken glass and uprooted bushes. Her breath hitched as she ran, calling, "Hvalla?" The girl had given herself over to the garden the last time Vynasha saw her, the last time she had called her *queen*.

Had Grendel ripped her up with the roots in his fury as well?

Vynasha sobbed as she reached a massive hole in the wall the glass garden shared with the castle. The inky shadows swirled and slithered like a living creature, stealing her breath as she warily approached. "Grendel?"

A jagged scattering of violet lightning illuminated the center of the hole, and Vynasha's hand shook as she placed her hand into the void. "Please," she begged as she closed her eyes and stepped through.

The shadows coated her like a second skin, caresses too intimate to belong to the malevolent manifestation she had expected. This was not Soraya's doing.

Vynasha gasped as she opened her eyes and found herself in what could only be the castle's throne room. She had never found this place before, but Bitterhelm did not easily share its secrets. She had certainly never walked through a hall so vast.

Great pillars carved in runes and effigies of mythical creatures rose up around her like an ancient stone forest. The floor was made of glass, reflecting the open sky slowly raining rose petals from an ocean of stars.

Vynasha should not have come through the entrance to the throne room but found herself facing the end of the long hall, with a set of onyx stairs and an illuminated throne made of gleaming obsidian. She barely recognized the hunched figure seated on the throne.

A deep, rasping voice reached her ears. "You are a ghost."

"Grendel?" Vynasha's steps faltered, then she quickened her pace until she reached the base of the stairs before the throne. Snarls erupted around her, and she froze as glowing eyes within the diaphanous shapes of beasts moved in the shadows. "I swear on the saints I'm not a ghost."

The figure on the throne slowly straightened, barking out a harsh command in the old tongue. The snarls tempered into low rumbles, and yet curious eyes watched on as Grendel lifted his head. His gray skin, which had been translucent before, now gleamed golden like a dark reflection of the sun. Violet eyes blazed as they slowly took in her appearance from head to toe. "So nearly perfect this time," he breathed.

A deep coil of hunger tightened in her belly beneath his

appraisal that she hated. She must remember what she had come for. Digging her claws into her hands didn't offer the pinch of reality she needed, the sensation muffled.

Vynasha willed steel into her voice as she said, "Believe what you want, it matters not. I am here because the spell blocking our connection has ended… for now."

Grendel's lips pulled back in a snarl and he gripped the arms of the throne. "You dare," he hissed, and the shades of beasts around his throne shivered and cowered. "You dare steal her face to taunt me yet again! Be gone, *Mother.*"

A frustrated growl escaped Vynasha as she climbed the short stair and covered his hands with hers. "I'm really here, you ass!" His hands spasmed beneath hers, the connection between them surging to life.

"Vynasha?"

"Grendel—" Vynasha yelped as he easily threw her grip aside and dragged her body against his.

"You are here!" Grendel pressed desperate kisses over her scarred neck. "I thought you lost to me, and I could not bear it, Vynasha."

She shuddered, breathless chuckles escaping her. "Still believe I'm a ghost?"

Grendel shook his head and smiled against her collarbone. "Ever since she stole you away, I have been going mad. I tried to hold on to hope, but when you did not return…"

"I'm so sorry, it wasn't my choice." Vynasha clasped the back of his head, savoring his solidness even when she knew she needed to pull away. It wasn't meant to happen like this, none of it. She should be stronger than this weakness of the flesh, this *sin* the village priest often railed against.

Grendel's hands tightened on her backside and the nape of her neck. "I know, my love. I know," he murmured, pressing his mouth to hers in a searing kiss.

Vynasha couldn't breathe, and she didn't want to. Only to exist in this moment, and for the moment to stretch into a small eternity. She kissed him back, knowing she would hate herself for this later. But for now...

"Grendel," she said as his mouth trailed to taste her skin and his hands moved over her curves. "Grendel," she moaned as he pulled her thigh over to seat her astride him and rocked his hips up against hers.

"I nearly lost all sense when the beast I sent after you did not return," he confessed as he pulled the bodice of her gown down, baring her breast.

Vynasha gasped as his tongue teased her flesh, fingers curling into his silken hair. "Beast?" She barely managed the word as her mind struggled to catch up.

Grendel hummed and urged Vynasha's hips to roll in time with his. Every moment they connected, she felt her control ebbing away piece by piece.

Wake up!

"I warned you what would happen if you did not give me this. With our bond severed, I will go mad. And I have struggled in vain to keep from wakening fully, Vynasha." He pressed his cheek against her breast, and his arms gathered so tightly around her waist until their dance stilled.

Vynasha caught her breath and blinked, taking in the obsidian throne she gripped with a free hand, runes illuminated with violet light. Ghostly shades of beasts wavered in and out of her vision in the black hall beyond the throne. Beasts.

"You sent the beast that attacked us?" she whispered against the crown of his head and prayed she had misunderstood.

Say it was a rogue. Say it was my fault because of the magick we dared use.

Grendel stilled, and his hold became painfully tight, his voice hardened and desperate as the prince he had appeared to be on his throne. "What else could I have done when Soraya stole you from me? When I had no inkling whether you survived?"

Vynasha attempted to pull back, to see his face, but he only held on tighter. She growled back, "You sent a rabid beast into my *home*, you bastard! I nearly died!"

"This is your home!" Had Grendel claws as well, her back would be torn to shreds.

"No!" Vynasha's fist closed over his hair in a tight grasp. He grunted as she pulled his head forcefully back to meet her gaze. There was little of the prince that had wooed her relentlessly in Grendel's eyes, only love burdened with madness. "My home is with my brother and nephew, not this hell you've cursed me to!"

Grendel smiled, his eyes shining with tainted adoration. "No, you do not mean that. You cannot believe that."

"This castle was my prison, Grendel. And instead of freeing me, you bound me just as surely as you did any of your pet monsters." She laughed and squeezed her eyes shut before her tears could fall. How could she want this man after everything?

She lost her tight hold of his hair when his fingers encircled her wrist and brought her hand to press against his cheek. Vynasha blinked until her vision cleared. "I hate you," she sobbed. "I hate you so much."

"Yes, hate me," he moaned as his hand slid up her thigh to the juncture between them. "Maim me. Only, never leave me, Asha."

"I must," she hissed. "I only came here to tell you I won't be coming back ever again." Her teeth dug sharply against her bottom lip as his fingers found her slick and desperate for his touch. She should make him stop. A part of her, a too-small voice at the back of her mind, nearly screamed for her inaction.

Wake up!

Grendel tugged at her skirts, the layers piling up between them. "Had *she* not interfered, I might have slept longer and given you time. But I cannot trust this not to happen again."

Her stocking-clad knees dug into the obsidian throne on either side of his hips. He tugged at her small clothes and dragged her up and over his covered length. Vynasha held on to his shoulder as her lips parted, and the stars above fell around them. "Saints, what are you doing to me? You do realize I'm telling you goodbye?"

Grendel smiled wickedly as he stole another kiss, his tongue darting to taste hers before he pulled back, lips still twined, to reply, "And I am telling you that you are a fool if you believe that will stop me. If you cannot give me this, I will not stop coming for you until you are mine again."

"I will never be yours," she snarled. "I'll find a way to break the bond if you don't leave me and the wylderfolk alone."

Grendel shifted their angle and flung his head back against the throne with a deep groan. "Neither gods nor your pithy threats will stop me, love."

Driven by fury, Vynasha kissed him. She drew his lip between her sharp teeth and bit down until she tasted his sweet blood on the tip of her tongue. The friction between them grew until every drag of his clothed member between her sex drew a keening whine from her lips.

Cursing him inwardly, she panted out, "This is the last time."

"Next time you will be in my arms, and I will never let you go." His fingers pinched her nipple, and he thrust against her as she lost herself.

"Grendel!" she cried as pleasure unlike anything she had known broke her apart, and left her aching for more. Her head fell to rest against his as she caught her breath.

And then he was moaning her name in return, pulling her tight as his member throbbed against her.

They clung to one another as the stars floated in and out of familiar constellations around them.

Vynasha blinked back tears and traced the almost boyish smile on Grendel's face. "This is the last time. I can't come here again, Grendel," she dared whisper.

His smile fell, and she watched carefully as his features settled and hardened. "I cannot let you go," he warned.

Vynasha grimaced. "You cannot or will not?"

Grendel's handsome features contorted into a cruel sneer. "I have been more than generous, Vynasha, but you try my patience. Shut me out, and I will come for you myself."

"But you can't!" She pushed off his lap and onto unsteady legs. *Please wake up!*

"Wait, Vynasha!" But he was too slow to catch her and rose to his feet as she stumbled down two steps, his arms outstretched.

"Stay away from me!" Vynasha pulled her dagger from thin air. The blade had not been on her a moment ago, she was certain, yet it was solid and real enough in her hand. The blade reflected starlight as she pressed the tip against Grendel's heaving chest. "Saints! I was so stupid to think I could come here and reason with you."

"It is you who are being unreasonable," he protested, eyeing Ferox's gift to her with clear disgust. "I warned you what would happen, and still you allow those *people* to hide you with their pathetic enchantments. When I have sensed your every moment awake or asleep since you left Bitterhelm."

She flinched at the knowledge he had been watching her all along. "You promised I could live a life for myself, and that is what I intend to do! Take this from me, keep me from my family, and I swear I will use the power you gave me to turn everything you love to ashes."

Grendel stepped into the blade, hissing as it dug into his chest and violet blood spilled from the fresh wound. His hand closed around her wrist. "We belong together. I was a fool to believe otherwise, and that is a mistake I intend to correct very soon, my love."

Vynasha backed down another step and pulled the blade free from his chest. "What do you mean?"

"Wake up!" a voice outside and all around them cried. It was the same voice she had heard at the back of her mind all along.

Grendel looked up with a roar. "Who is that?"

Vynasha smiled and ignored the longing that had not left her, that may never leave her again, as she listened for the source of the voice calling her name. "The one who's going to beat you one day, Grendel."

"No, wait! Do not leave yet, please!" He staggered down the steps, and the beasts hiding in the shadows surged forward as though sensing his need.

She tightened the grip on her dagger and took in his otherworldly features one last time. "In another life, I might have loved you."

Grendel shook his head, fury warring with desperation as he chased after her, his beasts at his heels. "You cannot leave me!"

"Goodbye," Vynasha said in the mirror world.

CHAPTER TWENTY-NINE

A Song of Death

"WAKE UP! YOU are scaring me!" Erythea cried as she shook Vynasha by the shoulders.

The real world was glaringly bright and harsh to her muddled senses. Vynasha welcomed the pain as she surged forward with a gasp.

"Oh, thank Crafter." Erythea sighed as she sank back to the edge of the bed.

Vynasha's hand pressed hard against the amulet searing painfully against her chest and turned to take in the door she had forgotten to bar. The dagger and stolen grimoire page sat on the bedside table beside the low-burning candle.

Erythea wiped her cheeks of tears and met her gaze with clear terror. Small, trembling hands covered Vynasha's, and a wash of soothing cold magick coated her skin. "I was so scared you would not come back," she said. "You were so far away, like the last time. I was afraid to try the spell on you again after Grandmother made me swear, but I should have. I should have—"

"Stop! It's all right, Thea." Vynasha cleared her throat and shifted uncomfortably to sit on the bed. Beyond the house, the skies crackled with distant thunder. Was the storm already here?

"I was so scared," the girl repeated.

Vynasha put aside her discomfort and covered the girl's hand with hers. "Your voice brought me back to myself. Don't feel guilty for doing the right thing. It's too dangerous for you to do magick, besides." She pointedly looked at her hand.

Thea ducked her head, nodding. "You stole the spell."

Vynasha rubbed her face and grimaced. "I did. I'm sorry, but I don't trust your grandmother to teach it to me, and I needed to do it before he could…" She had never talked about Grendel, or Ferox and the others, not even with Ceddrych. Not really.

Erythea lifted her chin, anger clear in her lilac eyes. "The prince."

Vynasha flinched. "You know about the prince?"

"Grandmother told me once. He helped the king kill our kind once. He killed us, but he is also one of us."

Vynasha had never seen anything resembling hatred from Balos's gentle girl until now. It called to her own hatred and guilt. "The prince created a bond with me before I escaped Bitterhelm," she carefully said. "It was the only way to save me from the curse, he claimed. But I didn't know until much later that our bond would also call my spirit to his each night I slept. And one day…" Her voice failed her and she shook her head. "One day, I will die, and my spirit won't join my loved ones. I'll be trapped with him in that forsaken place forever."

"No!" Erythea suddenly stood on unsteady feet.

A sudden crack of lightning sounded close to the village, thunder rumbling in its wake.

The spellbound child twisted and took Vynasha's ruby dagger and the ripped page from her mother's grimoire in hand. "I swear I will help you break this bond, no matter what it takes. We should mark you now, as you intended, before anything else happens. If he can pull you to him against your will even now, we cannot risk another moment."

Vynasha stared up at Thea and nodded. "Will you help me?" She didn't want to admit she was afraid, not only of Grendel's threats or marking herself too deeply, but of herself. After tonight, she could no longer trust herself to act alone.

Erythea nodded and glanced briefly about the room before pulling her apron from her waist and laying it in Vynasha's lap. "Begin now, quickly. I will guide your hand if you need me."

Ferox's dagger glinted in the dying candlelight. It was impossible to tell whether it was still night or if dawn had come while her body slept.

The storm raged high above them, snow falling in thicker waves overhead with a steady *tap, tap, tap*.

Vynasha closed her fist over the dagger with her left hand and bared the underside of her right arm. Her hands shook as she glanced between the spell and her uneven scarred flesh.

"Here. " Erythea closed her hand over Vynasha's fist and helped her begin the first rune. "Keep your intention in your mind, or the spell will not take."

Vynasha gritted her teeth as together they carefully cut her skin in a trail of runes, taking the shape of a fletched arrow.

Grendel's terrified face sat clearly in her mind, yet she didn't hesitate this time.

I can't trust myself around him, and I can't trust what I feel. Time to end this, before he ends me.

Wyll needed Vynasha to be whole when Ceddrych brought him home. There could be no more room for error or fear.

Her pain increased with each rune, her blood boiling and the amulet thrumming until it began to glow through her linen under tunic.

Erythea gasped but did not stop aiding Vynasha. Lightning struck again, closer to the village, and the rumbling of thunder grew louder. "Almost done," the girl promised.

Vynasha sobbed as she curled over her maimed arm, streaks of violet blood dripping over the sides and onto Thea's soiled apron.

"Hold on to your intention!" the girl urged, her grip tightening.

Vynasha flinched against the urge to recoil, as though someone else tried to take over her limbs. She growled as she fought back, the sound more beastly than human.

"Enough," she groaned as the final rune was drawn.

"It is finished," Erythea sighed as she pulled her stained hands free.

The mess of Vynasha's arm illuminated with sudden violet light.

They gasped in unison, then Erythea shrieked as the foundations beneath them began to tremble.

"That was not supposed to happen," Erythea said as she fell to her knees.

Vynasha caught her elbow and turned to the door as it was thrust open with multiple cracks of lightning echoing beyond the safety of their walls. Somewhere in the distance a bell tolled and shouts echoed their own as the trembling increased with a fresh wave.

The door slammed open of its own accord, bringing the muffled world outside to sudden life. What most frightened Vynasha were the fathomless black eyes of the Oracle, braced in the doorway with both hands and a look of horror on her face.

"What have you done!" Grandmother raged as she stalked into the room, unmoored by the tremulous foundations. "What have done, you foolish children!"

"Forgive us, but we had no choice! The prince nearly claimed her spirit again and would have if I had not found her." Erythea attempted to rise, and Grandmother aided her only to push the girl firmly toward the door.

"I shall deal with you later, granddaughter. Go to the room until I come for you. There you will be most protected." The Oracle turned her black eyes to Vynasha's bloody arm, fury once again rising with an unnamed emotion which pinched the old woman's eyebrows together. "Your recklessness will kill us all, you selfish witch. Come with me now, and for once in your life, *obey*."

Vynasha and Erythea struggled to follow the older woman down the stairs, catching one another's fall each time the quakes returned. "What's happening out there?" Vynasha called over the rumbling din. "Is it the storm?"

Grandmother cackled so madly that she paused and doubled over, turning to favor Vynasha with her predator's smile. "The storm, you say. I suppose you did not know, little fool that you are, blindly wielding your magick like a club with little care for the *consequences*."

Erythea gasped as they reached the bottom floor and the overturned furniture and kitchenware. "The bell only tolls for one reason." She chewed her lip as Vynasha met her gaze, and she whispered, "Death."

Erythea refused to part from them, taking Vynasha's bloodied hand in hers, fierce despite her slight stature. "You cannot make me stay behind," she hissed when Grandmother attempted to convince the girl otherwise.

The Oracle eyed the two of them as she shut the door and snatched a walking stick of ash in hand. "You will *both* obey me, no matter what I say, is that understood? No matter what we encounter in the village."

Grandmother's back straightened, the shadow of the powerful woman she must have once been in her regal bearing. So Vynasha found herself nodding along, despite her misgivings. And perhaps… a small part of her was grateful to lean upon someone else for a change, someone with greater authority that could make the difficult choices.

This feeling grew as they crossed the snow-drenched yard and reached the path leading to the village, just as four hooded, bobbing heads half stumbled and ran directly for them.

"Vynasha!" Asa reached her first, throwing his arms around her waist with a sob. "Something's wrong in the village! All the elders ran for the main hall."

Katya grimaced as she helped the raven feathered twins, Hugyn and Munyn correct their balance. "They tried to shut all the children into Elder Galtis's hall, but we had to come and warn you."

"Stay away from the village! I heard Grandfather talking about you with Aunty, and it scared me," Asa begged.

Grandmother huffed and barged between them, her walking stick a too-effective tool to pry the boy from his desperate grasp. "Enough! We have no time for this. You should *all* return to Galtis's hall, foolish children. The wards I placed there were set for such a dire occasion. And that is where I intend to deliver you."

Vynasha caught the old woman's wary gaze.

"You made them yours, so now they are your responsibility," the Oracle snapped as she pushed them farther along the path to the village.

Erythea squeezed her hand, and Asa quickly claimed the other. "I will not let them harm you," Thea vowed. Once, Vynasha would have doubted her. After all, what could a child do in a world cruel as this? But a child with *magick*, a child strong enough to overcome the prince of Bitterhelm?

Vynasha shook her head. "You heard the Oracle. I'm the one who will protect all of you, no matter the cost."

Katya turned and flashed an impish smile, opening her mouth to reply when the next tremor shook the earth. And the massive tree trunk before them cracked and fell.

"Run!" Grandmother cried as she ripped Erythea from Vynasha's hand.

Munyn screeched as she pulled her twin out of the tree's path.

"Asa, run!" Katya shouted as she lifted and shoved Asa into Vynasha's arms.

Vynasha stumbled, the air pushed from her lungs, yet she clung to Asa as the boy cried and struggled to reach his friend. "Katya, no!"

But it was too late.

It happened in a moment, and it happened so slowly Vynasha swore she could hear their heart beats somewhere beneath the din of breaking wood and the screams of the children.

One moment, Katya was reaching out to them, stumbling over snow and tangling roots. Then the massive tree swallowed Katya whole with a thud that knocked them off their feet. And she was gone.

Vynasha roared in denial as she lifted the trunk by one of the many great branches. It creaked but did not move. Her muscles strained and ached from abuse as she tried pushing instead.

Had Vynasha not fallen completely into the beast beneath her skin, she would have noticed the greater tree's fall causing others around them to creak and break like scattered tinder. Grandmother cried out in the old tongue, pounding her stick into the earth and ordering the others to "Keep close to me!"

As the forest settled once more, Vynasha's roar faded to a whine. "Help me! Please help me!"

Erythea approached first, her pale face gray as she took in the tree.

"Come!" Asa urged his cousins with their hands, the three bearing around Vynasha to help her push and pull.

"You cannot help the earthworn girl. Not anymore." Grandmother appeared before them, stick held tightly in her white-knuckled grasp.

"You don't know that," Vynasha grunted. "Don't you dare tell me to give up when she's right here. Now help us move this bloody tree before she suffocates!"

"We cannot help her anymore." The Oracle shook her head. "Countless others need our help in the village."

"Go help your precious villagers, then, you old hag!" Vynasha turned away from the only other people with real power. She didn't need Thea or her witch of a grandmother. "Come on, keep pushing," she huffed.

The raven twins jumped onto the log, feathers fluttering in place of hair, and hovered for longer than should have been possible. They screeched bitterly as their efforts to pull the log in the opposite direction failed.

"Katya! Hold on, we are here," Asa babbled nonsensically.

Vynasha sobbed and cursed the spell she had done to her arm, the weakness in her limbs. She had pushed and pushed too hard for too long. The fallen tree creaked and then trembled with the next, lesser tremor. Vynasha caught her breath. What had Grandmother likened her to, a club? If she was no better than a clumsy weapon, let her be a weapon this last time.

Vynasha growled as she bit down on her thumb, then coated the bark.

"What are you doing? Foolish child, you cannot!" The Oracle's protests faded as Vynasha pushed her *need* to move the tree behind it. And the other children raised their voices in a cry.

Together they pushed and *pushed*, and the tree slowly rose.

"Great Crafter," Grandmother gasped.

The tolling of the bell seemed very distant now.

Vynasha desperately wished the Dadas and Tarbus had been there too. Where was Balos, or the rest of the pack? Why had Balos led them all on a wild chase in the first place? A part of her raged and seethed that they could simply abandon their children.

Why do you always leave me, Ceddrych!

"They left you behind," she growled. "But I won't." She lifted her gaze to the Oracle's and bared her sharp teeth at the old hag.

Katya had laughed, saying that none of the grown-ups in the village cared for them. Ceddrych had been the only one to care for Vynasha after Wynyth died. Katya's people were folk of the earth. She would not be left behind as Vynasha was.

Never again.

As the trunk shifted, the branches broke and exposed a crumpled leg lying at a crooked angle. "Katya?"

"Grandmother," Erythea gasped.

Vynasha eyed the raven-haired twins. "Drag her out!"

"We have her!" Asa cried as he aided his cousins.

Vynasha released the spell and sank against the trunk, utterly spent and bone weary. She could only pant and stare with increasing worry as the children tried to prop Katya up.

"Are you proud of yourself, Wynyth's daughter?" Grandmother said as she released Erythea and glided over to Katya's prone form.

"You should not have given so much of yourself," Erythea softly chided as she knelt at Vynasha's side. "But I am glad you tried. It is more than any other would have done."

"She's going to wake up," Vynasha insisted.

The girl did not open her eyes.

"Katya, please wake up!" Asa pleaded, fat tears leaving clean marks on dirty cheeks. Asa's hands felt over the older girl's neck and slack features.

Grandmother placed a hand over the girl's pulse and her heart, bowing her white head a moment before sighing heavily. "We must leave her, for now. Better to have let the tree guard her until we could return. Come, children. Mourn Katya later. The bell has not stopped tolling, and we must hurry before more have perished."

"She is just sleeping, right, Vynasha?" Asa lifted his shaking, bloody hands—Katya's blood.

"Of course," Vynasha lied as she crawled to Katya's side and placed a hand over the girl's cheek. Her skin was cold and her lips turning blue. "Please, Katya," she prayed. "You are stronger than this. You're the strongest girl I've ever seen. You helped me lift that tree. I know you did. You have magick as much as I do, as much as any of us."

Grandmother's gnarled hands dug into her shoulders, pulling her from Katya and forcing Vynasha to meet the old woman's gleaming black gaze. "Enough! Return to your senses, child, before I rattle them back into you. Do you hear me, Wynyth's daughter? Stand on your feet and guide these children to safety. They already sacrificed because of *you*. Will you let the others come to harm as well?"

"How can you be so heartless?" Vynasha looked at her lap and the sleeping girl in her arms. Katya was so light when she should be heavy, for she was stronger than any girl Vynasha had met.

"None of us have the luxury hearts…" Grandmother rasped.

Vynasha blinked back fresh tears. She had brought Asa back from the brink of death, and Wyll from death's icy grasp. Yet when she reached for that place now, when she sought Katya's spirit, there was *nothing*. "I can't leave her like this," she sobbed.

Grandmother caught her chin and forced her to look up, past the trembling trees and to the ominous black sky, and the lightning illuminating the clouds above. "Do you see that, girl? That is not a natural storm, and it has been brewing all night and day. Hear my words and mark me, if we do not move *now*, there will be nothing left of our people."

"I don't care—we aren't leaving her behind!" Vynasha snapped.

CHAPTER THIRTY

A Reckoning

THE CHILDREN HELPED Vynasha lift Katya, though they could not carry her. None was tall or strong enough alone. Grandmother glared at them while muttering curses in the old tongue as Vynasha staggered beneath her unexpected burden.

"Can we not use magick, Grandmother?" Erythea begged, fresh tear tracks down her ruddy cheeks.

"Too much power has already been wasted here!" Grandmother thumped her walking stick against the broken earth and lifted her gaze to the heavy snow raining thickly above. "Now come, lest you wish to face the might of Bitterhelm alone."

Asa and the raven twins kept a hand each on Vynasha's back and arms, helping to steady her with each mild tremor. Erythea walked slightly ahead, ready to catch Katya if needed.

"Where are Dadas and Tarbus?" Vynasha asked as they neared the outline of the village houses appearing through the trees ahead.

"T-they were called to the g-great hall," Asa stuttered. "They told us to stay put, but Katya…"

Vynasha blinked and another tear slipped free. She hugged Katya's broken form even closer. "We're going to be okay, Asa. No matter what happens, we'll be okay."

"I wish we had all stayed in Wanderer's new house together." Asa's voice wavered.

Vynasha nodded and swallowed past the lump in her throat. They had raised her brother's dream together, and the protection ward had sealed it, forbidding beasts and people alike from entering.

I should have never left. If I hadn't left, Balos would have killed the beast, and we could have been safe.

No sooner did they break through the tree line than the wolves appeared. In their beastly forms, the pack could nearly reach her shoulders on all fours. Two of the pack snarled and snapped, hackles raised at their appearance and hatred burning in their beastly gazes.

"Let us pass, you fools!" Grandmother barked back.

A third wolf appeared, growling low and standing taller than the others. The first two wolves immediately backed down, and the third wolf shifted in a sudden rush of cracking bones, growls, and groans.

A tall and imposing man in a gray fur cloak stood in the creature's place. He was taller than Balos, the tallest man she'd ever seen, and beautiful in the way ice was both beautiful and deadly.

"Are you quite finished with your pointless posturing, boy?" Grandmother said as she stepped forward, blocking Vynasha's immediate view of the wolf.

The third wolf shifted on his mortal feet as another tremor shook the earth, flashing too-sharp teeth at them. "You should have stayed in your hall, Oracle, you and your cursed granddaughter," he sneered.

Grandmother chuckled. "You are certainly one to speak so harshly of *outsiders*, Vilhelm. I will not ask again, boy. Let us pass!"

Vilhelm bristled yet inclined his head in a shallow show of respect. "You are Balos's mother, so I will allow you and the children to pass, but the witch remains. Outsiders have no place in our hall."

Vynasha froze beneath the sudden burn of that terribly cold gaze. "I need to find my brother," she insisted, pushing through the ache in her throat. She shifted to ease Katya's weight in her arms.

Vilhelm's low growl eased as he noticed Katya for the first time, then Asa clinging tightly to her arm. The wolf's brow creased and he blinked rapidly before his expression flattened. "Come, then," Vilhelm gruffly beckoned as he turned. "But you have no authority to speak in village matters, do not forget, Witch."

"For whom does the bell toll, Vilhelm?" Grandmother insisted as she dragged Erythea by the hand, her walking stick swiftly marking their journey past the well.

Two other wolves replaced those that flanked their path to the main hall, and Vynasha recognized the twins by their pelts. Tarbus trotted closer, touching his nose to Katya's limp hand with a faint whine.

Vilhelm glanced over his shoulder, his sharp gaze passing the Oracle to Asa, glued to Vynasha's side. "One of our own has been slain. There is to be a trial."

Asa gasped and muttered something under his breath to his cousins. Vynasha stumbled slightly and attempted to shake her growing unease. She glanced up at the crackling of lightning. "Isn't the storm more pressing?"

"Mayhap you could ply your craft and make it cease, Witch," Vilhelm replied with only the faintest hint of disdain beneath his cold tone.

Vynasha lifted her chin and gritted her teeth. Her arms burned and every step was agony, but they were there at last. Torches set before the tall doors of the great hall quavered against another, harsher quake. Dadas and Tarbus turned their backs to the hall and faced the road, yet their eyes followed as Vilhelm shoved the doors open with a heaving groan.

The doors closed the instant they had passed the threshold. Only to face the furious storm that was Asa's aunt, Gira.

"There you are, you wicked younglings! I have been beside myself, Asa..." But the old woman bit her lip and clutched at the boy with far more force and even fear as she drew her nephew into her arms. "Same goes for you both, Hugyn and Munyn. How you could make your kin worry like this... and Katya—"

Gira gasped as she placed a hand on the girl in Vynasha's arms, then jerked it back as though burned. Wide eyes pale as Asa's caught Vynasha's, and a fresh wave of grief and understanding washed over the older woman's face.

Vynasha blinked, and more tears betrayed the heartache she was failing to keep at bay. "Will you take her and the others somewhere safe?"

Gira's mouth pinched, and something cruel and nasty twisted her features.

"Do as she says, Elder Gira. Or did you forget we have a trial to uphold?" Vilhelm barely shifted, but menace filled his every word.

"We are not leaving Vynasha!" Asa protested. "We need to stay together so we are safe. And I want to see Mother. Where is Mother? Is she with the pack?"

"Not now, Asa." Gira turned her head sharply, but not before Vynasha caught the woman's clear devastation.

No...

Vynasha's voice was too hoarse as she turned to Asa. "You must go with your aunt. I promise I will come and find you as soon as this... trial is over. But I need you to look after the others and especially Katya. Can you do that for me?"

Asa breathed heavily through his mouth and blinked back fresh tears, then his jaw set and he nodded. "You promise?"

Gira's expression hardened as Vilhelm hissed something to the elder.

Vynasha could only smile and lie yet again. "I promise." Her heart ached as she straightened, adjusting Katya's weight carefully in her arms and waiting for the boy's aunt to approach her.

"You—have my gratitude for returning Asa." Gira's shining eyes met Vynasha's as she gathered the girl into her arms. "Keep close, children."

"Katya was caught under a tree until we helped Vynasha move it," Asa informed his aunt as they began to walk away. "And we could not make Katya wake up, and the Oracle said there was no time because of the bell. Why is the bell tolling, Aunty?"

"I will explain everything soon. Come now, children. This hall is not for your eyes."

Vynasha ducked her head as the door behind them opened and shut once more. Once more she was adrift, without Katya's weight grounding her. She swayed. Her freshly marked arm burned hot like the amulet around her neck. She wanted to rip it off. She wanted to rip off her skin the way the wolves could, and race to that bloody castle and…

"Vynasha?" Erythea's soft hand pulled Vynasha's claws away from the fresh wound.

"Come, both of you," Grandmother insisted, placing a firm hand on either of their shoulders. "It is time we learn what has happened."

"You will come and observe, but you will not interfere in pack matters." Vilhelm instructed them as he led them through the chaos of the village hall.

Vynasha kept her feet, though she knew she must look a fright judging by the wary looks of the wylderfolk they passed. Some she recognized from before, and others nodded in respect, those whose children she had once saved. No other young children besides Erythea remained in the hall.

Good, this is not a place for innocence.

Rune-carved pillars surrounded the central square of the smoky hall, where a bright fire burned at the center of the room, benches and tables pushed back to the edges. Most of the townsfolk were gathered here, clutching one another, watching the roar of the wolves at their center with clear unease.

Folk of earth, built powerfully and marked by hair fiery red and gold, clung nearer the hearth. Folk of air seemed unable to hold still, flitting about the shadowed corners of the room on the tips of their toes. Folk of water were few and far between, though their slightly blue skin tones and scaled skin betrayed them. There were others whose origin she could not make out, singular beings like a man with horns and skin black as night watching her with a faint smile.

Vynasha caught her breath as she felt a slight pressure against her mind and broke their gaze to face the wolves at the center. A raised dais held three chairs padded with furs, bearing Galtis and two others Vynasha did not know by name who argued heatedly with the pack.

Her breath caught as she searched the sea of faces, unable to find Ceddrych. Erythea's hand squeezed hers, and Vynasha picked up her pace. She squeezed between two other wolves, reaching Grandmother's side just before the dais.

"Do not breathe a word, neither of you," the Oracle warned them before allowing Vilhelm to lead her to the edge of the circle facing the village elders.

"And I say the matter must be set aside for now, Balos! Before the storm makes it impossible for us to return to our homes," Galtis declared, sparing a surprised glance the Oracle's way.

Balos's fists were clenched, muscles taut in a way Vynasha had never seen before. "Damn the storm! We demand justice for the murder of Onya, *your daughter*, and all you have to say is we must wait?"

Vynasha choked back a sound as Balos shifted aside and revealed the prone body bound in linens and furs. Her claws bit into her palms, aching for Katya's weight in her arms, for Asa's hand on her arm.

The boy lost his friend and now his mother…

Erythea turned and buried her face in Vynasha's side, but she barely felt it nor noticed the ease with which she held the girl.

Who will tell Asa his mother is gone?

"This is worse than I thought," Grandmother murmured, black gaze darting between the cries of outrage from the pack and elders' desperate attempts to quail their fury.

Galtis stood, his feathered head bristling fiercely in the hearth light. "As an elder, the needs of our people outweigh my own. Something you seem to have forgotten in your bloodlust and endless quest for vengeance, Balos! Command all you wish, but even you cannot turn away from the evil at our gates."

"Coward!" Vilhelm cried out, the other wolves around them snarling in agreement. Whispers and jeers echoed from the villagers watching beyond.

Vynasha couldn't stop staring at the body of Asa's mother, lost in the fact the boy had lost both parents now.

The earth trembled, and the boards holding the hall together rattled around them as cracks of lightning flashed beyond the windows. The wylderfolk fell silent, wary, and fearful as they looked at the rafters above, at the metal cage swaying with great heaving groans.

The hairs raised along Vynasha's unblemished skin as the pervading scent of smoke and fur was shrouded by the cinnamon musk of magick. All these people held the potential, she realized. All of them were too terrified to wield it. To wield magick invited ruin and death. Magick required sacrifice, and these people had already lost so much, had given too much.

Like Asa. Like Erythea. And me…

The Oracle stepped into the circle between Balos and his pack and the elders on the dais. "I see I have been away too long, as your children continue to show abominable manners to their elders."

The elder women with silver-gold hair and pale eyes gasped and gripped the arms of her chair. "Oracle," she whispered and bowed her head immediately.

"Oracle." Galtis frowned heavily yet he inclined his head in respect, and then one by one, every person in the great hall shifted their stance and bowed their heads. All save Balos, who had at last noticed Vynasha and his daughter's presence, his mouth parting in surprise and his brow drawn in grief. Who had Onya been to him?

"You do us great honor, Oracle," the elder woman with silver-gold hair said. "But pray, why have you come?"

The third elder, with long, braided black hair, cocked his antlered head. "And why have you brought the witch?"

The woman bared her teeth. "She should not be here, nor should the blighted child."

The Oracle cackled at this. "You withering toads! None of you had the gall to approach me alone, content to borrow my predictions and tonics when needed. Yet now I tell you that your need of my aid, and of the witch, is greater than you comprehend." She leaned toward them on her walking stick.

Galtis eyed the branch of ash warily and shifted in his seat. "We are most grateful for your aid, but forgive us, what can you possibly do to ward against the full might of Bitterhelm?"

Balos stalked forward, green eyes blazing brightly as he interrupted, "You dare to bring *my* daughter into this hell, old woman."

The Oracle smiled. "You gave me little choice, boy." She looked past him to Onya's body on the ground and then to the cage above. "Onya's death is on your head, which is why you are so wroth. And why you abandon all sense to destroy when you should, *for once*, hold your fool tongue!"

Vynasha tilted her chin again to the cage, the outline of bodies pressed against the bars. A flash of pale eyes caught hers, and the dread she'd felt, the utter certainty she held but ignored like a fool, came crashing back.

Traitors, and Onya is dead.

A chain bound to a wheel somewhere above kept the cage aloft. She needed to slip back into the crowd, find a way to better see, and then plan. And pray it was not Ceddrych in that cage as she feared. But if not in a cage, where else could he possibly be?

Yet Erythea whimpered when Vynasha tried to move, tightening her hold, and whispered, "Please do not leave, do not go like all the others. Please wait, Vynasha."

Vynasha clenched her jaw and the spike of pain grounded her, keeping her touch on the girl's shoulder light. She tore her gaze from the cage to find the elders and the Oracle arguing in circles just as they had with Balos.

"Mayhap Balos has the right of it and we should convene the trial now, before all else," Galtis said. "A village divided cannot stand."

"Have you all gone blind?" The Oracle laughed. "We shall not survive the night if we do not bring all our strength to muster *now*. The boundary has been breached, and the cursed ones *are* coming, whether you are prepared or not."

"Tell us what we must do, then," Galtis replied, yet his birdlike gaze flicked to the motionless form of his daughter as the Oracle replied.

Grandmother tapped her stick to the planks at her feet with a resounding *clack,* and the elders flinched. "The pack must hold the line. The runes protecting this hall and yours, Galtis, are the strongest. No one may leave until we have pushed them back."

"And how can we possibly do this when they carry the might

of Bitterhelm with them?" The white and gold-haired woman's voice shook as she leaned forward.

Balos raked a hand over his silver hair as he shook his head and approached Vilhelm, to speak in his ear. "Be ready."

Vilhelm cast a dark gaze to the cage above, then inclined his head in a reverent bow. He cut an icy glare Vynasha's way before fading into the crowd.

Vynasha frowned and dragged Erythea along with her, ignoring the girl's protests as they reached Balos. "Wait," she snapped. She barely noticed her hand pressing insistently to his chest until she heard Thea's gasp.

"Beauty." Balos grimaced and caught her hand before she could successfully tug it away. Only a faint shadow of his usual amusement ticked at the corner of his mouth. "You should not have come."

"Tell me what has happened," she hissed and dared step closer, quickly eying the pack and the elders surrounding them. "Where is my brother?"

The abject fury she'd glimpsed in him when they first approached returned in every taught line of his body. Balos had not truly frightened her since the night he casually suggested she burn at the stake. Yet it took all the bluster she could muster to keep her chin lifted and her hand from trembling beneath his painful grip as he spat, "In a cage where the bloody traitor belongs."

CHAPTER THIRTY-ONE

A Trial of Beasts

"NOW!" BALOS THREW his command over the room, and the chain rapidly clicked above them as the suspended cage was lowered over the crowd. Wolves snarled and shouted as they leapt back to avoid being crushed. The cage's occupants were tossed against one another and back into the outer bars as the dust settled.

The Oracle whipped around quickly, her lip tugged back over her gritted teeth in a silent snarl. The elders rose as one on the dais, crying, "We have not yet consented!"

"You cannot simply do as you please, Balos," Galtis shrieked. "The council always takes precedence!"

Vynasha wrenched her hand, but the alpha refused to release her or acknowledge her struggle. Balos smiled coldly instead, proclaiming, "You called for action and I have delivered."

"Now is not the time, Balos," the Oracle barked back.

"I disagree, Mother! I believe now is the perfect time. Let the accused defend himself before the bones of his pack mate and beloved *sister*."

Though he lowered their joined hands, Balos kept Vynasha in a firm grasp, as though he thought she might leap onto the cage in the middle of a pack of vengeful wolves. He did not know her at all. For however much she struggled to find her brother and a strangely familiar, feral woman trapped together in a barbaric cage, Vynasha was not stupid. Not like her idiot brother, apparently.

Ceddrych appeared ill, his features sunken, his golden-green eyes haunted, and stared at her with so much regret she wanted to scream.

What happened to you, brother?

His features contorted as though he could hear her unspoken thoughts. How long had Ceddrych been trapped in that cage while Vynasha remained ignorant under Balos's roof? His dark hair was clumped together from days without cleansing and dried blood. And his companion looked even worse.

Balos forced Vynasha and Erythea to stumble along with him as he rounded the cage. "Here is the traitor! We welcomed Wanderer into our village, despite my warnings. And look how he has repaid us! With treachery, murdering one of *your* daughters," he declared, using his free hand to point at Galtis. "And colluding with the daughter of our greatest enemy, Wolfsbane," Balos spat.

Vynasha blinked and shifted her gaze to the small, black-haired woman in dark, bedraggled furs. What had her name been?

"Resha held my nephew held captive!" Ceddrych attempted to call over the buzzing crowd, his voice as hoarse as Vynasha's had been from screaming.

How long did you scream to deaf ears, brother?

"She had me in a bloody trap when Onya found us," Ceddrych

declared. "Onya may have followed my trail, but it was Wolfsbane's daughter who dealt the killing blow!"

Oddly enough, Resha did not appear to react to Ceddrych's accusations. Her amber gaze darted madly about the room, as though the woman didn't comprehend the danger they were in or no longer cared. She had been a wild scrap of a thing the last Vynasha had seen her. And it was then that she realized the truth of what Resha's presence, and Ceddrych's words, truly meant.

"Wyll?" Vynasha barely breathed her nephew's name aloud. Ceddrych's gaze snapped to hers, and his broken smile blurred as her eyes filled with tears she dared not shed. For Wyll was not in the cage with them.

"Convenient lies! Vilhelm has brought them to us for justice, and truth shall be found," Balos argued. The alpha did not bother to hide the slight curl of his mouth or the smug manner he kept Vynasha chained to him, so confident in his victory.

"*The most dangerous people are those who believe themselves righteous beyond doubt,*" Wynyth had warned her so long ago.

"Allow Wanderer to finish saying his piece, Balos," Galtis chided.

Balos turned to the Oracle, as though Galtis had not spoken. "What is the matter, Mother? Have you not foreseen this eventuality from the beginning?"

Vynasha twisted to peer over her shoulder at the Oracle. The old woman clasped her stick of ash wood with both hands and glanced knowingly back at Vynasha. And she realized whatever else was said this day, Balos would have his way. He would destroy Resha, might even do worse to Ceddrych. Rash action could not win the day here, no dagger to the alpha's neck, nor magick. Only reason.

"Who found them?" Vynasha murmured, too low for the others to hear, or so she thought. Balos grimaced down at her while the Oracle's lips turned up into a hidden smile.

"Answer the little witch, would you, son?" Grandmother prodded. "Or are you not here to shed light on the *truth*?"

Balos bared his teeth and tightened his grip on Vynasha's hand, his gaze never leaving his mother's as he said, "Vilhelm."

Whispers followed, and folk shifted nearer with a fluttering of feathers and crackling of firewood. The crowd parted easily as the tall man appeared with silent menace.

Resha's chapped lips moved soundlessly as she gripped the bars and stared up at the tall wolf with a curious blend of horror and relief.

Vilhelm came to stand on the other side of the cage yet did not meet her eye, only waited calmly for his Alpha's next command.

The Oracle thumped her stick, and all heads turned to the source of the sound as it reverberated through the hall. "Vilhelm, tell us how you came upon Wanderer and Wolfsbane's daughter?"

Vilhelm blinked and tilted his head to the side as he dispassionately began. "As our alpha's first, Onya was placed in charge of the hunt for our great enemy. Wanderer aided us in following our enemy's scent, and yet he began to act suspicious."

Because he found Wyll's scent, Vynasha realized. She breathed sharply through her mouth and pushed her feelings deeper within, to a place this trial and this bloody day could no longer touch her.

Vilhelm's cold delivery shifted, flickers of heat shining through as he glanced at Ceddrych. "I can only assume, now that we are aware of the boy, Wanderer suspected his kin to be in Wolfsbane's clutches. Wanderer wanted to find them first. And so he sneaked away in the night while I was away fulfilling our alpha's orders. I returned to camp to learn Onya had discovered his escape and flown into a rage so great she would not listen to reason. She hunted him as ruthlessly as we have hunted the hunters…" He paused, jaw tensing, and finally flicked his cold gaze to Resha.

"And you led the pack to shadow Onya," Balos urged.

Vilhelm straightened and inclined his head again at his alpha's words. "Naturally, we could not abandon her. We reached a part of the forest only the greatest of fools dare venture, lest they find their end at a forgotten one's hand. I went on alone and left the others to wait. And treacherous as my path was, I found Onya first… swinging from the very trap Wanderer claims to have been hung from."

Gasps and outcries filled the room, and Vilhelm turned a too-satisfied eye in Vynasha's direction.

Galtis called for order. "I shall hear the rest of Vilhelm's testimony, or this farce of a trial is at an end!"

The wylderfolk and pack quieted enough that Grandmother's voice rang loudly with her interruption. "We have no need to hear more, Galtis, for we have already had the facts, have we not? Oh, but wait…" She paused to hold up a ringed finger and tilted her head to turn a glittering eye upon Vilhelm. "There is one more thing."

The great wolf inclined his head and flinched as Grandmother slowly approached him, level with the cage. Resha cowered between them.

Balos cursed under his breath as the Oracle tapped the bars with a sharp *clang*.

"Many may have chosen to forget how you came to be part of our pack, mayhap even you, Vilhelm. Allow me to elucidate." She turned her back on the powerful man with no fear and smiled at her son. "Wolfsbane, loathsome creature that he is, is not so far removed from the wylderfolk as we might wish him to be."

"That is enough!" Balos stalked forward, dragging Vynasha and Erythea with him. The girl whimpered against Vynasha's side again, but her father seemed not to hear, too lost in his fury. "How does this matter when we are here to determine the murder of Onya, *my* first!"

"We are all kin," the Oracle declared, her gaze settling on Vynasha's. "All are bound by blood, and you must remember this or perish in the way of your ancestors."

Balos blanched and sucked in a sharp breath, and though he did not fully look at her, his chin jerked slightly in Vynasha and Erythea's direction. "No one else will perish. I refuse to allow it," he growled.

Galtis sighed and raised his hands. "Enough!" Thunder echoed his cry, and he waited for it to settle and all to face him before adding, "The Oracle makes a valid point. We often forget the hunter line merged with ours long ago. It is why Vilhelm joined our pack from the moment of his first scratch." He inclined his head sharply at the tall wolf's shaking form. "And if Wanderer used his kin as a means to hunt Wolfsbane, we must not forget Vilhelm has done the same to hunt his father and sister."

Resha covered her face with her hands and slumped against the bars.

"Sister?" Thea gasped, a nearer echo of the whispers stirring once more in the hall.

"As Wolfsbane's daughter cannot speak for herself, let her brother's testimony stand witness," Galtis said. "Vilhelm, you led the pack much farther west than any have dared journey in an age. Where did you find Wolfsbane's lair?"

Vilhelm sneered. "Across the river, near the base of the Diamond Caves, along the Silver Forest. We nearly lost two other pack members to the ancient ones before I went on alone..."

Ceddrych shifted and squeezed his eyes shut briefly as Vilhelm described the trap he laid for his sister. And how quickly after, Wanderer carried the boy to his waiting fire.

Balos chuffed at this, and Vynasha glanced between them with growing ire. Whether or not Ceddrych was guilty of Onya's death shouldn't matter. The storm was growing worse outside, high winds rattling the shingles overhead. "You could stop this if you wished it," she hissed, digging her claws against the back of his hand.

Balos glanced down and worked his jaw. "I could," he agreed. "But not without reason."

"Reason?" Vynasha frowned then froze as Balos turned the full force of his green gaze upon her, and all outside voices seemed to fade.

"Give me what I want… and I shall set your brother free."

Vynasha found her shock reflected in the black center of his irises. "What is it you want?"

Voices rose in protest around them, and Ceddrych's voice rose with them, but Vynasha couldn't make out their words, too lost in Balos's enigmatic smile.

"Marry me, Beauty."

Erythea gasped at her side as Vynasha choked on a laugh. "I hardly know you!"

Balos leaned forward until his forehead touched hers, and his free hand slipped around her waist. "Marry me, and I shall protect you and yours with my life. Your nephew may live with us, for the child is not at fault. And your brother may walk away, despite his treachery."

"Ceddrych didn't kill Onya." Yet even as she spoke the words aloud, they felt hollow.

Balos pressed on with a hint of his buried fury on his tongue. "His guilt was written on his face from the moment we brought her bones before him. You sense it as well as I."

Vynasha shuddered and her gaze shifted to Ceddrych. Her brother stood as tall as he could in his cage as he raged against a cruelly smiling Vilhelm. While Resha lay curled into herself, her tangled black hair masked her face.

"How do I know I can trust your word when you hate my brother so much?"

Balos's lips brushed against the scarred skin of her cheek. "I swear it on my daughter's life. I will not harm your brother, so long as you remain with me."

Vynasha's breath caught as the weight of eyes around them seemed to press against her skin, along with the growing weight of magick crackling in the very air they breathed. She did not dare agree to this.

But Grendel need not know, and you needn't marry the wolf immediately.

Vynasha licked her lips and watched the way those burning green eyes followed the trail of her tongue, and the black of his iris eclipsed the pupil. "Yes," she finally replied, barely noticing as Erythea covered her mouth with her hands and blinked owlishly between them.

Balos gasped, rocking back slightly before something infinitely brighter burned in his verdant gaze. "Yes?"

Vynasha swallowed and nodded quickly. "I will marry you."

Balos lifted Vynasha off her toes and…

Her world froze.

His mouth pressed against hers, a kiss so hesitant and somehow desperate all at once. His breath became hers as his hands cradled her face, and his lashes fluttered as he groaned as he slowly devoured her.

Vynasha's hands flexed against his shoulders as a sudden toxic rush of longing pumped blood through her body. One kiss, and she was damned to crave more. Voices rose in a tangled web around them.

"Take your hands off of my sister!"

"Do you make a mockery of this council?"

"Alpha may do as he pleases, old man!"

Grandmother's cackle rose above their protests, and outside the walls, wolves joined the wind in mournful howling.

Somewhere beyond yet far too near, the storm raged, and lightning struck furiously at every rune protecting the wylderfolk village.

Somewhere behind those most powerful wards, little Wyll was trapped with Katya and Asa, and the other children of the village.

Somewhere in the distant thunder came the roaring of beasts, the lullaby Vynasha had listened to for nights unending.

Part of Vynasha was aware of these things, but this part drowned beneath the consuming ebb and flow of flesh against flesh. It didn't feel like she imagined kissing a stranger might but rather a meeting of old friends. And there was something familiar about the way his fingers dug into her hip, the low, relieved chuckle as Balos trailed kisses down her neck.

"You have *ruined* me, Vynasha," he confessed against the raised flesh of her neck, just above her racing pulse. "Mayhap you shall allow me to return the favor?"

Vynasha ducked her head as he turned to face the stunned hall at last. She should keep her head high, for this was her choice. But that was before Balos stole her very breath away, and the power she'd wielded, holding her brother's fate in her hands, slipped through her fingers. She didn't dare look at Ceddrych.

Could she look anywhere else, anywhere but the pain creasing her brother's brow from the corner of her eye?

I did this for you!

Vynasha's limbs shook as she curled her hands into fists to keep her focus on Balos as he addressed the elders and the Oracle.

"The Oracle was right from the beginning," Balos declared. "How can we end the life of a man who was only protecting his blood? And how are we to know he aided Onya when she came upon Wolfsbane's daughter's trap?"

"Will you be my mother now?" Erythea's small voice drew her back to thin arms wrapped around her chest and bright lilac eyes.

Vynasha sighed and gathered the child in her arms. "If your father has his way," she said.

"I say we should give Wanderer mercy," Balos told his rapt audience. "Mercy for the wolf who has reclaimed his kin. But we cannot suffer him so near our home, and there must be consequences for his betrayal. And for Wolfsbane's daughter, of course..."

Vilhelm raised his head, a fierce smile on his face as he turned to hold his sister's gaze. "I ask the council, as Resha's kin, that we keep her as our prisoner rather than gifting her with a quick death. Let her pain lure Wolfsbane to us at long last!"

Balos smiled, and the elders exchanged glances as the people whispered. But Resha did not lift her head. And Ceddrych leaned against the bars as if he couldn't hold his own weight anymore. The empty expression on his haggard face made Vynasha's eyes burn.

Stand tall and don't let them see.

Balos would have his way, and Ceddrych would walk away free. But Wolfsbane would be forced to face both his children, it would seem, before the end. Once more, everyone would get everything they wanted, and Vynasha and her kin would suffer. Even Grandmother leaned back with her walking stick and a smirk on her face, content with how this sham of a trial had gone. Did the elders have any power, truly? Did it matter?

You made your choice. Now live with it.

Despite the pain of the amulet scorching her chest, Vynasha believed nothing could alter what her choices had set in motion.

She should have remembered, should have known after all she had faced in this land of cruelty and magick.

Yet not even the almighty Oracle was prepared for the vicious beast to suddenly burst into the great hall, shattering the doors and their fragile reality to pieces.

CHAPTER THIRTY-TWO

A Field of Bones

CHAOS REIGNED IN the aftermath as the beast burst through the doors, bringing the storm at last into the great hall. What wards had protected them for time beyond reckoning were broken in one terrifying instant.

Wylderfolk scattered in terror, pressing up against opposing walls, save for the folk of earth already carrying hammers and axes. Folk of air darted for carelessly discarded bows, while the pack not already in wolf skin immediately shifted and attacked their sanctuary's invader.

The leonine beast that had broken through roared so loudly that it swallowed up the people's screams. The golden-maned monster swiped right and left, uncaring who or what encountered its path. Snow flurries spilled into the hall with unnatural force as the beast fought its way closer to them.

"How many have come?" Vynasha hissed as her hand reached for the bloody dagger at her hip, then yelped as someone grabbed her arm.

"Too many for you to fight with magick," Balos said as he dragged Vynasha and Erythea to join his mother. "Watch over them with your life!" He commanded his mother before kissing the top of Thea's head. "Listen to your grandmother."

"I will, Father."

Vynasha shifted and watched the beast rise on its hind legs, taking great big sniffs of the air as though seeking something. Her magick rose flush to the surface of her skin, yet she didn't dare add the scent of her blood to the madness around them.

She jumped as Balos turned to her, unbothered by the press of her dagger to his chest as he closed the distance between them. "Do we really have time for this now?" she scoffed.

His eyebrow arched with amusement at the familiar sight as he pressed his forehead to Vynasha's. "Please do not do anything foolish. I gave you my word, and I shall protect you with my life."

Vynasha flashed her teeth and growled, "Don't you dare leave us, you old bastard!"

Balos ran a thumb under her eye, over her cheek and breathed her in deeply. "I will never leave you but cannot let you fight this enemy. Only I can drive this creature away. Remember the forest?"

"But I'm not strong enough to protect Thea on my own," she snapped, furious with her tears and the pressing reminder of the girl crying against her side. "How can you trust me with your daughter's life when we've only just met?"

"You are not alone, little witch." Grandmother laid a hand on her shoulder and squeezed briefly before drawing Thea away and into her protective embrace.

Balos nodded to his mother, then smiled as he ducked to quickly whisper against Vynasha's ear. "You know me better than you think, Beauty. You knew me once, long ago, as the voice in the wind. And though I wear a different skin in this place, I have never stopped wanting you for mine."

She gasped, her heart suddenly in her throat. "Ferox?"

But he was already pulling away, the man's body breaking and remaking before her eyes into that of a great silver wolf.

And Vynasha so clearly *saw* as she never allowed herself to see before: the curve of his brow, the shape of his wolfish face, and the perfect spring shade of his eyes…

Had she been blind all along, or simply not wanted to see?

Oh, Saints, Ferox.

Ferox, who had been bound from speaking truths yet asked her to give him all she was.

His voice in the wind had dragged her back to the cottage in time to save Wyll from certain death.

That same voice had urged her to follow the path into Wylderland and kept her sane when she should have gone mad from despair.

It had always been Ferox, who had cared for her horse Dragos and spent hours in glass gardens and frozen fields with her.

Ferox, who dined with her nearly every evening, until he tried to force her to claim the power of Bitterhelm. And when she refused, he'd locked her away with the other beasts.

Is this why you hated me so much when I first came to this village?

Vynasha watched as the silver wolf bounded into the fray, joining what could only be Vilhelm at his shoulder. Together, they herded the leonine beast toward the broken doorway.

"Grandmother, I am frightened," Thea cried.

Grandmother tucked the girl closer. "Your father will not let them touch you, mark me, girl."

The cage rattled at Vynasha's back, and she jumped as her

brother cried, "You can't keep us locked away in a cage, not with that thing loose. Release me and let me fight!"

"Even if Balos is right, I will never trust the safety of this village in *your* tainted hands again, boy," Galtis argued as he returned to his vigil at his daughter's side.

Vynasha finally tore her gaze from Ferox, gasping as she realized how close her brother was, near enough to reach through the bars and capture his hand with hers.

Ceddrych froze as she did just that, his expression pained as he met her gaze. "Ash?"

Vynasha squeezed his hand and pressed as close to the iron bars as she could manage. "Ceddrych…"

He sucked in a breath and then reached his other hand through the bars to embrace her as closely as he could manage. "Ash, how could you be so *stupid*! Whatever Balos promised you, don't believe him. Help me escape so we can find Wyll and flee this cursed place before it's overrun!"

"It's too late for that." Vynasha sobbed against her brother's turned cheek. Iron dug painfully against her skin and faintly burned.

"Don't—don't say that!" Ceddrych tightened his hold and choked on another sob while the world fell to pieces around them. "Saints, I should have never bloody left you! I was such a fool, believing I could reclaim Wyll and fight Onya without consequences. But I'll be damned if I'm forced to leave you in the hands of that monster. I can't do it, Ash, I can't bear to be parted from you or Wyll again, please, please…"

Vynasha shushed him, conscious of the ghastly battle making its way finally beyond the walls and the bright, curious stare of his cellmate. Her fingers pressed the cold burn of the amulet against her chest as she slowly pulled away from the bars. "I'm sorry, brother, but you're safer in this cage for now. I swear I will find a way. We always find a way."

"What? Where are you going?" Ceddrych's arm stretched beyond the bars, his teeth bared as he struggled to reach her.

Vynasha stepped just out of reach and glanced over to Wolfsbane's daughter. "Look after one another."

Resha frowned but still nodded even as Ceddrych pleaded with her. "Whatever you're thinking, you're wrong, Ash! Just—just wait a bleeding moment and talk to me!"

Vynasha hardened her heart and turned to flurries swirling through the broken hall. "It was looking for me, Ceddrych." She shifted on her feet and tightened her grasp on her dagger.

"That monster came to kill wylderfolk as they have always done, Ash. That's all!" Ceddrych cried.

Grandmother and Erythea had joined Galtis and the other elders near the raised dais. Vynasha would have one chance for this, and she knew it needed to be her. Did Grendel not warn her?

Wylderfolk poured from the compromised hall, darting into the blizzard rather than awaiting the next emboldened beast.

"Asha, don't be a fool!" Ceddrych snarled.

Vynasha glanced back over her shoulder one last time and forced a smile. "I love you, brother."

"Vynasha!"

She sliced her palm open with the tip of her dagger and ran over broken bodies and splintered wood into the snowstorm until her brother's voice was lost to the howling wind.

Violet drops of blood shimmered as they slipped from her palm and onto the snow. Sleet stung her cheeks, and though it should have been midday, heavy clouds illuminated by forked purple lightning blotted out the sun.

Vynasha kept Ferox's dagger in a tight fist and, with her other hand, pulled Grendel's amulet free from beneath her tunic. The amethyst at its center glowed brightly in the dim, a brilliant beacon of violet light.

She shook with every step, her lungs struggling for air after her race to the battle ensuing in the village. But only shadows of people and beasts took shape in the near white out.

Glowing eyes and screams surrounded her as she stepped over blood-stained snow and severed limbs. She pressed on, determined to keep moving, keep searching for another beast to approach her as they had before.

Please, just let it end soon.

Vynasha stumbled over a fallen corpse and caught her fall on the other side of the body. The fresh cut in her hand stung from the impact. She cursed as she snatched up the dagger and amulet. She focused on the stain of her violet blood in a sea of red as she struggled to stand. Anything to avoid looking at the person's face, lest she recognize them.

Climbing to her feet, she used the hand clasping the amulet to push back her hair, aided by the sudden gust of icy wind.

A wavering shadow waited for her not five paces ahead.

Vynasha froze, her heartbeat too loud in her ears as she rasped, "Grendel."

No snow or sleet touched the shadow as it stepped closer, growing more solid with every step. And the snow was pushed further out on every side, encompassing Vynasha in the shadow's shield. They were near enough to touch when Grendel appeared, a bronzed angel with wings fanning out from his back and eclipsing the field of bones.

Vynasha raised her dagger before his translucent hand could touch her. "Why are you here? Why are you attacking the wylderfolk after all this time?"

Grendel's features twisted, and his hand fell into a fist at his side. "I warned you what would happen. I begged you to listen, and you chose to act selfishly instead!"

"Selfish?" Vynasha leaned closer, confident he couldn't truly reach her. "Stop acting as though someone stole your favorite toy, you spoiled princeling."

Grendel lifted his chin, and his form flickered, brighter and more present as he seethed. "These *wylderfolk* as you call them dared to keep you trapped behind their wards when you belong to *me*."

"You already own my soul!" Vynasha threw her hands out at her sides, careless of the dagger in her fist. "I will be yours forever when I die. Why couldn't you give me this at least?" Her breath hitched, yet fury kept her tears from spilling over. "All I wanted was the freedom to dream, to live my life the way you offered. And now you've chosen to punish the people who took me in? Do you intend to finish your father's work, then? Will you destroy the rest of the wylderfolk because you grew impatient?"

Grendel's wings shifted and then wrapped slowly but surely around her. They were only shadow and should have been intangible. So why did she feel the caress of supple leather as she was brought forward? Why did his body feel so solid against hers?

"You're not here." She blinked stupidly up into his bright violet eyes.

Grendel's razor-sharp smile held a wicked edge, his sudden grasp of her neck deceptively gentle. "I warned you, Vynasha. I have never been a good man, not before my mother's curse and certainly not after. I refuse to wait another age for you to die. In fact, I refuse to *let* you die. And as your precious kin have proven too dangerous for you to remain among them, I find only one choice before us, my love."

Vynasha's heart squeezed painfully in her chest as his other hand encircled her wrist, easing her grip on Ferox's dagger.

Somewhere beyond Grendel's sphere of magick, a wolf began to howl.

"Please don't tell me it's my fault," she begged. "Don't lay the blame for all this senseless death on me. Don't make me hate you, Grendel, *please*."

Grendel caressed her throat, his cool touch dipping lower to trace his amulet hanging from her neck, bathing them in cool light. "I would have you willing, my queen. But as I am unable to cross the boundary of my prison, I shall continue sending my beasts. I will give them the freedom to ravage and make war until you agree to return to your rightful place."

In his smile, she saw the throne room, her seated upon his lap. She saw Hvalla in the rose garden warning Vynasha of a fate worse than death. And this gave her the strength to tighten her grip on her dagger and press it firmly against his side. Were he truly there, all she would need to do was push up and she could pierce his heart.

If he truly has one.

Grendel froze and clenched his jaw, nostrils flaring as she smiled. "Can you feel that, Prince? I will never be your queen, but you *will* allow me and mine to live in peace for as long as I choose. Or I'll destroy you."

Grendel tilted his head to the side and chuckled low. "You would destroy yourself, my love. Did I not tell you I refuse to let you die? And so you have afforded me no other choice."

A flicker of doubt made her hesitate. "What do you mean?"

Grendel's wings tightened around her. "Do not fear. My beasts will see you safely home. For now, you must rest."

Vynasha closed her eyes as a sudden wave of weariness struck her, then shook her head to dispel the urge to sleep. "What are you doing to me?"

"Are you not weary of expending all your power for these unforgiving people? Let me care for you as you deserve, my love." Grendel's features shifted and blurred before her eyes, more shadow than man.

"Stop," Vynasha protested as she lost control of her legs and slumped upon the snow. She twisted onto her side but Grendel was nowhere to be seen.

Only his voice lingered in the air, against her ear. *"Your suffering is near its end. Trust me. Love me, and I will give you all the glory you deserve."*

Vynasha blinked and lost the strength to hold herself up.

The storm abated slightly, the howling and roaring of the pack and beasts more distant than she recalled.

She watched helplessly as the golden beast from before lumbered toward her from farther down the empty street, blood coating his maw.

She blinked again and her tears spilled into the snow.

Grendel, what have you done to me?

Had he even been there? Or was he nothing but a phantom of her mind, a product of their blood bond twisted for his purposes?

Vynasha feared her return to the castle, certain she would lose what little remained of herself if she were taken now. Grendel would seal their bond so she could never leave his side again.

Ferox, why did you not prepare or protect me like you promised?

The golden beast huffed, blood and fetid breath wafting over her as the creature gathered her up into the crook of its arm and slung her awkwardly over its shoulder. And then, more swiftly than it should have been capable of, the creature slipped back the way it had come on three legs.

Vynasha stared numbly at the tattered village, aware she had lost her dagger and the amulet somewhere in the snow and that she was being carried to what would be the end of her.

Would Balos, or Ferox, whoever he truly was, allow Ceddrych to look after Wyll?

The tree line was just ahead, and the weariness she had fought—was still fighting—loomed closer. It would be best to give in, to sleep and pretend for a little while that her blood rune hadn't caused all this destruction.

It's all my fault.

"STOP."

The voice seemed to come from nowhere and everywhere. And the sheer power woven in the timbre of a single word was so great Vynasha's heart seized. The beast beneath her froze, impossibly stiff, not even breathing.

Vynasha clenched her jaw, and the point of pain was enough to allow her to draw in a sharp breath. She blinked, and her gaze darted around the ruined village.

"RELEASE THE WITCH."

The beast growled low as it dropped her instantly. More pain shot through her spelled limb,s and Vynasha turned her head, pushing off the snowdrift. The beast was far too near for her comfort.

"LOOK AND REMEMBER."

Vynasha and the beast turned their heads at once to the forest, and the storm abated to reveal the Oracle. Her stick of ash struck the earth, and the snows came to a standstill around them, thunder fading into a distant rumble.

The beast roared, great muscles bunching and heaving as though it wanted to leap at the woman. Other beasts appeared from the wood, covered in blood and intent upon Vynasha.

"STOP AND LOOK." The Oracle's mouth did not move, but the words came again as clearly and loudly as though she had shouted them.

The other beasts froze and the distant howling drew closer.

The golden-maned beast shifted into a crouch. Whatever power she held over them was fading.

Until the Oracle slammed her stick to the earth once more, and the stick became a sapling of ash.

Until the forest around them quickly withered and all color and life leeched from the earth. Lights flashed and traveled through the sapling and through the Oracle's gnarled hands, infusing her eyes with light, and her cloak ripped.

Until great translucent wings unfurled behind the old woman's back, and her silver hair turned white as the snow. "RETURN TO YOUR PRISON!"

The leonine beast snarled, and yet all the beasts in the forest turned and stalked away in swift albeit uneven movements. They roared and bayed, but the Oracle's command held.

The pack howled again, just ahead, herding the beasts to flee. The battle was won. And she was free.

CHAPTER THIRTY-THREE

A Battle Won

VYNASHA SOBBED WITH relief as she climbed to her feet and staggered over to the old woman's side. "How did you... Grandmother!"

The Oracle released her sapling, now a fully grown and flowering tree, and collapsed into Vynasha's waiting arms. Her wings no longer glowed but fell limply against her torn cloak, flickering slightly as the Oracle released a rattling breath. Her skin was paling, turning gray...

"No, no, please don't do this. You can't!" Vynasha's hand shook as she pushed the old woman's white hair back, staining it with her violet blood.

Grandmother's hand was soft as it pressed against Vynasha's cheek, her smile bright as she shook her head. "I always believed the one would come through Balos's clan, not a little fury of Wynyth's ilk. What I fool I was."

Vynasha swallowed thickly, desperate for a drink, for a potion to make Grandmother well. Yet there were wings on the old woman's back, and the magick she wielded smelled all too familiar. "Who are you?" she asked, but she already knew.

"I had a heart, once, if you would believe. I paid the ultimate price… my vengeance ran true and deep, as I knew it would. But I lost my youth, my power. All great magicks are beyond me now. That spell I used might claim my life, but it will have been worth it. Just to keep what my *spawn* wants from his greedy hands." She cackled but then coughed, and blood as blue as Grendel's had once been painted her lips.

"Soraya," Vynasha whispered as she held the ancient one closer. "But I felt you in the castle," she whispered. "I felt you everywhere…"

Soraya smiled, and the echo of her beauty still lingered at the corner of her mouth and the sparkle of her onyx eyes. "Much of me remains there. I gave of my spirit, and it is there what lingers here will go when my flesh gives out. 'Tis the price I paid and would pay again to keep my son from destroying our people."

"I understand why you did it." Vynasha lifted her head, searching for Balos, Erythea, anyone who could help her. "But I'm not letting you die," she said, echoing Grendel's words.

Shocked onyx eyes greeted hers. "You cannot, child. You have given too much, and I have lived for far too long."

Vynasha shook her head as she pressed her wounded palm to Soraya's cheek. "No one else dies today."

She drew in a deep breath, the rich and tainted power of Bitterhelm at the tip of her tongue. This mad woman's wicked son had gifted her with half of his power. What use was all this power if she was afraid to wield it? "I won't be afraid anymore," she vowed as she pressed a kiss to Soraya's forehead and breathed life back into her failing body.

Behind closed lids, she felt for the well within her, the rush of blood that she wielded like a hammer for her will.

She thought of Wyll, dying before the brilliant flames consuming the cottage.

She thought of Asa and the wylderfolk trapped by a demon.

Most of all, she thought of her father's broken body by a riverside. *"You weren't my child, but I promised her I could do right by you,"* Old Ced had confessed.

Life poured from her into Soraya's broken shell until the gray pallor left her skin, returning to burnished gold. Yet when the deepest wrinkles began to fade, Vynasha found herself ripped away from the old woman's body.

"What in the hells are you doing!" Balos thundered as he gathered Vynasha into his arms.

A bubble of laughter escaped her as she watched Soraya slowly rise and stare at her hands and arms in shock. "Child, what have you done?" The formerly rasping voice was smoother, and decades of age had been peeled away. Her glittering black eyes widened as the trailing wings at her back rustled with a sound like the tinkling of bells. "What have you done to me?" Soraya whispered as she took another step, wonder and awe in her slack features as she ran a hand over the skin of her neck.

"Crafter, why were you outside? Are you injured? Your scent is everywhere, you mad witch," Balos mumbled as he dragged her palm to his nose and sighed heavily.

The wound had closed at last, yet she yelped as he slowly licked the blood free from her skin. His eyebrow arched as his verdant eye found hers. Ferox's eye…

She shook her head and couldn't help laughing again as she cupped his cheek. "All this time, and you didn't tell me."

He grimaced, a slight shake of his head as he pressed his hand over hers, trapping it against his tight jaw. "I was furious with you in the beginning, for bonding with that demon. Yet how could I hope to stay away from you after you held my own dagger to my throat?"

"How is this even possible?" Distantly, Vynasha was aware she was still smiling and that Soraya was watching them with an unreadable expression. She was too giddy with relief to be herself and not a pawn. And she was aware she was using magick by instinct but little skill, and there would be consequences for this.

Soraya sighed as she turned to the rest of the pack walking the village streets on two and four legs. "We must burn or bury the dead soon if the frozen ground allows it. And we must remake the wards. No fear of *him* sniffing us out any longer. Our illusion of safety is gone, and we must prepare."

"Later," Ferox ground out.

Soraya nodded and then smiled at Vynasha, all traces of bitterness gone. "As soon as we put all this to rights, I am training you to wield your power properly."

Vynasha grinned. "I would have it no other way."

"Good." Soraya nodded briefly and returned her attention to the village with a heavier sigh. "I will begin with the wards as soon as I recover Erythea from Galtis. Our little witch has granted me strength enough."

Balos's arms eased their hold as all the tension fled from his limbs. "I cannot believe I nearly lost you again. I failed when I allowed the castle to fall to Grendel, and I would have failed you again if not for Mother."

Vynasha hesitated. "Is Grendel your brother, then?"

Balos blinked in confusion before a bitter laugh escaped his lips. "Not exactly. Soraya knew my father, Vonwere. And their union was a tool for them to bring Grendel down and reclaim the mirror." He shook his head and lowered her to her feet but kept his arm around her waist. "Ill-fated as it was…"

It felt natural, simple in a way that might have troubled her were she not so bleeding happy. Ferox had been her friend, had seen parts of her she had shared with no one else long before she reached Bitterhelm. No matter how contrary *Balos* had been, or how furious she had felt with both man and princely beast, Vynasha was too weary to hold onto her anger.

Vynasha blinked as she took in the pack working together to renew their broken home. How many times had the wylderfolk been forced to do this over the ages? "Was this why you wanted me to claim the mirror so badly?"

Balos pressed his chin to the crown of her head. "Claiming the mirror was the only way to keep Grendel from returning to his full power," he reluctantly began, "though the curse bound me from telling you. Placing you in that cell was the only way I could protect you from him, and yet it all still fell apart. There was nothing I could do to keep the wards from unraveling. The rule of Bitterhelm, even in its current state, was never intended for me. Only Soraya's runes and Grendel's unwillingness to challenge me made it possible to keep the bloody beasts in check. And when I thought you his creature at last... I had to flee while I had the chance, for Erythea."

"How many skins can you wear?" she wondered aloud. The rest was too painful to contemplate. She didn't want to think about Grendel anymore, or his promise to haunt her until she returned to his side willingly. No, she would rest, hold her nephew in her arms, and rebuild.

Balos pulled her closer, digging his forehead against hers as he opened his eyes. "You have seen all that I am and more than most in this village. Yet you should be aware that Bitterhelm is different. The curse reveals us for what we truly are... even you."

Vynasha turned to look up at the tic in his jaw, the way he avoided meeting her eye. "The tapestries," she murmured and recalled wolves that walked upright like men, women with wings, and similar beings of the forest had decorated the halls of the castle. "This isn't your true form."

Balos grinned faintly as he ducked his head and finally turned his gaze to her. "No, Beauty. Nearly all of us in the village are but shadows of our true selves."

Vynasha squeezed his waist and acknowledged the ache she had not allowed herself to contemplate until now. "I have missed you, Ferox."

"And I missed you, Beauty," he said, the same intensity she had glimpsed so often since taking refuge in his village. Was this what it meant?

"I'm still angry with you, I think," she confessed. "But I'm so tired."

Balos lifted her off her feet and carried her toward the hall once more. "Would you like to see your kin before you rest? The boy has been most anxious to see you again, from what Gira tells me."

"Yes," Vynasha choked out as she squeezed his neck, both eagerness and dread warring within her over the prospect of seeing Wyll again. She had abandoned her nephew with strangers as she had once been abandoned. Could he ever forgive her?

Seeking any distraction, Vynasha watched the pack remove the fallen beasts so scattered wylderfolk could search for their dead. She should feel sorrow for their losses. But the guilt was never far from her anymore, a crushing weight on the cusp of her consciousness. To give in now would be folly when Wyll needed her to be strong.

Balos held her closer as they passed the others, and a sudden thought occurred to her as her mind swam from exhaustion. "Which is your true name?" she blurted.

His smile smoothed, yet the warmth hadn't left his eyes. "Balos is the name my father gave me. Ferox is the name my queen gifted me when she made me as Bitterhelm's steward."

"I suppose it would be best to use the name your kin are used to," she said.

Balos pressed a swift kiss to her forehead. "Call me Beast again if you wish, so long as you honor your promise."

Vynasha stiffened and glared at the ruined opening of the village hall from over his shoulder. "You tricked me into saying yes."

Balos chuffed. "I need not rely on trickery when you had already promised yourself to me long ago."

Vynasha bit her lip as they made a sudden turn down a narrow path between houses. She had only been here once before, with Ceddrych. "Is my brother still exiled?"

"Is he truly your brother?" Balos growled back.

She dug her claws into his shoulders. "In every way that matters."

Balos remained silent and contemplative and so she pressed on. "You know Ceddrych is not guilty of killing Onya. If he's guilty of anything, it's doing whatever he needed to keep our nephew safe. It's nothing I wouldn't have done, or you wouldn't have done if it had been Erythea held captive."

Another growl rumbled through Balos's chest, the sound a much softer echo of Ferox that nearly made her smile. How had she not seen her friend sooner?

"Mayhap I was too lost in my grief… I will think on this." Balos inclined his head as a smiling Dadas appeared, opening the door to Galtis's home.

Vynasha's returning smile promptly fell as they entered only to find Tarbus on the floor with Katya's motionless form in his lap. Hugyn and Munyn sat on either side of Katya, holding her stiff hands.

Vynasha's breath caught, yet before she could speak, Balos's mouth pressed against her ear, and his words stilled her further.

"It has been too long. Katya's spirit is too far for you to bring her safely back. You will kill yourself trying, and your nephew needs you now."

She blinked, and tears spilled over her cheeks. "I'm sorry," she spoke to the room. Tarbus lifted his head, and his lips pursed as he nodded his head to her, while keeping a wary eye on his uncle. Asa's sobs came from the direction of the boy's room, followed by Gira's soothing hum.

She turned away from the dark hall leading to Asa's room and found countless familiar eyes already upon them. Many of these children had visited and even aided Vynasha in building her home in the woods.

To her shame, she had forgotten most of their names, yet she attempted a weak smile as she took in their weary faces. All the children took heart as they watched their alpha carry Vynasha deeper into Galtis's home.

And in a far corner, opposite the roaring hearth and isolated from the rest of the children, a curly-haired boy in furs lay curled in a tight ball. His chest rose and fell steadily, his lips parted as he slept away his exhaustion. His scars were of similar shape and texture to her own, and half of his face would always mark him as different in any village. But it was his scent that struck her most now.

Beneath the layers of the forest and deep, wild places, Wyllem smelled like *home*.

Vynasha's ears rang as she moved her legs and urged Balos to "Set me down."

Balos eased her to her feet gently, but she didn't linger long. Her vision blurred as she crouched and crawled to the narrow gap between her nephew and the wall. With practiced ease, Vynasha slipped her arm under his head and brought an arm around his middle.

Wyll stirred faintly and twisted his head to reveal the badly scarred side. "Aunty Asha?"

"Shh, go back to sleep, sweetling, I'm here. I'm here, Wyll, and I'm not going anywhere." Vynasha curled herself around his slight frame and drew her nephew into her arms.

Her boy hummed faintly, then his hand found hers and squeezed as he settled back against her chest.

Vynasha's chest shook with silent sobs as she pressed her lips to the back of Wyll's matted hair and breathed in the familiar scent of home until she fell into a deep and dreamless sleep.

CHAPTER THIRTY-FOUR

A War Begun

CEDDRYCH HAD BECOME numb by the time Vilhelm and the pack had brought them before the village elders. Balos had raged upon seeing Onya's body, so much so that a flicker of fear wakened Ceddrych from the howling emptiness.

Or was it the wolves howling outside the walls? No, it did not matter.

Nothing mattered anymore, not even after a screaming Wyll was taken from him—and *that* sound had almost been enough for him to lose control until he pushed the urge deeper within himself.

The moment Vilhelm found them and somehow discerned the truth of what happened to Onya, Ceddrych understood he would lose everything. This certainty was only driven home after the pack greeted them with Onya's hide-bound body near the Silver River.

The journey back was a blur after this, of his nephew attempting to speak with him and Resha. Eventually, Wyll gave up. At least the pack and wylderfolk would take better care of the boy.

Ceddrych thought he was prepared as the entire village appeared in the hall. At least Wyll would not need to witness this. At least...

Vynasha.

His nose caught her scent before he saw her, and she looked so exhausted, as though some of the life had been drained from her. Yet her beastly eyes were wild as they alighted upon his. And as she clutched Balos's unnatural spawn to her chest as a mother, Ceddrych knew he never should have left the village.

All numbness fled him with the sudden need to shout, to scream, to *fight*. But the elders would not listen, and bloody Vilhelm had to speak out.

Ceddrych had felt no end of fury with his fellow *captive* over this fine detail, though not even Wyll had known about Resha's forgotten brother.

"*She said all her family were killed, save her father,*" his nephew had said.

"*Clearly, Resha lied,*" Ceddrych had snapped back, all the while glaring at the hunter.

Though, to be fair—and he was woefully short on honor these days—it was plain the girl had been just as shocked by Vilhelm. What would she have said, if she cared to?

Ceddrych might have wondered, might have pressed the girl on the rare moments between their capture and their cage. But nothing mattered. He had failed.

Until Vynasha sealed an unholy pact with Balos and allowed the brute to maul her with unwanted kisses.

Ceddrych had seen red. Had they not bound them in iron shackles behind iron bars, he would have shifted into his beastly form in that instant. Something in his throat broke with his screams while something in his soul snapped.

How could she do it? How could she give herself over to that monster?

He watched, after the precious moment she clung to him through the bars, as she ran after the wolves and the beast.

He was numb to all the elders and their mutterings as the last of the fighting ceased beyond the walls and a fine layer of snow coated the inner hall. In the ensuing quiet, he found Resha had risen to stand as best she could beside him. Her gaze, too, was pinned to the break in the hall, to the fading storm beyond.

Much as he wanted to hate the hunter's daughter, he recalled what the Oracle had said about their peoples. She was not so different from the wylderfolk as they had been led to believe.

"Ceddrych? Are you well, brother?"

He startled and looked up from the crunch of his boots in snow to find Vynasha and Wyll watching him with concern. His breath stuttered at the sight. "Yes, I… was just… lost for a moment."

Vynasha exchanged a glance with Wyll and placed a hand on his shoulder before closing the distance between them. "Are you sure you're ready?" she spoke low. "We can delay a moment to rest if you need it."

Ceddrych shook his head and ran a hand over his tangled hair. "No. Your shadows will not like it." He barely managed to keep the bitterness from his voice but couldn't help his cursory glance at the surrounding forest. It was silent in a way that meant predators beyond themselves were nearby.

Vynasha sighed as she followed his gaze and twin wolves slipped from one tree to another. "Better Dadas and Tarbus than any of the others." She returned her gaze to his and pressed a warm hand to his cheek. "Think of it as a kindness. He could have sent Vilhelm instead."

Ceddrych groaned as he pulled her hand away. "I hate it when you're right, sister."

"No, you don't," she chided with a soft smile. It was the most either of them seemed capable of in the days following the attack.

Ceddrych grimaced as he found his mind stretching and the urge to wander once again. It had been happening more frequently of late, this losing himself to a past he couldn't change.

"Come," she urged, tugging on his hand until he picked up his pace. Wyll's smile brightened as they approached. "It's only a little farther."

Ceddrych shook his head and adjusted the pack on his back with a wince. He had only shifted once since his injury, and it had not been enough to fully heal all his wounds. The scars Onya's claws had left remained, but her death would always scar deeper. He would never forget the betrayal on Asa's face the first time the boy saw him since the attack.

Put it away, the voice in his head that sounded like hers seemed to whisper. Vynasha squeezed his hand and again offered that faint smile that didn't reach her eyes. She was often lost, too, he thought.

"Aunty Asha, are we almost there?" Wyll bounded ahead with an ease that brought a true smile to Vynasha's face.

"Just through those trees, I promise. Did you check every snare?"

Wyll held up two snowy hares with a gap-toothed grin. "Will we have time to prepare them?"

Vynasha shook her head and glanced toward their silent shadows trailing them. "We'll see." And something in the way she squeezed his hand and glanced nervously at him from over her shoulder gave him pause.

Ceddrych blinked, and the wonder of being outside again faded at last, and he became fully aware of the trail she had led them through. "Ash," he began then gasped as they broke through two thick trees masking a familiar clearing on the other side.

Ceddrych's heart raced as he took in the house that seemed to have grown overnight. It was two levels at least, with a peaked roof similar in style to the ruined village hall. And something about it recalled Grandmother Mayve's tavern in Whistleande. Runes had been carved over nearly every surface in arcing patterns. Someone had painted wolves and roses around each shuttered window and the door.

"Wow! Is this the home Asa and the twins helped you build, Aunty?" Wyll darted ahead of them to the covered porch, running his hands over the thick posts. The door swung open with ease, and Vynasha followed Wyll across the threshold.

She frowned and paused when he froze at the entrance. "Ceddrych?"

"I—I don't understand, what is this?" he rasped.

Vynasha faced him fully while Wyll explored ahead. "This is your new home, brother."

Ceddrych ducked and rubbed his eyes with his free hand. "How? I—Ash, this place… I *drew* this." He had started drawing out of desperation soon after settling in the village. Drawing kept his mind from going too far afield, kept him grounded. Naturally, this led him to drawing the home she had always wanted and the person who inspired him most.

Vynasha bit down on her lip briefly, then closed the distance to take both his hands. "I found it soon after you left with the pack, and the twins helped me get started. Then Asa and the other children I healed came…" Her gaze grew distant, and he knew she was thinking about Katya, the girl she couldn't save.

"I thought I was being exiled from the village," Ceddrych said, relieved when her focus returned to him and away from their many ghosts.

Vynasha's smile tugged up higher at the unscarred corner. "This is your exile, if you choose it."

"I found my room!" Wyll called, his steps a rhythmic thud over their heads.

"You aren't staying long today!" Vynasha called back with a shake of her head. But her eyes were sad. "Wyll and I can't stay yet, but this won't be forever. I'll find a way, I promise."

Ceddrych sighed and pulled her into his arms. He buried his nose in her unbound curls, needing to feel her solid and alive again. "I hate that you're staying with *them*," he growled.

He'd seen the Oracle in passing in the aftermath and felt uneasy with her shimmering wings and the years she had shed. He had liked even less the way Balos kept Vynasha at his side constantly, a smug grin on the alpha's face.

Vynasha smoothed her hands over his back, and he prayed she didn't notice his flinch as she brushed his new scars. "Grandmother can help me learn to control my magick, and Wyll will be safe with me. I swear it."

As though their nephew heard, Wyll's head appeared from the top of the wooden stair. "Can we eat?"

Vynasha's laughter startled Ceddrych. "Check the larder and see if Tarbus has left anything behind." Her wyldcat's eyes danced as she looked up, the vertical pupil contracting. "I should warn you, the children helped build this home, so don't expect a quiet exile. I believe they see it as partly theirs."

Ceddrych grimaced. "If any of them choose to trust me after what happened."

Her smile faded as she tugged lightly on his hands. "I know it wasn't your fault, and so do they. Give them time, and please come inside. Aren't you ready to get out of the cold?"

He hesitated even though this house and those within it were everything he'd ever dreamed. "I don't deserve this, sister. If you only knew—"

"So earn it, then," she interrupted, her grasp suddenly fierce. There was steel behind her eyes, and a dominance within her that he didn't recognize. "Live here for me and guard the village as much as you can. And trust me, brother, no matter what comes."

Strength infused his limbs with her words, straightening his spine, and gave him the courage to cross over the threshold into their new home. "Whatever may come, sister."

CHAPTER THIRTY-FIVE

A Beast's Tale

THE BEAST'S LIFE had been forfeited from the hour the prince had locked her in the dungeon.

She often dreamed of glittering gems beneath a canopy of starlight and soft silks against satin skin.

She dreamed of a perfect wolf moon gleaming in the glass skylight above, silvery beams blended together with the hazy glow of a dozen candelabra.

She dreamed dreams of joy filling her every step as they danced together, her hand in his, smile lines about his perfect silver-flecked violet eyes.

He was like the moonlight, and she filled with all the warmth of the sun. His words blurred together in her memory, full of promise and hope until her light died.

It was the last moment of her life she could remember and, though she could not explain how she knew this, the moment her dreams had died.

All dreams died in the damp dim of the dungeon of Castle Bitterhelm.

The beast woke to the echoing roars of her brothers and sisters returning from their latest failed hunt. Her same kin had been trapped half an age and more, some longer than she had.

The beast snarled at the lingering memories. Dreams and memories, like jagged pieces of broken glass, stabbed at her mind now and then at the worst opportunity. Just as she was enjoying the feeling of air moving through her fur, as she sat back to release her own cry to the moon.

In the endless black of their prison, she had forgotten much more than the name of the castle. Now it came to her as her last moments as a woman came to her mind, stalling her lumbering movements.

She froze, the cry escaping as a bitter whine, and she twisted her great head to the courtyard behind her. Bushes covered in bloodred blossoms surrounded her, and inside the castle, the combined stink of her brethren's blood and the blood of those they had slain permeated the air.

Darkness and pain had been her sole companions for so long, alongside the occasional cries of the others, until *she* had come to free them. Twin glowing eyes, like a wyldcat's, had blazed through the bars of her cell, piercing through the dark and stirring something long forgotten.

Curse breaker. The beast had tried to speak her name. The one foretold had come to them at last.

They were too far gone, she'd wanted to tell the girl.

Immediately, the beast had risen and stumbled as her chains were broken. The girl had smiled at her with sharp teeth and then left the door open behind her.

Come and be free, the curse breaker had said to their minds as she opened their cell doors, breaking both their physical chains and the magick blocking their free will.

The curse tied them together in malice yet, however. The eldest among them had had one conscious thought that quickly spread through to the others: vengeance.

Too long they had waited to be freed, and now they wanted revenge. Too late for the curse breaker to call them back. Now they would seek and find their pound of flesh.

She had followed the others like a wolf with its pack, up through the dungeon, seeking and sniffing out the one responsible. Often the paths were blocked by ruins, or enchanted to lead them back to dead ends. Her path had led her here, into the glass gardens.

How long have I been here? she wondered now as she looked about the graceful arches and noticed the darkness which had descended over the castle, over the grounds spread past the castle gate and to the forested valley and mountains below.

Time as a monster was meaningless. She hungered, fed, and slept, and while the others feasted, she ate the red blossoms that pricked her muzzle but filled her with increasing awareness.

Where is the curse breaker?

She knew this was not the first time she had asked herself this question as she turned back to the castle, then to the roses. Her memories before her time as a beast were still hidden behind a veil, thick as ice over the Silver River. But she did recall this much. The curse breaker had freed them, and then the Master had sent her away before she could heal them.

Now the power behind the curse was awakened and furious to have been so easily thwarted. Soraya may be dead, but her will lingered.

We must find the curse breaker, the beast girl thought with absolute and almost-human assurance.

A movement at the corner of the garden caught her sensitive ears, and the hairs on her back bristled as she twisted and snarled at the light between shadows.

The light flickered, and then a gasp escaped the bushes nearby as the beast approached.

Fury filled her as she breathed in the smell of the ones who had hunted and hated her people before…

She snarled as she pushed her head deeper into the thorny bush to reveal the gaping, frightened face of a young girl.

"P-please do not eat me," the girl pleaded.

The beast shivered, cocking her head slightly as though the motion would help her understand better. The girl continued, voice trembling and light flickering as she spoke.

"I have been watching you since you came here and began to eat Mistress's roses." Her voice came from far away, and when she shifted in place, the thorns and vines embedded in her faded flesh squeezed even tighter.

The beast snarled again, sensing the girl's disapproval beneath her pain.

The girl shook her head. "Do not fear. Mistress would not object, I am sure. As I said, I have been watching you, and you are not so savage as the others. I hoped… that is, if you understand me, I beg of you—please find our mistress. She has gone to the wolves, but she is in grave danger there and must return to us. Please go to her and, oh, please, do not try to kill her!"

The beast grunted with a bear like snort in what might have been a chuckle as the girl started.

"I can no longer dream, and I do not think I will last much longer in this realm. So few of us are left. You must go if we are to have any hope… If you find Vynasha, please tell her that Hvalla cared for her roses until the end."

The girl blinked back tears. Something about them pierced

through the fog around the beast's mind, and she backed away from the thorny bush at last. The girl's words were strange to her ears, but the beast found herself nodding her great head all the same.

"Thank you," the girl breathed.

The beast bowed her head to the girl and, as she approached the outer hedges of their sanctuary, felt a stab of pity for the fading girl. Her thin form flickered in and out of the moonlight. It would not be long before the curse claimed her too.

As the beast leaped and clawed over the hedge, she thought of her dream again and wondered at her reason for coming to the garden while her brethren haunted the rest of the ruin. Another unattainable memory, not to be grasped by beasts after all. This much she knew. None had come as close as she did—to what or whom, she was uncertain.

The curse breaker will know.

To her surprise, no magick nor beast barred her from slipping past the gates of the city once known as the Lost City.

Bitterhelm… it was called Bitterhelm.

The stars glowed brighter on her fur as she crossed the open downslope between the two mountains.

The fog that kept her thoughts hazy dissipated the farther she pushed into the forest below.

A lingering ache made her turn one last time toward Bitterhelm's crumbling towers. A bitter human feeling, that she was forgetting the most important thing of all by leaving, almost made her return to the garden with its sweet roses.

But the girl was right. Too many of her brothers and sisters were filled with violence alone now. They needed the curse breaker to help them remember.

With this final thought, the beast turned to the forest, trusting an otherworldly sense tying them to the one who had come to save and then abandoned them to madness.

Thanks for reading! If you enjoyed *Scarred Beauty*,
I would be beyond grateful if you could leave an honest review.
Long or fortune cookie length, either would be a big help in
spreading the word about this series. Thank you for supporting me
through this epic journey, my fellow wylderfolk.

Vynasha's journey continues with
Bound Beauty (Wylder Tales: Vol. 3)
For the latest news and updates follow my blog at
http://jennifersilverwood.com

Want to explore the world of Wylder Tales*?*
Visit http://wyldertales.com for more!

ABOUT THE AUTHOR

JENNIFER SILVERWOOD has been involved in the publishing world since 2012 and is passionate about supporting the writing community however she can. After studying traditional art at university, she began helping Qamber Designs bring authors' books to life. In real life, she's a mom of two, a prolific reader, and an occasional artist. Jennifer is the author of three series—Borderlands, Wylder Tales, and the Heaven's Edge Novellas—and the stand-alone romance titles *Stay* and *She Walks in Moonlight*.

Discover more about the world of Wylder Tales, along with Jennifer's blog on writing life and other bookish delights, at www.jennifersilverwood.com.

9 798330 227228